I0831926

INDISCRETION

WORKPLACE FLIRTATION CREATES UNIMAGINABLE CONSEQUENCES.

M.G.CRISCI

ORCA PUBLISHING COMPANY USA | 2020

This is a work of fiction.
Names, characters, business, places, events, and incidents are either the products of the author's imagination or used in a fictitious manner.
Any resemblance to actual persons, living or dead, or actual events are purely coincidental.

Cover design Good World Media
Edited by Holly Scudero
Manufactured in the United States of America

Library of Congress 2010929929
Copyright No. 1-414380231

ISBN 978-1-4566-3260-1

Also by M.G. Crisci

7 Days in Russia
Call Sign, White Lily
Donny and Vladdy
Ergonia. Land of the Giant Ants
Indiscretion
Mary Jackson Peale
Only in New York
Papa Cado
Papa Cado's Book of Wisdom
Project Zebra
Salad Oil King
Save the Last Dance
She Said. He Said.
Still Standing
The King of Violins
This Little Piggy

Learn more at

mgcrisci.com
twitter.com/worldofmgcrisci
YouTube.com/worldofmgcrisci
facebook.com/worldofmgcrisci

1.

When the phone rang, I had no idea my life was about to change forever.

A cheery southern drawl asked, "Y'all Martin Ruff?"

"What do you want?" I responded brusquely, assuming it was a cold sales call.

"I'm Marge Jamerson of American Financial Advisors [AFA]. My boss, Peter Maroney, spotted you on LinkedIn and wanted to meet. Thought you might be able to help him."

"You tell Pete I'm good—have an investment advisor and plenty of insurance."

Marge pushed back. "Mr. Ruff, you got me wrong. Mr. Maroney is one of Connecticut's successful young entrepreneurs."

"Okay, Marge, give me a hint," I said sarcastically. "What does Mr. Maroney do?"

"You need to talk to him directly." A phone rang in the background. "Sorry, Mr. Ruff, I've got to take this call. Back in two shakes."

I decided to hang up. Marge beat me to the punch. "Sorry about that; as you can appreciate, with 2,000 licensees in three time zones the phones never stop ringing. So, can we set a time?"

The "2,000" caught my attention. I decided, *What the hell.*

~

My first Pete conversation took place in his modest office in an industrial park overlooking Bridgeport Harbor, about fifteen miles south of snooty Southport, Connecticut.

The conversation quickly denigrated into a sparring match between titanic egos. I brought a one-page bio and an attitude. I wasn't selling; I was exploring. After all, based on the internet research I had completed, I had more big-time business experience than Pete and his partners combined.

"So, who are you?" said this rough-at-the-edges, athletically configured, forty-something guy with an out-of-date flat crew cut and a red, white, and blue American-flag tie.

"I'm sorry, but who are you?" I retorted.

"Nobody talks to me that way," said Pete, standing up and leaning by the conference table.

I tilted my chair back and returned the salvo. "Nobody talks to me that way, either."

Pete laughed. "Looks like you don't back down from a good fight."

He glanced at my bio for about 30 seconds and then did a complete 360.

As I was about to learn, Pete — a well-read security salesman with a high school education and sound business instincts — had a grandiose but straightforward vision: worldwide leadership in safe-money asset allocations

He realized that most broker-dealers merely processed and supervised buy-sell security orders placed by their licensed independent financial advisors. As per guidelines established by the Securities and Exchange Commission, they received a modest fee per transaction.

Pete's concept was to license the best of America's 1.1 million independent financial advisors and help them grow their practices using AFA investment and insurance products, along with its next generation lead and sales closing techniques. Pete offered the marketing and sales services as a "free added value," which permitted Pete to charge higher transaction fees to licensed advisors. His ultimate goal: become America's number one broker-dealer in total trading volume and net transactional revenues.

His five-year plan was to acquire twenty of the most profitable licensed firms, aggregate them operationally by removing administrative duplication, and then launch and cash out via an initial public financing (or initial public offering, IPO).

"My backup is to sell the new network to a strategically-aligned financial services company, such as Met Life or Northwestern Mutual, that has the appetite and the means."

"How's the plan coming," I asked.

"Moving in the right direction, just not as fast as I'd like."

"Why?"

"Our marketing programs are running out of steam," Pete replied, "and our in-house business consultants need a swift boot in the ass! Some are good; some are bad; some are willing to embrace new ideas; some wouldn't recognize a good idea if it came up and banged them on the head."

Pete paused. "Now that I've put my cards on the table, how about showing a few of yours?"

"Dad was a wholesale butcher who made a bunch of money with his cousins on the black-market during World War II. He decided he wanted better for his only son. We moved to Park Avenue — far from *the family*, if you know what I mean. I graduated from Penn undergraduate and got my master's at Wharton. That pedigree, my marks, and a few connections landed me on Wall Street, first as a trader at Merrill Lynch, which eventually led me to deal-making at Goldman Sachs.

"Within five years, I gained an unjustified, over-publicized reputation as a 'kingmaker.' Someone who could spot undervalued companies, advise them on how to grow, and design exit strategies that made the management wealthy. I made a bunch of money in the process and decided to strike out on my own.

"I started two public companies from scratch by consolidating undervalued companies in the same business space. My first foray made me wealthy. Maybe a $150 million net worth on paper? The second venture not only destroyed my paper wealth, but also left me $10 million in the hole. I sucked it up, went back to work at Goldman, paid everybody off rather than declare bankruptcy. In the next few years, I accumulated a few million dollars on the plus side of the ledger and bought a couple of multimillion-dollar homes. And here we are."

~

Pete found my candor refreshing; he leaned back in his chair. "Suppose you could get that hundred million, plus some, back in five years?"

"I'm listening," I replied.

"Problem is, you're already fifty-seven." He sat forward again.

"So?"

"So, I'm not sure you'd be willing or able to work that hard."

"And I'm not sure I believe your bullshit."

Pete smiled and leaned back again. "The hell with it; let's do it. You're the perfect cultural fit. I can see you'll charm the pants off my salespeople and the advisors, and intimidate the crap out of them at the same time."

I was leery; he sounded like a snake oil salesman. "How about we both do some due diligence? I'd like to meet some of your people, get a better idea of what you do. Maybe talk to a few of your field reps. At the same time, they can size me up and report back to you."

"Sounds good to me," said Pete.

Over the next two days, I met his three partners — Dawson Craft, Eddie Carr, and Jeremy Costas — who had no clue why I was there. As Pete explained, "they are sorta partners," which meant they received a share of the annual profits but made none of the big decisions, and they didn't own a share of company stock (Pete and his family owned 100 percent of it).

~

Pete's number two, the bald, cherubic Dawson Craft, considered himself a product-development expert who designed innovative securities offerings that fit the "just barely legal" bucket. He had never been married, was a high roller at Indian reservations, and usually fulfilled his sexual needs the "old fashioned way" – he paid for them. The only thing that didn't seem to fit was a rumor that he'd had a fling with a sexy, dirty blonde business consultant named Alexandria Plummet.

Pete and Dawson had met in high school; they'd waited tables together during their disastrous attempts to obtain college degrees and both loved fast cars. That's where the similarities ended. Craft, despite his rather homely appearance — 5′ 6″ tall, rotund, bald, with black-rimmed granny eyeglasses — loved to buy at least two women a week. The handsome, athletic Pete preferred one non-paid relationship at a time.

The two friends continually bantered about their approach to relationships. "Give me one reason why a beautiful woman would date a homely dude like you?" joked Pete.

"Pal, I'll give you three: money, money, and money."

Dawson fancied himself Pete's alter-ego, even though he had absolutely no day-to-day operating experience. He had been fired eight times in his career, primarily for telling his superiors they didn't get his latest product or strategic concept. "Dawson, I love you," Pete used to laugh out loud publicly. "But God, it's a good thing I'm here. Imagine if I let you run the company!"

When it came to money, the tables turned. Pete spent every cent he made; he thought money was for spending. Dawson was an oxymoron. He saved first; cold cash meant he'd never have to suck up to anyone. He spent the rest, after the cost of sex, at the blackjack and crap tables at the Foxwoods Casino on the Mashantucket Indian Reservation in Northern Connecticut.

~

Eddie Carr's name couldn't have been more prophetic. He was a former race car driver, built like a boxcar, and had a strong mechanical aptitude. His sumo-wrestler physique and happy-go-lucky attitude tended to offset the fact that he was, intellectually, the brightest of the three. "Dad was a neurosurgeon and believed my brother, sister, and I should all follow suit. Two years into medical school, I said, 'This isn't for me.' Dad was pissed, but hey, you gotta lead your own life."

Pete and Eddie shared an interest in extreme sports and souped-up, lightning-fast cars. They met at a NASCAR race in Old Lyme, Connecticut. Pete, needing a win to crack the top-twenty ranking, was having trouble getting the gearbox of his yellow Lamborghini to shift smoothly during the warm-ups, which could have led his car to stall at a critical juncture during the actual race. Carr, a friend of the event's promoter, was hanging around the pit area before the race and noticed Pete cursing and struggling. After a quick examination, he volunteered an unconventional adjustment to the intake manifold. "Pal, if we change the ratio of gas to air, your problem goes away."

Pete asked his pit manager what he thought of Carr's suggestion. "Pete, you've gotta be crazy to make changes like that at the last minute."

Pete instinctively felt Carr knew what he was talking about and overruled them. Pete won the race and the two became steadfast friends. With Pete, first impressions were usually lasting impressions, so Carr was now typecast as the guy who knew how to fix things. No more, no less. Pete knew his company needed one-of-those at the highest level.

Carr was AFA's version of a good-old-boy. His primary function was building and monitoring business processes, and modifying infrastructure. His self-effacing, easy-going personality also gave Pete an unexpected bonus: he was a natural at recruiting top salespeople across the United States. They were confident he'd teach them how to sell AFA products using easily understandable terms.

Carr believed the best salespeople were motivated by greed. He lived by a simple selling proposition: "Let me help you make more faster." In just five years, he had licensed more than four hundred top salespeople and grew AFA to $200 million annually, which was more than enough to support his increasingly grandiose lifestyle.

~

Jeremy Costas owned a state-of-the-art yacht repair shop in Norwalk, Connecticut, that catered to wealthy hobbyists. Unfortunately, he couldn't make a living in that role and, after filing for bankruptcy, he became an administrator at a national rent-a-truck company. Pete met Costas at the National Entrepreneurs Association's annual trade show in Orlando. He recognized that Jeremy was exceptionally good at day-to-day detail, something he knew was important but in which he had little interest.

Costas was a stickler for improving his knowledge base, yet at the same time, he was intimidated by rapid change. Pete thought Costas's volcanic temper tantrums were quite humorous. They reminded him of his past behavior, which he had eventually conquered. "Managing Jeremy is a piece of cake. When he gets nervous, he explodes. I tell him to take the rest of the day off. The next morning, he's cool as a cucumber. We never discuss the day before."

As the AFA head of operations guy, Costas started from the point of view that every office expense, every salary, every commission structure was too much, and that every employee wanted to cheat, lie, and steal.

The irony was that the buttoned-up Costas had had a second bankruptcy. He got talked into becoming a lobster boat captain near Prince Edward Island in Canada. After some initial success, he bought a shit load of boats about the time the price of lobster plummeted.

Like Craft, he was not exactly God's gift to women. At some point, a hot number named Joanne something-or-other had gotten him to invest in a group of five-star restaurants. Within two years, she had embezzled millions, leaving him holding the bag.

~

The business consultants were like a company within the company. They tended to be forty-five and older with significant sales management backgrounds, which gave them credibility with the independent financial advisors they were trying to license. The average consultant made four or five times any other employee.

~

There were ten on-staff consultants, eight men and two women. The men were sarcastic, know-it-all types who were income-complacent and change-resistant, but tolerated by the other departments because they knew Pete, the salesman, was the consultants' guardian protector.

The two ladies were as dissimilar to each other as the men were similar. They worked hard to know everything possible about their product lines. Give either of them a specific customer portfolio and they could spout product options in their sleep. When they didn't know the answer to a product question, they went and got the answer.

Barbara Brag, having never been married and in her mid-forties, believed most business people were empty suits, and thought *every* man wanted to get into her pants. Her strategy: tease them till their tongues hung out and their private parts were about to explode, then push them to sell more and more

AFA products. Her "insurance policy" was strategically revealing blouses designed to expose her well-endowed figure tastefully. Despite the book cover, Barbara was extremely stingy with her actual sexual favors. They were reserved strictly for absolutely, positively necessary situations. She was self-confident enough to project a what-you-see-is-what-you-get attitude.

Despite strong ties to Pete's second wife, Jolene, Brag eventually self-destructed. She decided she was so influential with AFA field advisors that she would start her own firm to compete with Pete, and the advisors would follow in droves. The evening after she resigned, she slipped back into the building and was caught stealing the company's advisor database. Charges were never brought, but there was no severance package and no competitive company.

The second female consultant was forty-six-year-old Alexandria Plummet. Her persona was the direct opposite of Brag. She was a well-groomed, conservative Midwesterner with two grown daughters. She looked at least ten years younger than she actually was, and preferred to date men of that age. She always said she never mixed business with pleasure. Business was business; pleasure was personal.

Once an advisor was assigned to her group, she built strong relationships based primarily on frequent contact and sheer personal charm, secondarily on the actual business advice she provided. At the time of my arrival, she was one of the highest-paid managers, earning about $350,000 a year.

The story was that Craft and Plummet did business at one of his stops along the way, and he recruited her to work at AFA. Supposedly they slept together on a semi-regular basis. However, evidence of such activity was highly circumstantial at best—most employees said they had a funny way of looking at each other whenever they were in meetings.

Despite her bright smiles, perky demeanor, and solid listening skills, Alexandria never bought into Pete's added-value mission. She believed that salespeople merely wanted product options so that they could make a quick trade and a big commission. She was stubborn as a rock. Interestingly, she quickly noticed that I could be equally stubborn when I wanted to make a point, so we operated at arms-length – at least initially.

~

My bottom line: AFA was populated by a bunch of business lightweights who were in the right place at the right time. I decided I'd take a pass; the company felt like a glorified Ponzi scheme filled with potholes.

A few days later, Marge called again. She wouldn't get off the phone until I confirmed a follow-up meeting with Pete. (Later, I discovered the source of Marge's intense loyalty. Pete learned from his wife that Marge's husband had beaten the shit out of her in a drunken rage and took their two kids with him. Pete hired lawyers, got the kids back, and had an injunction placed against the husband. Then he hired Marge as his administrative assistant and paid her $80,000 per year, which was more money than she had ever made.)

"So?" said Pete.

"Not sure," I replied.

"Name the amount. I'll pay you whatever makes you happy — *within reason*."

"Why are you so hot to hire me?"

Pete became candid. "I'm just a kid from the streets who wants to turn AFA into a Harvard Business School success story. I want Wall Street to love us so we can go public or sell to the highest bidder for an obscene amount of money. You've been there and done that. I want you to be my exit strategy coach."

I smelled blood! "Tell you what. I'll come on board as a full-time consultant for sixty days at absolutely no cost to you?"

"That's ridiculous," said Pete. "What's the catch?"

"If you like what I do, and I like what I'm doing, my compensation package kicks in. But — cards on the table — there must be a significant equity kicker in the deal. I'm not here for cash flow. That's just to keep you honest. I want at least five percent of the company on a fully-diluted basis."

Pete smiled. "And you have the audacity to tell me it's not about the money. How about $30,000 a month salary plus all expenses, five percent of the annual profits distributions, and a five percent equity stake after twelve months?"

The next day, Pete told his partners he had made the hire of the decade and sent a note to the office announcing my arrival.

He never mentioned my equity ownership agreement to anybody.

Pete placed me in the office next to his. This pissed off Dawson, Eddie, and Jeremy, who had smaller offices on a lower floor.

2.

My sixty-day trial went by in the blink of an eye.

On day sixty-one, Pete, his three partners, and I had an off-campus session at the Greenwich Inn on Long Island Sound. As the sailboats passed by, I explained my impressions and findings and laid out a no-holds-barred, three-year plan: step-by-step, year by year, department by dcpartment.

"To begin with, the data suggests you're spending far too much per head to recruit licensed financial advisors." Pete and Craft immediately became defensive, since this was one of their primary purviews.

"Buddy," smiled Craft cynically. "You don't fully understand our business model. But then, how could you? You've only been around sixty days."

"Give the man a chance," interrupted Pete.

"The fact is, despite your success, you've given the recruiting department no flak cover. You guys need a big-time public relations program so that every time a producer picks up a trade magazine, he sees something positive about AFA."

"That costs money and takes time," sneered Costas, "and there are no guarantees."

"Jeremy," I said, "You're right on all three counts. But if it works, advisors will want to visit Bridgeport. Your costs per recruit will drop dramatically, profits will soar, and you'll boost employee morale and productivity."

"How do we hedge our bets that it *will* work?" asked an intrigued Pete.

"We hire the best PR firm I know — Kekst, Slade, and Bitters in Manhattan—and create a corporate communications program that becomes the talk of the industry by exposing the humanity of your top producers."

"Are you telling us you want to send up our producers in public? They'll piss all over us!" responded Carr, tortured.

"Eddie, with all due respect, I've talked to a number of your top guns. I think they'd welcome the openness and lack of pretension. These guys have what I call 'the blue-collar millionaire mindset.' These are uneducated, unsophisticated entrepreneurs that are making more money than they ever imagined. Trust me; they'll love it."

Carr, Costas, and Craft were not happy campers — I had just described them. Pete tried to reduce the tension. "What else have you got, Martin?"

"I've analyzed your lead generation marketing materials. Your production costs are at a significant premium compared to current market rates."

"But our producers aren't complaining about the pricing," responded Craft, trying to make me look foolish.

"All I can tell you is that I estimate with a few modest changes in business practices, you can add $625,000, maybe more, to your bottom line. Since you all share in the profits, think of it as getting a free Lamborghini!"

Pete grinned and nodded his head. I continued.

"We also need to update the content and design of your consumer lead generation programs. Response rates have been slipping over the last eighteen months, so it's just a matter of time before your producers start complaining."

Carr, concerned about producer credibility, said, "How the hell do we fix that one?"

I laughed. "Our new 'AFA impact-maximization program,"

"Is there an English translation?" replied Craft.

"How the hell do I know? I just made it up," I responded with another laugh. "I need time to develop the details. But the sales pitch writes itself. We tell producers we tested the stuff with Pete's clients, and we've seen a significant increase in return on investment."

"Where do you come up with this bullshit?" smiled Carr.

"To be perfectly honest, I don't know. It just happens."

"I think a lot of what you're suggesting is terrific," said Craft. But it sounds like all the changes could overwhelm our guys; might cause a sales downturn and reduce out profit splits."

"Dawson, excellent point," I replied. "That's why my analysis also includes a few organizational changes to make the activities more turnkey."'

Carr and Costas seethed quietly while Dawson and Pete challenged my assumptions and suggested changes. Two hours later, Pete was satisfied, Craft was frustrated, and Carr and Costas were dozing off in the corner of the conference room.

Pete came to a simple conclusion. "Sounds good to me. Let's do it."

"I disagree," glared Costas.

"That's your prerogative," said Pete. "But as long as I'm the final vote, we do things my way." Pete paused. "Martin, stick around; we need to talk comp."

But Craft wanted to stay. "Pete, since I'm responsible for employee comp discussions, shouldn't I stick around?"

"Dawson," replied Pete, "Martin's not an employee; he's one of us," said Pete pointedly. "I'll handle the matter. Got it?"

3.

Life is full of ugly surprises.

I was stunned when I got the call early Saturday afternoon.

Our dynamic forty-five-year-old leader had died an hour earlier in a tragic race car accident at the Old Lyme Speedway in Northern Connecticut. A blue Maserati doing 190 miles per hour tried to pass Pete on the inside lane as they headed into the final turn. The driver lost control, bounced off the retaining wall, and crashed headlong into Pete's Lamborghini, doing some 180 miles an hour at the time of the crash. Pete was dead on impact according to his racing buddy and business associate Dave Lineman, who watched the tragedy unfold a hundred feet in front of him.

"One minute we were smelling the finish line, and the next minute Pete's skull was split open, bits and pieces splattered all over the car. I'll never forget it as long as I live."

~

Pete's funeral was vintage Pete. I could tell his first-wife, Dorothy, and their kids, Pete Jr. and Julia, had choreographed the whole thing. Pete's beloved yellow Lamborghini, covered in red, white, and blue carnations, sat front and center on the altar.

Pete Jr., sang his father's favorite song, "Smile." Julia reminisced about her "Pops." Dorothy talked lovingly about their roller-coaster life and his unequivocal love for his children. Notable for her absence at the altar was Jolene. She sat in the second row in a form-fitting black and white sequin dress, looking like a cheap trick from the Vegas strip.

~

There was also a parade of personal eulogies. Person after person, many who had flown in from all over the country, thanked Pete for changing their lives.

Unfortunately, Pete's fast-track philosophy had also attracted its share of charlatans. I can still remember Pete's phony friend Charles Bronson II monopolizing the podium for almost thirty minutes. He urged all to "follow the light," as the Bible said, if we wanted to visit Pete in the "Promised Land." Six weeks later, old Charles had his bulb dimmed. He was arrested for selling nonexistent payphone booths to senior citizens in a multimillion-dollar investment scam.

~

In the two weeks following Pete's death, there were surprise disappearances, nasty personal family disputes, and an avalanche of unconfirmed rumors.

Before the actual funeral, Jolene — on the advice of her father, Lou Marshman, and his attorney — declared Pete had died intestate, which technically, under Connecticut law, left sole control of AFA, independently appraised at $150 million, to Jolene.

She also visited Rhode Island Trust, where she and Pete had $1.9 million in joint accounts, and had the funds transferred into a father-daughter joint bank account at Boston Trust Company in Wellesley, where Marshman claimed official residence.

~

Days after the funeral, the Marshmans, Maroneys, and their respective attorneys entered a no-holds-barred, highly personal court battle to settle AFA ownership.

Jolene, in what appeared to be a rare display of largess, agreed to give the two kids 33 percent of the sale proceeds. In reality, she wanted an expeditious ruling because unconfirmed rumors surfaced that Jolene paid her father's attorney $500,000 to 'insure' Pete died intestate (with no will).

Daughter Julia, age 24, challenged the intestate characterization in court. She testified that she and her brother had signed trust documents which named them controlling owners (51%) of the business.

Since there was no supporting documentation, Marshman's attorney went straight for the jugular. "Your honor, this is a case of a disgruntled family who was rejected by their father, attempting to build a financial claim based upon loose recollections, nonexistent documents, and casual conference room conversations with Mr. Craft, the godfather of Mr. Maroney's money-mongering daughter. Judge, as difficult and tragic as this case may be, you must render a decision based purely on the facts as we know them. The lack of a will meant Mr. Maroney intended to leave the business and all related assets to his current wife, Jolene."

The judge ruled in favor of Jolene but did cut the Maroney family some slack. He ordered both families to meet privately to discuss the sale of AFA and determine an appropriate split of the net proceeds.

He cautioned, "If the families cannot agree on a fair share within three months, the courts will appoint an independent arbitrator to resolve the dispute."

~

Between Pete's death and the public legal proceedings, all the office employees were emotionally rattled and concerned about the loss of a regular paycheck. The most concerned were the senior business consultants — like Alexandria Plummet — who were making more than they had ever made in their life.

4.

Enter the perennially nosy Alexandria Plummet.

Alexandria Plummet was the whole package: smart, sexy, street-savvy, and insecure.

She also knew information was king. Before Pete's death, the rumor was she had made a point of befriending Jolene, using the trials and tribulations of being a single mom as their common bond. Much to her chagrin, after Pete died and Jolene fled, Alexandria's flow of insider information vaporized.

For reasons unknown to me at the time, she had decided I was going to be her new source of insider information. First, she began to *casually* drop by my office to chit-chat, beginning each conversation with a disarming "Hey, you." Before long, I noticed we were playing twenty questions. "As a single mom, should I be looking elsewhere? Who's going to own the company? Are commission rates going to be reduced?"

"Why do you think I know the answers to those questions?" I responded.

Alexandria crossed her legs, smiled her mischievous smile, stared into my light blue eyes with her bright blue ones, and said, "As a member of the *buy-out group,* I want you to remember that Mommy deserves her fair share. I want to be treated as an equal, not just as a woman."

"What buy-out group?"

"Mommy's not stupid; I can read between the lines. Dawson told me Pete's death could be a huge income opportunity."

"How so?" I asked.

"Dawson told me to schmooze my top producers into believing that closing a few new cases a month would be the best tribute we could give to Pete. As you can see from my production numbers, the guilt pitch is working like a charm."

As we talked, three things became clear:

- She was confident that the eight male account managers always received higher commissions than the two females.
- She was financially insatiable. Whatever she earned was never enough.
- She drove my testosterone level through the roof when she crossed her legs and revealed her shapely thighs.

"Gotta get going," she said. "Have a producer in town for dinner."

I had one last question. "Who's the head of your buy-out rumor committee, in case we need some professional advice?"

Alexandria smiled coyly. "No investigative reporter worth their salt reveals sources."

~

Enter brash, razor-sharp Courtney Street.

Courtney and I were like the original odd couple. When I arrived at AFA, she was an eighteen-year-old part-time clerk who was going to NYU full time. She was also Julia Maroney's best friend. I remember Pete laughing, "It's your turn in the box. Figure out what to do with her. She's pissed off everybody else in the company, but she's super smart." I spent about thirty days doing *Courtney trial and error.* Creative writing, marketing, accounts receivable, recruitment telemarketing, etc. There were peaks of excellence followed by valleys of highly vocal dissatisfaction – for Courtney *and* for her immediate supervisor.

Like Pete, I enjoyed her spunk and respected her intelligence. Hence, an unorthodox solution — I'd make Courtney *my* executive assistant! People thought I was completely nuts. Craft laughed, " Buddy, can't wait to see this rodeo. It will be like trying to tame a wild stallion."

When I informed Courtney of my decision, she went bonkers, "Me, work for you! Not a chance. You're too demanding. Too undisciplined. You try to do too many things at once. You…"

I asked her to shut up for a moment so that I could explain her options. I told her she could work for me and get a forty percent raise, or she would get fired. She decided to "try" option number one. To everyone's surprise, she became my loyal eyes and ears. Lauren became her second mom, polishing her rough edges and sharing my little quirks, woman-to-woman, providing Courtney with insights on how to work most effectively with me while bonding the two of them together forever. "Men," I overheard Courtney commiserating with Lauren one afternoon. "It doesn't matter what age. They need to be led around by the nose."

Whenever Alexandria "accidentally" happened by, Courtney smelled the testosterone percolating and made it abundantly clear she didn't approve. At the five-minute mark, Courtney would storm through the doorway brusquely. "Time's up! You've got your next meeting with so and so…. right now!" Then Courtney would stare at Alexandria until she left.

~

As I was to learn, Alexandria had a patented information collection *and* distribution system. When she felt her questions had unearthed worthy tidbits, she'd pass them on to her two closest cronies, Sam Cameron and Bill Johnson. They, in turn, would redistribute their version of what they heard to the rest of the account managers, who would then create their own versions of the truth.

In the end, what Alexandria initially understood and passed on bore little resemblance to the rumors that would resurface in my office days later. It was like the children's game of "telephone." They were so obvious that it was comical. My biggest concern, however, was not the rumor-mongering. In many ways, that was harmless, mainly since I was able to manage the content that went into the Alexandria newswire. The more significant concern was the wasted time that could have been put to more productive use.

Initially, I thought Alexandria and her trusted communications team were odd bedfellows. Cameron, a late-sixties conservative retired insurance trainer, collected a full-time paycheck while spending half his time enhancing digital photographs with Adobe Photoshop. Johnson, Alexandria's arrogant mid-fifties direct supervisor, was an average coach with a hushed past — two broken marriages laced with spousal abuse, a touch of alcoholism, and some unstated drug rehabilitation. As time went on, I would learn they had more in common with Alexandria than I initially imagined.

~

After Pete's death, I made it my business to stop by Julia Maroney's office every day, ostensibly to check on some business issues. But she and I knew it was about more than that. From time to time, we'd close the door and shed a few tears together.

One day, she seemed noticeably upset. I tried to cheer her up. "Young lady, you keep frowning like that and I'll have to buy you some Estée Lauder night wrinkle repair."

"Maybe there's a reason," frowned Julia. "This battle with my stepmother is driving me crazy. You know, she emptied Dad's bank accounts. Mom didn't even get her monthly child support and alimony payments this past month. I've been trying to help," she sighed. And then, all at once, she burst out, "I hate that woman!"

"Julia, you've got to stay calm. Things have a way of working out. How can I help?"

As I leaned back in the chair, Craft wandered in. He saw the tears in Julia's eyes. "Is this guy making you cry?"

She smiled. "Uncle Dawson, Martin and I were just talking about the situation."

He looked at me pensively. "No problem; just don't forget about the agreement."

She nodded.

"Gotta go," he said.

"Martin," said Julia, "I hope you realize I have no problem working for you. Dad wanted that anyway."

"I'm not sure what you're talking about."

"Oh, I'm sorry; I should have realized. We're all under the same gag order until the negotiations are completed. Sorry."

I didn't let on, but I had no idea what the hell was going on. But my absence of a full deck of cards was starting to become apparent. The partners were trying to work a deal to buy the company without me, then maybe dribble out bits and pieces via stock options to the peons, like me.

I'd been screwed before, and now AFA was starting to feel like *Martin Ruff, Wall Street Redux.*

5.

Marshman went for a quick sale; Croft had other ideas.

Jolene and her father decided it was the perfect moment to sell AFA to the highest bidder. Sales remained strong and the internal disputes had not yet become public.

Lou Marshman hired killer attorney Bubba McElhanney to act as the sole voice of the seller to avoid the appearance of a distress sale. Marshman, who disliked Craft, Costas, and Carr because of their public disdain for his gold-digger daughter, was giddy with delight when he discovered that Pete's so-called partners didn't own a drop of equity. That meant he could do what he wanted, when he wanted to do it.

McElhanney's first stop was offered the company to the firm's number one product supplier at a healthy multiple of annual profits.

Carr, Costas, and Craft were one step ahead of Marshman. They had already made sure that the highly compensated Patrick Defoe, president of Appalachia, knew that Craft et al. were the real key to AFA's future health. Craft suggested to Defoe that if he took a pass on Jolene's offer to sell, Craft would finance the purchase with his other partners, and they, in turn, would sell a substantial equity interest at a discount to Appalachia. "I think it would be the classic win-win for everybody," said Craft on the phone.

"I know you well enough, Dawson. That down-the-line equity interest will cost Appalachia more than buying the company outright from Jolene right now, so why the hell would I even consider your offer?"

Craft, a world-class risk-taker, then gambled the house. "Because Jeremy, Eddie, and I will bolt. And when sales start slipping, your board is going to ask you, 'What the hell happened to our number-one product distributor?' It's your choice, pal; no skin off my nose." Craft paused, "You know, pal, there may also be some founder's equity [lowest price insider stock value] lying around that could be transferred to you personally."

~

The next day, Defoe called Jolene Maroney directly, since they had met at several company functions. Now knowing Craft's intention, he figured he could bully Mrs. Maroney into a fire-sale and then take his chances with Craft, Costas, and Carr.

"With all due respect, Mrs. Maroney, most companies are looking at the current AFA situation and thinking to themselves, 'I'll wait to see if the current management can hold it together.' Because we worked so closely with Pete, we know AFA well. Even if Dawson, Eddie, and Jeremy were to leave, I'm confident that, after a few initial hiccups, we could make the company prosper. However, I don't know how big the hiccups might be or how long it would take to restore a healthy growth trend. Fortunately for you and your family, Appalachia not only has a vision, but we also have deep pockets. That's why we can make you a substantive offer right now.

"We'd still like to offer you fifty percent of book value paid upfront, fifty percent cash and fifty percent preferred Appalachia stock, plus a generous secondary profit-sharing formula." In plain English, Defoe was offering a quarter of what the company was worth before the Craft sales surge, and a minor share of profits after Appalachia took the majority of profits each year.

The streetwise Jolene Maroney smelled a rat. "What makes you think Dawson, Eddie, and Jeremy want to leave? They are making more money than they've ever seen in their lives."

"I didn't say they were leaving, but they sure seem confident you couldn't possibly run things without them. Not to insult you, madam, but you have no operating experience, no business relationships with the field advisors, and no apparent role with employees looking for leadership."

While he was correct, Defoe had insulted Jolene big time. She and her dad refused to make a counteroffer. Through an unnamed source at Appalachia, Craft learned of Defoe's double-cross and coolly filed it away for future retribution.

Lou Marshman heard the same story from the company's other product suppliers as his broker shopped the company around to the other potential buyers. Craft had gotten to everybody with the same speech he'd given Appalachia, including the illegal private stock offer.

As Marshman, his attorney, his broker, and his daughter began to sweat, Craft and company made their own unsolicited offer: $10 million in cash for forty percent of the company, plus an immediate share of profits, and a secondary note at two points below prime to finance the balance of the company over ten years.

An unhappy Jolene Maroney reluctantly accepted the offer as her only real option.

~

Despite my equity understanding with Pete and my growing importance within the company, Costas, Carr, and Craft were hell-bent on eliminating me from the purchase process. "Dawson, do you think we should apprise Martin of the deal?" asked Carr, torn between doing the right thing and concern that his equity position would be diluted.

"I'm not sure," said Craft. "He's done some incredible things in the past twelve months to improve the overall value of the company. At the same time, I can't help but feel Pete was just smitten with his Wall Street background."

As Craft and Carr seesawed back and forth, Costas sat quietly recalling the early days: how he agreed to embrace Pete's vision, with no guarantees; how he used his credit cards to live on during the zero-cash-flow days; how the financial pressures destroyed his first marriage and shredded his relationship with his kids. Most of all, Costas remembered sitting on the floor of an office the size of a postage stamp making homemade charts to sell Pete's vision to prospective financial advisors. It was now his turn to speak.

"Eddie, I agree with Dawson. We're the ones who did all the grunt work to get this company off the ground while Martin was out making his millions on Wall Street. I'm the one with the bankruptcy on my record. We should make him earn his place, just like we had to. As far as I'm concerned, he's been paid for his contributions to date. We owe him zippo!"

Carr, never known for his original thinking, played follow the leader. "Jeremy, you're right. If we do all the work and put up all the cash, why should we let him in?"

"I say we give him a share of the profits, as Pete gave us," proposed Craft. "But the company equity is ours. Just like Pete did with us."

"I can live with that concept, depending upon what share of profits you're thinking," said Costas.

"I'm thinking ten percent. As in ninety to ten," smiled Craft.

The three men looked at each other without saying a word.

"So moved?" smiled Craft, breaking the silence.

"Motion carried," responded Costas and Carr with shit-eating grins on their faces.

6.

Lies, bribes, and other good things.

Craft was well-prepared when I approached him about my verbal agreement with Pete. "Good news, buddy! We plan to honor the profit-sharing agreement, just like you and Pete agreed. After all, we're family."

"What about the equity part?"

"Pal, I don't know what you're talking about; do you have something in writing?"

"No, it was a handshake."

"Pal, I do not disagree that you may have *thought* you and Pete had some general understanding, but Eddie, Jeremy, Pete, and I had been working on an equity participation deal for quite some time. His death only added certain urgency to those conversations. Your name never came up, but there's no question about your contributions to the firm. That's why Jeremy and Eddie want you to have a ten percent share of annual profits." He then handed me a check for $500,000 and said, "*Trust me, pal.* They'll be lots more where this came from, and we'll eventually figure out something on the stock."

We shook hands as he joked, "Don't forget to remind your accountant that it's his job to keep your taxes to a minimum."

I decided to say nothing about my five percent agreement with Pete. "Dawson, I have an idea. Since you're trying to work out something with the family, why don't we use this check for my portion of the equity purchase?"

He seemed surprised. "How do you know about the purchase of the company?"

"I don't know anything. It's the other three hundred-plus employees who are telling me what's going on."

"Pal, this is a complicated thing. I understand your interest. It's appreciated and won't be forgotten; I promise you." Craft started to walk out of my office and then paused. "Oh, I almost forgot. Dawson, Jeremy, and I own a little jewelry company for fun." Craft handed me a little clear plastic bag with a 3.4-carat diamond ring set in an 18-karat gold setting. "This is for Lauren."

~

That evening, I filled Lauren in over a bottle of wine. I placed the check next to her glass. "Here's a little something Dawson gave us today."

She stared at the amount. "Oh my God, you've got to be kidding!"

"Oh yeah," I said deadpan, taking the plastic bag out of my pocket. "Dawson also wanted you to have this little bauble."

"I love it," said Lauren as she slid it on her finger. "These guys certainly know how to travel first-class."

"Don't be fooled by a few little crumbs," I replied sarcastically. "I'm still just an expensive hired gun with no equity stake."

"You know, honey," Lauren said sweetly, "You sound incredibly ungrateful. Maybe you heard what you wanted to hear about the stock thing with Pete. Remember, *you're* the one who said Pete was very reluctant about giving you equity since Dawson, Eddie, and Jeremy didn't have any either."

"Equity participation is not about seniority; it's about contributions. AFA is not a hospital, you know," I replied accurately but insensitively.

Her pained expression telegraphed *low blow.* To her credit, she maintained her composure.

"Don't take this the wrong way. I love you very much. I've heard the wonderful things advisors have said about you at the Pete and Dawson dinners but, let's be honest: you've only been there eighteen months, while the three of them started by making invoices and taking out the trash."

I countered. "Let's think selfishly for a moment. Why did I get involved? We felt we had enough to be comfortable, but this was our chance to be super-wealthy and to drive our Bentley GT off to our private hangar at Westchester County Airport before boarding our jet to our mansion on Lake Tahoe. Remember? At fifty-seven, how many more chances like this do you think will come along?"

"Maybe I'm missing something. Aren't you making a ton of money?"

"But you said it yourself: I'm not making what they're making."

"Martin, *how much is enough*?" countered Lauren. "Don't get me wrong. I love the good life just like you, and we've been fortunate to have more than most. But are money and toys the measure of a man? I thank God every day that he has given us good health and a beautiful family. But most of all, I thank him for my wonderful loving husband. You have been and always will be the love of my life. What else do we need?"

7.

An emotional crisis in Scottsdale.

Lauren and I decided to celebrate our thirty-fifth wedding anniversary and her promotion to director of surgical services at Cornell by spending two weeks at the Four Seasons in Scottsdale, Arizona.

Our son Bart and Valerie, his beautiful wife of five years, and our first and only grandchild, two-year-old Bianca, had decided to join us. Valerie had just officially retired from her position as marketing and design director at the Elite Baking Company in Stamford, Connecticut. For the past seven years, she had reported to the two financially generous but egotistical founders, Barry Self and David Toys, who rarely saw eye-to-eye. She and Bart had decided it was time for her to manage the family's expanding commercial real-estate portfolio while running the family and handling a few selected design projects.

Valerie's personality was mini-Lauren: gracious, soft-spoken, and certainly no pushover. I would joke with Valerie that she was a superwoman just like her mother-in-law... married to a difficult man-child, birthing a precocious daughter, and putting up with her father-in-law's bizarre sense of humor.

Unfortunately, Martin Jr., our other son, was now living in Manhattan and was unable to join us. He had just completed an extensive information technology needs analysis for RD Fluids, a midsized ethanol processor poised for growth because of the escalating price of oil. They asked him to present his finding at an off-site board meeting near their San Antonio headquarters.

The March weather and our two-bedroom desert-view casitas worked perfectly for us as a family. Lauren and Valerie were regulars at the spa and pool. At the same time, I hacked around the golf course (sans Bart) and took hundreds of sunset and sunrise pictures to add to my extensive, unorganized digital library.

The vacation was a slam dunk from Bart's point of view: *free* five-star accommodations and a central business location so that he could hop on a charter plane to close yet another real-estate deal and still be back for a *free* four-course dinner. There was also *unlimited* grandparent babysitting, which allowed our sophisticated, worldly children to savor the local Scottsdale evening hotspots without having to worry about Bianca or Donovan, their complacent, white cinderblock-shaped English bulldog who snored like a roaring lion.

Late Tuesday afternoon, the concierge paged Lauren to participate in a planned conference call with a group of hospital managers. I coaxed an invitation to watch superwoman in action, under one condition: "to keep my big mouth shut." The remote conference included two doctors, one in Boston and one in New York; two of Lauren's senior nurse managers, Darlene and Cathy; and the hospital's chief administrative officer, Lorraine Tremble.

Cornell's growing reputation as *the* place for complicated procedures was attracting patients from all over the United States and abroad, leading doctors to jockey for calendar time in the new operating rooms. This conference call pitted Dr. Samuel Crittenden of Manhattan — a caustic, arrogant, sixty-something man and one of America's lead heart specialists — against Dr. Gabriel Wentworth of Boston — an up-and-coming orthopedic sports surgeon who was about fifteen years Dr. Crittenden's junior. A third doctor, the polished, handsome, single Chief of Surgery, Dr. Winston Barnhorn, played the role of referee. I remember Lauren pointing out that when Dr. B. (his nickname among the nurses) entered the operating room, the nurses, particularly the single ones, had trouble concentrating on the surgery at hand.

Due to an honest administrative error, both Crittenden and Wentworth had wealthy international patients flying in for lengthy elective surgeries in the same operating room on the same day. Neither wanted to change his schedule since both booked months in advance.

As the three postured and haggled, Lauren offered a practical solution. She would reopen an operating room currently being remodeled on a one-time-only basis. Within twenty minutes, she had obtained hospital management approval and assigned experienced staff, who were delighted to be paid the overtime rate.

True to form, Crittenden harrumphed out of the room with not so much as a thank you, while Barnhorn complimented Lauren profusely. "Lauren, before you arrived, this place was a well-meaning zoo. I cannot tell you how appreciative I am of all your hard work and professionalism. I hope that husband of yours understands how lucky he is."

I looked at Lauren. "Now *that* was an impressive display of soothing two titanic egos. Maybe you can give me a few pointers."

Suddenly I was Lauren's straight man. "I thought you were never going to ask. Courtney tells me it would hurt your cause at the office."

"Ha. Little Ms. Abrasive thinks *I* need polish. Amazing how you women always stick together."

"Honey, let's not get all defensive," replied Lauren with a disarming smile. "We've joked about your style over the years. Sometimes you say things without thinking and people get upset until they get to know you better and realize your specialty is putting your foot in your mouth. Think about it. Our last name communicates all: '*Ruff*'"

I stared in self-denial. "Now wait a minute…"

"Honey," she interrupted, "Let's not argue. We've got so much to be thankful for; let's enjoy our vacation."

"Deal," I said, putting out my hand.

The phone rang again before we completed our handshake. I assumed it was the hospital. "I guess they can't live without you. They're probably fighting about bathrooms now."

She waved her hand as if to say, *Quiet.* It was Martin, Jr., calling on his cell phone from the San Antonio airport.

It was a call that would change our lives forever.

~

Lauren listened silently. Small tears began to form in her eyes. She stayed calm and composed as she spoke. "When did you first begin to feel this way? [Pause.] I see. I didn't realize it. [Pause.] Honey, there's no reason to be embarrassed. Dad and I love you very much. I think the important thing right now is for you to relax as much as you can, then figure out the fastest way we can get you. [Pause.] I'm not great on plane connections and such; let me put Dad on the phone. (Pause.) Yes, I'll explain what you just told me."

Lauren looked at me. "Martin's in San Antonio. He says he's having a mental breakdown — everything is spinning and he can't catch his breath. He wants us to come and get him. He's worried you're going to demean him on the phone."

"Mental breakdown? Are both of you crazy? You just don't suddenly get a mental breakdown," I bellowed incredulously.

"Listen, he said it's been coming on for years, but he just didn't know what it was. He thought he could handle it by himself. He's embarrassed and humiliated."

"That kid was always a little fragile. Are we sure he's not exaggerating?"

"Right now, that doesn't matter. Your son is sitting on the floor in the corner of a busy airport crying. Get him to his mother." She narrowed her eyes at me. "And for God's sake, be gentle!"

I took a deep breath. My hand was shaking as I put the receiver to my ear. "Hey, Son," I said in the calmest possible tone. "Mom says you're in a bit of trouble. Just relax; we'll get you home."

~

First, there was dead silence. Then sobs. Then a nearly-incoherent, crackling voice. "Dad, I'm so sorry, I didn't know who else to call, I'm so embarrassed… I can only imagine what you must think of me. A grown man…."

"Son, forget all that. Let's think about this as a basketball game. You've dribbled the ball up the court like you used to do so well, three defenders have trapped you, and you need to find the open man."

Lauren rolled her eyes as if to say, *What the hell are you doing?*

"Dad, you don't understand. I can't think clearly; my head is spinning. What should I do?"

"You're less than an hour plane ride from the Phoenix airport?"

"Plane? Can't you drive over and pick me up?"

I could see I was dealing with an irrational mind. "Son, it will take us five hours to drive over and another five to get you back."

"That's okay, isn't it?" he whispered.

Rather than debate him, I calmly responded in pithy soundbites.

"What airline were you on?"

"America West, I think."

"Good; they fly directly to Phoenix."

"Why Phoenix?"

"We are right there."

"Oh."

"Lookup. Do you see any airline signs?"

"Yes. American Eagle."

"Good."

"Do you see any gate signs?"

"Twenty-four."

"Good. Just relax; someone will be there to help you in a few minutes. Just hold on and talk to Mom. I'll be right back."

"Okay."

I grabbed my cell phone, called American Eagle, and explained the situation. They couldn't have been more helpful. We also had a little good fortune; there was a direct flight to Phoenix in less than twenty minutes. They booked a ticket, got him a wheelchair, picked him up, held the plane, and then placed him in an empty first-class seat near the front exit.

"Martin, I'm back." I tried to explain what was happening. He freaked out, thinking I was having him committed.

"Dad, don't do this to me," he pleaded.

I became impatient. "God damn it, Martin, listen to me. We're trying to help you."

Lauren, alarmed that I was making a bad situation worse, grabbed the phone out of my hand. She softly repeated the critical parts again and again until he finally understood.

"Martin, we're right here. We're having a friend make sure you get on the right plane. The airports are hectic and confusing at this hour."

"Yes, Mom, it is busy. But why?" asked Martin, like a befuddled ten-year-old.

"Let's not worry about that, dear. When Mom's friend picks you up and takes you to the plane, she is going to give you a little sleeping pill so that you can relax. Remember, Mom's a nurse. When you wake up, we'll be right on the other side of the plane's door. Understand?"

There was a long pause.

Lauren broke the silence. "Martin, do you understand?"

"Mom, please don't get mad at me. You know I hate taking medicine."

"Martin, please take the pill they give you. Everything will be okay, darling. We love you very much."

"Love you too, Mom."

"Dad wants to say something."

"Love you, Martin. Can't wait to see you."

Martin Jr. tried to respond but began sobbing instead. I just said calmly, "See you in a couple of hours." At that moment, I realized my first son, the witty intellectual, the handsome scholar-athlete with the world at his feet, felt he was a miserable failure. Not with our family, not with Lauren, but in my eyes. Our relationship would never be the same.

8.

Enter Dr. James Sherry.

The next six months were quite painful.

MJ morphed into an entrenched agoraphobic as soon as we arrived home. He wouldn't leave his bedroom for the first two weeks, which created the need for full-time help to cook for, wash, and feed him. Lauren took vacation leave in the middle of her busiest time of year to be near him. The psychiatrist MJ had identified refused to make house calls, which led Lauren on a professional search to find a suitable replacement, someone skilled at deeply entrenched cases.

Through a series of referrals at the hospital, Lauren was introduced to Minnesota-born Dr. James Sherry, a mid-forties psychiatrist with a gentle manner who had himself suffered from panic disorder during a particularly trying time in his life. After a few sessions in which MJ rarely spoke, Dr. Sherry declared privately, "Getting MJ back into the game of life is going to be a difficult challenge. He is intellectually brilliant but unbelievably stubborn. That's not an easy combination to deal with."

Guilt-ridden, we asked the obvious. "What did we do wrong as parents?"

Dr. Sherry's response was less than comforting. "First of all, you need to understand you did nothing wrong. MJ is suffering from an extreme case of acute panic disorder. Until the last twenty years, psychiatry spun its wheels trying to identify the root cause of the individual patient's affliction, using antidepressants as a crutch. Now we understand that cases like MJ are partially biochemical — something has changed in the fundamental makeup and order of his brain cells.

"Consequently, he reacts negatively to certain stimuli he feels he cannot control. Those stimuli vary by patient. For some, confined spaces cause anguish; for others, it's loud noises at sporting events; and for others, it's about suffocating crowds."

"What exactly is MJ afraid of?"

"Unless you have had one of these attacks, it is hard to describe, much less empathize. The patient thinks he is going crazy, or he's having a heart attack. They are unable to maintain control. Life becomes a distant haze. Their heart pounds; their skeletal structure becomes limp; they can't even hold a glass of water. The actual attack may last only a few minutes, but when we are in the eye of the storm, it feels like forever."

I wondered if Sherry's description was a subconscious slip.

"Mr. Ruff, I can smell the wood burning," smiled Dr. Sherry. "Yes, I have suffered from acute panic disorder. It became all-consuming. I had to take a sabbatical from my practice."

"How long?"

"Four years."

Looking around at the doctor's family pictures, I couldn't help but ask, "How did your wife and kids come to grips with your condition?"

"They didn't; she divorced me and took the kids."

"How did you get cured?"

"APD is like alcoholism," Sherry responded. "Once inflicted, you have to stand guard for the rest of your life. Some days are better than others. But living with it is certainly better than the alternative. We've also learned that trying to discover what causes the change is a professional waste of time. Changes in brain chemistry are irreversible. The only known cure is to rebuild your self-confidence by slowly regaining control of the situations that caused the attacks in the first place."

"How long does that process take?" asked Lauren, now fully realizing the gravity of the situation.

"Depends on the patient. Initially, some patients try to control their entire environment; eventually they realize that's not possible."

The more I listened, the more upset I became. "Can you at least give me a damn time frame?"

"Simple case, two to three years. Worst case, a decade or so."

"Jesus Christ!"

"I realize your son's condition is quite a shock, but there is some good news in all this. No patient has ever died or even experienced a heart attack or stroke from this condition."

"So, where do we go from here?" asked Lauren.

"You understand, for the moment, that he has to be treated as if he is disabled? He cannot work. He needs regular counseling, initially with the two of you, eventually by himself. He needs medication and a predictable course of rehabilitation. In other words, he can be institutionalized, or we can attempt episodic home treatment."

I bristled. "No son of mine needs institutionalization!"

"Calm down, honey."

Sherry responded calmly, "I was going to suggest we start by treating him at home. Let's see if the familiar surroundings help matters."

~

After twelve months of intense treatment and a few hiccups, MJ made some progress. He was now able to drive about a quarter of a mile to the grocery store, buy food for himself, and make a meal.

During that time, his brother Bart tried everything he could think of — from playing Madden NFL video football to gentle conversations recalling fun times and pleasant memories to stern admonishments about MJ's need to "get out of his funk." Bart desperately wanted his childhood role model to snap out of his mental malaise. Nothing worked. In time, Bart just stopped trying.

At age 58, I found I was feeling quite sorry for myself. We were restricted geographically. MJ had given up his apartment in Darien and moved into Southport full time. It was like having a child return home. MJ was always on the phone checking our whereabouts to avoid having a relapse. I was utterly frustrated, and it showed. Dr. Sherry suggested we practice driving to the airport. I'll never forget that first exercise. When MJ realized we were on the Throggs Neck Bridge across Long Island Sound, he completed wigged out, and then he cried all the way home.

At a subsequent session with Dr. Sherry, it became clear that MJ blamed much of his pain on my impatience, insensitivity, and overbearing personal expectations. He, the doctor, and Lauren all agreed Lauren should be MJ's "safe person," the person who would act as surrogate shrink when he experienced emotional duress, which was most of the time.

Effectively, I became a man without a family.

9.

The wisdom of Joanne Mathias.

While chaos and personal humiliation reigned supreme at home, the business couldn't have been more fun and satisfying. My twenty-five-plus years of diverse business experience fit the needs of post-Pete AFA like a glove.

Strategic insights and pragmatic solutions poured out of my head. There was something for everybody: lead generation programs for field producers, personal branding campaigns for our business consultants, new consumer promotional programs, new safe-money products with stable returns, and principal protection for investors. There was even an award-winning corporate advertising campaign featuring our field advisors that increased AFA corporate awareness by 213 percent.

By the end of my second year, AFA had been named the fastest growing financial advisory in America, and our consultants and their licensed advisors were making a ton more money. Everybody, that is, except for a few stubborn consultants who refused to keep up with the changes— people like Alexandria Plummet.

For me, the incredible respect I was accorded every day at the office replaced the growing emotional void at home. For the first time in years, I looked forward to work every day — equity or no equity. No problem was too significant, no business dilemma too stressful. Before long, as one of the account managers characterized it, "Martin, you're AFA's poster child. Your stamp is all over the company."

Lauren had decided to put her career on hold and focus on MJ; they created an impenetrable bond. Casual dinner conversation felt like a two-way affair between Lauren and MJ, with me an inconsequential bystander. Soon I was intentionally spending twelve- to fourteen-hour days at the office or on the road, searching for deals, visiting potential strategic partners, or stopping by to see top producers.

I felt I was about to explode. I needed someone to talk to, someone I thought I could trust. Enter Joanne Mathias, a red-haired firebrand and close friend whom I had recruited from the advertising industry. I figured she was a pro at marketing and building client relationships. She was a perfect fit, and in a short time, I promoted her to marketing director, reporting directly to me. We were riding home together one night, making small talk.

"Red," as I called her, "would you mind if I ask you something very personal?"

"So long as you're not going to ask me to leave John [her husband] and run away with you, I'm fine," she laughed.

"I've heard you talk about your alcoholic dad, how he divided you and your mom. I think I've got a somewhat similar situation brewing." As I described the current state of my home front and my feelings, she finished my sentences before they were formed.

"MJ is doing to you exactly what my father did to me as a teenager. He used his alcoholism as an excuse to shut me out. I was too independent, not what he expected in a daughter. He was constantly telling me I didn't have the sensitivity to understand his problems. We had an impossible time communicating. He had a twisted way of highlighting my foibles every goddamn chance he could. He was particularly good at talking trash when I was within earshot or hinting things to my mother; it was so humiliating. I tried to keep my cool, but my anger was always just below the surface. Eventually, I decided I needed a confidant. My psychiatrist helped me understand and accept that there is no such thing as a three-way relationship with an irrational person. Someone must be the odd person out. That little piece of wisdom cost about $20,000 and two years of my life."

All I could say was, "Holy shit!" I saw the parallels to my own situation.

She smiled her devilish smile. "My friend, that psychological insight is my gift to you, absolutely free, and unencumbered by a salary increase suggestion, although that would be appreciated!"

10.

Plummet starts to lay her foundation.

I was walking past Alexandria's office when she flagged me down.

"Hey, you, we need to talk to you." The administrative aides in the area chuckled.

I walked in with a big smile on my face. "You rang, madam?"

"I think I need some help."

"You think?"

Alexandria started to explain her business problem, carefully providing her version of the truth. "I've always prided myself on my close relationships with my advisors. When they talk to Alexandria, they know they will get an objective case analysis and first-class product solutions with options."

"So?" I chose not to divulge that I knew her income was down thirty-five percent versus a year ago, and that a management analysis suggested an even uglier trend line unless something was done. I just wasn't close enough to know what that something should be. I also knew we had received requests from some of her best advisors to be assigned to another account manager or, worse still from my perspective, leave the company altogether.

Her story was that the stock market was growing at a nice clip and interest rates were up, so people didn't want reasonable returns with principal protection. From talking to the field every day, I knew that was absolutely, positively *not* the case.

I explained while it wasn't my job to handle day-to-day operations, I would be willing to spend a few hours on the phone talking to her advisors so we could pinpoint what needed to be fixed. I explained that the approach was called "one-on-

one qualitative research" and was used by many large companies. All Alexandria had to do was to arrange back-to-back telephone appointments with a select number of past and present top advisors.

Her first response was predictable. "I don't think so. You'll screw things up. I've worked hard to build my field producer relationships."

I tried to disarm her belligerence. "Alexandria, trust me; I've done this kind of thing hundreds of times in my business career. And you're going to be right there with me."

She was expressionless. She turned her back to me and stared at the dry board on her wall, covered with names and sales targets. There was dead silence for more than thirty seconds. "Okay," she said. "Let's try it. I'll make the arrangements. When should we do it?"

"You know I've been forbidden to keep my schedule by Courtney," I joked.

"I don't get it. Courtney's a twenty-year-old loudmouth who intimidates you. How can you give me such a hard time and let her get away with murder?"

"Courtney's the smartest person I've ever met, and she's incredibly organized. She gives me the confidence I need to juggle ten balls at a time, and she will always have my back. I'd trust her with my life."

Alexandria leaned back in her seat. "I've never heard a man talk about a woman like that."

"And for the record," I said, "I didn't give you a hard time."

"Yes, you did."

"No, I just set up the damn calls."

As I left her office, I turned one last time. She smiled and mimicked with her lips, "Yes, you did."

~

I wandered around the office for an hour, talking to people to get a sense of what was going on. My objective was simple: push people to exceed their daily goals, an AFA tradition. My meanderings were also a platform to display my *other* management talents. I'd make paper airplanes and fly them over people's heads, play one-on-one basketball with pencils and wastepaper baskets, and crush paper into balls and toss them around. These silly little acts tended to boost morale by showing people it's okay to lighten up.

When I returned, Courtney was standing in my doorway, hands on hips. The stare was foreboding , "Martin, you're in deep, deep gaga." I didn't have a clue what the problem was.

"Alexandria called. She said you agreed to give her two hours with her producers on Thursday between ten and twelve. First, you don't have two hours that day. Secondly, isn't that Joanne and Bill's job? You know you can't please everybody all the time. You're driving me to drink."

"Let's go into my office and discuss the matter like adults."

She shrugged her shoulders, let out a gigantic URRGGH, and followed me in.

I explained calmly and firmly that I didn't set a time. "I told Alexandria that was for the two of you to decide."

"Alexandria is such a bitch. She always has to do things her way!"

"Courtney, I love you, but you just can't say that!" I spent a few minutes explaining that she represented me within the company and had to watch what she said. Then we arrived at the real problem.

"Now answer me this. Why does Ms. Plummet deserve special treatment? I see her production reports every week; the numbers suck!"

"I guess I just feel a little sorry for her," I responded sheepishly.

"Is that the real reason?" glared Courtney with her right hand on her hip.

~

Our first call was to Alexandria's highest-grossing advisors, a partnership in Missoula, Montana, run by brothers Michael and Dan Whitman. "These guys love me, plus they have lots of upside."

Michael and Dan were both in their forties. Over the past thirty years, their dad had built the largest property and casualty agency (house, auto, and fire insurance only) in the Northern Plains states. They had almost 20,000 clients. Dad, at age sixty-five, had decided to wind down, confident that his sons, who had worked in the business for twenty years, had the right experience to take over the practice.

Dan, the more conservative computer nerd, was going to manage day-to-day internal operations. At the same time, the outgoing, gregarious Michael would focus on identifying new ways to leverage the existing client base. Michael had been recruited by Bill Johnson, heard Pete's pitch, and was assigned to Alexandria. They cross-sold about $10 million in safe money products to existing clients during their first year with AFA. From Alexandria's perspective, they were more than just friendly people; they represented about $60,000 in annual income. She made sure she maintained a solid personal relationship in addition to advising them on business matters.

I was starting to get the drill with Alexandria. She was worried. They had been through their existing client database and weren't sure what to do next to keep their commission income growing.

Given our early talks, I was amazed at Alexandria's telephone introduction. "Dan and Michael, I want to introduce the company's strategic genius, Martin Ruff. You gentlemen will meet him in person at the upcoming conference in Hawaii, but I thought it was important that we get him thinking about taking your business to the next level right now. He's helped a lot of our advisors in situations like yours. I've given him some background, but why don't you explain your hopes and dreams in your words, and who does what to whom in your organization."

The two brothers couldn't have been nicer. In the end, they summed up their observations quite candidly.

"Alexandria is charming and a lot of fun. But when we ask about one of the new programs you guys have introduced to the field, her answer is always the same," said Dan. "'Why don't we let *them* work the bugs out of the new stuff before we just jump in?' Then we visit Bridgeport and meet other AFA advisors who tell us they have been using those new programs successfully for six months."

Despite being pained by the summary, Alexandria remained professional. After Dan and Michael left, she stood at the door to my office. "Okay, I get it. This forty-something babe has to make some adjustments. But honestly, where do I start?"

"How about drinks at Le Périgord?" I was surprised, but not sorry, as the words blurted out of my mouth.

She opened her purse, refreshed her lips with a deep red lipstick, and pushed her long, straight blond hair back from her face. I could feel a sudden rise in my pants. She noticed and smiled. "What time are you thinking?"

11.

The tortured love sonnet, and other bad choices.

As I drove to the Périgord, my phone rang. It was Alexandria. My first thought — she was canceling. "Just wanted to let you know I'll be a few minutes late. I just got off a long call with one of my producers."

"Listen, we can do it another time," I said.

"Not a chance; free drinks are free drinks. With the cost of cabs, a girl's gotta economize somewhere."

I loved her dry sense of humor and wondered what my real intention was. A middle-aged, ego-enhancing flirtation? The search for a new friend? A massive case of bad judgment? The desire to sample sex with someone other than Lauren? I concluded it was probably some combination of all four. *But even acknowledging those possibilities, I didn't turn around and go home.*

The bar was half-full when I arrived. I spotted a quiet table in the corner, far away from the main dining area. Alexandria arrived a few minutes later, dressed to kill. Her form-fitting leopard-spotted dress, long straight golden hair, confident walk, and sensual red lips turned every male head in the place. And she knew it.

"UMMM-UMMM," I drooled.

"You like?" she teased.

I tried to be cool. "So, how did your producer call go?"

"What producer?" She laughed. "Do you think I stashed this dress in my file cabinet?"

After ordering an Appletini and a Chivas on the rocks, we began to talk shop. She explained the telephone research conversations calls were an eye-opening experience.

One martini later, there was a second hint of honesty. "You make everything sound like success is guaranteed. I'm sick of hearing, 'What does Martin suggest?' Tell me, what happens when your damn suggestions blow up?"

I responded with bravado, "*You* pick up the pieces and get back in the batter's box."

She was concerned about her image. "So, *you* make the mistakes and *I* have to pick up the pieces as twenty years of building my credibility goes down the drain?!"

"Don't you think you're giving me a little too much credit by assuming everybody will try everything I suggest?"

"That's the scary part. You could sell ice to the Eskimos."

A second martini and scotch arrived. I launched into some esoteric diatribe about my business philosophy, as gleaned over the years. I sounded like a condescending, pompous ass; platitudes and clichés flowed like water. "Business is about survival through evolution. Good is no longer good enough. The best defense is a good offense."

She shook her head. "Do you believe all that bullshit?"

I became defensive. "As incredible as it may seem, the answer is yes. Think about it for a minute. I didn't need this job. I got involved because I thought AFA had a shot at being a big-time company with a big personal payoff. You know, I'm not a complete fool."

"Why is it when a guy asks a challenging question, it's just business, but when a woman does the same thing, it becomes highly personal? You men and your goddamn testosterone!"

"Another martini?" She nodded yes.

Either we were entering a different space or the martinis were wearing her down because she became less challenging, more conversational. She probed my background and seemed genuinely surprised at the depth of my operating experience and business accomplishments.

"Why did you stop?"

"I guess I was burned out from the nonstop business intensity. The lies. The posturing. The shades of gray." I raised my hand. "Waiter, can I have the check?"

"Where are you going?"

"I figured we were finished."

"I'd like another drink," she smiled.

I looked at her. Something was different.

"Are you intimidated by me? Most men are," she said.

"No. But then again, I'm not most men."

I decided to add some finger food to the drink order. "Listen, if you're going to keep beating the shit out of me, you need something nutritional to replace the lost energy."

She laughed and then turned dead serious. "Why are you here? You're married. Your wife's picture is all over the damn company. You're like the magical couple who has it all."

"You want an honest answer, or just an answer?" I then gave her a *Reader's Digest* version of the MJ situation. "So, I guess down deep, I just wanted somebody to talk to."

She apologized, "Sorry I've been a bitch to you all evening,"

"Actually, from the very first day we met."

"So why bother with me?"

"Maybe I'm just attracted to smart, beautiful, combative women."

"I think that means you want to have sex."

"I didn't say that."

"You implied."

~

Alexandria gave me a respite. "So, how much do you know about me?"

"For better or worse, I never got on the gossip train on Wall Street, and I'm sure as hell not going to start in Bridgeport. I do my *own* research and come to my *own* conclusions. No need to get clouded by someone else's agenda."

I touched a chord. I could feel Alexandria reaching out. She was born in the heart of Middle America — Lincoln, Nebraska — and had an older sister, Tori, who never left home. Alexandria was also a proud single mom with two grown daughters, Melissa and Shanti.

"My first husband was a real shit! We met, married, and lived in Boston. The two girls were born during the first three years. I worked part-time as an airline administrator in town. He was in outside sales and traveled Monday to Thursday. One day he came home from a trip to announce that he was leaving, and *I could have the girls.* We wound up in alimony court. He made a few payments then disappeared altogether.

"I was desperate to earn more money, since I'd decided to stay in Boston. I preferred the cosmopolitan lifestyle to the grim reality of small-town America. After some job interviews, I was hired by an insurance company that wholesaled fixed annuities to field marketing organizations like AFA. I broke my butt learning product lines, studying for licensing exams, and becoming a salesperson. Despite all the effort, I still had credibility problems with the mostly male target audience, a bunch of horny old middle-aged men. But I was determined to succeed, so I decided to use my looks and personality to my advantage.

"Most times I had to tease my way to that initial appointment. True to form, most guys wanted to get in my pants first and hear about my product line second. I never once mixed business and pleasure. Word got around I was for real. Before long, I had an envious customer list and was making pretty good money.

"Did the girls eventually get to know their father?"

"They haven't seen him since they were two."

"How does a father disown his children?"

"You think that's pathetic? Guess what this 'smart, combative woman' did next? I got married again to a nice guy, and the girls liked him. He was ten years younger than me, so the sex was great. Unfortunately, he turned out to be a drug addict. The girls were teens by then and I wanted them to have some semblance of a father, so I foolishly supported his habit for three years. Eventually, we reached a stalemate — he wouldn't enter rehab, and I was tired of the financial burden. I was also concerned he'd screw up the girls and turn them into addicts. We reached a rather bizarre court settlement: he would forgo all visitation rights in exchange for three years of alimony payments.

"I got stung financially. The girls were rejected again. After those three years, he just dropped off the face of the earth. Maybe now you have some sense of why this 'smart, combative woman' is so belligerent."

There wasn't much to say after that. I blurted out the first thing that crossed my mind. "So, how did you meet Dawson?"

She assumed I was referring to the generally salacious rumor making the rounds. "I was selling triple-A investment contracts. He was one of my prospects. He liked my spunk. My product lines. My pitch. When AFA started to grow, he made me an offer I couldn't refuse."

"Interesting."

"In-ter-est-ing." She had a phonetically peculiar way of enunciating the word. "Is that all you can say? And, no, despite what you may have heard, I never slept with him. It never even crossed my mind. Haven't you noticed? The guy is homely, bald, and chubby. Not my type. If you and your buddies are going to play a game of rumors, at least make it somebody I'd actually consider."

"I'm bald."

"No, you're married and bald."

"So, why are you here?"

"I find you kind of sexy," she purred.

I wanted to reach across the table and kiss her. Instead, I wrote a poem on a napkin and handed it to her. "Here's a memento of the evening. Thanks for the time."

She opened the white cloth napkin and read the title out loud, *Should, Shouldn't.* "Sounds interesting. I'll read it in bed later."

Lights, action, camera.
Unreal set,
Noisy, crowded bar.
Surreal situation,
Dead silence.
Consuming dilemma
Can, can't
Should, shouldn't…

I paid the check. We got our cars from the valet. I kissed her gently on the cheek and we drove our separate ways.

~

A few minutes later, my mobile rang. It was 9:30 P.M. Lauren asked, "Are you all right? I was starting to worry."

"God, baby, I'm so sorry I forgot to call. Two of our top advisors, Dave Lineman and Jim Cleveland, just dropped in out of nowhere, looking for a free dinner. Dawson was busy and I was standing nearby. Next thing you know, I'm the evening's master of ceremonies."

"No, you were asked because you're his top schmoozer. And he knows you'll do anything for AFA. Just be careful and don't fall asleep; I want you home in one piece."

"I should be home in about a half-hour; I'm just leaving downtown."

As I drove, I wondered which was worse: *lying to Lauren for the first time in 35 years, or the fact that she believed me, implicitly.*

When I arrived home, Lauren was sleeping peacefully. I slipped in bed next to her soft, warm body. Instinctively, she knew I was there. She rolled over and kissed me gently on the lips.

12.

The inappropriate acquisition.

It was no accident that the weekly sales production board resided in a place of prominence. We all believed that good salespeople were very competitive *and* very sensitive. The production board served two purposes.

First and foremost, posting weekly results stimulated sales activity. Every account manager wanted to be at or near the top of the board every week; it was a public disclosure of their success with assigned advisors, and how much they made.

Second, the board was a slump-reducer. When an account manager was in a sales slump, their sensitivity meter would kick in and they would break their tail *not* to be near the bottom. We had an unofficial slogan: "Middle means slump, top means drinks for all."

Alexandria had been mired in the lower half for eight straight weeks.

One late afternoon, I happened to be looking at the latest posted numbers on the way to my car.

"I know what you're thinking. I'm not worried," said Alexandria softly from behind. "A lot of my guys have been on vacation. It's summertime. They'll roar back in the fall."

I nodded.

"There's also something else I want to talk to you about that could be gigantic for the company… and for yours truly. Dan Whitman has been perfecting it for some time, so it's field-tested."

"Are you going to give me a hint?" I replied.

"No, we're going to do this *your way*. I have some interesting materials, and I made a date with Courtney. Surprised?" She batted her eyes ever so slightly and slithered away.

~

I knew Alexandria wanted something when she appeared right on time, an unusual occurrence. She started with a few pleasantries. "I enjoyed the other night, and the poem was in-ter-est-ing. Nobody ever wrote me a poem." Then she headed into her pitch. "What's a financial advisor's most important asset?"

I thought to myself, *Who gives a damn? She turns me on.*

Alexandria answered her own question. "Their time. That's why an AFA-ContactPro partnership."

"Contact who?"

"ContactPro. Don't worry; we'll get to that part in a minute. First, you need to understand their patented software package. It's all based on the concept of merging toll-free telephony with the 24/7 capability of memory-based remote servers."

I began to smirk.

"Why the shit-eating grin?" she asked, half-kidding. "This girl's trying to make some money. I want you to listen!"

I couldn't resist responding. "How does a woman who prefers phone calls to email suddenly know about the capability of memory-based remote servers?"

"Okay, okay, so Dan helped me with my presentation. But this thing is cool. ContactPro is a small technology company based in southern Litchfield, about thirty miles north of here. They've created a single-point communications application software designed for the road warrior. The advisor calls his own dedicated 800 number from anywhere in the United States, day or night, seven days a week, to access his emails, telephone messages, databases, client profiles, and whatever else he so chooses to have programmed into ContactPro servers."

I asked a few basic questions. *How long have they been in business? Who are their corporate clients? How many financial advisor subscribers do they have? How does the information get programmed? Can calls be forwarded from the client's office to the 800 number? Is there firewall protection?*

She smiled. "I don't know. That's what you're supposed to figure out. I just talked to the president and negotiated the revenue-sharing deal. We get ten percent of the first month revenues for every advisor that signs on to the system. Then we get five percent for the next eleven months, and yours truly gets a nice commission from AFA on every sale. So, everybody wins."

I had quite a dilemma. The concept was irrelevant to our current business model, and she had absolutely no authority giving third-party vendors the impression she spoke for the company. On the flip side, I didn't want to dampen her business enthusiasm in case I was wrong, or squelch what I perceived might be a budding personal relationship.

"I know. You're skeptical. That's why I arranged a meeting with the president, Gil Rodman. He'll give you a complete demo and answer all your questions. He sounded very nice on the phone. Plus, I checked where you live. They are less than three miles from your home."

"Alexandria, I appreciate what you are trying to do, but…"

She had anticipated my next objection and was ready with the appropriate retort. "I made the meeting late in the day, on your way home. I was thinking that maybe after the meeting you could buy this girl a little dinner, since I'll have to drive back to the city. You wouldn't want me to do that on an empty stomach?"

"Okay, okay. But for Christ's sake, don't tell Courtney."

13.

The first lie.

ContactPro Ltd. was in the middle of one of the picturesque Litchfield's hottest office complexes, called Technology Center Research Park. The mirrored facade of the ultra-modern ContactPro building was a vibrant crimson and dark gray. However, once inside, there was an eerie silence, as if everyone had been evacuated. The feeling reminded me of the late nineties dot-com boom, which left venture capitalists with bankrupt internet businesses and empty re-wired landmark buildings up and down Manhattan's Silicon Alley (West Broadway between Houston and Canal Streets).

There was no receptionist, just a set of locked double-glass doors with a bright red button that said, "Push me." A young man with wire-rimmed glasses, a full head of groomed hair, and a rumpled jacket with a non-matching shirt and tie greeted us. "I'm Gil Rodman; you must be Alexandria and Martin. Thanks for coming."

Alexandria was already in venture-building mode. "Oh, no, the pleasure is all ours. Thanks for spending the time with us."

"I've set up a presentation and demonstration in our boardroom."

As we walked down the hall, I couldn't help but notice more than half the seventy-five or so work stations were empty cubicles. "Looks like you've invested for growth. How long have you been in business?"

"We've been around for about four years. We've had to do some retooling of our business model since we discovered our primary prospect is the corporate enterprise rather than the internet community's end customer. We're also in the middle of another round of financing."

Translation: they wasted a ton of stage-one venture capital, maybe between $10 and $20 million judging from the facility, before they had a proven business model. Then they cut operating costs to conserve cash and were again running out of money, probably because they hadn't sold zilch to anybody.

The presentation and subsequent discussion went pretty much as I expected. There wasn't a salesperson to be had, and Rodman had no idea what we did or whether his model was appropriate for us. He was suggesting that our advisors, who had long-standing offices in their communities, shut them down and convert to virtual storage of their sensitive sales information, databases, etc., on his remote servers.

I explained that people like to visit the offices of financial advisors. He said he didn't know that and looked at Alexandria. I told him most advisors were marginally computer-literate and got most of their communications through a designated administrative assistant. He said he didn't know that either and again looked at Alexandria. I told him we were not in the business of selling branded third-party proprietary software with no headquarters controls.

Later, standing in the parking lot outside the building, I said, "The ContactPro situation is not right for us. Let's discuss it tomorrow at the office."

"What about my dinner?" she asked.

~

I decided on dinner at the Tomiyama Sushi Grill at the edge of the 79th Street pier, across the river from the Pacific Palisades. The sunset was spectacular, the George Washington Bridge twinkled, and the sushi was fresh. Importantly, Lauren hated sushi, so there was zero chance of an accidental encounter.

As always, the conversation began with the business issue du jour — in this case, ContactPro. I reiterated the same points I had made to Rodman about a lack of strategic fit. Alexandria uncharacteristically acquiesced. "Now that I understand better, I'm sorry about wasting your time."

"Oh, my God," I joked, "Does that mean you trust me?"

She smiled. "No. It just means I *may* be *beginning* to trust you." I touched the hand she placed on the table. "What did you think of Gil's business acumen?" she asked.

"Very smart, but he has no clue what the financial marketplace needs, and I seriously doubt whether he'll raise anymore venture money in today's environment." I paused and smiled mischievously. "And he seems a bit young for you."

"That's a terrible thing to say!" Alexandria said in mock-outrage. "Besides, Gil's not my type."

"Well, I'm trying to figure out why else we're here."

"Bill Johnson suggested we meet. He may be an early investor in ContactPro. I'm not sure."

"So, we're here because your boss is using you to recapture his investment, and then some?"

"You make Bill sound dreadful."

"And let me guess: Johnson promised you a finder's fee, a bonus commission, or some future favor if an AFA-Contract Pro deal closed."

"Well, there was some of that," she admitted, "But Gil Rodman also sounded cute on the phone."

"I thought you said he wasn't your type?"

Alexandria just glared.

Dinner was a terribly quiet affair. As I signed the check, Alexandria finally spoke. "How did you explain the other night to Lauren? I mean, what did she say when you got home?"

"I had to lie."

"That's terrible. What's worse is, I know Lauren."

14.

A single mom's dilemma.

Alexandria stared into space. "I was thinking about Shanti."

"Shanti?'

I was beginning to learn that Alexandria's thought process could go any which way, and sometimes her most direct route connected two seemingly unconnected dots. This was one of those moments.

"Remember, I'm a single mom; I worry about my daughters all the time." Alexandria explained that Melissa was straight, worked hard, paid her bills, was looking for a nice guy, and had decided, after graduating from Oregon State University, that she preferred the Pacific Northwest and its lifestyle. She was working as an assistant editor for an innovative boutique publisher, The Intelligent Press.

Her sister Shanti had declared she was gay about two years ago, had dropped out of college, and had held a string of low-paying, dead-end jobs as she traveled from town to town, seeing the United States.

"I'm not upset about the gay thing. That's a lifestyle preference; Shanti's a grown woman and has the right to make her own choices. I've always tried to balance being a caring mother with disciplined values, while at the same time allowing my daughters the freedom to grow through personal experience. But Shanti is very lazy. She figures I make good money and has no problem with me subsidizing her…regularly. She's got a bit of her father and stepfather in her. Whenever she needs money, a thousand dollars here, two thousand dollars there, I give it to her. The other night I finally said enough is enough. I'm sending you one more check. That's it."

"What did she say?"

"I told her, 'You've got to be like everybody else in this world. Go out, get a steady job, and stand on your own two feet. Just like your mom and sister do.'"

"Sound, practical advice. How did she respond?"

"Horribly. First, Shanti got irrational and vindictive, said I loved Melissa more — that I never wanted her in the first place. Then she became downright nasty, claiming my failed marriages to 'two worthless younger husbands' invalidated heterosexual relationships. She then explained the benefits of gay relationships: 'Partners are carefully chosen for the right reasons — love and loyalty; they are less promiscuous and more faithful; they are better listeners and more sensitive to their partner's needs.; Then she slammed the phone down and hasn't returned a call since."

~

I had no idea what had just happened. All she said was, "Just hold me." We sat silently for a couple of minutes, then she said, "Thank you; time for this girl to get home."

We walked to her car at the end of the parking lot. She looked up. The stars were twinkling brightly in the clear night sky. "My goodness, what a beautiful night."

I put my arms around her waist. She put hers around mine. I hugged her. She hung on for dear life. "God, why is life so complicated?"

We kissed gently. Alexandria got into her car as I stood and watched. My cellphone started to ring. I didn't want to answer. She rolled the window down and smiled, "Hey, come here, you."

I did as she said. "Don't you answer when Madam rings?" She got out of her car and kissed me again — this time a bit more intensely.

15.

Going to Hawaii, alone…

Lauren decided MJ's emotional fragility required her to miss her first AFA advisor conference in two years. It was in Hawaii, and she felt he shouldn't be left alone that far away for seven days.

We had a session with Dr. Sherry to weigh the pros and cons. In the end, he concluded MJ had made little progress in the past year, so pushing him at this stage could do more harm than good.

MJ's timing was most unfortunate. We had spent six months planning AFA's biggest and most expensive thank you ever — 1000 of our top advisors and their spouses were being feted for six days at the opulent new Four Seasons on the Big Island of Hawaii. Former New York Mayor Rudy Giuliani was our keynote speaker, and the Beach Boys were booked for a private concert.

From a purely personal standpoint, this was also my major coming-out party. I had ninety minutes of podium time to present four innovative, industry-leading programs we had developed and tested, and we'd made sure each presentation contained the same important subliminal message: AFA (post-Pete) was financially stronger than ever, more innovative than ever, and in very capable management hands.

With the long hours and the familial stress, I had forgotten one important thing. All the advisor entertaining had grown my neck size from 16 to 16½. I needed a few new dress shirts and ties before I got to the podium. I told Courtney to adjust my schedule because I needed to leave early and go shopping the next day. She led me to believe there was nothing important on the calendar that couldn't be shifted.

On my way home that afternoon, my cell phone rang. It was Alexandria. "Blowing me off again?"

"What are you talking about?" I said.

"I was on your calendar to get a sneak preview of what you were presenting at the conference, so I'd look like I knew what I was doing. But Courtney called me an hour ago to say we had to reschedule after the conference."

"Look, I don't know anything about that. All I know is that Lauren bailed on the conference, and she's tied up working late, and I need two new shirts and ties because I'm getting too fat."

I could smell the wood burning on the other end of the phone. "Did you ever read the book *Whenever God Winks* by Reverend Jonas Bond?"

I'm stuck in a torrential rainstorm, traffic is moving at a snail's pace on the FDR, and this zany broad wants to talk about some crazy book? I knew if I hung up, she'd call me back! "No, Alexandria, can't say I have."

"Reverend Bond says when one door closes, it's because he just opened another one. Don't you see? I am going to help you shop, and you're going to fill me in."

The idea didn't sound half bad: shopping with some attractive eye candy on my arm. Besides, based on the way she dressed, she'd probably do a better job of color coordination than I would alone. It was just the "business fill-in" part that sounded like it could be painful.

"Hey! Are you still there? Calling Martin, calling Martin. Yoo hoo."

"Saks Fifth Avenue," I blurted.

"Perfect," she said. " I need a new pair of Jimmy Choo's for the Giuliani opening-night black-tie dinner dance."

~

We had a great time shopping for me. She asked me what color the suits were; then she began looking at every shirt on the floor, in price categories ranging from expensive to very expensive.

"May I help, madam?' said the well-mannered, very gay salesman.

"*Pleaaase*, I'm fine," responded Alexandria curtly as she rummaged through the counter and glass racks.

"Come here; I think we have just the right thing for your gray pin-striped suit." She placed a Giorgio Armani fawn-camel shirt on my chest. "Perfect. I also think I found the tie to match. See, it's got some black, muted grays, and touches of yellow to accent the shirt. Look in the mirror." There was no question it was an attractive combination, something I would have never imagined.

"What was the color of the other suit again?"

"Dark blue pin-striped."

She went back to work. I noticed the price tags. "Christ Almighty, $275 for the shirt and $150 for the tie?"

"What's the problem?" she said with a straight face.

"I've never spent that kind of money on this kind of stuff in my life!"

"Stop," she paused. "You can afford it. You've earned it. Occasionally spoiling yourself is a good thing."

She had a point. Then she threw a dagger, just for fun. "For goodness' sake, *at your age* how many more of these conferences do you think you're going to headline?"

Two shirts and two ties heavier and $1023 lighter, Alexandria and I headed to the shoe section. As we passed the costume jewelry section, she said, "Do you mind if I browse a minute?" I nodded okay. After all, Lauren was away at an overnight conference, so there were no deadlines.

She tried on a half-moon shaped necklace made from thin strands of silver.

"That looks fabulous on you!"

She watched my eyes. "You think so?" When she was confident I wasn't kidding, she glanced at the price tag.

"It's nice, but I really need a pair of shoes."

I knew she didn't want to say the necklace was too expensive. I walked behind her and looked at the price tag. At $425, it was a bargain compared to my shirts and ties.

I handed my credit card to the saleslady behind the counter, "We'll take it."

"I couldn't.'

"Consider it your fee for helping me shop."

Alexandria turned around and looked me straight in the eye. "This doesn't mean I'm going to sleep with you!"

"I didn't ask."

"You were thinking it."

"Alexandria, you have such an original way of saying thank you."

~

When I packed for the trip, I made sure Lauren didn't see the new shirts and ties. I wore both during my two speeches on the stage at the conference. It also realized that Alexandria and I never went shoe shopping.

16.

Getting deeper into the hole…

For a real change of pace, we opened the conference with a black-tie dinner dance. Since I was solo, I made sure to work the room. My goal was to chat with virtually every important producer. Courtney made me a floor plan that listed advisors by the amount of production and where they were located.

Next up was Dan Whitman. Alexandria, not surprisingly, was sitting at his table. "Martin, so glad you could grace us with your presence," smiled Alexandria as she made the introductions. "This is Dan and his wife, Margaret. You may remember we were on the phone recently?"

"Dan, it's a pleasure. Where's your brother Mike, and Roxanne?"

"Mike's not been feeling well lately. He and Rox decided to stay home, but he sends his best."

"I've been thinking about your situation with all those P&C clients. I think I have a few ideas that can bump the needle this coming year. We should talk when we all get back. Alexandria, I assume…"

"Done," smiled Alexandria.

"Martin, don't tell me you're a workaholic like my husband?"

"I wouldn't say that. But I'm guessing you'd look great in one of those new Bentley Silver Streak convertibles. That's why Alexandria and I need to talk to your husband and his brother when we get back."

As the table laughed, the band began to play "The Way You Look Tonight." I looked at Alexandria; she was stunning.

"Can I tear you away from your clients?"

We tucked ourselves into a corner of the dance floor.

"I'm impressed. That was masterful. I had no idea you were that smooth."

"You don't survive on Wall Street for as long as I did without some ability to suck up. But keep in mind, I did my homework. I didn't just accidentally stop by. I have two new ideas I've already bounced off Joanne."

"Why Joanne?"

"As my marketing director, she's in charge of Whitman business building initiatives."

"Is that all?" she teased.

"Do I detect a streak of jealousy?"

"Shut up. Just dance."

She *was* stunning. The hair, the eyes, the lips, the dress, her smile, the necklace. I put both arms around her as we danced to the classic, "The Way You Look Tonight…"

Someday, when I'm awfully low.
When the world is cold,

"These lyrics were made for you," I said. She put her head on my shoulder. I could feel her soft flaxen hair.

The music stopped. We just stood there looking at each other. The dance floor was almost empty. "We better get you back to your guests." She smiled.

As we made our way through the crowd back to the table, I could see Margaret's eyes following the two of us.

"Wow," said Margaret, looking right at Alexandria. "I could feel the sparks from here."

I was about to move on when our events coordinator, Karen Archoa, stopped by with the photographer. "Martin, we are trying to get pictures of each table. Sort of a memento."

I joined in for the table shot. The photographer was about to leave.

"Karen, would you mind one more picture?" said Margaret. "Dan and Alexandria, come here." The three of them stood together. "Martin, you're supposed to be in this one. And I want you to get close to Alexandria."

~

Two weeks after the conference, a picture collage was sent by the photographer to each member of senior management. I wasn't home when the picture arrived, but Lauren was. There were the Beach Boys, Rudy Giuliani, selected shots of advisors, and the four-shot of Dan, Margaret, Alexandria, and me.

"Your conference collage arrived today in a very nice frame. It looks like you all had a great time, Lauren or no Lauren. Who is the couple?"

"That's Margaret Whitman and her husband, Dan."

"Why was Alexandria with you?"

"She's not with me. She's Dan's business manager."

"She sure looks like she's with you."

17.

The first taste of serious money.

The AFA management team constantly reminded employees that their attendance at our conferences, despite the glamorous venues, was work. It was everybody's job was to enhance existing relationships by providing our guests, their families, and their significant others with a memorable vacation experience and new business ideas to grow their practices, thus increasing AFA's gross revenues and their net take-home pay.

In the five days following that dance, Alexandria and I spent about sixty seconds together, as we stood in line early one morning with a dozen advisors at the cappuccino walk-through. A soft, protracted "helloooo" and a smile was the extent of our conversation.

Alexandria had invited about fifteen advisors and their families to the conference. When she wasn't wining and dining or attending breakout sessions, she was researching outings and other free-time options.

As for me, when I wasn't rehearsing my presentations and preparing for follow-up breakout sessions, Courtney had filled every waking minute with one-on-one appointments with our most important advisors. She acted as traffic cop, scheduler, waitress — she had food and beverages delivered, so I wouldn't waste time at lunch or on a coffee break — and scribe because, as she explained, "Somebody has to take notes on what you promise, so we can actually get the work done when we get back to the office."

Initial conference feedback appeared quite positive, but I had no idea how positive until Craft walked into my office and closed the door two days after we returned.

"Martin, that was a masterful selling job at the conference. Almost eighty percent of the advisors signed up for the new business building programs you developed and presented. You are one hell of a salesman. Before we arrived, I thought twenty-five percent would sign up, and we'd double the business next year. God only knows what kind of business the eighty percent sign-up will drive."

And I was thinking, Y*eah, that also puts a shit-pile more money in your pocket.*

"I've been talking to Jeremy and Eddie, we've decided that now that the family squabbles are behind us, and we've bought the company, we'd like to share the wealth and make you an equity partner. After all, without you, we wouldn't be where we are today, much less tomorrow."

My response was measured. I figured I was about to be thrown a tiny bone. "That's very nice of you; I appreciate that."

"For a man who's about to be wealthy again [Pete had shared my professional roller-coaster], you don't sound very excited. We want you to have ten percent of the company at no cost to you, and a ten percent share of the annual profit distributions in perpetuity."

"Holy crap!" That was twice what Pete and I had agreed, plus an unexpected profit distribution.

"I'm guessing you're worth $20 million more this morning than you were worth yesterday, plus an additional half million per year in increased cash flow."

I reached out to shake hands. He gave me a big warm hug instead. I said, "You guys have made me feel like family."

"Pal, you *are* family," he responded. "The attorneys will be sending over the agreement for your signature. It's pretty much the same boilerplate Jeremy, Eddie, and I signed. You might want to have your attorney look it over for tax purposes and so that there are no misunderstandings." Craft headed for the door. "Gotta go. I have my weekly Dave Lineman call in a few minutes." Craft made sure he talked to key advisors regularly. He understood that ego-driven entrepreneurs craved recognition. A call from the president and CEO was just that. "Oh, I almost forgot. I told Amélie to organize a celebratory partner dinner. Just the eight of us: Amélie and Craft, Costas and Mona, Carr and Evelyn. Tell Lauren to look out for the call. Let's do it real soon."

I decided to break the news to Lauren after dinner with a bottle of champagne. She was as giddy as a kid. "Told you, told you, the cream always rises to the top!"

"Funny, that's what all the doctors say about you."

"Really? I guess we're just two nice people."

MJ heard the excitement and wandered in with the now-familiar scowl on his face, "Why the champagne?"

"Dad got some great news today. They made him a partner at AFA."

MJ looked straight into my face. "How come I'm always the last to hear about everything?" He walked away.

"Goddamn it," I said.

"That's not your real son talking; that's your *other* son. He'll be better once he starts on the medication."

"And when is that?"

"Dr. Sherry and I are discussing the right time."

"With all due respect, we've been discussing that issue for the last $8000 in session fees. I'm starting to wonder, why do I have to put up with Sherry's condescending attitude? The good doctor makes me feel like an insensitive, idiosyncratic fool who's supposed to pay the bills and keep his mouth shut."

Based on our recent history, Lauren knew our discussion was one step away from a full-blown argument. Again. So, she tried to lighten things up, "I understand the dumb, but idiosyncratic?"

"Listen to MJ next time I'm driving the car. 'You're too far right, too far left; driving too slow, too fast; turning from the wrong lane, turning into the wrong lane.' I feel like a student driver being admonished by the instructor."

MJ, Lauren, and I went to get a pizza at a local family-style Italian restaurant. The food wasn't great, but the place was usually quiet, and the owners knew MJ by name. Traffic was heavier than usual. It began to drizzle, which slowed traffic even further. MJ started to squirm.

"Relax, son," I said empathetically.

"Relax. How can I relax? You constantly pick the slowest lane, then you let everybody turn in front of you at the traffic light and beep your horn."

I exchanged glances with Lauren. Nothing else needed to be said. MJ had made my point.

~

The next day, the stockholder's agreement arrived from Craft's attorney, Jonathan Friedman, the managing partner of Friedman and Matson, a midsized Bridgeport firm.

Courtney, who took her role as my executive assistant, mother protector, and personal confidant very seriously, opened the package (marked personal and confidential), marched into my office, and announced, "It's official, boss: here are your partnership papers."

"Don't I have any privacy?"

"Whoa, don't get so snotty. You told me to open everything, remember?"

18.

A partner's agreement dotted with landmines.

Lauren retired early; she had a 6:00 A.M. staff meeting the next day. I sat down by the fireplace with a glass of 1970 Fonseca Port and the long-anticipated shareholder agreement. I wanted to savor the moment; unfortunately, the more I read, the more it felt like Craft and Friedman assumed I was a corporate rookie.

I decided to withhold final judgment until I spoke to my attorney, Tom Kugle, the next day. At 2:00 P.M., I closed my door and made the call. "Tom, have you had a chance to read the agreement?"

"Yes."

"As the layman, let me tell you what I think the agreement said. I'll own ten percent of the company in the distant future. I'm vested two percent a year beginning twelve months from signing the agreement. If I leave, become disabled, or die any time before completing the five years — effectively six — my family and I lose all accumulated vesting.

"Second, since I will have made no contributions to the purchase price, I have no voting rights but am personally liable — for ten percent of the $50-million loan balance if the company goes belly-up.

"Third, the ten percent profit distributions don't begin to accrue until 24 months after the signing of this agreement, which in plain English means three years."

"I must compliment myself," joked Tom. "I've taught you well. You get an A+ for that concise summary."

"A+ for accuracy. F- for the terms. This is like a bullshit, phantom equity agreement," I said.

"It isn't *like* a phantom agreement.; it *is* a phantom agreement. It's designed to protect the majority shareholders," replied Tom. "They want to make sure you stick around to earn the equity, which speaks to your importance to the company."

"Tom, I'm starting from a different place. I've already earned the equity stake based on my past contributions. And I'm committed to making sure my partners' equity grow over the next five years."

Tom smiled. "Given this agreement, you're a partner in name only. Example: the fine print in Section II, Paragraphs 2 and 3, says you have no tag-along rights. So, if they decide to sell the company or go public, they can buy you out at the pre-event price and personally pocket the spread, which is almost certain to occur."

"They wouldn't do that!"

"Martin, this is business. Everyone tries to screw somebody."

I was starting to get the picture.

"So, we need to agree on a negotiating strategy before you respond. I've got to ask you a few very personal questions. Do you and Lauren need the cash flow from your current position with the company?"

"It's nice. Pays for a few extra trips, but no, not really; we're fine."

"Good. And what about the equity agreement? Suppose we can't reach a satisfactory compromise."

"I think I'd rather maintain my dignity and just walk away than accept their terms."

"Given those circumstances, what do you want?"

"I want the ten percent, now, with no strings."

"I thought you and Pete agreed on five percent."

"They volunteered ten, so the new number is ten. Consider the extra five a penalty assessment for playing games."

"And what about profit distributions?"

"Let's compromise. I'm willing to wave distributions this year as a contribution to equity and start receiving distributions at the end of next year."

"They're proposing no distributions for three years."

"I'm aware of that. But I have a high-powered New York attorney while they're using some yahoo in Bridgeport."

After a mutual chuckle, Tom, having negotiated hundreds of agreements, suggested an approach. "Since Craft seems to be the ultimate decision-maker, I'd take him aside privately and explain your concerns. Don't be confrontational. We need to determine if the lawyers initiated the terms to protect their client or if Craft had them draw up the document to his specifications. Let's hope it's the former, because this is a poorly written agreement. I don't think they have a lot of experience in these matters. So, if Craft's in your camp, I'm fairly confident I can get his counsel to capitulate."

"Suppose Craft put them up to it?"

"Then we have a different issue, and it will probably get a little testy."

19.

Contract negotiations drag on, and on, and on.

Next day, I walked into Craft's office. "Dawson, I'd like to talk to you about the agreement."

"No problem, pal, just close the door."

I unemotionally cut to the chase. "Dawson, I think the vesting period is too long; it ignores past contributions."

Craft's take was different. "No, pal, you've got it all wrong. Giving you ten percent of a company valued at $200 million in recognition of your past contributions. But to make the company grow, so we're both worth a lot more, I gotta make sure you're by my side for three to five years."

I knew that was Dawson's way of saying, let's compromise the vesting to three years, which was probably his goal in the first place. He was quite unprepared for my counterproposal. "Dawson," I said, balancing indignation and determination, "I'm going to make it simple. The stock has to be fully vested because this is my last corporate rodeo."

"Jeremy and Eddie will flip. That's not reasonable."

I decided to gamble the house and throw him a life raft. I knew from Craft's dealings with our field advisors that he abhorred confrontation. He preferred that others do the dirty work. He fancied himself *The Great Compromiser*, a modern-day Henry Clay. "Dawson, if that doesn't work for you, I understand. We can just part friends. It's been a great three years."

"You'd leave me over this?" he said, totally befuddled.

I ignored his question. "If it would help, I'm willing to give the three of you my profit distributions at the end of this year as an equity payment. Based on my projections, that should put another million or two in everybody's pocket." I knew with fifty percent of the stock — after my ten percent — that meant about $4 million more in *his* pocket.

"You know something, Martin, I'm thinking while you're talking. We're friends; we shouldn't be negotiating against each other. I've got a business to operate, and I need you to focus on staying one step ahead of our competition. That's really how we all win. Let's have the attorneys wrap this thing up."

~

The push back from his partners was more than Dawson imagined. Carr was concerned about not having strings on me, but liked the profit distribution. He had just bought a $4 million house and was in hock up to his eyeballs. He, like Craft, was willing to eliminate the twenty-four-month waiting period that Friedman had incorporated into the agreement.

Costas was considerably less docile, since he was the least convinced about my past, present, and future contributions. "There is no way in hell I'm giving up any of my equity under those terms. Eddie, I can't believe you'd even consider such a stupid thing." He stared at Craft. "If you're so damn sure about Martin's added value, then take the equity out of your share." Craft owned sixty percent while Carr and Costas owned 20 percent each. "You can afford it."

Craft brought the debate to a screeching halt with one sentence. "Fine. I'll transfer ten percent of my equity and my profit distributions to Martin; that way we don't have to vote on anything."

Costas had no choice but to acquiesce.

~

This laborious process continued for six months. The attorneys would talk concepts; then Friedman would talk to Craft and Tom would talk to me. With each document revision, Craft figured he could deftly insert a counter-clause, which Tom promptly identified and modified to the point of neutrality.

While I was becoming impatient, Tom remained cool as a cucumber. Whenever I pushed, he'd push back, "Hey, I'm picking up the tab, so please let me do it my way." Tom's ultimate strategy was to take ownership of the agreement section by section, paragraph by paragraph, sentence by sentence, with

Friedman confined to executing redrafts. By the third month, Dawson was getting antsy. By the fifth month, Friedman dreaded returning Tom's calls because he knew Tom had "just one more little detail that required a modification in the wording." By month six, Craft and Friedman were exhausted; Craft had spent a small fortune in personal legal fees. To Tom's credit, we got everything I had originally wanted, plus some: immediate vesting, tag-along rights (whatever the other three could do, we could do), no liabilities for outstanding notes, and no binding employment contract. In all, there were 181 revisions to the original agreement.

Early one morning, Craft walked into my office with "enough" written all over his face. "We've got to end this thing. Jeremy and Eddie are furious. I'm tired. And if we keep this up, we'll both be bankrupt. My attorneys are expensive, but I understand Morrison's hourly fees are off the charts."

"I know. That's why Lauren is so upset when she sees the bills. But here's the good news. We're done" I said, handing Craft four copies of the executed agreement. "You guys need to countersign. As you can see, I've already put my John Hancock."

Craft, Carr, and Costas signed the agreement later that day.

20.

Lavish spending makes strange bedfellows.

Despite the protracted equity negotiations, we all agreed the partner celebration should take place as planned. The eight of us toasted our future at La Grenouille on East 52nd Street, one of New York's most elegant eateries. We sat boy-girl-boy-girl in the elegant room's corner banquette. Craft, a genuine wine aficionado, ordered a $1,500 bottle of Chateau Margaux and Chateau Beycheville '61 as if they were bottles of Evian.

Mona Costas, a well-proportioned, five-foot ten-inch workout fanatic, sat to my right. I discovered she was a woman with an aberrant split personality. During the first few courses, she projected the carriage of a former New York debutante – which she wasn't.

She began by heralding her new-found fascination with ballroom dancing and expressed her disappointment in the uncultured public's inability to embrace the revival of Wendy Wasserstein's play, *The Sisters Rosenzweig.* and, her opposition to many of the "non-consequential."

I started to find her a bit overbearing, so I drank my wine and remained uncharacteristically quiet as she rambled on, "I love everything about the Museum of Modern Art's stunning renovation; but I must say some of their exhibits are out there… Martin, have you seen Elio Oticica's *Box Bolide 1965?*"

I shook my head.

Mona suggested I don't bother with it; it's not real art. "It looks like 'a small plywood box partially filled with dirt.'"

The more Mona rambled, the more she drank. By the time we got to the entrée, she had raised her voice quite a few decibels and was noticeably slurring her words. Hubby discreetly whispered in her ear, "Honey, maybe you better take it a little easy on the wine; we've still got a long evening of celebrating ahead."

She stared at her husband blankly and then turned to me. "Do you agree with Jeremy? Don't tell me you didn't hear. You've been avoiding me all night. Why?" She exploded. Then she punched me on the arm.

"Easy," I smiled, trying to make light. "You've got quite a right."

"So, I'm not as sophisticated and polished as your wife. Who cares? I'm goddamn rich."

An increasingly embarrassed Costas grabbed Mona's arm. She ripped it from his grip. "You want to see my goddamn right." She cracked me right in the jaw. I saw stars. Jeremy tried to restrain her, but it was too late. She again swung wildly. I ducked. She knocked the wine and some plates to the floor. The place was dead silent.

The evening was over; we were asked to leave. As Costas dragged Mona out the door, she looked at him and said loudly, "Why shouldn't I crush him? He's what you said he was — an arrogant, condescending little shit.'"

~

"I'm going to do some real damage to that $1 million distribution check Dawson gave us," I said. "I've organized five nights in the Bahamas, starting next Thursday."

"Honey, that's very sweet of you, but I just can't take off," Lauren replied. "We've got the Department of Health coming for their biannual inspection in less than three weeks. Everything has got to be letter perfect. They're just a bunch of $50,000-a-year bureaucrats, and this is their chance to flex their muscles."

"Too bad," I replied matter-of-factly, "because I organized a jet charter to the pink sand beaches of Harbor Island in North Eleuthera at tip Bahamas. I even booked five nights at a boutique retreat called the Dunsmore Beach Club, which tends to attract entertainment types trying to get away from it all. One of our new advisors, Ray Hurley from Savannah, told me about it; he's been there three or four times and loves it."

Lauren's eyes bugged out of her head. "Well, let me see what I can do about departmental coverage tomorrow morning."

There was no Ray Hurley from Savannah. Alexandria had mentioned Harbor Island and the Dunsmore at one of our dinners. She said it was her favorite place in the whole world.

"What do I have to bring?"

"Not much. The place strongly suggests traveling light. The weather is mid-eighties during the day and mid-seventies at night, virtually no humidity, no television, no fax, no radio, and no telephones. Just crystal-clear aquamarine waters, pink powder sand beaches, gourmet breakfasts, candlelit dinners, and every imaginable spa treatment."

"Ahhh!"

I followed my own instructions, packing one small get-a-way-from-it-all bag with a few shirts and swim trunks. Lauren brought two standard 22-inch pieces of luggage, one brimming with evening dresses, beachwear, and shoes; the other bursting at the seams with cosmetics, moisturizers, perfumes, and such.

Arriving at the small launch across the bay from Harbor Island, the hotel guide said, "Maan, veree heavee; need second boat." Lauren and her bags were inseparable. She insisted he bring the bags on board. "Please, they're not that heavy." She assumed the help wanted a larger tip, so she began to dig into her pocketbook. The hotel guide was insulted. "Mum, no disrespect, don't need moneee; do our best."

Halfway across the bay, the rear of the little craft tilted downward, flooding the rear where the bags were sitting. Within seconds, the boat capsized, and Lauren's bags fell about forty feet to the bay floor, which was covered in coral. Surprised, but not in any danger, we laughed and paddled our way to shore in our life vests. The locals did their best to retrieve the bags, but they had no real deep-water diving equipment. Every time the men struggled to raise the heavy, water-logged bags off the coral, their flimsy ropes would slip out of their hands. A young boy, probably no more than twelve, attempted a deep-sea dive with nothing other than a bonefish harpoon with a u-hook on the end. After about ninety seconds, we all became worried. The little boy surfaced with a smile and my bag. "Able to get ladies little bag, mon, but heavy mon's bag no move, sorry."

By the time the boy resurfaced, we were on our second fabulous mai tai, made with local coconut milk and 151-proof dark rum. I decided to thank all the help that participated in our boat journey. "Mai Tais for everybody!" We sat for another 45 minutes laughing, drinking, and befriending the locals. By the time we were ready to go, our little twelve-year-old diver had quite a buzz.

Since there were no retail shops on the island, the hotel manager, a European-educated Brit named Dennis, convinced one of the residents to hand-make a few brightly colored bathing suits, shorts, and wraps for Lauren. The entire six-day wardrobe cost $35, and she never looked more beautiful.

21.

Five-star resort anger.

Dunsmore Beach Club only had five private suites and five dining tables, which could be clustered into any configuration the guests wished. In the evening, we could dine with other guests, or we could have our table placed on one of the tiny sand perches above the empty, pristine beach. Our choice that first evening was the privacy of the beach. We dined course by course — at our pace — on deliciously fresh, inventive cuisine under the light of the moon, with a small antique candle-lit lantern a few feet from our table. Hours later, after a nightcap, we strolled the beach while looking at a clear, star-studded sky.

While the locals were diving for our luggage, I'd made arrangements with a local musician to serenade us on his guitar as we walked down the beach. Fortunately for me, he knew the quintessential Eric Clapton lyric:

> It's late in the evening
> She's wondering what clothes to wear
> She puts on her makeup
> And brushes her long blonde hair
> And then she asks me
> Do I look alright?
> And I say yes, you look wonderful tonight…
> © Eric Clapton

Each evening — private table or no private table — ended in the same delightful manner. We made love in our down feather bed to the rhythm of the ocean waves, gently cascading on the beach some twenty yards away. As we turned our separate ways to catch a few winks before sunrise, she would whisper, "You are the love of my life."

~

The next morning at breakfast, a thin, heavily bearded gentleman asked if we'd mind if he joined us for breakfast. He had a familiar look, but the facial hair masked his real identity. "I gather you folks had dinner near the beach last night. Great experience, isn't it?"

Lauren smiled at me then nodded.

"I loved your choice of music. How times flies; I wrote that song more than 30 years ago."

~

The trip did have a few detractors.

MJ was angry with me for absconding with his safe person — Mom — and finding the only five-star resort in the world that was completely isolated from everyone. MJ spent hours researching communication possibilities. He was assuming some combination of email and Skype internet calls would keep him in constant touch. Based on past experience, that meant at least one call each morning, afternoon, and night, usually to explain his latest symptom to his mother. To his dismay, MJ learned the island had no internet service, and that my iPhone and his mother's cell phone weren't working. (They were at the bottom of the bay, and replacement devices would take a week, with no guarantees of reception.)

Bart and Valerie applauded our impromptu romantic interlude, but didn't like the notion of being MJ's defacto care-takers and babysitters. MJ understood their concerns; he had been through this before with his younger brother. In his fragile state, the last thing MJ wanted was a challenge from his brother.

So, he feigned business. "I hope you don't mind, but it's going to be tough trying to get together while Mom and Dad are away."

"Really?" said a pleasantly surprised Bart.

"For the last sixty-nine days, I've been talking to a coal mining company in Texas about developing some application software that will allow them to estimate production flow more accurately. Damn if they didn't decide they want to do the project right now." There was no project, but MJ made it sound plausible.

"Well, let's keep in touch. Maybe we can have dinner," said Bart.

"Sounds good. But I'll have to let you know. The Texans have set a pretty tight deadline."

Bart was now certain his brother was bullshitting him, as he had done so many times in the past.

~

Alexandria felt outraged, neglected, and ignored because:

...I disappeared without so much as a goodbye.

...Courtney blew her off when she asked where I was.

...She had a serious question for me about renewing her auto lease.

...She was depressed about her declining income.

...I took *somebody else* to *her* favorite hideaway.

When I returned to my office a week later, there was a small envelope in my right-hand drawer addressed, "Hey you." Inside was a colorful bookmark featuring a Pizarro painting, *The Garden at Madame Jardin*. Alexandria knew I loved the Impressionist painters. On her last trip to France, she had brought me back a Matisse bookmark. The brief unsigned note inside this envelope said, "Hope you had a nice time."

22.

Terminal cancer arrives, uninvited.

Suspended anticipation, as defined by me, is the confluence of noncontrollable circumstances randomly clustered around a malleable mass — i.e., me!

I was surrounded by MJ's nascent desire to establish an emotional divide; Lauren's Pollyanna-ish commitment to *All's Well That Ends Well*; and my poorly placed, flirtatious behavior with the complex, intelligent Alexandria.

And, if that wasn't enough, I cast my financial fortunes with a collection of rejects from the biblical Sermon on the Mount who loved contaminated fish and stale loaves of bread.

At noon, I did something I rarely do. I decided to stop for a sandwich and take a walk around the research park where AFA resided — alone. My route to the door accidentally passed Alexandria's office, where one glance communicated all was not well in her world. Tears were cascading down cheeks lined with smudged mascara, and bloodshot, sullen eyes stared blankly ahead. I asked Alexandria's administrative assistant, sitting outside her office, what was going on. He just shrugged his shoulders as if to say, *Got me.* So, I stepped inside.

"Hey, sunshine, how's it going?" I asked nonchalantly.

"My mascara is running down my face, and all you can say is 'how's it going?' Do you know why Mike Whitman didn't attend the conference?"

"Didn't Dan say he was a bit under the weather?"

As it turned out, the real reason was that Mike, at the tender age of forty-two, had been diagnosed with stage-four pancreatic cancer. The prognosis? Three, maybe six months. Michael would leave behind a wife and three boys, aged three, five, and seven; a thriving business; hundreds of clients who loved him; a mom and dad not yet retired; his best friend; his brother Dan; and a brilliant life, only partially fulfilled.

"When did you find out?"

"Dan called late yesterday, right after they got the results from the doctor. My mom believes everything happens for a reason. 'It's part of God's master plan,'" said Alexandria bitterly. "But really, what possible good can come out of Michael's death? With all the crap that's happened in my life, where is God's goodness?"

"Have you talked to him?"

"I'm afraid. I mean, what would I say?"

"Did Dan have any suggestions?"

"He said Michael plans on living as normal a life as he can for as long as he can, including going to the office; that I should call and act normal."

"So, why not follow his lead? Have your assistant call his office to schedule a phone appointment, and then let the conversation take its course."

The call the following afternoon was surprisingly upbeat, yet ironic.

"Alexandria, I'm relying on you to help Dan build our business; remember, he's a bit of an introvert."

That's all she had to hear. Tears began to pour from Alexandria's eyes. She stumbled, unsure of how to respond. Mike broke the awkward silence with a personal request. "Martin, I wondered if you might do something for me."

"Whatever I can."

"My seven-year-old, Errol, is really into baseball. I told him my hero was Cal Ripken because he never played hooky in over twenty years. I want Errol to understand that, as my dad taught me, 'Good things come to those who do.' Dan tells me you announced Cal Ripken would be the keynote speaker at the next AFA conference. Congratulations. I've heard he's extremely articulate and motivating. I figure it's unlikely I'll be around for that one, so I was wondering if you could pull a few strings and get me an autographed baseball? Hopefully, whenever Errol looks at that ball, he'll remember what I told him."

"Consider it done," I said. Then I called Ripken's agent, Frank Vuono, who also happened to be a close personal friend. Vuono said Cal would not only be happy to sign the baseball, but that if I'd like, he could organize a phone conversation between Errol, Mike, and Cal.

The conference call took place about five days later. Cal couldn't have been more gracious. He even tried to send a little hope and inspiration Mike's way. "Yogi Berra said something to me when my dad was fighting the Big C," said Cal. "'It's not over till the fat lady sings.' My dad lived five years more than anybody expected, enjoying his grandchildren. It was a special time for all of us."

Unfortunately, the fat lady sang for Mike just ninety-three days later.

23.

The pitfalls of married men.

Alexandria and her best friend, Stephanie, were sitting in Stephanie's East 67th Street penthouse, searching for some meaning in Mike's death, as well as Alexandria's two difficult marriages, her strained relationship with daughter Shanti, and her inappropriate flirtation with a married man.

Despite her wealth, Stephanie was real. She was born, raised, and had lived in Manhattan all her life. She had been married almost twenty years to her childhood sweetheart and soulmate, Ryan, a successful investment banker who had died about seven years ago in a private jet on route to New York, shortly after completing the largest transaction of his career in Bombay, India. Ryan left Stephanie a substantial and well-organized estate, a world-class book of contacts, and a handsome son, Ryan, Jr., who followed in his dad's footsteps as a Rhodes Scholar and an investment banker. His dad had been Ryan Jr.'s role model and best friend.

Stephanie and Alexandria had met at a mutual friend's party. They had become steadfast friends despite their apparent differences. Alexandria's dry wit made Stephanie laugh, while Stephanie's sanguine advice usually helped the more fragile Alexandria overcome what seemed to be a never-ending series of emotional crises. On numerous occasions, Stephanie had asked Alexandria to join her company, but Alexandria would always explain she was having too much fun and making too much money to shift gears.

Stephanie was president of a highly profitable niche business: a thriving, concierge-style Manhattan property-management firm with 96 high-end residential properties in her portfolio. Her clients were wealthy foreigners who used the properties as second and third homes for themselves, their families, and their friends. On occasion, some of her clients, for tax and or publicity reasons, wanted their places used for prestigious, high-profile events.

Stephanie was pleased to oblige. Her business philosophy was to *deal with wealth; they can afford it.* Stephanie's staff took care of every last detail for her clients, from paying the mortgages and real-estate taxes, to stocking refrigerators with beluga caviar and rare Cristal champagne, to organizing butlers and chauffeurs, and even arranging custom spa treatments or hair appointments.

Stephanie's contacts and imagination were second to none when it came to planning and implementing unique events. For example, when friends wanted to celebrate music impresario and legend Leonard Bernstein's sixtieth birthday, Stephanie called some old friends, Gilbert and Maguy LeCoze, the owners of New York's haute-cuisine landmark Le Bernardin. They arranged to have award-winning chef Eric Ripert prepare and serve a five-course meal to thirty-eight of New York's crème de la crème at the twenty-two-room Park Avenue penthouse of one of her out-of-town clients, the Saudi Ambassador to the U.S., Prince Bandar. Stephanie had world-renowned flutist Jean Pierre Rampal and twelve of his orchestral friends stop by for a small personal concert.

This particular Friday evening, the girls had decided to have a two-person pajama party. Alexandria was exhausted from her week of sparring with advisors on the phone, cajoling them to sell her financial solutions and products instead of a competitor's, while Stephanie had a rare, free weekend with no outrageous requests from her pampered clientele.

"Sometimes it feels like I took a detour to a foreign land when I left Nebraska," said Alexandria wistfully as she searched the twinkling Manhattan skyline.

"Don't you have a lot of family there?"

"Virtually my entire family. Mom, my sister Tori, a few aunts and uncles, nieces and nephews. And now my daughter Shanti."

"So why did you leave?"

"Please! Lincoln, Nebraska: where all the men aspire to make tires in the Dunlop factory and drink beer on Friday at the 12th Street Pub, and the girls all look like something out of *Grease*."

"Well, what *do* you want?"

"Regarding what?"

"Life. Men. Career."

"Men are always a good place to start. It strikes me they're always a prime target for our wrath and frustrations. But unless you're a lesbian, it seems we all want a good one." She smiled wryly. "Okay, your turn. What makes a good man?" asked Alexandria.

"I guess my standard will always be Ryan. He was smart — I find average intellects boring, devoid of challenge. He knew how to make money — that adage 'the best things in life are free' is pure drivel. Living well is expensive, and living in New York? Even more so. I'm not about to fall in love with some widower in a three-bedroom, one-bath house in Seaford, Long Island. A man has to make me laugh and to be able to laugh at himself — every life has ups and downs, nobody escapes that. We're only here for a moment, as your friend Mike learned. Most of all, my 'good man' knew how to make me feel important — a lot of little things, like a quick phone call on a busy day, the single red rose, and the poetry. My larger-than-life tycoon was so sweet; he'd read me a sonnet or two in bed and suddenly all would be right with the world."

Stephanie got up, walked over to the bar, and poured herself another drink. "Okay, Miss Twenty Questions; now it's your turn."

"How would I know about good men? Look at my track record. The first one — that trash Johnny — left me high and dry with two kids in Los Angeles. And Keith, number two, became a goddamn drug addict."

"Alexandria, cut the 'woe is me' crap. You're attractive, successful, smart, and…"

Alexandria interrupted. "And intimidating to most eligible men in their fifties with money and relationship baggage. They are looking for a submissive, zero-body-fat lay in their twenties that shrieks and moans. Haven't you noticed?"

"That's why I was so delighted with Curtis," said Stephanie.

"Curtis? I've known you for four years, and I've never heard you mention the name."

"Maybe there's a reason," said Stephanie.

"Give it up, girl," smirked Alexandria.

"I met him about four years ago. He was an intelligent, sensitive, rich, handsome investment banker who needed a memorable thank you event for his blueblood, old-money client list. The event was a big success, one thing lead to another, and before long we were an item. Three years into the relationship and I still got excited when he held my hand," said Stephanie wistfully.

"So when do I meet dreamboat?" smiled Alexandria.

"Do I have to draw you a picture? He was, and is, very, very married to a lot of money. He kept promising me that after the next deal, we'd have enough to head off into the sunset. Just like the movies. I never wanted something so much in my whole life."

"I can't believe you were so naïve," said Alexandria.

"I know, I know. Curtis wasn't about to give up his fifty acres, his neat, orderly life, or his stables and country club in New Canaan. The other night he called and said we needed to meet *somewhere discreet*. It was important."

"Meet where?"

"We never got that far. Curtis was quivering in his boots. Rather than even give me the courtesy of a fact-to-face conversation, he dropped his bombshell right then and there. His wife had hired a private investigator to track his whereabouts. Guess she had a suspicion. He followed Curtis to my place. The private eye either bribed or tricked the doorman into documenting the frequency of visits to my apartment. When the wife got the completed report, she told him to cease-and-desist or she'd emasculate him financially. She told him she was also ready, willing, and able to have him professionally blackballed, so he'd end up selling pencils on the street."

24.

The vixen that screwed up a perfectly good marriage.

The women had two more Cosmos. They decided Stephanie needed to clean out the master bedroom closets; Curtis's wardrobe was history. First, they cut his custom-made English suits into strips of cleaning cloths for Stephanie's maid service. Then they took Curtis's shirts, removed the collars and cuffs, and made a very professional noose in case Curtis stopped by to pick up his belongings. The plan was to drug him, put the noose around his neck, drag him to the deck, and let him dangle by the throat thirty-nine stories above Manhattan.

As they sat on the floor in Stephanie's bedroom among the ruined clothing, Alexandria commented, "We may be more alike than I thought."

"I'm almost afraid to ask…"

"Well, I sort of got involved with this guy at the office. We've gone out to dinner a couple of times. The chemistry is phenomenal. I can feel it."

"*Sort of* involved?"

"Actually, he's not just *a guy*. He's one of the partners. He's smart, he makes me laugh, and he isn't intimidated by me — although God knows I've tried. And he writes me poems over dinner. Unfortunately, he's very married — like 35 years. They grew up together and his wife's pictures are all over the freakin' office."

"This has disaster written all over it."

"We've never slept together. Martin's been a perfect gentleman."

"How many times have you seen him?"

"Maybe a dozen times in the last six months."

"A dozen times and you're telling me the subject of sex has never come up."

"I didn't say that; I said we haven't had sex yet. I'm trying to get him to commit before…"

"Before what?"

"I'm not sure. I really like his wife. One side of me wants to be good friends; the other side wants it all because I think this is the man I've been waiting for all my life."

"Just out of curiosity, what do you guys do when you go out?"

"Sometimes it's dinner. Sometimes it's drinks. Sometimes we go shopping and have coffee. One time he needed shirts and ties for an AFA conference; another time I needed shoes. He's also bought me some plants for the house and some very nice costume jewelry."

"You sound like old married farts. What do you want?"

"Him."

"Then what are you waiting for?"

"It's just not right. Imagine if word got around the office. The rumors would be gruesome. *I'd be the vixen that screwed up a perfectly good marriage*."

"Perfectly good marriage? Then why is he chasing you?'

"He's not exactly chasing me. I always try to stay in his face without being too obvious. He knows I'm there."

Before Alexandria could continue, the phone rang. "Yes, it is. Yes. Oh, my God. How?! Are you sure there's no mistake? He doesn't drink. I see. I'll be right down."

Stephanie hung up and burst into tears. "That was New York Hospital. Ryan Jr. is dead! He was speeding down the FDR under the influence and crashed into a concrete divider column."

Alexandria was stunned.

In the cab to the hospital, Stephanie told Alexandria, "Ryan Jr. detested my relationship with Curtis; he felt the affair was cheap, tawdry, and an insult to his dad's memory." Ryan Jr. had apparently left after a heated debate, then drank himself into oblivion at the Le Périgord Restaurant, where he was a regular. The restaurant owner, long-time friend Georges Briquet, had begged Ryan Jr. to leave his Bugatti in their garage, saying that they would hail a cab and call his doorman to help him when he got home.

But Ryan Jr. refused. The police report said he ran a series of red lights before heading down the FDR 62nd Street ramp at 80+ miles an hour. He was dead two minutes later amid a mangled mass of metal, concrete, and glass. The speedometer froze at 110 miles per hour.

25.

Forced to downsize.

Alexandria stared at the computer screen as she thought about the latest challenge in her life.

The biweekly salary transfers into her checking account were becoming smaller while her outgoing expenses were increasing, forcing her to draw more and more out of her savings. At forty-eight, and at the rate she was going, it would just be a matter of time before there was no emergency cash, no vacation fund, no retirement savings.

Despite Martin's offers and her supervisor Bill Johnson's chiding, she refused to accept the obvious prognosis. She was struggling to retain advisors because the market had shifted, and more of them demanded the kind of business counsel she was incapable of delivering without significant retraining. She saw her two-year slump as a series of misfortunes among the advisors who represented much of her income: Michael Whitman had, unfortunately, passed away; Bill Evans in Fairbanks, Alaska, who had sold his practice to run for public office; and Gloria Frontin of New Orleans, whose practice was destroyed by Hurricane Katrina.

The fact was that *all* account managers lost advisors, sometimes for the right reasons and sometimes otherwise. The best ones understood that and made sure they had fresh replacements at the ready. Alexandria's dogged determination worked against her. She would try to retain an advisor long after he or she stopped returning calls and placing their business with her.

To renew or not to renew? That was this evening's question. Alexandria loved her metallic black Mercedes convertible. The car exuded success, which was good for her career. The car also turned heads when she drove down the street with her blonde hair blowing in the breeze. That was great for her ego. At issue was her $925-a-month lease payment. Her current cash flow suggested she could realistically afford only $325-a-month. Alexandria translated her shortfall into daily activities. "Do I forego my twice-a-week apple martini with the girls at Jennings's Lounge and my Saturday night club-hopping until sunrise?"

She decided that friendships were more important.

~

Alexandria called Martin from the car dealership.

"Hey you, it's me. Listen, I need a favor."

"Now that's something new for you."

"Don't be such a smart ass. You're the one who stole my Harbor Island suggestion and took another woman there right under my nose. I assume my trip is in the planning stages."

I didn't dare bite on that bait. "What's the favor?"

"My auto lease expires next week; I've decided to downsize my car. You know, these days a *single* woman has to save money for a rainy day. I've just taken care of the paperwork. And I thought maybe we could get a little dinner."

"It's a date."

"No, it's not a date. It's just a favor and dinner between friends."

~

The first order of business was to drop off Alexandria's new car at her apartment in Chelsea since, as Alexandria would say, it was "sorta on the way" to La Fortuna in Battery Park, which I had suggested for dinner.

I couldn't even bring myself to ask how she wound up with a Toyota.

The restaurant wasn't particularly busy, so we had a ringside table on the Hudson River. It was a beautiful, clear night with a full moon that seemed to make Miss Liberty all the more striking.

One appetizer platter and bottle of Brunello di Montalcino later, Alexandria explained the car thing in her own inimitable, slightly dyslectic fashion.

"I know, I know, I could have afforded a nicer car, but I figured if I was going to downsize, I should look the part. I know I'm a little wacky, huh?"

"A little?"

"Compliments like that will not get you any closer to my bed."

"Will anything?"

"I don't know." Then she leaned forward in her low-cut blouse, "What do you think of my boobs?"

"Nice nipples," I chuckled.

"You missed my point."

"No, I think I got your point — both of them!"

Alexandria then began her newest excursion into circuitous logic.

"I've set a new goal. I want to be married by the time I'm fifty; that gives me eighteen months to find someone I can enjoy living with as I grow old. I don't want to be alone at the end; that's why I asked you about my boobs."

Alexandria was on a roll, so I ordered a second bottle of wine and listened. "You know women my age have a hard time finding an intelligent, eligible man with similar interests. My friend Stephanie and I were talking about that the other night. It's a mathematical thing. There are simply a lot more eligible woman out there than men. It's a vicious competition if you don't want to settle. So, you've always got to look your best to play in the game. If I looked like frumpy Betty Martin in the office next door — who, by the way, is two years younger than me — do you think we'd be sitting here tonight?

"My boobs are just not distinctive enough," she went on. "I know what you're thinking. It's not just about size. It's about properly enlarging and contouring, so they are a more complete expression of the woman I am."

"Sounds like you've already met with the plastic surgeon."

"How did you know?"

"Remember, my wife deals with them all the time."

"Ahhh yes, your wife. I'm curious; what do you tell her when you're with me?"

"I lie."

"How does it feel?"

"Not particularly good."

"If we were married, would I have to worry about you lying to me?"

~

Given the hour and the fact that I had to drive to Southport, she offered to take a cab home. I welcomed her offer. She had made the afternoon and evening a mentally exhausting event. I needed a little quiet time. My cell phone rang on the way home.

"I almost forgot. I need your opinion on something else."

"Alexandria, I've got to be careful about Lauren. I can only see so many out-of-town advisors."

"Then meet me for coffee after work."

"It's gotta be just coffee," I insisted. " In fact, can't we discuss whatever it is over the phone?"

"It's more complicated than that."

What a surprise!

26.

Champagne taste and a beer pocketbook.

"I need a bigger apartment."

The New York real estate market, particularly Manhattan, had been on fire for the last four years. The one-bedroom, one-bath prewar apartment on East 33rd Street that Alexandria had originally purchased for $240,000 had been unofficially appraised at about $520,000, even though it was on the third floor with no particular view. She figured her $350,000 in equity would allow her to purchase a bigger apartment with a million-dollar price tag.

"The girls are grown up now and would like to visit New York City more often. Two bedrooms and two baths would make everybody more comfortable. Plus, I've got a ton of out-of-town friends who sleep on my couch when they visit."

Personal gratification also was a motivator, if not the prime motivator. Alexandria believed it was essential for making a success statement to friends like Stephanie. Besides, why should she be cooped up in 700 square feet while they played in spaces two and three times larger? Hadn't she paid her dues?

Alexandria also figured that regardless of whether the whole marriage thing did or didn't work out, the growing equity in her new home would be like a forced retirement savings plan. She had been looking and had found the perfect apartment building. It was called the Horizons, a brand-new building just south of the United Nations on the East River Drive. The 1,300-square-foot apartment itself was on a high floor with great views, and the two-bedroom unit had two full marble baths and lots of closet space, a rarity in Manhattan. Plus, the amenities as she explained, were to die for: white-gloved concierge, a complete health club, outdoor sun decks, running tracks, on-site tailor, hairdresser, and masseuse.

I said, "You just downsized on the car to improve cash flow. Where is the money going to come from for the increased mortgage payments?"

As always, Alexandria wanted advice, but there were no guarantees she would take it. To her credit, she had done some homework.

"Look at the comparatives that the builder's bank provided. As you can see, a new $650,000 interest-only, two-year fixed mortgage at three percent is only $500 more a month than my current $168,000, eight and three-quarters fixed-rate mortgage. And my auto downsizing should cover much of that difference."

At the risk of sounding negative, somebody had to mention what the bank hadn't said. Her real estate taxes were about to go from $3000 a year to $18,000 a year, and her condo fees from a modest $300 a month to $1,400 a month. Then there was the matter of high closing costs, estimated at $20,000, and the fact that her variable mortgage would be tied to the prime rate for 15 years. Even a modest increase in that rate could her raise her mortgage payment another $1,000 a month.

"I'm not trying to be overly dramatic, but in reality, you're looking at a monthly increase of $2500 and $3000 now, plus a lot of unknowns a few years down the road." I didn't even mention her current declining income.

Alexandria's face turned ashen. "Oh my God, I didn't think that far. I've already put a $25,000 deposit on the apartment.

"How long ago?"

"About ten days."

"Christ, why didn't you at least think to ask me first?"

"I did. But you were basking in the sun on Harbor Island, remember? So, I did the next best thing: I went to Bill."

"The same Bill who brought us the ContactPro fiasco?"

"Listen, you and he disagree; let's leave it at that. The fact is he's bought and sold a lot of houses." Bill had bought two houses with his ex-wife, both in Atlanta. The first was declared part of an eminent domain relocation two years later. They'd lost $14,000 on an $85,000 purchase. The second and larger home was during Johnson's business success period. They paid $400,000 in Buckhead with $100,000 down.

Two years later, she filed for divorce. To fund the settlement, the couple was forced to sell the house. To accelerate a sale, the real estate agent positioned Johnson and his wife as cash-strapped, highly motivated sellers. When the dust settled, the house netted $390,000, leaving $40,000 in cash to be split equally before paying $16,000 in divorce costs.

"Did you and he discuss all the facts?"

"I just caught him in the hallway. He said, 'Just do it, you can never lose on real estate.'"

~

The next two weeks were consumed with trying to get Alexandria's deposit back. Not surprisingly, the developer said she had signed a binding contract and that her free-look period had expired. She used every bit of her interpersonal skill to reach a compromise but to no avail. The developer, who was starting to experience a sales slowdown, didn't want to create a precedent that his binding purchase contract had loopholes, so he stood fast. The initial deposit would be forfeited unless she wanted to continue the purchase process. In that case, the balance of the ten percent down payment, another $80,000, was due within thirty days.

Like a bad dream, interest rates also started to rise, so Alexandria saw firsthand the difference between 3 percent and 3½ percent on $650,000. Additionally, the condo association announced a homeowner fee increase of 20 percent in the second half of the year to cover rising energy costs and to maintain the building's luxury accouterments.

Her final recourse was respected attorney James Townsend, whom she hired to represent her in the closing transaction. After thirty years of Manhattan real estate transactions, he had pretty much seen it all. "Alexandria, I'm prepared to fight for your deposit, but the absolute best we'll get is a negotiated settlement because you notified them ten days after signing the contract. *Maybe* they'll refund $5000, strictly for PR purposes, after raking you over the coals. BD Development is a billion-dollar organization that cannot afford to look weak. But I must advise you that your legal fees and court costs will run two, maybe three times the settlement. As painful as it is, my best advice is to move on."

27.

Alexandria becomes a real headache.

Alexandria was becoming more than a tangential flirtation; she was a complicated friend whose life was starting to unravel, financially and personally.

No matter what course our quasi-sexual relationship ended up taking, the best way I could help her in the short term was to get her income growing again.

First, I asked my marketing director Joanne to assign one of the best marketing associates to help Alexandria with her agents. And maybe also to get her some specialized training so that she could catch up.

"Martin James (what Joanne called me when she wanted my undivided attention)," said Joanne, "how the hell can we train someone who hasn't bought into our philosophy?"

"What are you talking about?" I responded naïvely.

"Martin, Martin, Martin, what am I going to do with you? You're such a schmuck, despite all your sophistication. That little blonde probably batted her eyelashes and you promised her the world."

"That's not it; she just lost a pretty significant real estate deposit, as her employer, we can try to improve her commission income."

"Martin," glared Joanne. "I've been around the block a few times — Bill Johnson is her boss, not you. and her real estate gains and losses are none of our business."

Joanne was right, but Alexandria did need help.

"Listen, Martin, Alexandria is a friend of mine. We've been out to dinner, had drinks, and picked up guys, the whole nine yards. Don't kid yourself; behind that gentle feminine exterior beats the heart of a stubborn broad. For Christ's sake, I'm little Miss Flexible compared to her!"

~

Bill Johnson was a different matter entirely. He didn't trust me, and I didn't trust him. But I didn't take it personally. He was also pissed at me for passing on the ContactPro venture. As I learned later, Alexandria had not explained my reservations to Johnson. She simply said that I was a rude bull in a china shop to his friend Gil Rodman.

Johnson was known in management circles as a pen-ultimate cynic who would rally behind the company flag, its strategy, and its culture only when he agreed with them. His damnation by faint praise had a finite employer shelf life. Like clockwork, after three years, no matter how successful he was, his current employer would conclude Johnson's internal divisiveness more than offset his effectiveness. Bill had moved seven times during his twenty-year career. AFA was his eighth; he had been with the company for about eighteen months.

Johnson was also the critical link to Alexandria's potential income. He was her immediate boss and trusted advisor. Alexandria had known Johnson for more than twenty years. To her, he walked on water. More importantly, if he thought she needed to do something professionally, he would tell her and she would do it.

I invited him to lunch, as I had done with the three other group heads. I knew I had to balance discretion and interest. The lunch was billed as a management bonding experience and a chance to get some feedback on how each group direct reports. I figured in that context Alexandria's name and performance would inevitably surface, allowing me to convince Johnson that my accelerated training program for Alexandria was a creative business idea.

Bill was cordial but cautious. He was delighted to report that he figured his group would do more than $520 million in revenues, an increase of about twelve percent over projections. We discussed every one of his reports — except Alexandria.

"Is there a reason we've discussed everyone but Alexandria?"

"She's trouble. Everybody knows that."

"Bill, there's no reason to be defensive. She's a pro. Pros have slumps. Look at the way we fixed Tony McCormick in Dee's group and Lorraine Ward in John's group."

"Sorry. I've been wracking my brain trying to figure out what to do," said Johnson. "I know she's hurting financially; that's why I suggested the ContactPro partnership."

"ContactPro isn't the answer," I responded. "Let me explain why."

He listened; I could tell it was all news to him. My burst of candor seemed to open the door. Although, as I was to find out, not quite enough.

"So, do you have any other ideas?" glared Johnson.

I told him that an analysis of Alexandria's advisors suggested they used less of our practice-building services than any other AMA financial manager because she probably knew less overall about the menu of services we now offer.

"And your conclusion is…?" Johnson continued glaring.

"I guess, in plain English, she hasn't yet got what we do. She needs an accelerated cram course to catch up," I replied. "Johanna has agreed to assign one of her best marketing executives to work with Alexandria."

"And why do you think we should follow this course of action?" queried Johnson with the air of a tenured college professor challenging a failing student. "Are you that worried about her performance?"

"We both know she lost a ton on that new apartment; hopefully we can help her earn back that deposit." As soon as I said the words, I knew I had made a mistake

"Oh, really," said Johnson. "Our earlier conversation led me to believe you didn't know much about Alexandria personally."

28.

Enter one charming, handsome Cuban doctor.

Forty-three-year-old Dr. Gabriel Wentworth was more than just a handsome, articulate doctor who made nurses swoon. He was considered by his peers to be one of the world's most exceptional orthopedic sports surgeons. He had repaired, rebuilt, and given second careers to professional athletes all over the world.

He was born and raised in Cuba, although he was now a naturalized American citizen without even a hint of an accent. As early as in high school, he had become a student of international cultures. His father, Hernàn, was a doctor, so it was hardly surprising that Gabriel decided to do likewise, attending the University of Bologna Medical School in Italy and completing his residency at the University of Havana Medical Center in Cuba, thanks to his family's Cuban citizenship.

The sign over the entrance to the medical center became his professional credo.

La Vida De Un Solo Humano
Vale, Pero Millones De Veces Mas,
Que Todas Las Propiedades
De La Personas-Mas Rico De La Tierra.

Translation:
The value of a single human being
Is worth millions of times
More than all the property
Of the rich people of the world.

After completing his residency, he wanted to help his beloved Cuban citizens, so he established a practice in the town of Cienfuegos, about eighty-five miles from Havana and fifteen miles from Rancho Luna, home to one of the country's most beautiful white-sand beaches. Castro, for all his faults, believed one of the obligations of the state is to provide its citizenry with quality healthcare services. Wentworth's professional reputation grew quickly as *El curjano Americano con un mano dulce y un carazon grande* (a Caucasian surgeon with a gentle hand and big heart).

In his spare time, he also surfed and scuba dived in the Galapagos Islands of Ecuador. It was while celebrating his birthday on the Galapagos that he met a beautiful olive-skinned Dominican named Moravita Benuti. She quickly became the air he breathed. They'd been married for five years when she died in a small plane crash while delivering medical supplies.

Gabby, as his friends knew him, decided to move his practice to the United States, initially in La Jolla, California. About seven years after obtaining his citizenship, he visited New York City for the first time. He fell in love with the culture, rhythm, and medical challenges the city had to offer. His practice there flourished as it had abroad, again attracting top-tier professional athletes from all over the world.

Initially, he was wooed to New York Hospital by its president, Dr. John Savarese, long recognized as one of the world's finest anesthesiologists — and a college roommate of Martin Ruff. As part of his pitch, Dr. Savarese assured Gabby that the hospital's Director of Surgical Services, Lauren Ruff, would personally see to it that all his needs would be met.

~

Within three months, Gabby was performing more procedures at New York Hospital than Lauren's operating suites could handle without bumping other surgeons. Concerned about losing operating room time, Gabby scheduled a meeting with Lauren, who was the OR (operating room) gatekeeper.

"You know the word is spreading among my colleagues all over the world that their most complicated orthopedic procedures cases should be performed at New York Hospital because the service, the staff, and the infrastructure are second to none."

"That's nice to hear," said Lauren modestly, "although I'm not sure how much additional business we can handle. As you've probably seen, there always seems to be some other priority."

"Understood," said Gabby. "And what about technology? Shouldn't the hospital have a leadership position in the practical application of orthopedic innovations?"

"Again, I agree in theory. But, Dr. Wentworth, do you have any idea how much this new technology costs to own and maintain?"

"Lauren, therein lies our *mutual* opportunity."

Lauren understood that her compensation was based on doctor and patient satisfaction. "I'm listening," she replied. Besides, he was so handsome and charming.

"I estimate my colleagues and I will need two dedicated operating suites for sports orthopedic surgery with select advanced equipment — like the Olympus Robotic Assistants — permanently stationed in those suites to reduce prep time. In return, we'll guarantee the hospital a certain amount of additional cases each year to more than cover costs."

Gabby continued, "I'm willing to act as the hospital's spokesman, poster child, and public relations spokesman at medical conferences and in medical journals to increase the hospital's brand awareness and capabilities among my colleagues around the world.

"My increased activity, plus your current backlog, plus all the new business, should provide the financial projections you need for the hospital management."

Lauren knew Gabby was right, but she had no idea where to start. Financial projections had never been part of her skill set.

Gabby kept pouring it on. "Plus, I'd like to donate a portion of my time to worthy pro bono cases. I'm sure I could get my colleagues to do likewise. New York Hospital would be king, a wonderful social statement about the human condition."

"Doctor, you're a wonderful salesman; you may have missed your calling," joked Lauren.

Gabby was a touch insulted. "The more you get to know me, the more you will learn I don't live by hyperbole or exaggeration. I simply see things as they are and do what I can. No more, no less."

Gabby's integrity and humility were quite refreshing, particularly given the titanic medical egos Lauren had massaged over the past thirty years.

Gabby noticed the framed pictorial poems of Lauren and Martin on the walls.

"These are beautiful and so touching," said Gabby. "Where was this?"

"The Rocky Mountains, near Aspen."

"And this?"

"St. Tropez."

"You do travel a lot?"

"It's one of our hobbies."

"Who wrote the poems and designed the photography?'

"The same person: my husband."

"Very loving; I can feel the emotion."

"He's the love of my life. Thirty-five years."

"I understand."

Lauren assumed 'understand' meant he, too, had a long and happy marriage. "How long have you been married?"

"Was. My wife died about seven years ago. Plane crash. She was the love of my life also."

"I'm so, so sorry."

After a moment of silent bonding, Gabby returned to the business at hand. "So, do we have a partnership?"

"I guess so," said Lauren, wondering where the conversation was going.

"I propose we develop an overall presentation with my revenue projections and my requirements, and your needs and costs. Then you get us a board meeting. I may bring another well-known colleague or two to add additional credibility. We all know administrators love to hear what doctors have to say."

Lauren agreed in a heartbeat. During the next two weeks, they worked after hours, constructing a persuasive presentation.

For Gabby, the project was a labor of love, and he got to learn more about Lauren in personal sound bites sprinkled here and there. She also learned to call him Gabby.

The actual meeting with Gabby, Lauren, Dr. Savarese, and the Hospital Board went off without a hitch. "Doctor," summed up Savarese, "You and your colleagues project New York Hospital will generate $50 million in incremental revenues annually if we invest $20 million in new equipment, build eleven new operating suites, and absorb the increased maintenance costs, which you estimate at $10 million per year."

"That's correct, with one caveat. We will undertake our best efforts; I can't guarantee."

"I understand Doctor; forgive my choice of words. But your reputation does precede you."

Within two weeks, the Board approved the plan, and Lauren was named the hospital's project manager.

29.

Chicago trip turns very personal.

Step one was to hire an architect to begin design work. Lauren organized an internal team and invited Gabby and his staff to participate.

The next step was to meet with the technology suppliers who Lauren thought most appropriate at a mutually convenient site. Chicago was selected because of its transportation accessibility. Since the initial order was expected to be in the tens of millions, companies had no problem sending their best sales representatives from all over the United States. The evaluation committee consisted of Lauren and her two top managers, Kathy and Darlene, and Gabby and his two critical team members, Jonathan and Dorothy.

The meetings and presentations were scheduled over two days at the Hyatt Hotel conference facilities, adjacent to O'Hare Airport. For convenience, rooms were also booked right at the hotel. Lauren and Gabby took one cab, and the staff took the other.

"Ritz Carlton in the Water Tower on Michigan, please, " said Gabby to the driver.

"Ritz Carlton? Downtown? I don't think so," said Lauren.

"Relax, my dear. I just thought it would be great to celebrate our victory in the style to which you've become accustomed."

"Listen, it's a wonderful gesture, and I love the Ritz, but I'm very married."

"Lauren, relax. Don't you think I know that? I've reserved separate rooms on separate floors so that you would feel comfortable."

"I'm not sure."

"Ni hagas rogar un viejo?"

Lauren surprised Gabby with her command of Spanish. "That's the first time I've ever heard a grown man beg in Spanish." She paused. "How many floors apart are we?"

~

Dinner was politically appropriate with impromptu flashes of personal candor. Lauren learned Gabby's wife Moravita had been a Dominican native and a registered nurse who was deeply concerned about the availability of quality medical care in the neighboring countries of Haiti, Guatemala, and El Salvador, which she considered less fortunate than her motherland. "She died doing what she wanted to do: delivering medical supplies. Her cargo plane crashed in heavy fog while trying to land at a dirt airstrip in the northwest portion of Haiti, near the isolated towns of Rambaz and Riaribes." Lauren also learned Moravita loved mountain climbing and scuba diving.

"Your wife and I had virtually nothing in common."

"I'm not sure that's completely accurate. I sense you love Martin, as Moravita loved me, unconditionally and without reservation."

She noticed his unusual aquamarine-colored eyes for the first time.

"So, tell me how a health care professional winds up marrying an artist."

"What do you mean, artist?"

"I just assumed, given what I saw in your office."

"Martin's quite a successful businessman. He's started companies, built companies, and invested in companies. In many ways, he's an oxymoron — a type A businessman with creative sensitivities."

"Now that's a unique combination."

"You mean, like a doctor who listens?"

They laughed. It was 10:00 P.M. and time to go. As they walked by the lounge on the way to the elevator, Lauren noticed her favorite saloon singer, Steve Tyrell, performing.

"Oh, my goodness, Steve Tyrell!"

"Who's Steve Tyrell?'

"He's been a successful song producer for people like Frank Sinatra and Tony Bennett. I have every one of his albums. His wife, Stephanie, died of cancer just before the third album, so at least she got to see a measure of his commercial success."

Her passion for the artist was obvious.

"So, how about a nightcap with Steve?" suggested Gabby.

"I shouldn't; it's getting late. We've got an early morning."

"Let me rephrase. How about two decaffeinated low-fat lattes with Steve?"

He made a half-circle with his arm on his hip. She placed her arm in the opening and said, "How did you know this girl never passes up a low-fat latte?"

As they entered the dimly lit lounge, a relaxed Tyrell stood center stage in his signature black suit, white shirt with open collar, black tie, and a warm, friendly smile. He urged the audience to come up on the dance floor. Lauren agreed. Tyrell began to warble "One Kiss to Build a Dream" in his distinctively deep, raspy voice.

Gabby held Lauren close but not too close. She could feel his breath. Neither said a word as they danced. When Tyrell finished, Lauren, beginning to feel emotionally out-of-control, said, "Let's finish our lattes, and then I think it's time to go."

As she began to leave the elevator on the fourth floor, he took her hand and gently kissed it.

The elevator door closed, and Gabby got off on the sixth floor.

After a quick call home to say hello to Martin, a guilt-ridden Lauren tossed and turned in bed for the rest of the evening.

30.

Enter Shanti, Alexandria's troubled daughter.

Shanti Plummet, twenty-six, was depressed and confused. Which may or may not have contributed to her never-ending malaise and the belief that her mother somehow owed her because she was gay, partner-less, and struggling financially.

Shanti's early years were not exactly a storybook childhood. Her biological father, Douglas Whitman, left Alexandria when Shanti was four months old, so she never really knew him. Perhaps worse still, Whitman either changed his name or was never actually legally named Whitman, because Shanti's repeated attempts to locate him failed. When Alexandria's second marriage ended in divorce, she decided both daughters should bear her maiden name, Plummet.

Physically, the unattractive Shanti was a cross between a scarecrow and a nerd. She was thin, gangly, and bony. Her eyes looked like two oversized light bulbs that wanted to pop out of her head. Her red, curly hair and thick, dark brown eyebrows did little to add to her allure. Not surprisingly, as a teenager, she became a loner with few close friends. Academically, however, her insecure behavior had led her to place virtually all her energies in her studies, so her grades had been outstanding.

The kids in school nicknamed her "beetle nerd," which hurt her deeply. To seek relief from the constant snickering, she did most of her homework, studying, and research at the library near home rather than at school. It was there she met another gay woman named Lily Rodriquez.

Lily found Shanti's fragility alluring. "I notice you study like hell," said Lily brusquely one day as she made it her business to leave the library the same time that Shanti did.

"I wouldn't say that. But I do want to get good grades."

"Why are good grades so important to you?"

"Because I want to get into a good college."

"Obvious, dumb fucking answer. Truly bourgeois thinking," responded Lily waving her arms emphatically. "Did you know Van Gogh never went to college? Ditto for Manet, Monet, and Degas."

Shanti's first instinct was to be intimidated. But she wasn't. She found Lily's brashness honest and refreshing. "Let me guess: you're going to be an artist?"

"Going to be," responded Lily confidently. "Going to be! One is either an artist or not an artist. I am the former."

Shanti chuckled shyly.

"A nonbeliever! Why not stop by my studio and see for yourself?"

The two entered a small, dimly lit one-bedroom apartment next to the Erie Lackawanna Railroad tracks. "Voila, my studio," said Lily, pointing to the converted living room neatly filled with canvases, paints, and other art supplies.

"Very nice," said Shanti, trying to remain upbeat in the depressing surroundings.

"Temporary, of course, until my discovery," said Lily. "Would you like to see the rest of the place?" Lily stood in the center of the room and pointed. "In front of me is the kitchen. To my right is the bathroom. And, behind me is the master bedroom. Truly, it is not a Manhattan penthouse, but it's a start."

Shanti nodded. "A slow start."

Lily felt an emotional connection. "Do you feel it?"

"Feel what?"

"Our connection," responded Lily warmly and confidently.

Shanti paused nervously, not sure what she felt. After all, Lily was another woman. "I think so."

Lily slowly placed her arms around Shanti. Shanti didn't resist. Lily kissed Shanti on the lips. Shanti opened her mouth and returned the kiss. Moments later, they were undressing in the bedroom.

Shanti felt guilty, like she was doing something wrong. "I've never had sex, much less with another woman."

"Darling, you poor thing," smiled Lily. "Just relax; let Lily handle everything."

Before long, Shanti had forgotten Lily was a woman. They made love for almost two hours. From that moment, they became inseparable lovers. In time, that became clear to Shanti's classmates and friends, and to her mother and sister.

Shanti finished school at the top of her class and was selected as class valedictorian. Over her mom's objections, she decided to pass on scholarship offers to the University of Iowa in Ames and Northwestern in Chicago.

~

Then Alexandria decided to move to New York to build her career. New York was the center of the financial services industry. She could make more money there and ensure a comfortable old age, since she was starting to believe that she might never find mister right, get married, and live happily ever after.

Alexandria also assumed the move would force Shanti to break up her relationship with Lily, which she found troubling. To her surprise, Shanti decided to temporarily stay with her aunt Tori and her husband in Lincoln.

"Mom, I wish you well, but I'm not going with you. For the moment, I'll be waiting tables at Shoney's till *we're* ready to move."

"Shoney's! You're joking."

"It's not like forever. It's just until Lily sells a few paintings."

"Lily! Jesus Christ. My daughter is living with a goddamn starving dyke artist. Have you gone completely mad?"

"Listen, Mom. Don't lecture me about relationships. Your straight ones have been goddamn losers. I mean, we can't even find that deadbeat father of mine!"

~

With Shanti's accumulated savings and her high school graduation cash, she and Lily moved to New York a few months later to pursue Lily's dream of becoming a commercial artist. She was rejected by galleries large and small in Soho, Midtown, and the Upper East Side.

The politically correct response was always the same, from every gallery: "Your work just doesn't fit the profile of our work at this time." Privately, the gallery buyers thought Lily was a hack. No central themes, no continuity of technique, and no real inspiration. To make ends meet, Lily resorted to selling tourist watercolors of Central Park, the Statue of Liberty, and the Empire State Building to tourists at the entrance to Central Park and 59th Street, for five and ten dollars each. The more watercolors she sold, the angrier and more depressed she became.

Shanti, with no skills of her own, started as a file clerk at Time-Warner Cable. She hated people telling her what to do, so she lasted about two months. They lived in a dump on 22nd Street and 11th Avenue with two mattresses and one lamp. Lily began to blame Shanti for her lack of recognition, and once Shanti's money ran out, Lily left. Shanti had no alternative but to move in with Alexandria.

"You're my daughter and you can stay as long as you want. It'll be fun," said Alexandria, trying to remain upbeat. "We'll be roommates, the female version of The Odd Couple! But there are a few ground rules. You must have a regular job and contribute to household expenses. It has to be something regular, so I know you're standing on your own two feet."

Shanti's life disintegrated into a series of jobs found and lost, money earned and wasted. The more Alexandria admonished, directed, and suggested, the lower sank Shanti's self-esteem and motivation. This painful roommate arrangement lasted three years. Finally, Alexandria gave Shanti an ultimatum. "Clean up your act and get in the game of life, or leave."

Shanti chose to leave and return to Nebraska, where she again cajoled Aunt Tori into letting her stay with her, her husband Louis, and their three kids. "I promise I won't be any trouble. You won't even know I'm here."

The weekly calls to Alexandria were always the same.

"Mom, things are going pretty well. I've got a little job at the [names changed every two months]. I've decided to go back to college, so I'm taking a few courses at a time. I was wondering if you could help me make ends meet?" Shanti discovered it was easier to extract cash from Mom by declaring the funds were earmarked for some positive life-enhancing experience. With every check sent, Alexandria and Tori hoped.

Everything seemed to be progressing nicely until Tori, Louis, and Alexandria discovered there were no college classes. Shanti was earning money as a prostitute. Louis was furious; he threw her and her bag out the front door 24 hours later, "No whore is gonna live in my house and eat my food."

Out in the cold again, Shanti went to live with her grandma, the fiercely independent Cecelia Plummet, a determined eighty-three-year old who chose to live in her house rather than an adult or assisted-living community.

"Grandma, promise, I'll make you proud."

"Shanti, child, Grandma has always been proud of her smart, beautiful granddaughter."

Grandma Cecilia loved having company, since Alexandria's dad Fred, a life-long fireman, had died of heart failure a few years back. Shanti felt comfortable in the house where she and Melissa had spent so much time as children. Grandma had never even changed the wallpaper in Shanti and Melissa's room, so it was like coming home. Grandma's attention and unconditional love made Shanti's spirits soar. She got a regular job as a waitress in Lincoln's landmark Silver Spoon Diner on the corner of Main and Harbor, a few blocks from the heart of town.

One afternoon, she was serving a bearded, blue-collar patron a heaping platter of franks and beans. The man stared through the cloud of steam. "Shanti Plummet, is that you?"

"Yes? Do I know you?"

"It's me, Rocky Stein. Remember?"

Rocky Stein was the sixteen-year-old junior who was Shanti's first French kiss when she was fifteen.

She started to smile until he opened his mouth again.

"I heard you became a goddamn dyke. I hope it wasn't me. Imagine, Rocky French-kissing a dike!"

He started to roar, as did most of the other male patrons. And an embarrassed Shanti ran out the door and went home crying to Grandma's.

31.

Shanti's not-so-shocking demise.

Alexandria was dressing for the office when her cell phone rang. She assumed it was me calling to say good morning while driving to the office, a little routine we had started after one of our dinner dates.

"Sis, this is Tori."

"What a nice surprise."

"Sit down. I don't know exactly how to tell you. We just came from Mom's."

"Oh, no! What happened? I knew we should have put her in that assisted care facility."

"It's not mom. It's Shanti."

"Shanti?"

"Mom went into Shanti's room to wake her because she hadn't heard the alarm clock go off. She didn't want Shanti to be late for work; she was doing so well. Mom found Shanti hanging from the light fixture on the ceiling. She must have used her sheets as a rope."

Alexandria fainted. Tori called the manager at Alexandria's building and explained what had happened. He rushed upstairs, opened the door, and revived her with some smelling salts.

As soon as she was conscious, she started kicking and screaming on the floor. "I knew it! I knew it! It's all my fault! Ahhh!"

"It's not your fault!" screamed Tori into the phone.

"Shanti called last night. Said she wanted to move back to New York. It wasn't going to work in Lincoln. Would I buy her a plane ticket and let her stay with me again? I told her no way. 'Be like your sister Melissa; go figure something out.'"

Alexandria could feel herself hyperventilating. Her heart began beating erratically, and she saw her pulse pounding in her wrist — he was having a panic attack. She hung up, shut the curtains so the room was completely dark, and then mustered all her emotional resources to take twenty deep breaths, inhaling through her mouth and exhaling through her nostrils in one fluid motion, just as the psychiatrist had suggested.

~

As her exhausted body began to calm down, her brain turned into a digital slide projector, as images of happier times flashed in her mind. Shanti the determined three-year-old engineer building a sandcastle on the beach at Southampton. Shanti, the tomboy, playing t-ball in Central Park with the boys. Shanti the Girl Scout proudly returning from an overnight outing with a pet snake in a bucket. Shanti the idealist singing "Over the Rainbow" at a high school concert to raise money to feed the less fortunate.

As the light in Alexandria's mental projector dimmed, images of an older, more pensive, reflective, jaded Shanti appeared. Alexandria, now a guilt-ridden mass of personal confusion, wondered how she had missed all the apparent cries for help from her flesh and blood.

~

The family held a quiet, dignified funeral — a one-night wake, closed casket, with family and a few friends and no newspaper announcements.

Somehow, one of Shanti's old high school friends got wind. She contacted other friends, who contacted other friends. About twenty minutes before the final service was to begin, the room was full of Shanti's friends. Each had brought their favorite picture taken with Shanti and placed it at the foot of the casket. Meanwhile, Shanti's best friend, Kristen, an attractive, petite, dark-haired girl with a silky soprano voice, sang Shanti's favorite song, *In the Arms of anAngel.*

Spend all your time waiting for that second chance
For the break that will make it okay
There's always some reason to feel not good enough
And it's hard at the end of the day

I need some distraction, oh beautiful release
Memories seep from my veins
They may be empty and weightless, and maybe
I'll find some peace tonight
In the arms of the angels, fly away from here
From this dark, cold hotel room, and the endlessness
that you fear
You are pulled from the wreckage of your silent reverie
You're in the arms of an angel; may you find some
comfort here

©Sarah McLachlan

A tearful Alexandria was so moved she asked the mortician to unseal the casket so everybody, including herself, could have one last look at this beautiful life lost.

The last person to pay his respects was a young, bearded, curly-haired man.

He stood in front of the casket and stared for almost sixty seconds. Then he turned to pay his respects to the family. "I'm so, so sorry. I'm so, so sorry."

"I take it you knew my daughter pretty well?" asked Alexandria. "And your name is?"

"Rocky Stein."

"Oh, my goodness. I didn't recognize you with the beard. God, did Shanti have a crush on you in high school."

On the way home, Rocky stopped at the local watering hole. He had a few scotches, then a few more, and a few more after that. It began to pour as he got in his car. The next morning, Rocky and his vehicle were found three hundred feet down an embankment not far from his home. The police were never able to determine whether it was the drinking, the rain, or an intentional decision that ended Rocky's life.

~

An emotionally drained Alexandria fell into a deep sleep. When she awoke, it was nearly noon. She felt embarrassed and didn't want AFA to know just yet. She called Bill Johnson to tell him that her 83-year-old mom in Lincoln had suffered a massive stroke and she needed to take the rest of the week off; she would return to the office on Monday.

"Alexandria, you do what you have to do; don't worry about anything. I'll get some of the other managers to cover for you this week."

32.

The Jets, Patriots, Alexandria, and MJ.

I decided to take a punt.

Lauren and Dr. Wentworth were in Chicago, looking at medical robotics, and I had an extra ticket for the Jets-New England Patriots game at the Meadowlands.

"Alexandria, it's me. First, I want to offer my condolences about your mother. I assume you're exhausted from this week's ordeal. But it just so happens I have an extra press-level seat for the Jets-Patriots game on Sunday. I remembered you telling me your dad turned you and Tori into pro-football junkies at the Pro Football Hall of Fame in Canton. It's okay if you want to take a pass — no pun intended. It's not even necessary to return the call. I'll understand.

"I thought you might get a kick out of meeting my two sons. We've been avid Jet fans since they were eight and nine years old. We typically make a day out of it by meeting at the Stadium Club an hour and a half before kickoff. This is the only activity MJ will attend with his big, bad father. I guess we have to be thankful for little things. Hopefully, Melissa and the family handled the funeral okay. By the way, if you decide to go, the invitation includes pick up and drop off service."

Alexandria caught an earlier flight out of Lincoln. She arrived home around noon. She listened to the message several times, then started asking herself questions. *Should I go? Is meeting his sons a good or bad thing? Do I want to meet them for lunch?*

I was busy doing a distinctly New York thing — standing twelve inches away from Van Gogh's *Starry Night* at the

Metropolitan Museum of Art — when Alexandria left her response.

"I think I'd like to go. But if you don't mind, I'll meet you at the Meadowlands. I have a few errands to run in the morning." An hour later, she called again. "I think I'd like to join you for lunch. Be a dear and meet me outside the Stadium Club at 11:30. See you!"

~

As my sons and I drove to the stadium, I mentioned I invited a friend from the office to use the extra ticket. I didn't say it was a woman. "You guys get our table; I'll wait for our guest." Alexandria arrived at the Club door in a sweatshirt, sneakers, and a ponytail in her hair topped with a Jets hat.

"You look like a real football buff."

"I can't believe what you guys pay for this stuff. I could've bought a nice Louis Vuitton bag and had money left over."

"That was the errands?"

"Plus, I wanted to give you time to figure out how to tell your sons you gave the fourth ticket to a *woman* friend."

"Well, I didn't exactly …"

"Great. Do you think they'll notice?" said Alexandria.

My sons were very calm when I introduced a surprisingly self-conscious Alexandria. "Boys, this is my friend Alexandria from the office. Alexandria, these are my sons, Bart and MJ."

Alexandria's big blue eyes stared at the two boys. "Nice to meet you guys. Your dad has told me a lot about you."

MJ, the more intuitive of the two, tried to put her at ease… Ruff-family style. "Did he tell you he loves Bart more than me?" quipped MJ.

"That's because I work harder than you," retorted Bart.

"So, you must be MJ," smiled Alexandria as she reached out to shake his hand.

"And, I'm Bart, the illiterate son who never reads my dad's ultra-left-wing *New York Times*."

Alexandria cackled. "You boys certainly have your dad's peculiar sense of humor."

The ice was broken; I just sat and marveled at the show. Alexandria's quick wit established her parental savvy. Before long, the talkative, uninhibited Bart was discussing his marriage, his wife, his job, his hopes and dreams, and his favorite subject of all — the acquisition of money.

"Nothing wrong with money," said Alexandria. "As a single mom, I learned you simply better make enough of it. Your dad's been twisting my arm to learn some new things. He keeps telling me I'll make more money."

"How's it going?" asked Bart.

"With somebody as stubborn as me, it might be easier if I just married some wealthy old guy." She turned to MJ, " And what do you do?"

I cringed.

MJ, to my surprise, responded candidly. "I work out of the house because I'm battling a biochemical condition called acute panic disorder."

Alexandria was surprisingly empathetic. "I've had a touch of that myself, "I've found the damn thing is so hard to explain — people think I'm crazy."

"I know what you mean," responded MJ empathetically.

I interrupted, thinking Alexandria might be feeling uncomfortable. "Boys, topic change. We might be getting too personal for a first conversation."

"Martin, it's fine," said Alexandria. "The doctor told me the more I talk about it, the more I'll be able to minimize recurrences. I discovered this is something you have to learn to live with, to manage."

MJ nodded as if to say, *Finally, someone who understands.* "Have you had any serious recurrences?"

"You know, the most difficult thing for me is how, when I have one of those attacks, I feel all alone, even in a crowded room."

"Me too. That's why I avoid crowds."

"That's another thing I've learned. It's unrealistic to believe you can control all the circumstances around you all the time."

"I'm not ready to accept that statement."

"What statement?"

"That I must get back into the workplace. I've done just fine running a business out of the house."

"I didn't say that," responded Alexandria with just the proper hint of indignation. "Don't put words in my mouth."

MJ was shocked that a woman challenged him. His mom, his safe person, would have never done such a thing.

A determined Alexandria pressed forward. "This woman says you're kidding yourself. *Pas possible* long-term."

MJ, fluent in French himself, smiled. "*Le temps passe vite. Le temps passe vite.*"

My concern was now MJ. Would he freak out because of the challenging conversation?

"Dad, relax, we were just having a little *tète à tète*," smiled MJ.

"*Votre père savoir à ennuyer homme*," she teased.

"*Merci beaucoup, merci beaucoup.*"

Bart, simultaneously impressed with Alexandria's mastery of MJ and bored with the incomprehensible French one-upmanship, decided a subject change was in order. "Alexandria, I'm curious. Dad can be quite overbearing at home. How's he at the office?"

Alexandria got the message. "Absolutely the same. Maybe worse."

I felt compelled to defend myself with a touch of humor. "With friends like you, who needs enemies?"

"My, my, my," said Alexandria. "Sooooo sensitive."

"Alexandria, said Bart, "You sound like my *mother*."

"Boys, I'm joking. I find your father to be a fascinating man. His experiences, his creative ideas; he's just full of surprises. You never know what he's going to say next. Most of all, he makes me laugh and feel important."

I could sense Bart wondered what that statement was all about.

MJ was now completely taken. "Alexandria, do you think I should venture outside the box?"

"It's going to be a little scary at first, but you're a bright man. I'm sure you'll figure it out."

MJ thought about it.

"I can smell the wood burning," chided Alexandria.

"Oh, I was thinking. I just had an offer for a sixty-day freelance project. I told them I'd have to think about it. Candidly, I'm not sure I can maintain my focus for that extended period. I don't want to let anybody down."

"Take the job; you won't let *anybody* down."

"So, Alexandria, how old are your daughters?" said Bart.

She paused and bit her lip. "Twenty-eight and twenty-six."

"What do they do?"

"One works in Portland as an editorial assistant. The other does nothing." Tears formed in Alexandria's eyes. "Nothing. As in she committed suicide last Monday. She hanged herself in her room at her grandmother's house."

There was an eerie silence at the table. Alexandria was so matter-of-fact that the self-consumed MJ wondered if this was a psychological ploy.

"I'm sorry, fellows. It's been a hell of a week for me. I didn't mean to spoil your game."

"Listen," I said, "Why don't I take you home? The boys can stay for the game and get themselves home. Right, fellas?"

"Absolutely not," said Alexandria. "We came to see the Jets whip the Patriots' ass. It's almost time for the kickoff."

The boys were impressed with her emotional tenacity. So was I.

On the trip home, Alexandria openly discussed who Shanti was, how mother and daughter had drifted apart, and how it was to lose someone that was a part of you. Mostly, we all just listened. I could see it was therapeutic.

"By the way," said Alexandria as we arrived at her apartment, "MJ, if you ever want to talk some more, here's my business card with my cell phone number. You can call anytime."

MJ smiled a smile I hadn't seen in a long, long time.

The Jets beat the Patriots 34-0, and Alexandria cheered and screamed like a weekend jock.

33.

Stephanie evaluates the situation.

Monday morning, on the way to work, I called Alexandria. " I had no idea."

"How could you know?"

"Is there anything I can do?"

"Yeah, how about a TLC dinner? I could use some about now."

Under the circumstances, I thought I'd pull out all the stops. "How about La Dolce Vita on the water at Battery Park City?"

"How about we do something simple? There's a little steak house that just opened in my building."

Fortunately for me, Lauren's Chicago trip had spilled over into Monday, so there was no explaining to do other than to tell MJ I'd be late. From the tone of his voice, he'd sensed I wasn't dining alone.

"Business dinner, son."

"Another out-of-town producer."

"Yeah, sure."

"What's his name?"

"What is this, twenty questions, and you're the dad?"

"I was only asking. How come when I ask a question, you always explode?"

~

Carmine's was just what the doctor ordered: a charming little Italian steak house with maybe a dozen starched white tables, soft lighting, a warm bar, and delightful kitchen aromas that were one-part garlic, one-part marinara sauce, and one-part broiled New York strip steak on the bone. I arrived first and mentioned

Alexandria's reservation. It seemed the entire staff knew and liked her. "Senorita Plummet, bella, bella."

As I sipped a glass of Pinot Noir, I felt a gentle tap on the shoulder. "Hey you," she said, kissing me gently on the cheek. With minutes of ordering a drink and an appetizer, we had a surprise visitor: Stephanie. Alexandria introduced me to "her best friend in the whole wide world."

Stephanie hadn't talked to Alexandria since she went back to Lincoln. I could see she wanted to say something to Alexandria but wasn't sure if I knew; she didn't want to embarrass her friend.

"It's okay; he knows everything," said Alexandria.

"I'm your best friend, and I don't know everything."

"Stephanie," I interrupted, "you need to understand I have two sons about Melissa and Shanti's ages. Alexandria's difficulty with Shanti mirrors my experience with my son MJ, who suffers from acute panic disorder. They bonded yesterday."

"Excuse me," said Stephanie caustically, "Who are you again?"

"Don't be so rude, Stephanie. Martin's my boss's boss. He's one of the owners of my company."

Stephanie quickly put two and two together. Martin was the married man that Alexandria talked about in her apartment.

"Maybe we should turn this into a shrink session about Shanti, MJ, and my Johnny." Stephanie looked at Alexandria. "I assume he also knows about Johnny?"

"No," replied Alexandria.

Stephanie laughed. "Well, what the hell; you're already like family, so I might as well fill you in. I have, I mean, I had, this fantastic, handsome, successful son. All we did was fight over the fact that I was the kept woman of a married man. He said it was an insult to his deceased father's memory. One night, after one of our nastier spats, he drank himself into oblivion and crashed his 24-valve something or other into a concrete divider on the FDR at 100 miles an hour."

"You know life is a series of misadventures," I said. "Somehow, we survive. The fact is, we have more than most despite our disappointments and tragedies. But look at me: here I am with the two most beautiful women in the place sitting across the table from me. How about we all stop wallowing in our martinis and order some dinner? But first I have to make a guy stop. Where are the restrooms?"

~

"That's quite some mystery man," said Stephanie. "My God, Alexandria, he's perfect — sensitive, honest, successful, handsome, experienced. Go get him!"

"Are you crazy? We're just good friends. He's my boss. Besides, Martin's married. I've even know his wife."

"Let me tell you something: *he's not that married.* Otherwise, he wouldn't be here. Did you see the way he looks at you?" said Stephanie.

"Men like Martin don't just leave their wives. Not after all those years. They're too comfortable. Look at what you just went through with that heel Curtis."

"Alexandria, let me tell you something. They were four great years. When we were together, the world and all its frustrations seemed a million light-years away."

"Stephanie, you should hear yourself."

"Listen, Miss Proper, look at your love life — two shit marriages; broken homes; a bitter, confused child."

"I'm warning you, just don't go there."

"I'm so, so sorry."

"Apology accepted. But what about the lies, the deceptions you endured?"

"Hey, I'm a grown woman. I knew the ground rules. *Je ne regrette rein.*"

While Alexandria pondered the implications of Stephanie's observations, Stephanie gave her friend's relationship a little helping hand when I returned.

"Martin, while you were away, I remembered something rather important. I've got someone waiting for me up at Lincoln Center. Thank goodness for cell phones. I just called him to apologize that I was running a little late. It was nice meeting you. Hope you don't mind if my friend walks me to the valet."

"No problem."

Once out of earshot, Stephanie urged, "Alexandria, this is your time."

"Suppose he's not ready. I don't want a Curtis on my hands."

"Honey, this is a completely different situation. If he blows out, you've got the perfect claim for a sexual harassment suit. So, you win either way."

"You're kidding, right?"

"Don't be so naïve. This stuff goes on all the time in today's workplace. Why do you think companies carry beaucoup millions in liability insurance? You're just the poor victim. Cry foul in the right way and you're an instant millionaire. It's better than winning the lotto."

~

Dinner and drinks took the better part of two hours. I suggested, "How about a little dessert?"

Alexandria countered, "How about coffee at my apartment instead?"

34.

Sending and receiving mixed signals.

Alexandria opened the door to her apartment with a clear disclaimer. "Now, don't get any ideas. It's just coffee."

Except for the oversized windows and a clear view of the East River, the apartment was a typical 1-bedroom, 1½-bath luxury New York condo with a small island kitchen and a combination living room-dining room.

"Would you like the 25-cent or the 50-cent tour?" smiled Alexandria as she stood in the center of her living room. "This is the living room, over here is the dining room, you're standing in my entrance hall and kitchen, to my right is my bedroom and bath, and behind you is the guest bathroom." Then she walked into her bedroom, with black walls and ceiling, and pointed to a small alcove under a double window. "And there's my office."

"What's with the black walls and ceiling? Does it make the sex more intense?"

"One-track mind. It helps me to sleep better. My doctor suggested it as part of my insomnia regimen."

I wasn't in the mood for a dissertation on black. "It's cute. The apartment, I mean."

"It's claustrophobic."

"That's New York."

"No, that's *my* New York. You're the one with the 2500-square-foot apartment and six acres in Southport."

"Where did you hear that?"

"I have my sources."

She began making coffee as I sat on one of the bar stools at the kitchen island. "Do you prefer coffee or espresso?"

"You know, with a little space management, you can make the apartment more spacious and more functional."

"You've got my attention, now that I'm $25,000 poorer from the apartment debacle!"

"Take your office. That nook is perfect for a built-in desk, filing cabinets, and shelves with a mini-stereo system. And if I'm not mistaken, eliminating the filing cabinets in the closet will also make some serious additional space for your clothes."

"I'm impressed; all that in less than five minutes. Let me get a pad before I forget some of those ideas."

"There's more. If you got rid of that monster TV across from your bed and installed a flat-screen, you could get a dresser more in scale with the room, which would then give you room for a queen-size bed."

"And, why would I need a queen-size bed?" she teased. "That brings me to ground rules." She paused. "How long have we been doing this once-in-a-while thing?"

"About a year."

"Would we say I've been a good girl in that year?"

She went over some familiar ground — she wasn't a home-breaker, she'd never mixed business with pleasure, etc. — until we reached new territory. "So, we have choices and ground rules. Option number one is we can just be friends. No more sneaking behind Lauren's back, no more lying, and no hinting or joking about making love. Ever."

"Can straight guys and girls be friends without eventually having sex?"

"Girls can," she smiled.

"What's my next option?"

"You can decide if you love me. No more implied hints. You tell Lauren, and we begin to have a real-life together."

"Isn't there some reasonable compromise? Like Curtis and Stephanie."

"That was not a compromise. Curtis wanted it all. The comfort of his wife's money and a piece of attractive eye candy he could lick when it was convenient for him. That's not the way I want to live my life."

I thought privately: there's a third option — just maintain the status quo and wait for Alexandria to wear down. Like Curtis,

I'm in a comfortable space; why screw it up for Cinderella's slipper?

"Forget it!" said Alexandria. "Standing pat is not an option. I am not interested in a part-time emotional commitment. Like I've said before, I plan to be married, with or without you, by the time I'm fifty."

It was like she read my mind and assumed I could read hers.

35.

Wham, bam, then along came Frank.

Cecelia Plummet died just a few weeks after Shanti's death. It wasn't much of a surprise given her age, her two defective heart valves, and her acute diabetes. She passed away quite peacefully with Tori and Alexandria by her side, as well as Tori's husband and the four remaining grandchildren.

The funeral service reflected the life and times of a woman who was born and had spent her entire 83 years in Lincoln. The room was filled with modest yellow bouquets and yellow floral arrangements, because everybody in town knew her favorite color was yellow.

The walls of the funeral parlor had been turned into a giant bulletin board, so people could put whatever pictorial memories they had of Cecelia and her loving husband of fifty-three years, Fred the fireman, who pre-deceased her by five years.

By the third day, when the fire department came to pay tribute and the priest said last prayers, there wasn't any space left on the bulletin board. Melissa decided she would have all the pictures digitized back at her publishing company, so all the grandkids could have a record of Grandma and Grandpa.

A representative group of firemen, past and present, placed copies of all the awards and citations that Fred had been awarded over his forty-three years — first as a firefighter, then as a battalion chief, and finally as fire chief.

After everyone left, Alexandria stayed a few more moments. She thought about all the values her mom had passed on and wondered how she had driven so far off course.

A gentle hand tapped her on the shoulder. "Alexandria," said a tall, distinguished, gray-haired man who looked quite a bit older than she. "I just wanted to offer my condolences. There were so many people on the receiving line; I figured I'd wait until the end. You don't remember me, do you?"

"I'm sorry. But any friend of Mom's is a friend of mine."

"I was your friend. It's me, Frank Graves, the wide-eyed boy who took you to our senior prom. Remember that white wrist corsage? The pin I almost plunged through your wrist?"

Alexandria's first reaction was to think of how old Frank looked. That living in the Midwest and chomping on cheeseburgers had transformed a teenage hunk into a slovenly, bent physique with a massive protruding pouch.

But despite his physical shortcomings, he still possessed a boyish, innocent gleam in his eyes that demanded Alexandria do the right thing.

"Frank. Frank Graves. Oh, my goodness, I was mad about you," said Alexandria as she gave him a firm hug and a broad smile. "Captain of the football team, those tight pants. You had the cutest bum." Alexandria turned to the casket. "Sorry, Mom."

"Are you doing anything now? Maybe I could buy you and your husband a cup of coffee at the old Silver Spoon so that we can catch up on the last thirty years."

"I'm divorced."

"Sorry."

"Nothing to be sorry about; they were both deadbeats. Let me buy *you* and *your wife* a cup of coffee while we catch up on old times."

"I'm a widower. You may remember her. Mary Lou Vuono. She was the prom queen."

"Of course; she was beautiful."

"That she was. She died of breast cancer at thirty-six. Today, with all the medical advancements, she'd still be alive."

They dropped Alexandria's rental car at her house and drove to the diner in Frank's car, a chocolate brown Infiniti G35, a duplicate of the car Alexandria wanted to lease at the Mile of Cars.

"Nice car," she said.

"Thanks. I just bought it after spending a month doing new car research. I narrowed it down to this and a hybrid, the Toyota Prius. Given the price of gasoline these days, I decided to buy the Toyota. Next thing I know, I'm pulling into the Infiniti lot. I figured it was destiny or whatever, so here we are."

Alexandria just smiled. "Nice choice. I'm sure you'll be happy with it."

They took a corner booth in the Silver Spoon. "Gee, this is amazing. I haven't been here in over twenty-five years. It still looks the same," said Alexandria.

"That's the way things are around here."

"So, let's get started," said Alexandria with the charm of a schoolgirl. "Thirty years is a lot of catching up to do. What time do they close?"

"They're open all night, and that's a change. About fifteen years ago, the mattress factory at the end of Main became a Goodyear tire factory. It's so busy that they have three shifts. Old Milton, who owned the diner, thought he died and went to heaven. This place is now a gold mine. And they still don't take credit cards."

"So, where did you go to work after we graduated?"

He smiled. "Oh, I got a scholarship to the University of Pennsylvania."

"I'm sorry; I don't recall what position you played."

"Went there on an academic scholarship. Once I finished my undergraduate degree, I got my master's in statistical theory and a Ph.D. in behavioral sciences at Wharton."

Alexandria was starting to get embarrassed by her dumb assumptions. "With those credentials, the world must have been your oyster. Where did you decide to live?"

"Fortunately for Mary Lou and me, Texas Instruments decided to open a futures research center right here in Lincoln. The job was great, and we were near our family and friends. Before I knew it, they had me running the place. Mary Lou was happy, the boys were happy, and I was making enough to buy three houses in a row over on Sumner Street. I put Mom and Dad in one and my brother Chas and his wife and their three kids in the other. Everybody's still kicking and screaming, although the kids are all out and about, leading their own lives. And we still get together once a month, since everybody's within driving distance." Frank smiled warmly and paused. "Just out of curiosity, how long are you planning on staying in Lincoln?"

"Tori and I figured we could wrap everything up by the middle of next week. I took a few weeks' vacation time."

"Perfect. You're invited, and you can't say no; this Sunday is our monthly family dinner."

"I don't want to intrude."

"Intrude? Wait till I tell Mama I *finally* got the damn prettiest girl in school to visit after all these years." He paused. "You don't remember, do you?"

"Remember what, Frank?" smiled Alexandria, getting more comfortable with each passing minute. "What are you babbling about?"

"You dumped me for Richie Vitale the day after the prom. I came over to get you for the class picnic at the lake, and you told me you preferred Richie's red Mustang convertible."

Alexandria held her hand to her mouth. "Oh my God, it's coming back. I'm so, so sorry."

"You damn well better be. But as Shakespeare said, *All's Well That Ends Well.* It was at that picnic that I got to know Mary Lou better, and the rest is history."

It was Alexandria's turn. She felt so comfortable, so secure that she couldn't stop talking: twenty years of frustrations, disappointments, and pent-up emotions oozed out of her pores.

The waitress came over. "You folks want a fresh cup of coffee? I just made some. Plus, old Milt's just getting the morning muffins out of the pan. Want a couple while they're still hot?"

"Morning muffin," said Alexandria. "What time is it?"

"About 5:30. The night shift should be barreling through those doors any minute now…"

"Aren't you Alexandria Plummet, Shanti's mom?"

"Why, yes, I am." But Alexandria wasn't prepared for what followed.

"I was so embarrassed what that little shit Rocky Stein said to your daughter — calling her a dyke and laughing about her first French kiss. She was so embarrassed; she just ran clean out the door. I tried to catch her, but she was too young and fast. God have mercy on me, but I jumped for joy when I heard the little bastard drove off the road that night."

Alexandria was speechless. Then she started to cry, and then to hyperventilate. Frank took her outside. He held her quietly in his arms till she calmed down.

~

Alexandria had a great time at the Graves family dinner that Sunday. She hadn't heard so much chatter around the dinner table in years. There was love in the food, love in the voices, and love in the walls of that old house.

Frank's mother, Joanne, paid Alexandria the penultimate compliment: "Goodness, child, you look fabulous. How could that old son of mine and you possibly have been in the same graduating class?"

Alexandria also spent Monday, and Tuesday, and Wednesday with Frank before she got on the plane for New York. When she arrived home, there was a flower box wrapped in yellow foil paper waiting in the lobby. She opened it right there and then. It contained two dozen roses. The card read, "Just because." It was signed, "from that guy in Lincoln."

36.

Courtney's going away party turns into Peyton Place.

Much to my delight and dismay, Courtney decided it was time to explore other opportunities. "Heck, there's a big world out there; I'm twenty-four and have lived in New York City *all* my life," said Courtney.

She decided she wanted to try Southern California — the perfect fit for a hyper, New York type A! Rather than debate the matter, I got her a bunch of contacts in the financial services area, and within two months she had landed a job as a relationship manager for a major broker-dealer. It was a natural fit: she could leverage her knowledge base and skill in dealing with the AFA financial advisors. She even managed to negotiate a $20,000 raise.

Jeremy, Dawson, Eddie, and I decided it was only fitting to throw her a super sendoff party because, despite her tender age, she was one of the firm's five most tenured employees. We rented a yacht for the evening, which circled Manhattan Island, and stocked it with a wide variety of spirits, fine wines, and gourmet food, plus a Jamaican steel band. We told everybody we were going out until the wee hours of the morning and that there were only three ground rules: no drugs of any sort, no sharp or potentially sharp objects, and no objectionable behavior.

"One strike and you're out," I explained. "Our for-hire bouncer will escort you to shore in his dingy, and *you'll* receive a major league ding in your personnel file." For the weak of stomach, we also brought a stash of complimentary seasick tablets.

~

The entire office decided to attend. Amélie Craft, Mona Costas, Evelyn Carr, and my Lauren all decided to come as well.

While some people brought wives and significant others, it was 53-year old systems consultant John Dodone who turned the most heads. For the past year, Dodone, married with three young children, had been having an affair with Tiffany Blanchard, a 22-year old equally married marketing assistant. While the relationship was supposedly discreet, Dodone told ten of his closest associates at AFA. They, in turn, told ten of their closest associates that he was madly in love with the young lady and wasn't sure how to handle the situation at home. The entire office scratched their heads because Dodone's wife Mildred was beautiful, well-educated, and from serious money. At the same time, Tiffany, despite her alluring pen name, was plain-Jane-homely, had barely graduated from community college, and had $229 in her checking account.

Thin-legged Tiffany showed up in a mini-mini skirt; when she leaned slightly forward, you could see her flowered, unseemly rose-colored panties.

With three margaritas already under her belt, Courtney was in late-evening form. "Lauren, will you look at that tart, Tiffany? It's a giraffe in red panties!"

Ever the lady, Lauren tried to quiet Courtney down. "Courtney, that's not very nice."

"Lauren, I understand what you're trying to do. I appreciate that. But I hate that girl! I mean, John Dodone should be ashamed of himself; he's as old as my father and Tiffany's younger than me!"

Lauren looked.

"Lauren, don't tell me you don't know? Doesn't Martin make conversation when he comes home? Hello?"

"In the 37 years I have known him, he's just been oblivious to rumors. His attitude has always been, if something's important enough to know about, go right to the source."

"I've gotta tell you, the thing I'm going to miss the most in leaving is your husband. I've learned so much from him. He's a real keeper!" said Courtney.

"I know," beamed my wife.

Courtney was warming up. "Sorry for the digression. Back to John. Rumor has it Mildred Dodone threw John out of the house last week when she was finally confirmed what she had suspected for some time: her husband was having an affair with Tiffany. The following week, she had him served with divorce papers right at the office. It was quite a scene. Imagine the dinner conversation between those two. Tiffany's talking about the new pieces she's going to add to her playhouse, and he's explaining the new codicils he's adding to his last will."

Even Lauren had to laugh at Courtney's depiction. Before long, the slightly inebriated Courtney had recruited ten of AFA's most vocal employees to play a robust round of *Dodone dumping*. Each player presented their Dodone dump. The other nine gave it a score of one to five. Then the scores were added. The person with the best Dodone dump got $5 from each of the other nine players. The winner was marketing associate Adam DeChristian, an Alabamian whose dad was a Methodist minister. The winning dump: "Dodone's dick is suffering from midlife *limp-boner* while his brain has terminal, encroaching senility."

As the evening wore on, Dodone started to pick up the vibes and made like Sir Lancelot. "Fellas, cut the shit. Enough is enough."

Pushing and shoving could be heard in the rear of the yacht. Suddenly, DeChristian came running. "Stop the boat; man overboard! Stop the boat; man overboard!" A concerned, out-of-breath DeChristian explained. "John has had a lot to drink. Man, he was pounding them down. I told him to ease up; we've got the whole evening ahead of us. He told me to shove it. John got angry and started pushing me. He's an old guy, so I tried to keep my cool by just moving out of the way. He swung so hard he lost his balance and fell over the side of the boat."

The captain's mates pulled a shivering Dodone out of the water and wrapped him in blankets. Dodone told his version of the story to Costas and Wasserman, who had appointed themselves heads of their newly created AFA Morality Force. Dodone claimed he had been pushed overboard because of defending his relationship with Tiffany. After they finished interviewing Dodone, Costas and Wasserman talked to anybody who had seen or even heard the incident. Everybody corroborated DeChristian's version of the facts.

A half-hour later, Dodone, accompanied by Tiffany, was on a dingy back to shore. As they disappeared into the darkness, Wasserman mumbled under his breath, "What a travesty; he should be ashamed." Costas nodded silently.

At the rear of the boat, DeChristian was laughing as he asked his band of nine, "Are there any other assholes on this boat that need to disappear?"

Lauren then looked at me with a twinkle in her eyes, "Some men just never grow-up."

I felt a twinge in my stomach.

~

Evelyn pressed her ear against the uninsulated wall in the ladies' room. She could hear Adam. She was hysterical as she headed back to Lauren, Amélie, and Mona. "You will not believe what I just heard. The Dodone accident was planned. Those stinkers wanted him and his little girlfriend off the boat."

"Can you blame them?" said Evelyn. "Imagine that's your husband."

"I'll kill Jeremy first before he'd embarrass me like that," volunteered Mona. Lauren had seen that fire in Mona's eyes before. She was starting to believe Mona might be crazy enough to do something like that.

"You know, those things are happening more and more in the workplace today," declared the more understanding Amélie. "The long hours, the proximity. In a lot of cases, the people you know at work become your friends after work. I mean, look at Dawson and me." Dawson and Amèlie had met when she came to work as an executive assistant to one of the account managers. He very discreetly asked her out for a cup of coffee. During the next six months, they started seeing each other frequently and secretly. Martin had said nothing — he didn't want rumors flying around that the president slept with his employees.

"That's different. You were both single," said Mona. "The way I see it, two married people in the same office having an affair, regardless of their age, is downright stupid. I think that's what the *AFA Vigilantes* are trying to say. I would have let the bastard drown. He would have been a shining example for all those men in midlife crisis."

"Wow," smiled Evelyn, "Ain't no messing with you, girl!"

"AFA is starting to sound like that sixties television series *Peyton Place*," said Lauren. "All we need now is a middle-aged married guy hitting on some middle-aged single woman, and we've got a trifecta."

"Why would a married guy do that?" challenged Amélie. "That's dumb!"

"Haven't you ever heard of dangerous liaisons?" said Mona. "Some guys need to feel they're still attractive to someone. Some are just sexually curious. And then there are the head cases who think something's missing at home."

"You sound like an expert on the subject," teased Lauren.

"Remember, ladies: I was the middle-aged single woman before I met Jeremy."

"Mona," said Evelyn, "based on your vast experience and our distinguished cast of bald, pudgy, inarticulate leading men at AFA, I dare you to name me one viable candidate."

"I think Martin's kind of sexy," smiled Mona. "Plus, he's in great shape, because we know he can take a punch."

"Hey, hey, Mata Hari, hands-off; he's mine. Always has been and always will be."

37.

Trying to undo a dumb mistake.

My cell phone rang on the way home. It was the call no parent ever wants to receive.

"Dad," said my near-hysterical daughter-in-law Valerie. "Bart collapsed while he was jogging. He's in the emergency room at New York Hospital. I tried to call Mom, but I got her voice mail. I'm on the way over with the baby."

"What the hell happened?"

"He blacked out completely and fell face-down on the street. A biker spotted him in a pool of blood and waved down a good Samaritan, who stuck him in his car and took him right to the emergency room."

Twenty minutes later, I stood in front of my thirty-three-year-old son, lying in a hospital bed with tubes attached to him and breathing through an oxygen mask.

"His EKG was normal, as were his pulse, blood pressure, and oxygen intake. So, he didn't have a heart attack or stroke. It appears he may have collapsed from heat exhaustion and stress. We've given him a sedative because it took thirty-six stitches to stop the bleeding in his chin and forehead. I want to suggest we keep him overnight for observation and to complete some more tests, because it's very unusual for someone his age to completely blackout during exercise."

Lauren and Valerie concurred with the doctor despite Bart's protestations that he was fine. It was 8:00 P.M.; everybody was starving and the hospital cafeteria had long since closed.

"How about some dinner with the baby, and then we bring you back something?" said Lauren. "Dad, stay and keep your son company," she said, pointing to me.

It had been a while since Bart and I had spent any private time together. Despite his discomfort, we enjoyed the next half hour, chitchatting about nothing while we watched the Knicks and Pistons on the television.

"You know, Bart, I've never forgotten how proud you made me feel by asking me to be your best man. That made…"

Bart interrupted. "Dad, Dad, I'm fine. Don't start with that corny Clark Griswold stuff.

I shut up. Within a few minutes, Bart was sound asleep. As I looked at him, I recalled some of the great moments our little family had shared and all the possibilities that lay ahead with Lauren, our daughter-in-law, and our granddaughter.

As I sat quietly, my mind began to wonder about Alexandria. Were my silly middle-age flirtation and the lies and the deceptions worth destroying the memories created over the past thirty-five years? Was my stupid unconsummated tryst worth risking all that we had built, all that we had accomplished as a family?

What did I think when I got on the Alexandria merry-go-round? I guess at first, there was the testosterone charge of an illicit affair after thirty-five years with the same woman. Okay, she was beautiful and sexy, charming and intelligent, and, lest we forget, challenging, irrational, and unpredictable. The idea that someone like that could find me attractive was in itself an attraction. I didn't regret a moment of the time we spent together, although I'm sure Lauren would find that statement in itself repulsive, perhaps demeaning and embarrassing. But it was how I felt.

Alexandria is fundamentally a decent human being, I thought, a conscientious single mom who deserves a better hand than she's been dealt so far. When I thought of her roller-coaster ride through painful marriages, unfulfilling jobs, and Shanti's tragic ending, I realized how tranquil my life had been — even with MJ's nagging illness, which sometimes made me feel like a stranger in my own house.

I also had to give her credit when it came to "crossing the line," as she termed it. She was steadfast in her resolve, yet always managed to handle the issue with style and class. Unfortunately, or fortunately, she wanted more from me than I was prepared to give. We both probably knew that maybe all along.

I compared the tumultuous peaks and valleys of our unconsummated relationship/affair to the tranquility and support of my loving family. "Comparison" sounds like an insensitive businessman analyzing an inanimate balance sheet, but that's what I was thinking. Men would kill for a woman like Lauren, my measure of financial stability, and my legacy: two intelligent sons, who I'm confident will leave substantive markers that they once passed through here.

Making my decision was easy. Now came the hard part—telling Alexandria in person. After all, she deserved that courtesy. And, crazy as it may sound, I hoped we could remain good friends.

~

I decided it might as well end at my favorite restaurant, Le Périgord, with my friend, the owner, Georges Briquet, within hailing distance if the seas got tumultuous. My call was direct and straightforward. "I've made some decisions; we should talk."

I knew I was in trouble the moment Alexandria walked in. She was dressed to the nines. The eyes of every man in this very upscale eatery followed her as she approached my banquette. I realized she assumed I was about to tell her I was going to tell Lauren, perhaps that I had already told Lauren that I wanted to start life anew with her by my side.

She bent over and gave me a warm kiss. "Waiter," she said confidently, "could we have a bottle of the Veuve Cliquot '95. I feel like celebrating."

I sat back in my chair and took a deep breath. Then I wolfed down three glasses of champagne with her faded, one-way conversation acting as a distant room tone.

"What is so important that we needed to talk right away?"

"Well…err…I've been thinking…"

"That's always dangerous," she jokingly interrupted.

"Will you please stop? This is hard enough. Look, we've had a great time this past year or so, and I am so very, very fond of you, but…"

"Fond of me? What the hell were all those flowers, those poems, that I adore you stuff? That's your idea of fond!"

"Look, I didn't want to do what Curtis did to Stephanie and just make a call."

"So that's it. Poof, I'm done."

"You made a point when we started the non-business part of our relationship: 'men don't want just to be friends with women.' . . . Well, I'd like us to remain friends."

"That's bullshit," she responded angrily. "I don't want to be your friend." She tossed her champagne in my face and walked out.

38.

Johnson helps Plummet create Plan B.

Alexandria felt confused and alone: the disturbing suicide of daughter Shanti, her mother's sudden heart attack, and our unexpected dinner conversation.

New York seemed more grueling, the streets noisier and dirtier, and the people more aggressive and obnoxious — particularly after reconnecting with Frank Graves in Omaha.

Johnson noticed her lackadaisical attitude and decided it was time for Motivation Class 101.

"Alexandria, we should talk," he said, closing the door to her office. She began to weep about her mother and Shanti. Johnson would have none of it. "Alexandria, we all have rough patches; that's part of life. You need to be aware there's a witch hunt underway."

"What are you talking about?"

"While you were away, management decided to eliminate the bottom third account managers and hire some new blood. Each of the four partners selected a systems supervisor to work with; I got that hard-nosed bastard Martin Ruff. He has already been through my producer group one by one. He's identified three low performers; you're on that list."

"That's outrageous after what I've done for this company."

"Alexandria, as much as I dislike the guy, the numbers don't lie. Your production has been in a tailspin for the last eighteen months. I've been trying to coach you, but I'm not getting through." Johnson continued to hammer on her truculence and inflexibility. She recalled similar assessments from Dawson Craft and Martin, although she thought they were delivered with more of a sense of humor. "Don't be ridiculous; I'm not inflexible."

Johnson realized he hadn't even pierced her psyche. He had to shock her into submission. "From Martin's point of view, the difference between you and the other struggling consultants is that 'you don't get it.' You refuse to accept there's a problem, you refuse to modify your business tactics, and you refuse to listen to anybody's advice."

She was stunned. "Do you believe that?"

"Absolutely not! But, right now, it doesn't matter what I think; it matters what Martin thinks."

"After all we've been through, I can't believe that."

"What do you mean, 'after all we've been through'?"

"I'm sorry, I'm rattled. After what *I've* been through." Alexandria continued her soulful lament. "You might understand intellectually, but you can't possibly feel…."

Johnson impatiently interrupted, "Bullshit! I've been dealing with the fact that I'm gay since my wife dumped me for another guy because I was sexually unsatisfying. You don't see me hanging myself, do you?"

Alexandria's eyes popped, "I had no idea."

"That's because you don't see me moping around. I know it sounds corny, but nobody is interested in helping those who don't want to help themselves."

"You're right. I've got to get out of my funk. I've got mortgage payments, credit card bills, obligations."

"I have a potential Plan B," said Johnson. The plan, incidentally, had an attractive financial incentive for Johnson. "Look, let's be candid. The odds of you turning your book of business around in the next ninety days is slim to none. But the fact that you've been seeing Martin after hours can work in your favor."

"Martin? Me? Bill, you must be joking!"

"Look, I've seen you in Shun Lee Palace and at the Algonquin Bar. I'm not blind."

"You must have been mistaken."

"Alexandria, stop. I saw your arms around him on the deck outside La Fortuna. The way you kissed him. The way he held you."

She sheepishly acquiesced. "It's a crazy relationship, and maybe I shouldn't have gotten involved, but Martin's such a nice guy when you get to know him."

"Look, despite all that, my read is that it's just a matter of time before he dumps you. You don't think he's going to give up everything for you? Get real," said Johnson convincingly. "Why do you think he's trying to get you fired? It's his way out. Trust me; I know how guys think."

Johnson now had Alexandria's undivided attention as he revealed the specifics of Plan B. Alexandria would file a sexual harassment suit against Ruff by depicting his off-site social encounters as sexually-motivated rendezvous forced upon her.

"But it wasn't like that," Alexandria responded.

"Who's going to know that other than you, me, and Burton James Moss of Moss, Twilliger, Thompson? He saved me from being raped financially by my ex-wife."

Alexandria hesitated. "Bill, Moss sounds expensive. I'm not sure I can absorb a big legal bill in my current financial condition."

"No worries. Burton has a customized contingent fee program. It worked for me. But you should hear about it from the horse's mouth, since your situation is a little different."

"Will I have to lie?"

"Do you think I'd ask you to lie under oath? We're just talking about how the AFA Corporate harassment workshops opened your eyes to inappropriate behavior on the part of a senior officer."

"You think we can win a case like that?"

"It's not about winning; it's about settling. From what Burton tells me, harassment suits filed by female employees are a piece of cake today. You can't lose. It's your word against his. Since every company wants to be known as a great place to work, they'll settle with you in a heartbeat. You walk off with a nice lump sum and everybody's happy."

"You make it sound like a foregone conclusion."

"Because you're the one with the star witness who will corroborate everything you allege."

Alexandria stared blankly, "Star witness?"

Johnson broke into a devilish smile as he tilted his chair back. "What are friends for?"

It was now time for the *implied close*, a sales technique Johnson had taught his advisors.

He calmly looked directly at Alexandria. "It's your choice, my dear. Get yourself fired and wind up with nothing, or become financially independent, compliments of the company you helped to build."

Alexandria agreed to "explore the opportunity" with Moss. Unbeknownst to Alexandria, Johnson had already briefed Moss, since there was a potentially significant success fee.

39.

Enter the amoral ambulance-chaser.

The distinguished-looking Burton Moss was thin and tall with a full head of wavy gray hair, and he was impeccably dressed in a custom-made, striped suit from Essex Street in London.

Moss's statesman-like appearance masked the fact that he was a ruthless personal and corporate ambulance chaser with known ties to the Mafia. His practice specialties were corporate settlements for on-the-job injuries and sexual harassment claims.

Once upon a time, on-the-job injury settlements were confined to *guaranteed* situations, such as a UPS driver *accidentally* being hit in the rear by another car.

Moss changed all that. He created a regenerating cadre of *freelance* victims, who filed suits against companies with big pockets who carried significant liability insurance policies. As part of Moss's service, each claimant received discreet *prior-to* personal coaching by Moss to avoid embarrassing slip-ups on cross-examination. His fees were contingent: he got 40 percent, including reimbursement of all legal fees and expenses. Conveniently, winning claimants disappeared after each case settlement.

Sexual harassment suits also had specific ground rules. Moss only accepted sexual harassment suits where the plaintiff was a woman, senior management was male, and men controlled the Board.

He also had developed a proven process for extracting significant settlements and accelerated payments from intimidated managements. He'd ask a member of "The Family" to dig up a little dirt on all the corporate decision-makers and threaten public exposure. In those rare cases where no dirt existed, he knew people who knew people who could manufacture the required documentation.

Prospective plaintiffs also found his performance-based fee plan incredibly attractive. There were no upfront fees, no out-of-pocket expense reimbursements. When the case settled, he received fifty percent of the gross proceeds plus all his expenses, including finder's fees. Johnson's undisclosed fee for delivering Alexandria to Moss was fifteen percent of Alexandria's 50 percent.

Moss's office, located in the prestigious Olympic Towers on Fifth Avenue, was modern, efficient, and technically advanced to give plaintiffs the confidence he and his firm were not typical lowlife ambulance chasers. While technically a graduate of Brooklyn Law School's correspondence course, Moss stocked the office with counterfeit certificates from Harvard Law School. In fifteen years of practice, nobody had ever called his bluff.

His initial impression was that Plummet checked out fine. A heavily female jury, another Moss strategy, would certainly believe most men would find Plummet attractive.

~

"So, Ms. Plummet, tell me about your abusive relationship with the defendant."

"This was supposed to be an exploratory conversation."

"Right, sorry." He sensed her ambivalence, so he decided to hold his pressure tactics.

Alexandria explained things as they were.

"Ms. Plummet, that's not interesting for our purposes. There's gotta be more *emotional distress.* For example, the boss insisted on having dinner after checking out the ContactPro opportunity. It was a *quid pro quo.* To your complete surprise, he tried to physically accost you in the parking lot on the way to your car. Didn't he? Fortunately, someone else entered the parking lot, which caused him to pull back."

"It wasn't like that. Martin walked me to my car because the parking lot was very dark."

"Ms. Plummet," said a frustrated Moss. "May I be blunt with you? As I understand your situation, you can use a substantial settlement for personal reasons. AFA should be ashamed of itself for having no formal sexual harassment policy. Don't you agree they should share in your pain?"

"But I think there is a policy in the employee handbook."

"Not to worry, we can just claim nobody administered the policy. The proof of the pudding is the relationship Ruff forced upon you."

"I see." Alexandria was starting to get with the program. "Just out of curiosity, if I decided to go ahead with this claim, what kind of money are we talking about?"

"I figure we can *settle* for about two million. That's the part I love about harassment cases. The process is so orderly and predictable. You approach the company to settle your grievance. They respond that you don't have a case. We file a formal complaint with the court. Now they know we are serious. They examine the company's directors' and officers' liability insurance policy. They discover they are covered. Enter the timid insurance adjuster. I'll outline the cumulative costs to the insurance adjuster, including legal fees if he loses, and they come running with a check. It's like taking candy from a baby. As part of the settlement, we agree to dismiss the case, and the court records are sealed. Nobody can verify your suit and the company can't reference the matter with anyone. As I started to say, I always like to begin with a big number. Based on my research, I think $5 million will catch their attention."

"What research?"

"Let's just say we've been able to identify last year's partners' profit distributions."

"I thought AFA was a private company."

"Let's not worry about those details."

"Jesus, how could I continue to work at AFA after demanding that kind of money?"

"Work there? Ms. Plummet, at the risk of sounding condescending, here's the way it works in the real world. You present your claim. You continue to scream and yell foul, and remain fully employed since they don't want to appear biased and open the flood gates for other potential suitors. When they settle, you quit. We split the proceeds and you go off into the sunset to start life anew. You get sixty percent of the settlement. I get 40 plus my legal expenses."

"Sounds like you make out like a bandit," said Plummet.

What Moss didn't mention was that on a $2 million settlement, in addition to his plaintiff settlement split of $800,000 and his expense reimbursement, he earned another $300,000 in legal fees from the insurance company, using generously padded timesheets at $650 an hour.

Moss paused and smiled. "Maybe next time you find yourself a nice, unmarried guy, somebody like me."

Alexandria was personally repulsed by Moss, but mesmerized by the allure of financial independence. After all the crap she'd been through, she felt she deserved nothing less. "What if something goes wrong?"

"Wrong? Nothing can go wrong! Our case is solid as a rock: juries today love to side with the intimidated female employee who has been verbally and physically abused by her boss."

"He's got lots of women reporting to him, and I can't remember hearing much about his behavior."

"Turns out he's clean as a whistle, but that doesn't matter. Harassment cases are like political holy wars — there are no ground rules. Nothing and no one is off-limits.

"We're going to focus on the sexually permissive environment fostered by the CEO Craft. My guys are pretty sure he's been screwing somebody in the office. Identifying her will go a long way towards establishing a corporate pattern and discrediting Martin."

"I'm not sure that's the case; the partners are pretty straight," said Alexandria, not wanting to expose her own prior relationship with Craft.

"My dear, just leave that to old Burton. My guys think they are very close to identifying the woman. And one more thing," said Moss, raising his voice, "you've got to knock off that holier-than-thou shit. Our *mutual* goal is simple — absolutely, positively humiliate Ruff in front of the whole world. Remember, the bastard is trying to get you fired. We're not playing games."

Moss explained the rules of engagement. "You give me a complete debriefing. I will determine which facts best support our case. Then I draft the complaint letter, complete with typos. You sign the document and present it to the company."

"Typos?"

"Another little trick of the trade. It communicates that you have not escalated the matter, as of yet. Over the years, I've learned that small details ensure big settlements."

"I'm not sure I'll be any good at presenting the claim."

"Don't worry; by the time we finish rehearsing, you'll be a poster child for the emotionally and physically distraught. The idea is for you to sound conciliatory but determined to receive your just due."

"Suppose they don't buy my story."

"Remember," said Burton, "It's all in the delivery. These days, a successful harassment complaint is like playing poker. If the other players believe you have a better hand than you do, they settle. It's easier, faster, and cheaper than increasing the bet."

40.

Gathering documentation for Moss's deposition.

"What is this?" asked Burton at his first discovery session with Alexandria.

"Oh, that's just a corporate ad featuring me. The idea was to try to recruit other female producers by showing my success, despite the pressures of being a single mom."

"Wrong," said Burton. "It's a degrading exploitation of your role as mother and breadwinner. And, despite comments from your peers and friends, you said nothing to management for fear of being fired."

"I understand," replied Alexandria.

"So, as you review your papers and documents, remember what I said: 'Small details ensure big settlements.'"

"That's great; I love it. I love it. Give me more."

Two days later, Moss and Plummet reviewed his draft of their deposition.

Alexandria paused. "This section isn't true. He didn't force me to go out with him. I was attracted to him."

"Don't you dare say that! You feared for your job; he was your boss; he made you go."

Alexandria looked at the section dealing with dinner after ContactPro, stating he forcibly molested her. "God, the guy has never done anything physically inappropriate. Lauren will flip if she ever sees this."

"Alexandria, you're making me nervous. Who the hell is Lauren?"

"Martin's wife."

"Martin's wife! Who gives a shit about Martin's wife? Who gives a shit about Martin's kids! Who gives a shit about his mother, father, aunt, uncle, cousin?"

"You're right, you're right," said Alexandria, intimidated.

"I need more specifics. You've got to help me here. Any letters, notes?"

"Well, he wrote me poems on restaurant napkins; they were so sweet. I saved them all."

"Poems. Burn them. They've got to go. The relationship cannot have any good memories. We can't afford to have you slip and perjure yourself. One mistake will kill your credibility and our case. Come on; think. There's got to be more. Think, think, think!" Moss's face reddened; he pounded his hand on his desk.

Alexandria stuttered. "Well, there are the messages." She explained that they called each other quite frequently to stay in touch: sometimes to chat on the way home after work, or to confirm a dinner time, or to pass the time when he was on the road traveling. "I've saved a few of the messages because they make me feel good. Whenever I'm down, I play them, because they tell me somebody I care about thinks about me."

"Fantastic!"

"No, not really, they're just little bits and pieces of our unusual relationship."

"Honey, you've got it all wrong. Those messages are proof the guy was constantly harassing you. You kept the messages because they were so disturbing. You just weren't sure what to do with them until you feared for your well-being. Honey, always remember — it's your word against his. Think money! Think independence! Think revenge!"

"I understand. But will you stop calling me honey? It's denigrating. I need some time to decide."

"Decide what? It's not like you've got all the time in the world. The faster we accelerate the process, the better."

~

Leaning, but still not convinced, Alexandria needed to talk to someone she could trust, preferably a female. "Stephanie, can we get a drink? I need to talk to someone."

They met at the Oak Bar in the Plaza Hotel later that evening. "You've got my undivided attention," said Stephanie.

"I've been talking to this attorney about filing a harassment suit against Martin and the company. He thinks I could get a million dollars for my quasi-relationship by modifying the facts slightly. I wanted to get your opinion. You've met the guy, and you know me."

"Alexandria, you've got me at an odd moment. I'm afraid my response might be a bit jaded. Curtis's wife Mildred just slapped me with a bullshit $20 million lawsuit for financial damages caused by emotional distress. She's claiming my affair with Curtis caused him, as executor of her family's trust, to make bad investment decisions."

Alexandria shook her head in disbelief.

"It gets worse. The lawsuit was filed with Curtis as co-plaintiff!"

Alexandria left a voice-mail message for Moss later that evening. She was ready to begin rehearsals at his earliest convenience. She closed with, "I'm looking forward to nailing the bastard."

In the morning, Moss put a copy of the recorded message in Alexandria's file, just in case.

~

"Bill," said Moss from his office, "I'm worried your ditsy broad is going to foul up the first approach to the HR guy. I've rehearsed her statement fifty times, but she always takes some detour — it's like she has a built-in self-destruct button."

"Nah, she's just stubborn. Leave it to me. I'll convince her to let me pave the way with Wasserman. You know, poor Alexandria is embarrassed to approach the company. I've known her for twenty years. She'll pretty much believe anything I tell her."

41.

Alexandria and her advisors establish the battle lines.

Johnson sat across the desk from HR director Colton Wasserman. "Alexandria wouldn't tell me exactly what the problem was. She just said that it involved a fellow employee," said Johnson. "I've known her for almost 20 years; she tends to be a very private person."

"Bill," said Wasserman empathetically, "Tell Alexandria that we'll handle the matter with the utmost discretion. I could see her at 5:00 P.M. tomorrow. That way, most of my department will be gone and she doesn't have to call to make an appointment."

~

"Colton," said Alexandria with the appropriate pained expression, "this is very difficult for me." She then pulled out two copies of her harassment complaint. "After five years, this place has been such a part of me."

He assumed from her opening comments she was about to quit and negotiate a severance package. Even he was aware of her declining performance.

"I am formally filing a sexual harassment claim against Martin Ruff."

"That's a pretty serious claim. Do you have a supporting statement?"

She handed him a copy of the complaint Moss had prepared.

He sat back in his chair stone-faced and spent about ten minutes reading the letter. The room was dead silent, but Moss had prepared Alexandria well. She remained cool, calm, and collected; she knew Wasserman was watching her body language.

Dawson Craft
President, CEO
American Financial Associates, Inc.
380 Ferry Street
Bridgeport, CT 06604

Dear Mr. Craft,

The purpose of this letter is to lodge a formal complaint against Senior Vice-President Martin Ruff for committing physical and emotional acts of sexual harassment during the past 24 months of my employment at American Financial Associates ("AFA"). His repeated actions have led to a severe decline in my earned income and my quality of life and have caused me countless hours of untold stress and the need for professional counseling.

I seek damages for all the above.

My difficulties with Mr. Ruff began when I introduced him to a potential business venture with ContactPro, a business services software company. As a former field sales rep, I thought such a strategic partnership was in the best interests of our 3,000-licensed independent financial advisors, and a significant source of income for AFA.

Mr. Ruff and I met with company principals on October 12, 2011, in Westport, Connecticut. The meeting took place after hours — at his insistence. The meeting was quite successful: ContactPro principals expressed serious interest in a strategic alliance. Afterward, Mr. Ruff suggested a drink to discuss possible next steps at a nearby restaurant. Since Mr. Ruff was one of AFA senior partners and third-party alliances was one of his areas of responsibility, I agreed — although my instinct told me the discussion should have taken place at our offices during business hours.

During this conversation, Mr. Ruff made it clear he was not interested in a venture with an underfunded start-up. He assumed the reason I was determined to forge the strategic alliance was that I was sleeping with the ContactPro president. Furthermore, when we returned to the parking lot to enter our respective cars, he surprised me by grabbing me firmly and kissing me. Rather than cause a commotion in the parking lot, I chose to enter my car and leave.

We never consummated a deal with ContactPro, but I did see Mr. Ruff on several occasions socially because I feared job loss, given his position of influence within the company. However, about a year ago, I decided to stop because his continued calls to my home caused me severe mental anguish. I am attaching to this complaint three such phone calls that I recorded.

This personal rejection of Mr. Ruff led to a deliberate and continuous process of mental harassment during business hours. This behavior has affected my income-earning ability and my overall quality of life. In one instance, he had personal performance conversations with my immediate supervisor, Bill Johnson. According to Mr. Johnson, Mr. Ruff stated I "didn't get it," implying I was seemingly unable to keep up with the new products and services being offered to our licensed advisors. Clearly, Mr. Ruff was retaliating for my rejection of his advances.

On other occasions, he would intentionally walk by my office and throw crumpled paper at or near me to communicate his continued displeasure. Knowing I was under this aberrant form of surveillance added additional stress to an already uncomfortable situation.

Finally, since I continue to reject his advances, he has begun a tactic of employee manipulation to regain my favor. An example of such underhanded behavior was a call I received recently inviting me to dinner with him, and a new manager, Joseph Boston, recently relocated from Cleveland. His rationale was that Mr. Boston was also from the

Midwest, lived next door to me in Westport, and didn't know a soul in the area. Again, I politely rejected the offer, stating I had a long-scheduled plan to host several outside advisors from Atlanta. Mr. Ruff wasn't pleased. At that point, I knew I had to file a formal complaint.

Given that Mr. Ruff is a senior partner and member of the board at AFA, I believe the Company is liable for substantial damages as well as a stern reprimand or dismissal of Mr. Ruff. His behavior should not be repeated with another AFA employee, female or otherwise.

My attorney, Mr. Burton Moss, and I would like to discuss the Company's specific offer of retribution as soon as possible.

Sincerely,

Alexandria Plummet
120 E. 83rd Street
New York, NY 10028

cc. Burton Moss, Esq., Moss Twilliger Thompson, PLC

"You say here, your 'difficulties with Mr. Ruff began when you introduced him to a potential business venture with ContactPro, a business services software company in Westport.' Why would you do that, since it's not part of your job description?"

"As I said earlier, I've been with this company for a long time. I've known Dawson Craft even longer than that. As a senior account manager, I take pride in the fact that I'm always on the lookout for ways to add value for our licensed field advisors that create profitable new revenues for AFA."

"And how did the meeting come to take place after hours?"

"He insisted, since this was one of his corporate areas of responsibility and he was one of the company's senior partners; I agreed, although my instincts told me otherwise."

"How many drinks did you have before you returned to the parking lot?"

"Colton, I understand where you're going. I probably had one too many. My only defense is that I was passionate about the ContactPro possibilities; once Martin made that crack about me 'sleeping with ContactPro president,' I knew it was time to go.

"We returned to the parking lot to enter our respective cars. That was when he surprised me by grabbing me firmly and kissing me. Rather than cause a commotion in the parking lot, I chose to enter my car and leave."

"Did you resist?"

"At first, I did, but he played football at Colgate; he was too strong."

"I didn't realize he played football in college."

Alexandria sensed she might have gotten a little too personal. "I'm not sure about the football thing. I think somebody at the office may have mentioned it."

"Despite that alleged compromising situation, you continued to see him after hours?"

"I saw Mr. Ruff on a few other occasions socially because I was fearful for my job, given his position of influence within the company. But his continued calls to my home caused serious mental anguish on my part, since he was a married man."

"I see from your complaint that you have some of those messages?"

"Yes, I brought the three I have. Would you like to hear them?"

Wasserman nodded.

She pulled a small recorder from her pocketbook.

Tape #1. "Hey, it's me. I'm in Toledo. I think the deal is almost done? So, where are you while I'm out busting my tail?"

Tape #2. "It's raining like hell here. I'm exhausted. Maybe if I close this deal and you make another $50,000, I'll get a reward."

Tape #3. "Me. I'm driving to O'Hare as we speak. Or at least as I speak to myself on your voice mail. The traffic is all backed up as usual. I'm sitting here thinking about you having a nice long dinner with me at La Fortuna. The wine is great. You look sensational."

Wasserman thought the tapes sounded friendly, like a friend teasing another friend. He wanted more. "I hope you don't mind, but I need to ask you a few very personal questions. "

"Understood."

"Did Ruff ever force you to have sexual intercourse?"

"No."

"Did you ever have sexual intercourse of any type?"

"No."

"How do you explain that?"

Alexandria remained on-brief. "As you can imagine, my rejection of him led to a deliberate and continuous process of mental harassment in the day-to-day working environment, which has affected my income-earning ability and my overall quality of life."

"Can anybody corroborate these accusations?"

"I think so," said Alexandria innocently. "During my performance reviews with my immediate supervisor, Bill Johnson, he told me Mr. Ruff stated I didn't seem to 'get it.'"

"What did you take that to mean?"

"Mr. Ruff was attempting to retaliate for my rejection of his advances by telling my boss I was unwilling to utilize the new AFA products and services offered to licensed advisors."

"Do you have any problem with me verifying that with Mr. Johnson?"

"Be my guest; I have nothing to hide. Which reminds me, on several other occasions, Martin would walk by my office and throw crumpled paper at or near me to communicate his continued displeasure. Knowing I was continually being watched added additional stress to an already uncomfortable situation."

"Did anybody witness these incidents of displeasure?"

Alexandria was in uncharted waters, so she bluffed, "Anybody in the administrative staff near my office probably noticed."

"Anything else?" Probed Wasserman.

"Yes. When Martin got desperate, he even tried to gain favor by manipulating employees. As an example, when our new training manager, Joseph Boston, arrived from Cleveland, he invited the two of us to and dinner. His rationale: Mr. Boston was also from the Midwest, lived next door to me in Westport, and didn't know a soul in the area."

"I see. And how did you handle that situation?"

"I politely rejected the offer by stating I had previous commitments that couldn't be changed."

"Is that it?"

"Yes."

"So, what are you thinking?" asked Wasserman. "What would you like the company to do?"

"I think Mr. Ruff should receive a strong reprimand so that other female employees are not subjected to his abusive advances."

"I assume you mean fire him?"

"No, I don't think he should lose his job over this."

"So, what are you thinking?" replied a surprised Wasserman.

"I believe in cases such as this, the company is liable for damages for emotional distress and loss of income."

"Is that what your attorney told you?"

"I haven't hired an attorney yet. I was hoping we could settle this thing amicably. I realize Martin is far more important to the long-term growth of the company than me, so I am willing to settle and leave quietly. I am not trying to wreck the company or Martin's personal life."

"Are you trying to tell me you are also suing the company for damages?"

"I wouldn't put it like that."

Wasserman responded sarcastically, "That's gracious of you… what's the magic number?"

"I figure this whole incident will cost me $250,000 in emotional distress and another $750,000 in loss of income. And, then there is a loss of reputation and my future earning potential."

"Let me get back to you."

42.

Wasserman turns Plummet's threat into a power grab.

"Son of a bitch," said Costas. "What a pompous hypocrite! For two years, he was our poster child for the happily-married male."

Wasserman had disliked Ruff from the day he discovered — compliments of Costas — that Ruff cast the lone vote against hiring him. Ruff sensed he was too political for what he incorrectly assumed was an apolitical company culture. This was Wasserman's chance to *give back*. He combined that with another vital fact he discovered — Craft, Costas, and Carr's entire net worth was tied up in the company, while Ruff appeared to have less of his wealth at stake.

The polished Wasserman used the indirect approach. "I spent an hour with Plummet asking the hard questions. I think her claim may have merit, or at a minimum has settlement written all over it."

"I can't believe he could have been that stupid," said Craft. "How much does she want?"

"A million dollars."

"Not a chance, pal!"

"I'm guessing she'll settle for half that without getting an attorney involved," said Wasserman. "That could reduce our exposure by a hundred grand in legal fees. You know how these things go."

"Whatever it turns out to be, we're going to figure out how to get it out of Martin's hide," said an angry Costas.

"Let's slow down here. Have we checked Alexandria's story? This has hold-up written all over it," said Carr. "I still don't understand what Martin did other than exercise some bad judgment. Has anybody asked Martin his side of the story?"

"Not yet," said Wasserman. "I figured I'd better advise you gentlemen first."

Blunder and Wasserman met with AFA corporate counsel Jim Shamus, who advised them to settle quickly. "In those harassment suits that have gone to court, the jury almost always sides with the employee. So, unless you have a substantive case beyond *she said-he said*, it's better to just move on." The only question in Shamus's mind was, *What was the right number?* He suggested Wasserman do some discreet fact-gathering with AFA employees before the partners talked to Ruff, and before they made a counteroffer to Plummet.

Wasserman's first stop was Bill Johnson. He disclosed the claim, subtly corroborating those portions of Alexandria's complaint that fell directly within his domain and cleverly adding a little topspin to the rest. "I thought it was a little peculiar that Martin focused exclusively on Alexandria's performance, but I had no idea. You know I just work here," he smiled.

Wasserman's mind was made up, but he had to be a dutiful human resources director and interview a few other employees. That's when the trouble began. Alexandria's close friend and senior consultant Sam Cameron was too honest to participate in the ruse, despite Alexandria's subtle request. "To be perfectly candid, Colton, I'd prefer to stay out of the matter. I'm just two years from retirement and don't need the grief."

Wasserman persisted. Cameron acquiesced. He explained he knew of no instance where Ruff was abusive to anyone, male or female. It was his impression there was no more to it than a few *consensual* dinners.

As for Alexandria's interpretation of Martin's crumpled paper tossing, at least a half-dozen employees commented they participated in the activity with Martin. Alexandria's next-door neighbor, sixty-three-year-old Betty, laughed, "Gotta hand it to Martin: he makes the best paper planes. He gets them to go twice as far as my twelve-year-old grandson!"

From Wasserman's standpoint, the most damaging anti-Alexandria testimony came from Joanne Mathias, delivered in her inimitable no-bullshit style. "Please, Colton, let's not play games. I've been with Alexandria on numerous occasions — dinners, lunch, drinks, theater, concerts, the beach. You name it; we've done it. She has never mentioned being harassed by anybody, much less somebody at AFA. The only thing she said about men in her life was that she had met 'this positively wonderful married guy who was in the process of getting a divorce.' I know the next question is, did she mention a name?

"The answer to that is no, despite my pushing and probing, both sober and under the influence. That's why I know there was no chance in hell this guy would leave his wife for some stubborn broad with fake boobs and tons of excess baggage from a lifetime of bad judgments. Take it from another stubborn broad with her own baggage. Is that clear enough?"

Wasserman's last stop was Gil Rodgers at ContactPro. Rodgers took the call immediately and assumed it was about the venture. "Listen, Colton, thanks for the call. Tell Martin I'm so sorry about wasting his time. If Bill Johnson had given me the right input at the outset, I would have never dragged him up here. We are strictly a corporate business-to-business sale. Tell Martin I owe him and his wife dinner at the Four Seasons whenever he wants."

43.

Kangaroo court now in session.

A stone-faced Costas marched into the office and effectively shut down my weekly department-head meeting by barking, "We need you downstairs. *Right now.*" The room was hushed.

Sensing the tension he had created, I responded cheerfully, "No problem-o, just give me a few minutes to wrap things up. As you know, Jeremy, Lauren and I will be in Australia and New Zealand for the entire month of April. I want to make sure nobody misses a beat." Costas cared nothing for employee sensitivities or my extended vacation, which he was against from the outset. His face turned beet red as his infamous temper exploded — a rage so hostile that he had discreetly undergone anger-management counseling on three separate occasions.

"I said Dawson and I need to talk to you *right now*!"

My direct reports scattered. As we walked briskly down the stairs to the boardroom, I asked, "Give me a head's up; what's so urgent?"

He just sneered.

As I opened the door, I detected the pungent odor of a freshly-skewered rat. There sat Dawson Craft and Costas's celebrated hire, HR Director Colton Wasserman, whom I had already profiled as a condescending backstabbing scumbag and who kissed Costas's ass 24/7. I had survived Manhattan's corporate jungle for twenty-five years, so I could smell a dead rat and spot brown noses from a mile away.

Costas and Craft sat at one end of the table while Wasserman sat across from me, clutching a slightly crumpled multiple-page typewritten letter. To his left was an oversized black stereo boom box. Wasserman acted as Roastmaster General.

"Martin," he said, with sarcasm dripping in his voice and a twinkle in his eyes, "I want to inform you that a sexual harassment complaint has been brought against you and the Company by our business consultant, Alexandria Plummet. I have an obligation to read the complaint and the related evidence. Then I'll ask for a preliminary response."

"You guys have got to be joking! I've made you rich men during the past five years; I've been eating, sleeping, and drinking this business. Two billion-dollar companies don't grow on trees."

A Cheshire grin covered Wasserman's face. "Trust me; this is no joke."

Costas leaned back in his chair and stared blankly. Craft tilted his granny glasses forward, "Pal, this is pretty serious stuff, so listen closely."

~

After reading the complete letter, Wasserman turned to the boom box. "In addition to the allegations noted herewith, Ms. Plummet has provided these audiotapes, referenced in her complaint, as further documentation of your continued acts of harassment.

I listened — all three tapes were mostly the same — tongue-in-cheek messages left on Plummet's voicemail. In the context of the interrogation, though, they sounded dreadful.

"Is there anything you'd like to say?" asked Wasserman, employing the tone of a headmaster admonishing his student.

My mind raced. Either all the time we had spent together was a lie, or she had been setting me up all along. I couldn't believe that was the case. Not Alexandria. Yet, the facts, as articulated, were so inaccurate and one-sided, my initial response was solely emotion-based. "We had such a beautiful friendship. I can't believe she'd do such a thing."

"Are you saying Ms. Plummet's allegations are correct?"

I looked around the room. My initial response had been trite and inconsequential.

"I didn't say that. Yes, we had a personal relationship. And maybe it was poor judgment on my part. But it was nothing like that twisted depiction. It was a warm, consensual relationship."

"I understand from the partners that you and your wife have planned an extended vacation to the Southern Hemisphere."

"We leave in three days."

"Given the circumstances, we'd like you to provide a formal response in writing before you go. When you return, we will have completed our investigation and will let you know your status," continued Wasserman matter-of-factly.

"My status," as I looked around the room for the life-raft that never appeared. "For Christ's sake, this whole thing is a trumped-up grab for money. Aren't my partners going to give me the benefit of the doubt? We worked side by side like brothers for the past four years to build this company. What happened to loyalty? I feel like you guys have already abandoned the ship."

Their body language and their silence rendered the verdict: *guilty as charged.*

~

"I know, I know," said Craft, imitating deep sincerity. "Buddy, this is difficult for me. You and I are more than business partners; we're friends."

Costas tapped his pencil on the table. Craft ignored him. "But you gotta agree, what you did was pretty stupid. Now we're looking at a serious claim against the company. As its primary stockholder, I'm responsible for the financial health of the whole company and our 350 employees. You've made incredible contributions to the growth of this company. We want to keep you. We just need time to figure out things."

"Dawson, with all due respect," interjected Wasserman, "We need to follow the due process. Let Martin respond to us formally, and *I'll* take it from there."

"Martin, I've gotta ask you, did you sleep with her?"

"No. Never." I looked at Wasserman. "I have no problem providing a factual response to the fiction you just read. Just give me a copy of the complaint so I can respond to every accusation."

"Martin, this is a complaint against the company with you as an employee. Counsel has suggested we withhold dissemination to you unless and until Ms. Plummet files a formal disposition."

"What the hell! How am I supposed to offer an intelligent response?"

"I presumed you took notes as I read the complaint."

I was furious. To add insult to injury, I wasn't allowed to return to my office. "It's probably better for all concerned if you left without any fanfare," Wasserman intoned. My partners just nodded their heads limply like bobblehead dolls.

"While I'm disappointed by your initial reactions, I can also understand your disappointment with me. But when all the facts are in, you'll see that Alexandria's claim is frivolous and without merit. I'd appreciate it if we could keep Lauren out of this."

"Pal, not a problem," responded Craft. "I understand completely. The last thing any of us want to do is wreck a perfectly good marriage."

44

Expensive defense attorneys front and center, please.

Wasserman and Costas escorted me to the back door like a common criminal, brusquely whizzing past several stunned, wide-eyed employees.

I then called my good friend and trusted advisor, corporate attorney Tom Morrison — managing partner of Conner, Smith, and Spencer LLC, Manhattan's penultimate blue-blood law firm since 1911 — to discuss what had just transpired. Tom and I had met fifteen years earlier. He became my corporate counsel on two IPO deals. A Washingtonian by birth who graduated at the top of his class at the prestigious University of Virginia School of Law, Tom knew how to get through the bureaucratic maze at the Securities and Exchange Commission. He saved me millions on delay fees and such.

More importantly, his ethics were beyond reproach. He was a workaholic who prided himself on never being outfoxed. He made sure he knew more than the other guy, then used it to his advantage. *Forbes* magazine had voted him one of New York City's top-ten attorneys, and his fees, at $975 an hour, were also top-ten.

Tom didn't hold any punches. "While harassment claims are not my area of expertise, I know enough. We are about to travel a road cluttered with landmines. These days, harassment cases are the ambulance chaser's plat du jour and a plaintiff's dream — easy to accuse, sure to sympathize, impossible to defend, and begging for settlement.

"As your friend, all I can say is, what the hell were you thinking? Lauren is a wonderful wife; you've got two great kids, friends who care, and financial independence."

Tom's logic was irrefutable, so I chose to concentrate on the legal battle ahead. "I may be naïve, but doesn't the truth ultimately take precedence?"

Tom harrumphed. "What's the truth? A pretty employee walks down the aisle. You compliment her. She claims you were thinking wicked thoughts. You mentally harassed her. She gets a lawyer to write a complaint. She threatens to bring you to court. How do you defend yourself? Do you want the potentially large legal bills? Do you want the emotional strain on your marriage? What about your reputation with the other employees? And then there's the internet. If the claim is filed, you're marked for life. Anybody can Google the public records!"

"So, what do you suggest?"

"Let's make the whole thing go away for a few bucks."

"What's a few bucks?"

"Probably a couple of hundred thousand dollars."

"You have got to be kidding! For what? That's down-right outrageous!"

"Martin, think about it before you do something stupid. You and Lauren have been together for a long time. Marriages like yours don't happen every day. Take it from three-times-married Tom. Let me check around the firm and get you a killer attorney who specializes in these sorts of matters. At the risk of sounding incredibly jaded, harassment cases assume *guilt unless you can prove innocence*."

The more Tom talked, the more I realized the gravity of the situation.

"I guess I'd appreciate a referral at your earliest. My so-called partners gave me three days. They wanted a written response to the complaint before Lauren and I headed to Australia."

"I must say that sounds a bit strange." said Tom, "I am surprised at Craft. He seems to be bailing on you big time. When we had lunch with him just last year, he implied in no uncertain terms you walked on water."

"The sense I have is my three partners are in hock up to their eyeballs. They all went on multi-million-dollar house shopping sprees. You wouldn't believe Craft's spread. He went from owning a two-bedroom condo in Larchmont to buying a

$5 million, 8000-square-foot house on three acres in Greenwich."

"There you have it," said Tom. "It's all about self-preservation. You know for some people, money supersedes friendship."

"Not Dawson."

"That's what I love about you, Martin. With all the corporate backstabbing you've survived, you still prefer living in your *Alice in Wonderland* glass bubble."

"What are you suggesting?"

"That you develop a dispassionate, factual response and let me review it. We'll have to do the best we can before you leave. By the time you're back, I'll have identified your specialist. Your attorneys will then act in tandem."

~

Two days later, Wasserman and I met at a local coffee house to discuss my formal written response. The eight-page document incorporated the facts as I knew them. I attached over one hundred pages of exhibits that supported every statement.

Wasserman reviewed my document point by point, asking questions, and taking notes while generating undecipherable, primeval morality grunts, groans, and moans.

"As you can see, the relationship was completely consensual," I concluded.

"Her version of the facts is quite different," responded Wasserman.

It took all the restraint I had during the next month to reveal nothing to Lauren; I figured, why mess up the trip? I remained optimistic that once my partners knew the real facts, we — collectively — could make the whole thing go away. Or worst case, as Tom suggested, settle for a reasonable amount of blackmail money to keep Lauren and the kids ignorant of the whole nasty affair.

45.

Visiting Australia and New Zealand.

On the surface, Craft's bon voyage phone call was a pleasant surprise.

"Pal, I just wanted to wish you and Lauren a safe and memorable trip. The travel department told me your first stop is Sydney, so I sent you guys a bottle of Dead Arm 2000 to kick off the trip before you start drinking that Aussie swill." Dead Arm was Craft's favorite Napa Valley vineyard, which specialized in using fifty-year-old vines to make intense, flavorful Shiraz.

But there was always another agenda with Craft. "Don't worry about a thing. I'll make sure we take care of Alexandria discreetly. Your position in the company will be waiting for you when you get back, although I suspect you might have to eat some humble pie and throw the boys a bone." Translation: *Expect to cover all the legal and settlement costs, since we're not planning on taking a dime out of our annual profit distributions.*

Tom Morrison concurred with my instincts. "Given the testy negotiation I had with Jim Friedman on the immediate vesting issue in the stock agreement, the boys probably see this as an opportunity to renegotiate some of the provisions or reduce your share of annual profit distributions or some combination of both."

"Can they force me to do that?"

"I'm fairly certain the equity agreement is free and clear of encumbrances and punitive calls. But let me reread the document."

The following morning, while standing in the Qantas Lounge waiting for our departure to Sydney, I received the answer.

"It was as I suspected," Tom explained. "Your agreement is bulletproof. You own one hundred percent of your equity position and annual profit distributions in perpetuity, with absolutely no strings."

"Suppose they fire me, or I'm forced to resign?"

"It doesn't matter. They've got two options: pay you as per the agreement or offer to buy you out at some discount to the fair market value."

"Why at a discount?"

"Lots of legitimate reasons. The company is private, so there is no ready market for the stock, and you can't pledge it as collateral. Also, during the negotiations, you agreed to be a nonvoting partner. That's not something an outside investor finds attractive. On the flip side, the fact that you have the same tag-along rights as the voting partners effectively provides you with the same protections and privileges as the voting partners. I believe the company today is valued at about $200 million. A fifty percent equity haircut is reasonable, which nets roughly $10 million-plus whatever we negotiate on profit sharing."

The only issue, according to Tom, was if the partners attempted to void the transaction based on misrepresentation — that I had negotiated my equity deal while actively harassing Alexandria. "Frankly, given the facts as I know them, they have no basis. People get involved in office trysts all the time. The board may ask the executive to resign, but I do not know of one case in American business where a fully-vested executive has been legally stripped of that asset. About all they can do is create a public relations nightmare for you and Lauren. And I'm not sure they'd want to bring that kind of attention to the company, since their own exit strategy involves its eventual sale."

Tom's advice was, "Have a great vacation and don't spoil Lauren's trip." In the interim, he would discreetly search for the appropriate lawyer to represent my interests.

Naïvely, I hoped that, while we were on vacation, the facts as I presented them would be validated, Alexandria would be muzzled or would disappear from my life completely, and things would return to what they had been with my partners. At the same time, given Tom's advice and assistance, I felt I needed to be prepared for the battle of my life.

During our vacation, Tom's research all pointed to attorney Margo Margoles of Margoles, Williams, Ephraim. The firm had an impeccable record of emasculating corporations in shareholder claims and humiliating all those who brought claims against companies in workplace harassment suits (sexual and otherwise). Margo's reputation was as a "tough as nails" defense attorney who left no hostages, hence her nickname: "The Killer."

~

The trip across the Pacific to the land down under was uneventful and relaxing for both of us. After a three-course dinner and a few champagne toasts, Lauren fell asleep in my arms for hours. We awoke to an Aussie captain announcing "G'day mates, we're about ten minutes from the mainland and about thirty-five minutes from Sydney International Airport. For those of you who are coming home, the shrimp should be on the barbie in less than two hours."

~

Our recollection of the Paddington section of Sydney was street after street of multicolored stone terrace houses, reminiscent of the antique townhomes in Manhattan's West Village.

Lauren was so excited. As the plane was landing, I could feel her heartbeat. The first thing we did after checking into the hotel was to take a cab to visit the house where our children had spent three of their formative years. The exterior looked the same: the architecture, porches, color scheme, landscaping. All was as it had been. As we stood and stared, a middle-aged lady came out of the front door. "Can I help you?" We explained we once lived there; a cordial invitation followed. The interior looked familiar. We learned Mr. and Mrs. Wright were, in fact, the people who bought the house from us, liked what we had done to the place, and simply freshened things every few years. The only exception was the kitchen, which had been modernized.

It was about lunchtime, and we were hungry. "Mrs. Wright, I'm curious," said Lauren. "We used to love a neighborhood restaurant called the Queen Street Tavern. I don't suppose…"

"Dearie, it's still there. The menu's a bit more sophisticated, but they still make the best lamb burgers in Sydney."

A few minutes later, we were sitting in front of two lamb burgers and chips (Australian for French fries) and schooners of Toohey's Gold (22-ounce glasses of a popular local beer). We began to chat with the distinctly Australian waiter — friendly, smiling, muscular, blonde surfer-type with beach wrinkles from over-exposure to the sun. It turned out he wasn't the waiter, but the original owner, who remembered the day a mischievous, curly-haired American kid, our son Bart, had crashed into the etched glass front door with his bike.

Lauren's eyes twinkled with joy. All the beautiful memories of those times came flooding back. We walked the neighborhood hand in hand. My iPhone started beeping. One was a message from Costas confirming a meeting "on the matter at hand" for the morning after we arrived home.

~

We visited friends in Melbourne, then toured the Great Barrier Reef, Ayers Rock, and the Red Centre, before moving on to New Zealand, where we had never been. Some experienced traveler friends had recommended the Delamore Lodge on the island of Waiheke, a ferry ride from downtown Auckland, which they described as "the most romantic place in the world."

The Lodge was a five-star plus accommodation perched atop a lush floral hill, surrounded by green rolling hills and lakes. Directly in front sat a private emerald-green harbor with a white-sand beach. The lodge had only four suites, each with spectacular views and expansive carved stone patios. As for the public spaces, it was as though we were sitting in a luxurious Manhattan penthouse dining on five-star meals for breakfast, lunch, and dinner. No amenity had been spared; no luxury missed.

At the owner's urging, we watched a sunrise — simply the most spectacular view we had ever seen. We sat silently while drinking cappuccino and nibbling on fresh kiwi, passion fruit, and pineapple. The yellow morning sun reflected off Lauren's face. She was as sexy, sultry, and beautiful as the day we met. I smiled at her. "This incredibly happy guy is staring at the most beautiful woman he's ever seen."

46.

Wasserman builds his version of the truth.

During the three weeks after my departure for Australia, Wasserman was the model of a proactive company sleuth, interviewing whomever he saw fit. He assumed the boys had given him carte blanche. To cover his ass, each interview began the disclaimer, "Rest assured; this conversation is being held in the strictest of confidence."

When the dust had settled, Wasserman had interviewed just enough people to send misguided rumors through the halls that AFA was a quick-to-settle company on matters relating to harassment. No one was quite sure who was in the line of fire, which created endless rounds of speculation.

The two emails Costas sent to update me were premature. The first was related to a twenty-seven-year-old female employee who had asked me to dance at a company Christmas party. She claimed that I had been looking at her funny ever since. Unfortunately, not one person she knew was willing to corroborate her story. She quit seven days before I returned, and three days after Wasserman had discovered an alarming pattern — the grieved employee had brought similar claims at her two prior places of employment. Each claim had been deemed frivolous, and she quit shortly after.

The second email again involved Johnson. He saw Wasserman's interrogations as a chance to double-dip by getting a half dozen of his professional cronies to cry emotional harassment, then establish a Moss referral with his usual finder's fee. The anonymous group's story collapsed when they all refused to testify under oath. Wasserman also wondered about

Johnson, since his name again surfaced as an employee advisor on such matters.

Wasserman presented his report. "Based on my findings, Mr. Ruff exhibited bad judgment as a member of the management team and should be reprimanded."

"Colton, with all due respect," interrupted Jim Shamus, "we're a little off brief here. Your mission was to determine what specific support existed to support *Alexandria's* allegations, that would also dispute Mr. Ruff's version of the facts. Remember, this woman is demanding a multi-million-dollar settlement. The company has to believe she has a legitimate case to the dollars."

Wasserman fumbled for a moment. "I didn't undercover any other corroborating witnesses besides Mr. Johnson."

"Are we talking about the same Johnson that just tried to screw us *and* spoke out of turn to Alexandria about her performance?"

"Well, she has the tapes," responded Wasserman.

"You mean three of the calls that Martin documented were among the one hundred calls between them?"

"What about her claims of office abuse?" asked Shamus.

"Best I can tell, that's a dead end. Everybody I talked to said Martin loves to keep things light to maximize personal productivity."

"And, the Boston allegations?"

"Absolutely nothing to them. Boston's recollections were the same as Martin's."

Shamus then turned to Craft and Carr. "Unless there is something we don't know, I'm inclined to advise you to tell Ms. Plummet she's entitled to nothing. A goose egg. It's her word against Martin's, and he has more real documentation. I'm guessing he could also produce witnesses that would support his version of the facts."

"Her production sucks," blurted Carr to his partners. "Strikes me that this incident has been disruptive to the company's growth. So, let's get rid of her."

"You can't want to do that," said Shamus. "*That* could be classified as harassment."

"You've gotta be kidding."

"No, the wisest course is just to keep our cool. Tell Plummet that despite our refusal to provide her a settlement, she is welcome to stay and work for the company as long as she wants."

"Let me get this straight," said Carr. "We allow a person who wanted to sue the company and defame a partner to remain an employee in perpetuity."

"The short answer is yes. But my guess is the indirect personal embarrassment combined with Alexandria's declining income will eventually take its toll."

"That's bullshit!" said an angry Carr.

"Eddie, Eddie, relax; that's what we pay counsel for," said Craft calmly. "I vote that we accept Jim's recommendations concerning Alexandria. All in favor, raise your hands." Costas and Carr agreed.

~

"There's still the matter of Martin and any potential unknown future exposure to the company, and to us personally," said Costas.

"I agree," said Wasserman. "Based on my investigations, we have no idea if someone else might step forward with something he might have done in the past."

"Jim," asked Carr, "am I missing something here? Martin's guilty of terribly bad judgment: no more, no less. He's also got an impeccable twenty-five-year corporate record in companies a hell of a lot bigger than ours."

"True," responded Shamus, "But the cat is out of the bag. You need to protect yourself if somebody else decides to come forward. And suppose Ms. Plummet finds a greedy ambulance chaser to take her case?"

Shamus continued. "One remedy is to insist that Martin sign an at-will employment contract that makes him personally liable for any legal and settlement expenses not covered by AFA's Director and Officer Insurance Policy in any claim related to his general behavior. The contract should include a clause that the company retains all rights to initiate and agree to the actual settlement."

Everybody nodded.

"I'd also like to restrict his freelance authority. Right now, he can initiate and reevaluate business strategies across the board," added Costas.

"Pal," said Craft. "Martin's a genius when it comes to building companies. Why do we want to restrict his creative juices?"

Wasserman again interrupted. "I agree with Jeremy."

An annoyed Shamus looked at Costas, "Isn't this guy supposed to be your human resource director?"

Costas became defensive. "Colton Wasserman is an experienced business mind. I hired him personally after an exhaustive search. Nobody in this town knows how to handle corporate subtleties better than Colton. I'd trust him with my life."

Shamus had seen Costas's beet-red face before. He wanted to move on. "Look, to save some time and fees, why don't you guys add selective clauses to Martin's employment contract?"

"And I want a strong reprimand in his file," said Wasserman, "signed by Ruff, and his commitment to attend and personally pay for harassment classes for two years."

"Agreed," said Costas. "Hands?"

"Now wait a Goddamn minute!" said Carr, rising from his chair. "Why embarrass him by sending him to a class if he didn't do anything?"

"I couldn't give a shit less about him. It just makes a statement that the company's ass is covered, and *my* wealth protected in case something comes up in the future," said Costas.

"Agreed," said Craft.

"Guys, the key is for the company to appear to distance itself from Martin. That implies we don't condone anything that's transpired while also defusing a potential plaintiff claim of investigative whitewashing."

Craft looked at Friedman. He saw a huge positive opportunity in the waiting. "I guess I've got one for you, pal. Let's follow that same line of reasoning. Can we create an addendum to the founder stockholder agreement that says if someone files a claim against Martin, frivolous or otherwise, we have a right to rescind his equity and return it to us on a pro-rata basis?"

"You can try," said Friedman. "But if I was him, why would I sign that? Besides, based on the terms of the current agreement, you would also have to get his wife to sign the addendum."

"Let's forget it. I promised we'd try to keep Lauren out of this; after all, he's our *friend*, and he's been married to that lady for over thirty-friend years."

"Bullshit," said Costas. "He's not *my* friend. Let's get the stock back."

"Does that mean you want me to draw up the addendum?"

"Yes," responded Costas, glaring at Craft as if to say, *and you keep your mouth shut.*

Costas looked at Friedman. "Jonathan, one more question. Can we claim the agreement is null and void because he was fucking around with Plummet during our stockholder negotiations?"

"Not a chance in the world," replied Friedman. "According to the *laws* of the State of Connecticut, the guy hasn't done anything wrong."

"Personally," said Wasserman, "I am confident Martin will capitulate to *our* demands. He's sixty years old; where's he going to go? What's he going to do? I'm betting he needs the cash flow."

"Jesus Christ," said Shamus. "Talk about discrimination and harassment. Don't ever say anything like that in or outside of this room again."

~

Wasserman called Alexandria down to his office. His job was to tell her to take a hike in the most careful possible manner.

She was already spending the settlement on the new condo she had missed the first time around.

"Alexandria," started Wasserman, with his assistant Maria Gonzalez in attendance as a witness. "The partners have reviewed the results of our investigation and met with our attorneys. It is their considered opinion that while you and Martin Ruff had a relationship that was inappropriate, given his senior role in the company, the relationship appears more consensual than abusive. Consequently, your claim has been rejected. However, I have been asked to tell you that we consider you an AFA employee in good standing and we do wish for you to remain in your role as one of our senior system consultants."

Alexandria was furious. "Don't you understand the pain I've been subjected to?"

"The facts suggest…" Alexandria interrupted Wasserman.

"How *could* you understand? You're all men! You people always get away with everything. This damn place doesn't even have a sexual harassment policy. How could you have an investigation? Against what criteria?"

"Alexandria," said Wasserman calmly, "I beg to differ, but we do have a policy. It's in our employee handbook."

"That creep humiliated me, and you're going to do absolutely nothing about it."

"We are discussing appropriate actions with Mr. Ruff."

"You're telling me he's still working here in the same role?"

"I said we are discussing the appropriate actions with Mr. Ruff."

"I want my money, and I want that smug bastard fired," shouted Alexandria.

"I don't understand," said Wasserman. "When we first met, you told me you didn't want Mr. Ruff to lose his job over this."

Plummet glared, got up, pushed the chair over, and walked out. "You'll be hearing from my attorney."

47.

Plummet goes into battle mode.

"I told you, honey, this is a fucking war! We've got to load the planes and bomb them into submission."

"Goddamn it, will you stop calling me honey, you chauvinist pig?! And stop with those stupid war analogies."

"Listen, honey, and I do mean honey," said a now-incensed Burton James Moss. "I'm your only shot at big money. You've got to decide if you're in or out. And if you're in, from now on, you do precisely as I say. Do we understand each other?"

Moss spent the next two days loading the brief with every nasty charge he could muster, including twisting numerous facts and highlighting misrepresentations about who was directly responsible for Plummet's compensation and the company's lack of clear sexual harassment guidelines. Moss's strategy was to generate a final settlement figure by heaving multiple accusations against the wall, many of which couldn't be proved or disproved. His goal: inflicting maximum psychological doubt and inner turmoil to extract the biggest settlement.

Moss also figured he might as well sue the company *and* me, as an individual. It would just make things that much messier and probably add more to the ultimate settlement because he was certain the company carried director and officer liability insurance. He had been through enough of these cases that he knew the speech by heart for the claims adjuster.

~

Lauren and I returned from vacation to a vibrating email. Wasserman suggested a meeting at Webber's coffee shop in Westport, almost ten miles from the office.

When I arrived, Wasserman and Craft were already seated with a small manila folder was on the table. After the exchange of a few pleasantries about my trip, Wasserman turned spokesperson. He explained that they had not yet gotten back to Alexandria, nor had she filed a formal legal suit in the courts. They were "happy to report" that they had concluded their investigation of the Plummet matter as a "nebulous claim" and that two "non-Plummet" incidents had been withdrawn by the unnamed parties after further consideration.

"So, pal," said Craft, "we need you to get back to work after you sign a few documents, including this employment contract which is *essentially the same* as Eddie's, Jeremy's, and mine."

Having been through my share of documents in my day, I quickly scanned the document for landmines, which I knew had to exist. All seemed standard fare until I reached the indemnification provision on page eight, the boilerplate or standard-clause section. The provision said I would "defend and indemnify the company for any reasonable expenses, etc., for any claim brought against and satisfied by the company by any employees — past, present, and future, including Ms. Plummet — without regard to the company's ability to secure insurance coverage of indemnity for any said claims."

I looked at Wasserman. "This clause suggests that should any opportunist bring a claim against the company on behalf of me, I have no right to defend myself against such claims, and the company, in its sole discretion, can settle or not settle as they see fit. Then, I'm responsible for reimbursing the company for settlement and legal expenses, whether or not you get reimbursed through director and officer insurance."

"That's correct," said Wasserman handing me a second document.

"Dawson, you're telling me Eddie, Jeremy, and you signed essentially the same agreement with the same indemnification clause?"

Craft nodded sheepishly. "Absolutely, pal." *The first lie among friends.*

The second document was entitled, "Employee Final Written Warning." It included such tidbits as:

"You engaged in an inappropriate relationship with Ms. Plummet that will not be tolerated by the company. Consequently, you will no longer have employees reporting to you.

"You will hold meetings in limited view and access; You will limit interaction with other employees to and from your office;

"You will attend sexual harassment training weekly at your expense for 24 months."

I stared at Wasserman, who stared right back.

"Pal, there's one last document, which is really between you and me. I need you to sign this also."

It was a stock assignment agreement, which said upon the occurrence of an "event"— broadly defined as "any of the aforementioned activities or any other activity deemed negative to the company's interests"— all of my rights, title, and interest in the shareholder agreement, previously signed by Costas, Carr, and Craft, shall revert to Craft, without further action. And Craft would be free to redistribute said interest in any manner he deems appropriate, at his sole discretion.

"Lauren also needs to sign this agreement."

"I assume this assignment agreement is the same as everybody else's, and the wives have countersigned?"

"Absolutely, pal," said Craft. *The second lie among friends.*

"I noticed all the documents you just showed me are already signed."

Craft took off his glasses. "Martin, this is important. This is not a negotiation. We've spent a lot of time with the lawyers. I hope you appreciate that while I love you like a brother, I'm also the president, and as such I have an obligation to the other two hundred or so employees."

"Buddy," I said with a hint of sarcasm, "some of the clauses seem incredibly harsh, given your conclusion that Alexandria has no case."

"Martin, the documents are what they are. I wrote every word of them on advice from counsel. I did everything I could to make them fair. Selfishly, I need you back to work as soon as possible. We have lots to do." *The third lie among friends.*

It took all I had not to throw the documents in the trash right there and then. I had no intention of ever signing those documents.

~

The voice on the other end of the phone was surprisingly warm and friendly, given "The Killer's" reputation. "Tom said to expect your call," said attorney Margo Margoles. "How was the vacation?"

I started to explain our itinerary in detail, but Margo, all business, interrupted. "So, tell me about the facts in the case…as you know them to be."

I pushed to meet in person. Margo resisted, with an explanation. "Tom may have told you I have a pretty good track record in these kinds of matters. Unfortunately, these cases become very personal and nasty, so I have to make sure I want to take the case. I hope you understand."

"I'm not going to tell you a story, just the real facts, all of which are either already documented in writing or can be documented through third-party interviews."

There was a pause on the other end of the phone. "You certainly sound sure of yourself."

"I'm quite unsure, actually. I don't know what to do. And I'm angry as hell at myself, the plaintiff, and my partners."

"Why don't you just tell me what happened."

I explained who I was, the business, Lauren, Alexandria, my partners' proposal, etc.

"You're telling me what you just represented is in writing? And with all those dates, you never had intercourse?"

"Yes."

"And Ms. Plummet is still working at the company?"

"Yes."

"That all seems hard to believe. What does your wife think about the situation?"

"I haven't told her yet. I'm so embarrassed; we've been married thirty-five years and I did a dumb, stupid thing."

"That's a long time," she responded empathetically. "But she'll need to know. Let me give you some advice. Try not to beat yourself up; I've seen a lot worse."

"That was very kind of you."

"Don't be too complimentary, or I'll raise my hourly fee."

"Which does bring up the subject."

"It's $400 an hour plus expenses. While I'm certainly not inexpensive, compared to Tom's fees, I'm a bargain. Who represents the company?"

"Jim Shamus of Osborne, Reed."

"They're a pretty good firm. I know Jim. I'm surprised. It's very unusual for an employee to sue an employer and stay."

"I don't mean to be rude, but do I have an attorney or not?"

"Let's make that decision when we meet. In the meantime, send me all the documents you have, including the shareholder agreement. That way, I can do some research and perhaps talk to Jim and Tom. Does 2:00 P.M. on Thursday at my office work for you?"

The real question was, *How do I explain all this to Lauren?*

48.

Lauren's professional standing grows.

Lauren's boss at New York Hospital, Peter Braun, a product of the 1960s peace-and-love movement, had decided to return to his beloved Oregon. His rationale: "The skies are clearer, the ideas are more liberal, the environment is treated with greater respect, and the hospital administrations are apolitical."

The board decided to promote Lauren to Nurse Administrator rather than hire from the outside. I could never forget the expression on her face when she made the announcement. "I have something to tell you," she said, beaming ear to ear as she handed me a glass of champagne. "Your wife is now in senior management." She explained the details. Our glasses clinked. "But don't worry, honey; nothing will ever change with us. I know my priorities."

"Lauren, I couldn't be prouder. Wow, have we come a long, long way. I can still remember that evening twenty years ago when you sheepishly told me you had been asked to interview for an assistant manager position. Do you remember what you said to me?"

"Not exactly."

"It was a thousand to one shot. And do you remember old Doc Hayes' toast at your congratulations party? 'Cream always rises to the top.'"

~

The next day, the shit hit the fan at the hospital. Some instruments used in a late-night kidney transplant procedure turned out to be defective. While the surgery was successful and the patient spared discomfort, Lauren, to the chagrin of the staff, felt a full disclosure should be made to the family.

Unfortunately, the family then chose to hire a ruthless attorney who threatened to leak the story to the press to pressure the hospital into settling his inflated claim for damages, lest a torrent of bad publicity smear the hospital's impeccable reputation.

Calmly and coolly, Lauren laid out her proactive plan to the board. "I've already talked to the president of the instrument company. They have prepared for the claimant and his lawyer. You will notice that they accept full responsibility and have asked the claimants' attorney to direct all financial claims to them. Separately, I have worked with our public relations group on a balanced, factual press release, which should neutralize the press's tendency for sensationalism.

"I would also respectfully suggest we send a letter to all prior and upcoming surgery patients explaining what has transpired and our commitment to remain New York City's finest in-patient surgical center. The PR department also worked with me on a draft release, which we're handing out right now."

Lauren's proposals were approved. In the following weeks, the matter was handled flawlessly by all concerned. In the end, Lauren was credited with avoiding a potential financial and public relations crisis. Her reward for handling the matter so professionally: more money and more responsibility.

"Needless to say," said hospital president Robert Hawkins, "everyone was impressed with your grace and intelligence under fire. Consequently, the board has suggested that we move all of the communications departments under your supervision. All departments that communicate with our vendors, the press, the public, our patients, our donors, and our benefactors."

"Oh my God, are you sure you want to do that?"

"Initially, we realize the job may take some time away from your family, but we know that your husband is a Type A businessman, so he should understand. We'd also like to make you our fifth senior vice-president and give you a substantial raise. As an SVP, you become eligible for the executive management bonus pool. I'm guessing that, all told, you'll make another $150,000 annually, which, as you know in hospital land, is a major, major increase."

"You're joking."

One of Lauren's senior reports, Cathy Childress, crashed the meeting. "Mr. Hawkins, I'm sorry, but we have a real situation upstairs. We need Lauren *right now*."

"We can finish this later. It sounds like you've got another impending patient crisis that takes precedence!"

"Oh, it's not a patient problem," said Cathy.

"Then what's so urgent?" asked Hawkins.

"It's Dr. Crittenden. He's storming around and giving orders and making even more outlandish demands than the last time. The entire staff is terrified and frozen in their tracks."

Hawkins leaned back in his chair and smiled. "Ah, Dr. Crittenden. Lauren, it looks like you have another public relations crisis on your hands! Deal or no deal?" said Hawkins, his hand extended.

"Deal."

Lauren got an earful from the good doctor. "Twenty-two days ago, to be precise," said a condescending Crittenden right in Lauren's face, "I asked for a Da Vinci Robotic Surgical Assistant to be available in the operating room for this particular procedure. I brought students from Europe to observe my work. Can't you people get anything right?"

"Doctor, I can understand your frustration," said Lauren calmly. "Why don't you and your students have a latte in our lounge? I'm sure we can get the matter squared away before your patient completes the pre-ops. Cathy, be a dear and make the doctors some of your wonderful mocha lattes. Would you gentlemen prefer regular or low-fat milk?"

The doctors followed Cathy to the lounge. Lauren authorized an immediate search to locate an available robotic Da Vinci machine. A team of technicians found one. He was up and running before the patient was finished with her pre-ops, just as Lauren had predicted.

Dr. Crittenden held his latte glass in the air. "A toast to the lady who knows how to get things done." The doctors clinked their glasses. Lauren took a modest bow.

49.

The moment of truth arrives.

"There's something I need to tell you." I began with a soulful reaffirmation of my love and the fact that we had thirty-five years of good times sprinkled with remarkably few bumps in the road. I watched her body language for clues.

"Tell Mommy," she purred. "Nothing can be that bad, because we've got each other 'till our bones creak, our memories fade, and our hearts stop."

I was overwhelmed by guilt. Tears formed in the corner of my eyes as I took a deep breath. "About a year ago, I began to have dinner with one of our system consultants, Alexandria Plummet. You know her, the blonde lady in her late forties with the straight hair."

"The one you asked me to recommend a plastic surgeon?"

"Yes. At first, it was all about business; then, it became more personal. I had feelings, she had feelings, but we never crossed the line."

"What the hell does that mean?"

"We never made love. It wasn't like a real affair."

"How many times did you see her?"

"About a dozen."

"You broke *my trust* a dozen times, and somehow that's not an affair?"

"I'm so, so sorry. It was a terrible lapse of judgment on my part. I never meant to hurt you."

"Explain how you lied and cheated and never meant to hurt me. After all these years, I find I have a husband who's a fraud, a goddamn hypocrite." She got up and walked over to me and started smacking my arms, my chest, my head, and my face. She kept swinging and crying until she slumped in the chair, head in hand, emotionally spent. "There's more, isn't there?"

"Unfortunately, yes."

"You're lying about the sex. You must have had sex."

"No."

"Then why, why, why?"

"There's no perfect answer. Part of it was she paid attention to me; she made me feel important. You were so busy with MJ and your job…"

"That is the biggest bunch of horseshit I've ever heard. If you felt that way, why didn't you say something?"

"I did, but you just didn't hear me."

"Tell me when. Just tell me when I didn't hear you!"

"At this point, it doesn't matter. It doesn't excuse what I've done."

"Do you realize you've turned my whole world upside down? How am I ever going to trust you again? And what about *my* self-esteem?"

I remained calm so as not to exacerbate the situation. I dreaded moving on. "Honey, I need to tell you the rest."

She closed her eyes and whispered, "The rest? Dear God, what else?"

"Alexandria has brought a sexual harassment claim against me through the company."

"On what basis?"

"That after we stopped seeing each other, I caused her emotional angst that led to a significant drop in her income. That I frightened her around the office, acted strange, made her lose focus."

"Everybody I talk to at the office thinks you walk on water."

"Trust me; I've got some enemies."

"Please don't use the words 'trust me,'" said Lauren. "When the hell did all this happen?"

"Eddie, Dawson, Jeremy, and the HR guy, Colton Wasserman, read me the charges and played some audiotapes before we went on vacation. They asked me for a written response before we left."

"Audiotapes, written responses, and you said nothing for thirty days."

"I didn't want to spoil your vacation."

"You're telling me all this was going on, and you made me believe I was the only woman in the world for a month in Australia? I just can't believe it. How gullible can I be?"

I opened my arms to provide a comforting shoulder.

"Don't you dare touch me!" She pulled back. "I want to see the complaint and your so-called response."

"I've got a copy of my response in the upstairs office."

"And her complaint?"

"They wouldn't give it to me."

"Who's they?"

"Jeremy, Colton, and Dawson."

"But they're supposed to be your partners. You're a team. I've dealt with some sexual harassment cases at the hospital; they have to give you her complaint."

"You've never mentioned that before."

"These are very private matters that get messy because of all the verbal allegations and denials, and they're none of your damn business," glared Lauren. "How could you write a response to something you didn't have?"

"I responded from memory and then sent a draft to Tom for his input before I submitted my response to the company."

"So, you hired a lawyer without even consulting me?"

"Remember, Tom negotiated our stock agreement, which is all part of this thing too. He just did me a favor as a long-time friend and tried to make sure that what I wrote made sense. He thought it was well put-together, but he strongly suggested I hire counsel as soon as we got back. He even did some research and identified a harassment specialist."

"What's all this talk about a deadline?"

"They said they wanted to do an arms-length investigation and would have something to say when we returned."

"Investigation? Aren't you getting a little melodramatic?"

"I didn't make up the term; that's the term they used."

"They're supposed to be our friends."

"I'm learning that protecting their money comes above all else. I guess if every dollar I had were invested in the company, I'd do the same thing."

"You mean every dollar *we* had! I can't believe you did all this right under my nose. I'd like to kill you. With all I have going on in my life, now this!" Lauren got up, walked over to the fireplace, and stared silently with her back to me for what seemed like an eternity. "So, where are we right now?"

"I met with Dawson and Colton yesterday. They said the findings of their investigation were inconclusive; that most of her allegations could not be documented. They told Alexandria they had no interest in settling her claim, but she was free to stay and work at American Financial."

"How much did she ask for?"

"A million dollars."

"My God, what a money-grabbing witch."

"They want me to return to work ASAP…."

"Well, at least there's some measure of sanity to all this!"

"I'm not sure that's the case," I said as I placed the employment contract, the stock assignment, and the final warning memorandum in front of her. "They want me *and* you to sign these documents."

Lauren sat quietly and read every word…twice. "Are they crazy? There is no way I'm going to sign these documents."

50.

Meeting our new defense attorney.

Attorney Margo Margoles was precisely as Tom billed her — a cold-blooded killer with an impeccable reputation for destroying plaintiffs. She had specialized in sexual harassment suits for more than a decade, long before it became fashionable.

After graduating from Harvard Law School, she began as a paralegal at Scadden Apps, a major law firm on Wall Street that specialized in corporate affairs. It wasn't long before she recognized that the firm's partners were lining up to represent plaintiffs on a contingency basis in the burgeoning area of sexual harassment. Previously, the firm had resisted contingency cases. Margo was curious. Why the about-face?

"Pretty simple," said her boss, Senior Partner Patterson Edelman. "We're typically paid forty percent of the settlement, plus all our expenses. That's a hell of a lot of hourly fees. And it's easy money; most companies just want to settle and move on. Publicity is bad; no publicity is good."

"What about the defendants? Suppose the case is a frivolous claim?"

"Most are; so what?"

"What about the rights of the accused employee?"

"Not my problem."

Repelled by her boss's smug attitude, Margo decided she would build a practice defending the underdog. Within five years, her solo practice grew to become Margoles, Smits, and Cane, a twenty-eight-person firm that specialized in representing defendants in a wide variety of employment abuse cases. She was quite proud of the fact that after twelve years, her firm had never lost a case. And in those few situations where she deemed a settlement was proper and fitting without admission of guilt, she accepted fifty percent of her usual fees as consideration.

~

The Thursday conference in Margo's office was enlightening for both Lauren and me. Lauren trusted Tom's legal recommendations, but this suit involved her life and her money. She was going to be deeply involved in case strategy and decision making. From my standpoint, Margo was more reserved than I had imagined. She also seemed a bit surprised that I was sitting in front of her with Lauren by my side.

"I've read all the material you provided. This case seems to have some unusual twists. Normally, the company and the employee act as co-defendants. That does not appear to be the case here."

An emotionless Margo then stared at Lauren. "I know this may be a little uncomfortable for you, but before I take a case, I need to hear the defendant's side of the story." She wanted to make sure what I said on the phone matched what I said in person. She had an aversion to deceitful clients. I summarized what I knew the facts to be, slowly, logically, and dispassionately, although, for the sake of Lauren, I tried to understate my sexual attraction to Alexandria.

While I was talking, I could see Lauren sizing up Margo. The fact that Margo was strikingly attractive — long black hair, porcelain complexion, an athletic figure attired in a conservative black suit — didn't help Lauren's comfort level.

Given the Alexandria fiasco and our thirty-five years together, I could hear her mind churning. *Is she as good as she looks? How did Martin come to select an attractive female attorney to represent us? Is there something going on behind my back…again?*

Margo glanced at Lauren. She sensed Lauren was uncomfortable, so she broke the ice. "Mrs. Ruff, what do you do?"

"I'm a senior manager at Cornell Medical Center."

"She's not just a senior manager," I said proudly, "She is one of the hospital's rising stars. They don't schedule surgery or issue a press release without her blessing."

"I'm impressed," said Margo.

Lauren felt a bit self-conscious about my description, even though it was true. She wanted to change topics. "You have a nice family," said Lauren, looking at the photos on the mahogany cabinet behind Margo's desk. "Looks like you're outdoor aficionados," she added, referring to the picture of a handsome, obviously fit man and two teenagers on a snowy cliff.

"I like to hike and mountain climb. I find it physically challenging and mentally stimulating. It's a great way to leave the office behind."

"Have you always loved the outdoors?"

"Mom and Dad were Virginia horse farmers. I don't think I even knew what a snow-capped mountain was until my first trip to Colorado."

"Is that where you met your husband?"

"Lauren, I don't mind answering your questions, but since I bill by the hour, shouldn't we focus on the issues at hand?" Margo never directly answered any of her questions. I wondered if I had an attorney.

"So, where are we?" I asked.

"I'm willing to take your case, if that's your question," Margo said matter-of-factly, which I took to mean she believed me, or she at least thought a jury would believe me. "But we have to have an understanding. First, as I said on the phone, I'm not cheap. My hourly fee is $400, with an upfront contingency of $10,000. Should the case wind up in court, my contingency increases to $25,000."

I was looking for odds of success before I simply agreed. "What are my chances of getting out of this mess?"

"Until I get a better handle on all the facts, I don't know. I can only tell you that you've been accused of serious misconduct and this kind of situation can get very personal." Margo stared at Lauren. "Are you prepared for that?"

"To be honest with you, I'm furious with my husband. But we've been married for a long time. I *think* I want to stand by him."

Both Margo and I heard the "think."

"Secondly, we all need to understand something: Martin is my client. Mrs. Ruff, do you understand what I'm saying? There will be times when I must talk and meet separately with your husband. You will have to respect those confidences."

Lauren looked at me, and then at Margo. "I understand."

51.

Building a defense strategy gets very personal.

"I took the liberty of calling Tom," said Margo the next day. "We agreed there should be a two-attorney attack plan. Tom knows the subtleties of your equity agreement and profit distributions, since he worked closely with Jonathan Friedman at Logan Lane Smith on the actual drafting. He's more qualified to protect those interests, which I understand are quite substantial. My focus will be to bring the Plummet matter to a satisfactory conclusion as quickly and as painlessly as possible."

"That sounds like you've already ruled out challenging her allegations."

"I'm not sure I like the tone of your voice," she snapped.

"What did I say?"

"You accused me of taking the easy way out."

"I simply asked a question. I have no idea how the process works. So, if I said something wrong, how about giving me a little slack?"

Lauren smiled. "Margo, you have to excuse Martin; he's famous for putting his foot in his mouth."

"I can see that," replied Margo with a sly smile.

After the two ladies had a good chuckle at my expense, Margo continued. "According to court filings through last night, Plummet has not yet filed a formal claim. My guess is she's looking for an attorney to represent her. But that might not be so easy, since the company has already rejected her claim based on their investigation. Assuming she engages counsel, they will most likely try to intimidate you, the company, or both of you by preparing a formal brief and suggesting a settlement before all parties concerned are dragged through the embarrassment and costs of a public court proceeding."

"What do you estimate it would take?"

"It's hard to say until I talk to Jim Shamus. Ideally, both you and the company would work cooperatively to discredit as many of Plummet's allegations as possible to minimize her chances of a substantial court award or a large private settlement or both. Why don't we talk again after I tell Shamus you have hired counsel, and after we get some of the documentation the company utilized to reach their conclusions?"

~

Shortly after we left, I received a call from Margo. "Are you free to talk? I need to ask you something that would have made Lauren very uncomfortable."

"The answer is yes, I wanted to have sex with Alexandria on some occasions. Why else would I have gone out with her on all those dates? The bizarre part was I was in no hurry. It's not like I was sexually deprived. I just figured she was stringing it out. I think she did struggle with the fact that I was married, and she knew Lauren. I also think she was expecting me to tell her I was going to leave Lauren for her."

"Did you ever imply that?"

"Probably."

"Did you or didn't you?"

"Yes."

"You realize that makes those tapes even more credible as support of their stalking claims."

"But if you subpoena her phone records, you'll find between her calls and mine that there were many out-of-town conversations. They were part of the entire relationship, not isolated instances."

"To obtain a subpoena, we would have to go to trial. Do you realize the publicity could seriously damage your wife's career? Do you want to drag her through that kind of embarrassment?"

"I didn't think so; I'm proud of Lauren's accomplishments."

" Is there anything else I need to know?"

"Like what?"

"Have you had affairs before?"

"No."

"Is there anything, absolutely anything else I should know? Remember, it's better that I have all the facts in advance so I'm not surprised. A surprised attorney is like the kiss of death. The other side smells the blood."

I paused. "I'm not sure if this is relevant or not, but probably fifteen years ago I was told my management style was too overbearing. There were some unnamed complaints."

"Were they from men or women?

"The company I was with at the time never revealed that information."

"What happened?"

"Nothing. I turned my dial down and never heard another word from anybody."

"Do you think there is anything in a file somewhere?"

"Unlikely. The company has ceased to exist."

"Were there any ramifications with Lauren?"

"She never knew about the situation."

"Did it hinder your career growth?"

"No. In fact, I was named the company's youngest senior vice president."

"Well, it doesn't sound like anything we need to worry about right now," said Margo, "but it fits with the email you received from Costas on vacation. There may be somebody or some group out to get you at AFA, and that doesn't help matters."

52.

Attorneys jockey for the lead position.

"Jim, this is Margo Margoles. I'm calling to advise you that I'm representing Martin Ruff in the Alexandria Plummet matter."

"What Alexandria Plummet matter?"

"Jim, we've known each other for a long time, please…"

"Margo, Alexandria brought an informal complaint to the company about Martin. We investigated the matter, including talking to your client, who provided us with some potent documentation about their consensual relationship. We concluded two months ago that her claim was unfounded and told her to get back to work. As far as the company is concerned, the matter is closed, except for some outstanding paperwork issues with Martin."

"The documents he never signed?"

"The documents he *has* to sign. You can appreciate the fact that the company needs to distance itself."

"Are you telling me the company's intention is to continue to employ both of them at AFA?"

"Martin is a member of senior management, and we have no gripe with Ms. Plummet."

"A person tries to hold you up, and she's rewarded with the promise of continued employment?"

"Margo, with all due respect, you're on the wrong issue. You should be concerned about protecting your client in case she decides to come after him individually. In her current financial and emotional state, I believe she is capable of that."

"Point taken. The other reason for my call was to obtain some of the findings of your investigation, as well as a copy of

Ms. Plummet's original allegations. Martin tells me that even though he was asked to respond, he never actually received a copy of her complaint."

"I can't release any of those documents. As I said, the matter is closed as far as we're concerned. Providing any such materials would be an invasion of Alexandria's right to privacy under Connecticut law."

"Do I understand you to say you acknowledge Martin is a member of AFA senior management and could be personally sued for sexual harassment? But the company will not assist Mr. Ruff in defending himself by releasing the very evidence it used to dismiss Ms. Plummet's claim?"

"Yes."

~

"There's a pompous ass by the name of Burton James Moss on the phone. He insists on talking to you," said Jim Shamus's assistant, right after the Margoles conversation.

"Yes," said a guarded Shamus.

"I represent an AFA employee, Alexandria Plummet, in her claim against one of your senior managers, a Martin Ruff."

"What do you mean, 'your senior managers'?"

"It's my understanding you represent American Financial Associates in such matters."

"I'm AFA's corporate attorney; I do not represent its employees. We've discussed the matter with Ms. Plummet and provided the company's point of view. If you're looking to talk to someone about Mr. Ruff, I'd suggest you talk to attorney Margo Margoles at Margoles, Smits, Cane."

"Thank you. By the way, what is Mr. Ruff's current position at AFA?"

"I think you should ask Ms. Margoles that question."

Moss had been around the block enough times to know that response suggested there was tension on the AFA front. Something he looked forward to learning more about from snitch par excellence Bill Johnson, so that he could pour some additional fuel on the fire.

~

Margo sent me an email summarizing her conversation with Shamus. Unfortunately, Lauren saw the email first, since I was on the phone.

She came storming down the hall, waving a piece of paper. "I don't understand what the hell is going on," said the normally even-tempered Lauren. "My whole world has been turned upside down," she said, placing the email in front of me. "My husband, my partner, my best friend turns out to be a fraud; people I thought were friends are heading for the hills; AFA is disavowing us; and the hospital has turned into a political zoo. I don't know how much more I can take. I just feel like screaming!"

53.

Moss begins his quest for big bucks.

The following day, Margo received a call from Burton Moss.

"Ms. Margoles, I understand from Jim Shamus you represent Mr. Ruff. I represent the plaintiff, Alexandria Plummet, in the sexual harassment claim, Plummet versus Ruff, employee, and American Financial Associates, the company."

"I am not aware of such a complaint."

"That's the purpose of my call. I wanted to inform you that we are sending you two documents via certified mail: a copy of the Department of Fair Employment and Housing Complaint and Notice of Case Closure/Right to Sue Letter. The latter document has been filed; the former has not. We thought you and your client might like to review the claim first since we are amenable to a pre-filing conference."

Translation: *We have the documentation for our right to sue, but we have not done so yet because we thought we could blackmail you into a settlement rather than drag us both through the expense and pain of a public trial.*

"After you've had a chance to review, you are free to forward it to Jim Shamus at Osborne Pine."

"Why would I do that?"

"Well, the claim is against your client *and* the company. I assume they would like to know they are being sued. Since I assume you'll be working as a team, I thought I'd try to low-key the process as a professional courtesy."

From her prior conversations with the uncooperative Shamus, Margo knew the suit would come as a complete surprise. She was in no mood to do favors. "Burton, I appreciate your concern, but I think it would be best for you to communicate directly with Mr. Shamus."

Margo's response was just another clue to the mercenary Moss that the defendants may not be on the same page, which boded well for his client.

~

The complaint was a highly professional agglomeration of demeaning and disgusting accusations, half-truths, innuendos, and twisted misrepresentations. Moss was determined to humiliate Ruff and his business associates into a settlement that created a nice nest egg for his client while leaving ample fee for his "professional guidance."

The litany positioned Plummet as "a plaintiff who loved her job and found personal fulfillment in her daily contact with her co-workers and clients. Her job was a significant factor in her enjoyment of life. She had become psychologically disabled because of mistreatment, harassment, discrimination, and a hostile work environment." Moss further alleged that Ruff had engaged in a pattern of unwelcome and offensive physical contact and provided unsolicited gifts.

Their mutual indiscretions were depicted as forced behavior, and Plummet's voluntary participation in client business dinners with other team-members was positioned as forced servitude, which, if rebuffed, could have had severe impact on her income and advancement.

To Ruff's surprise, even their after-hours conversations had been recorded. While he had telephone records to document Plummet's many calls to his cell phone, it had never occurred to him to record their conversations. After all, why would he?

It was also clear from the complaint that Bill Johnson had been an integral contributor to the general allegations, as his name was mentioned on numerous occasions as the confidant that Plummet turned to during these "emotionally taxing days and nights."

The complaint also alleged that Ruff's partners knew of and condoned his behavior. Moss positioned that corporate insensitivity as tantamount to mutual compliance. Bottom line: the suit demanded a financial judgment against the defendant Ruff and his partners:

1. For general damages according to proof.
2. For medical and related expenses in a sum according to proof.
3. For the loss of earnings, past and future, and other employment benefits.
4. For interest as allowed by law.
5. For reasonable attorney's fees.
6. For punitive damages in an amount according to proof.
7. For costs of the suit herein incurred.
8. For such other and further relief as the Court may deem proper.

From Margo's perspective, defending Ruff would be difficult because of the emotional nature of the allegations. Ruff's strategy would factually discredit specific allegations, but the strategy was a two-edged sword. If she swung it too far, it would reinforce Ruff's alleged abuse behavior; if she swung too lightly, the courts would side with the bereaved and troubled plaintiff.

~

It was a sunny Friday afternoon. Despite recent events, I had convinced Lauren to spend her birthday weekend at the picturesque Washington Inn in North Litchfield County, Connecticut, where we could view the brilliant fall foliage.

As we drove along the winding country roads, I decided to retrieve my voice mails. I wanted to regain some of Lauren's trust, so I put the iPhone on speakerphone. It was my way of saying, "See, I'm hiding absolutely nothing."

As luck would have it, the first voice mail was Margo. She carefully and unemotionally explained the events of the past twenty-four hours. I was stunned by Shamus's uncooperative abandonment and the Moss-Plummet blackmail strategy.

Lauren never used vile language. Until now. "That miserable little bitch! She's just ruined another vacation. I hope she rots in hell."

54.

Lauren tries to keep it together.

Things were deteriorating on the home front. There were no good mornings, no gentle touches, no warm hugs, no tender greetings of, "I love you." The smile that greeted me at day's end had disappeared. "Hi, I'm home" had been replaced by a blank stare. When it was time to turn out the lights, Lauren simply got into bed and turned her back.

When I attempted to break the silence, she'd say, "Not now." Her days were consumed by life at the hospital, and her evenings with making small talk with her sons and daughter-in-law Valerie, with whom she had become especially close. Neither Lauren nor I said anything to the children, although they, too, sensed something had changed.

"Lauren, I can understand your anger."

"No, you can't!"

There was no appropriate retort. "We've got to make some decisions about AFA. Together. We're sitting in no man's land. The company wants me to sign those papers before I return."

"I told you no way. They were insulting and salacious."

"If I refuse to sign the papers, I'm fired. Because I have no contract, I'm sure our friends will contend there's no severance package, because I still have my stock and profit distributions. If I resign, we're in essentially the same place except, according to Margo, the company will be better positioned to dispute Alexandria's claims against them."

"At this point, I couldn't care less about helping that company."

"I also think Dawson, Eddie, and Jeremy might take one more pass at trying to get the stock back. Agreement or no agreement. Tom advises standing firm since they don't have a legal leg to stand on, and to be prepared to bring all the resources of Conner, Smith, Spencer against AFA for defamation of character, should that be necessary. There's maybe one other long-shot compromise: try to convince Dawson that if I create a settlement with Alexandria on behalf of both of us, he'll drop his demands about signing those documents and we'll all just go back to work."

"Christ, are you talking about us actually paying that's bitch's blackmail?"

"Yes. If the case goes to court, the dispute becomes very public. I probably will not be able to find gainful employment in the future, and I'm not sure how it would affect your standing at the hospital. Then there are all our friends. The embarrassment, the..."

"I get it. I get it. The question is, how much?"

"Margo and Tom think that, worst case, it could be a million dollars."

"A million freakin' dollars. For what? Your midlife crisis stupidity?"

"That's why suits are so popular with the legal community. They assume nice people want to get on with their lives. The only saving grace is that we might be able to negotiate a payout over time. Say three years. The AFA annual profit disbursements should cover most, if not all, of the payments."

"That means our financial independence is three years further away, assuming those idiots don't take the company down," said Lauren. "Without you, there isn't a shred of real management experience there. Just three happy-go-lucky guys who happened to be in the right place at the right time."

~

"Boss," said Courtney, who had returned to her old post a few short months after concluding she was a cultural mismatch for the Southern California surfer dude set. "When the hell are you coming into the office? People need direction. Are you sick, or is something else going on? Rumors are flying. One day you've had a heart attack; another day you're forming a group to buy out the partners. Today's rumor is you've been fired. Does that mean I don't have a job?"

"Courtney, relax. When we came back from Australia, we discovered I had a torn meniscus. We're setting up an arthroscopic procedure for sometime next week. The doctors say I should be out and about in a week. So, I should come in part-time in about two weeks." I figured the imaginary medical timetable would give all parties concerned enough time to conclude matters, or at least to figure out where I fit into the AFA picture going forward.

Courtney knew some part of what I said was a lie; she just wasn't sure which part. So, she began a process of elimination. She cleverly checked New York Hospital to confirm if I indeed was a pre-op patient. "My boss is a workaholic," explained Courtney to the hospital's operating room scheduler, Margaret Sands. "I'm trying to figure out when we can deliver his laptop so that he can retrieve his emails. My job is to make his life as easy as possible."

The scheduler bought Courtney's act entirely. "I understand, my dear. We have a few of those types around here also. Mr. Ruff's surgery is scheduled for next Thursday. I expect he'll be in a bit of discomfort for the first thirty-six hours. I wouldn't restart his business activity until Saturday at the earliest."

"Thanks, Margaret; you've been a real dear."

The surgery validated, Courtney ran into another dead end when she searched the executive calendars to see if any long-distance conferences between my partners and me had been scheduled. As she discreetly probed the halls, all she could discover was that Alexandria Plummet had taken a sudden two-week vacation. The general assumption was that her waning performance suggested she was looking for a new job while still gainfully employed.

~

Craft readily accepted my dinner invitation. "Dawson, I think we need some closure before the office rumors start drifting out to the field and hurting business. How about we break bread at Le Périgord tomorrow evening? I'm buying."

"So, pal, I'm glad you're ready to go back to work," said Craft as he uncorked a bottle of Chateau Margaux 1984. He then made his usual fuss over the wine with his favorite sommelier, Jacques Dubayère. "Jacques, decant this baby and let it breathe until we finish our appetizers. I want Martin to experience the intense berries in this vintage."

"Dawson, I've got to hand it to you," I said jokingly, "you're full of shit about a lot of things but you sure know your wines. It's the only plausible reason why Amélie married you."

"Speaking of Amélie, she's one of the reasons I want you back as quickly as possible. She's pregnant; she's due in six months and ten days."

"Congratulations."

"Pal, I'm excited about having kids. Imagine: less than two years ago, I was a forty-six-year-old confirmed bachelor. I just hope everything works out with the pregnancy. We discovered she has a narrowing of the uterus, so she has to have a remedial surgery to prepare her for childbirth, and then the delivery has to be a caesarean."

"I wouldn't worry; it's amazing what they can do today."

"Assuming all goes well, we plan to have a bunch of kids. My goal is to be a great father like Pete. So, starting right now, you and I need to develop a plan that will allow me to spend more time at home."

"I've been thinking about the same thing, but for different reasons. I'd like to start winding down from day to day."

"Martin, you've been the hardest-working guy in the company for these past five years, so I can understand that."

"I think there are lots of options. I just happen to have a favorite. My sense is we are nearing the peak of our profitability curve unless we dramatically change our business model. Specifically, instead of just marketing to individual financial advisors to wholesale our product lines, we need to market to groups of financial advisors."

"You're talking about going directly to competitive broker-dealers?"

"Yeah. My research suggests there are at least 5100 firms around the US with at least 1000 independent advisors that sell securities. But we must make them feel important by visiting them on their turf. They won't come to us."

"So, we use our current business model to continue to capture one-offs while we create a separate parallel effort to sign up BDs?" asked Craft.

"Precisely. And it just so happens that I began to test the viability before I took off for Australia. I've already met with a half a dozen BDs, and I've created a prototype contract. I think we can sign up all six of them. I've also got some ideas on how to motivate the account managers to assist us without getting in the way."

"That's what I love about you, Martin; you're always a step ahead. But now I've got one for you. I agree with your profit analysis, but that can be our little secret. I think the time is ripe to sell the company in the next few years, while we are at the top of the hill. I figure I'll head into the sunset with $300 - $400 million. You should do pretty well also.

"By the way, the boys and I read that bullshit harassment claim Alexandria cooked up with some ambulance chaser. We are going to bury the fucker!" said Craft.

55.

Costas turns nasty, nasty.

After two bottles of Dead Arm, Craft let it all hang out. "I don't know if you're aware, pal, but when I was single, Alexandria and I were quite an item. I imagine we did it about four times a week for twelve months straight. She was surprisingly uninhibited for a mother of two!"

"What happened?"

"Let me put it this way. She is one wacko broad, with all her baggage from her two ex-husbands plus God knows who else. To me, she was a convenient lay; no more, no less. But when she started talking marriage and stuff like that, I said adios."

"What was her reaction?"

"She was going to go public with our affair, tell people she was forced into the relationship unless I gave her some hush money and that expensive car you see her driving. In exchange, she signed a non-disclosure agreement."

"Dawson, can you trust her?"

"I told her if she ever crossed me, I'd make sure she couldn't get a job anywhere in the industry."

I changed the subject. "Dawson, my lawyers have thoroughly reviewed the documents you want me to sign.."

Dawson's expression turned dead serious as he peered over his granny glasses. "Lawyers? I told you the terms were not negotiable."

I ignored his comment. "We have a counter-proposal that should work for everybody, since Alexandria seems to have a history of other indiscretions."

"This better be good," replied Craft.

"I will take the responsibility to settle the suit with Alexandria and pick up the costs. In exchange, I come back to work and we just tear up your proposal. My guess is that she desperately needs the money and will keep her mouth shut with me just like she did with you."

Dawson had spent considerable time with his attorneys trying to figure out how to make my equity position vulnerable. As Tom had suggested, our agreement was bulletproof. His only potential strategy was intimidation. Like Wasserman, or because of Wasserman, he concluded that I needed the monthly cash flow from working at AFA, but he made no allowance for the fact that my annual profit distribution still provided ample cash flow — it was just paid in a one lump sum rather than in monthly installments.

"Does that mean you're not going to sign the papers?"

"Dawson, look at my perspective. Two of the papers embarrass and humiliate me in front of the staff, to say nothing of making me go to harassment classes for two years at my own expense for something I didn't do."

"Pal, you understand we have to protect the company in case somebody else tries to sue."

"That brings me to the second point. The wording of the suit suggests somebody inside the company helped Alexandria with her attorney."

"That's probably true."

"You and I both have a suspicion who that might be."

"Could be."

"And you want me to sign a piece of paper that says if *any* employee creates an event — in other words, a financial claim against the company involving me — I automatically lose my entire equity position. Let me ask you a question. If you knew someone in the company was out to get you, would you sign that assignment?"

Dawson paused and stared at me silently.

"But you want me to sign it."

"Does that mean you're not going to sign it?" asked Dawson again.

"Yes."

"You know Jeremy and Eddie want me to initiate an action that says you received the equity under false pretenses."

"Don't you think my attorney and I considered that possibility? He told me the same thing that I'm sure Jim Friedman told you. My ownership is rock solid. If you want to challenge the agreement in court, be my guest. Remember, the loser pays all legal costs."

Craft backed off. "Nah, I understand, pal. I wouldn't do that either, but I can't back off our lawyers' demand that you sign everything."

"Here's your alternative," I replied. "Tell the boys I resign, effectively immediately, and I'll see you at the partner bonus distributions meeting in February."

56.

Gracious and ungracious exits.

To Craft's credit, he handled my abrupt departure quite professionally by preparing an email announcement with my picture that was sent to all employees. It read:

> To All AFA Employees,
>
> It is with great difficulty that I announce a vital member of our executive team, SVP Martin Ruff, has decided to pursue other interests at this time. Reluctantly, we have accepted Martin's resignation.
>
> Martin has been a respected member of the AFA team for the past five years in a variety of roles. Without Martin's innovative strategies, brilliant executions, and operational diligence, AFA would not be where we are today. I want to thank Martin for his years of service and dedication to the AFA mission and wish him all the best!
>
> Thank you, Martin; you will be missed!
>
> Kind Regards,
> Dawson Craft
> CEO/President

Since he wanted to make a proper announcement via teleconference with AFA advisors across the country, he asked employees not to release the information about me piecemeal.

All two hundred AFA employees followed Craft's request. After the teleconference, I was deluged with emails, letters, and notes thanking me for my contributions and wishing me well.

~

"Colton," said Craft the following day in a meeting with his other partners, Costas, Carr, and HR Director Wasserman. "I think we need to find out who's for us and who's against us. I want the landline and cell phone records of every employee that we reimburse, and we'll have somebody cross-check their activity to see if anyone else contacted Alexandria's attorney, Burton Moss. I have a hunch somebody may have gotten sloppy."

Three days later, the four men again sat in the conference room. Wasserman had a single piece of paper in front of him. "I had records cross-checked for the last six months. There were no matches for the first three. Then about three months ago, one employee started making calls to Moss's office on his cell phone after business hours. There were nine outgoing calls that all followed the same pattern. They all averaged a minimum of ten minutes each. There were also five calls from the same cell phone from Moss's office itself."

"So, who's our outstanding employee of the month?" said Craft sarcastically.

"Bill Johnson."

"That son of a bitch," said Carr. "He walks around here complimenting us on what a great work environment we've created and then screws us behind our back. Why the hell would he do that?"

"I'm guessing it's about the money," said Wasserman. "He's probably got a revenue-sharing arrangement with Plummet. Maybe even Moss. Alexandria and Bill have made a deal to split the settlement her lawyer expects to extract from us in exchange for Johnson helping Moss dramatize the case."

"Get Johnson down here right now," demanded Craft.

"Shouldn't we talk about this first?" said Costas.

"There's nothing to talk about," responded Craft angrily. "This is my fucking company. I've got my life savings invested in it.."

"Colton, go get Johnson," said Costas.

Johnson bounced into the room. "So, what's up, fellas?"

"Did you know Alexandria Plummet has filed a sexual harassment suit against us?"

"I wasn't sure. She had come to me about some of the terrible things that Martin Ruff had been doing to her. And I discussed the matter with Colton. Remember, Colton?"

"How did you decide to get in the middle?" said Costas in an accusatory tone.

Johnson got the drift immediately. "I didn't get in the middle. She came to me for advice. She said she was losing sleep and income over his harassing behavior; she asked me to talk to HR to find out what she should do."

"Did you know you were quoted in her initial complaint?"

"No, I didn't realize that."

"So, you knew she was going to file a complaint."

"No, I only heard about it after the fact. I'm guessing sometime in April."

"And did you know she hired an attorney?"

"No."

"Then how do you explain these lengthy phone calls on your cell bill to her attorney, Burton Moss, before she filed her initial complaint and before Moss threatened to file a formal claim six weeks later?"

Johnson was flabbergasted that the boys had done their homework. His tone turned conciliatory. "I was just trying to help an old friend. She ……"

"At the risk of holding up your employer!" blurted Costas.

"Look, I wasn't born yesterday. The company has D&O insurance. A settlement is no skin off your nose," said Johnson.

"And what about Martin?"

"That arrogant fuck deserves whatever he gets."

"Did you help prepare the attorney's claim?"

"I may have made a few comments to fill in some gaps."

"Do you personally benefit from her claim if there is a settlement?"

"No. Alexandria gets one hundred percent of the settlement, less her attorney costs."

"As her direct supervisor, you are aware her income has been in a steady decline."

"Yes."

"How do you think Alexandria is paying her attorney fees?"

"I wouldn't know. That's none of my business."

"I'm going to ask you again," said Costas. "Do you personally benefit from her claim… from anyone?"

"Like I said before, no."

"Interesting coincidence then," commented Wasserman. "According to publicly available court records, Mr. Moss represented you in your divorce proceedings."

The four men looked at each other. Craft nodded to Wasserman. "Bill, thanks for clarifying matters. We'll get back to you."

"Back to me about what?"

Costas flipped. His face turned beet red. "You lying son of a bitch. How could you sit across from us and keep a straight face? I want you the fuck out of here in the next twenty minutes. Does anybody in this room disagree?"

"Colton," said Craft, "Please accompany Bill to his office to gather his belongings, and then escort him out of the building."

57.

Telling our sons about my indiscretions.

Lauren and I agreed our sons, Bart and MJ, needed to be apprised of the situation. "You created the problem; you explain it," said Lauren.

I decided it was best to meet both in person at Bart's office. There I explained all the gory details: my unconscionable quasi-affair, the company's reaction, the harassment complaint, and so on.

MJ's first question exposed his real concern — himself. "I can't believe she'd do such a thing. She seemed to understand my situation and was so nice at lunch. You must have pissed her off."

Bart was shocked by his brother's self-centeredness. "MJ, stop thinking about yourself! Mom and Dad have got a serious situation here." The brothers glared at each other. Bart then turned to me. "How is Mom doing?"

"Not particularly well. She's confused and disappointed."

"Do you blame her?" said MJ angrily.

"Look, I'm not saying what I did was particularly intelligent, but I'm not the first married man who has dated another woman."

Bart took control of the meeting. He began asking a series of dispassionate questions, as if evaluating one of his commercial real estate transactions. "Dad, what's done is done. We can talk about that some other time. But I need to understand the situation better. Do you still love Mom?"

"Yes, I do."

"That's a relief. Did you ever tell Alexandria you were going to leave Mom for her?"

"I'm going to tell you guys things I haven't revealed to anybody else because you're my sons. You deserve the whole truth. From our conversations, I knew she was chomping at the bit to remarry. I figured suggesting a willingness to switch partners was a pragmatic approach to getting her in bed.

"It didn't work, but she kept dangling the carrot. Alexandria's point was 'you commit first; then I'll let you enter the pearly gates.' She kept talking about her girlfriend Stephanie's situation. Stephanie had a passionate affair with some married guy because he told her he was going to leave his wife. In the end, the guy's wife had too much money to leave behind. Alexandria concluded Stephanie wound up more miserable than if she had never met the guy. Alexandria vowed she would not let that happen to her… again."

"If you weren't going to leave Mom, why did you continue to see her?"

"After a while, it became a personal challenge. It wasn't like my marriage was in shreds. I was satisfied at home. In some ways, I was playing a game of who would give in first. My assumption was she'd eventually wear down, and I'd get my way."

"Why did you stop seeing her?"

"After being with her so many times, I realized she had more baggage than I wanted to deal with, so I just stopped seeing her."

"So, where does the harassment come in?"

"She took what was a deeply personal friendship and twisted it into something grotesque. She claimed I was stalking her, that I forced her to go out with me because of my senior position. She even saved some of my voice messages and positioned them as support for her harassment claim. She claimed her income dropped precipitously because of me, that she couldn't work at the office because I frightened her."

"Dad, you are a bit of a bull in a china shop; are you sure you didn't …."

"Absolutely, positively not."

"How much does she want?"

"She said $500,000."

"What's the company's position?"

"They did their own investigation, which included my statement with documentation that supported a purely consensual relationship. But their investigation also suggested that one or more employees friendly to her helped her prepare the claim. Identified an attorney, that sort of thing."

"Why would they be so vindictive?" asked Bart.

"Petty jealousy. We've got some egomaniacs on staff who hate my guts for rejecting their business proposals, which made no strategic sense. The company told Alexandria there was no conclusive evidence to support her claim. They told her they weren't going to offer any settlement and that she should go back to work."

"That should have given Mom some comfort."

"At that point, Mom still knew nothing. But when we returned from Australia, the company said I had to sign three separate documents as a condition of continued employment. That they needed to cover themselves."

"To tell you the truth, that doesn't sound unreasonable from what you've said in the past. Those three guys stepped up and put their entire net worth on the line to buy the company. I'd probably do the same thing."

"That may be true. But from my standpoint, I told my partners the conditions were unacceptable. They wanted me to sign a nonstandard employment contract that said I was liable for all expenses related to any alleged harassment suit that might be brought against the company on my behalf in the future.

"Secondly, they wanted me to sign a letter to the file which said nobody was working directly for me, that any meetings with employees must be held in plain sight so they can be monitored, and that I had to attend sexual harassment training twice a week for two years at my own expense.

"Importantly, they also wanted me to sign a stock assignment that said if anyone brings any kind of complaint again — past, present, or future — my equity stake and profit distributions revert back to the company."

"Wow!"

"It gets worse! They also wanted Mom to sign all the documents."

"So, what did you do?"

"At this point, it's all about the money. Alexandria wants her pound of flesh, my partners see this as a chance to recapture their stock at no cost to them, and I want to protect my retirement assets."

"But you said Alexandria's claim was rejected."

"Her initial claim was, but she subsequently hired an ambulance-chasing lawyer who has escalated the matter dramatically by preparing a formal suit, which twists the facts and sues both me as an individual and the company. Rumor has it that his settlement number is between one and five million."

"Jesus, what a damn mess. How much does Mom know?" asked Bart.

"I explained everything and showed her all the documents. But you know Mom; she's dealt with life and death at hospitals her whole life, and she has a unique capacity to remain calm under pressure."

"I don't understand. Usually, company management puts up a united front and supports one of its own," said Bart astutely.

"Over the last few years, your dad became the company's agent of change to stimulate growth, which made Jeremy Costas and some account managers uncomfortable. Then there's the new HR guy, Colton Wasserman, who Jeremy hired. He flat-out doesn't like me or my management style.

"There was no way I could sign those documents, so I was forced to resign. I wanted you to know that before you heard it secondhand."

58.

Bart performs his due diligence.

"I can't condone the mess that got you to this point, but it sounds like the right decision," said Bart.

"If you went back to work, you would receive a monthly draw against your annual profit distribution, but it would be open season on your equity position. By resigning, you keep the stock with no restrictions and get the same profit distribution in one lump sum at the end of the year."

"That's about right."

"Do you have the cash flow to live annual to annual?"

"We're in pretty good shape, financially. In practical terms, we are just talking about the first year. After that, we can live comfortably on the prior year's distributions, plus our other investment income, plus Mom just gotten a big raise."

"And you can always get involved in another corporate situation."

"Probably not. I'm assuming the boys will drop a few discriminating negatives to anybody who wants to check me out. Besides, I'm not sure I want to deal with business politics anymore. I've had almost thirty years of this bullshit."

"Well, that's your decision. What are you doing about counsel?"

"I had to hire experienced counsel to represent me in the harassment suit. Her name is Margo Margoles. She seems pretty buttoned up."

"What's her point of view?"

"Just settle the mess for as little as possible. Keep your marriage together and get on with your life."

"Sounds right to me," said Bart. "Even if you have to give up some or all of your profit distributions for a year or two. You and Mom don't live over your head like your partners do — I mean former partners."

"Your logic is unassailable, except for one thing. I am being blackmailed and embarrassed for something I didn't do. That's not fair."

"Dad, to be blunt, at your age you should have known better. From what I've read, right or wrong, the woman always wins in these kinds of cases."

MJ finally broke his silence. "Has Mom met Margo?"

"Yes. Why?"

"I think it's critical they get along — this is so incredibly personal," said an incisive MJ. "The look in Mom's eyes tells me she's worried about her abilities."

"What makes you say that? I hired Margo via telephone conference and a strong recommendation from Tom, based on his firm's research."

"So, what's the problem?" said Bart.

"It turns out Margo is drop-dead gorgeous."

"Great. Just great!"

"Mom took some solace in the fact that she's got family pictures all over the damn office. But I get the feeling Mom would have preferred a traditional family man."

"Dad, what do you want us to do at this point?" asked Bart.

"I think you guys should have your own conversations with Mom. I think she'd appreciate it. I'll keep you posted on developments as they happen."

"And if I were you," said Bart, "I'd make a conscious effort to talk to your daughter-in-law about this, too; you owe her that. She's an important part of this family. The fact that you didn't invite her today probably didn't advance your relationship."

~

"Mom," said Bart, "we've just talked to Dad. Do you want to talk about the situation?"

Lauren decided life had been good, and she was determined to make lunch with her sons into an honest but pleasant affair.

Bart and MJ arrived at the Bryant Park Café first. It was a sunny, crisp autumn day. The Café's large picture windows provided a uniquely Manhattan experience — tall elm, spruce, and maple trees surrounded by towering glass and stone skyscrapers.

The boys wondered about their mom's current mental state. How should they begin this awkward conversation? How did Mom feel about Dad? What kind of support should they offer?

To their surprise, Mom approached them beaming ear-to-ear. "How are my two little men? You know, we're all so busy with our lives that sometimes we forget to stop and thank the Lord for all we have. I want you both to know there isn't a prouder mother on the face of this Earth."

Mom's mood made the conversation almost natural. She continued, "I gather Dad filled you in on the situation."

"Step by gory step."

"Let me make it a little easier for you, boys. I'm still stunned by what your dad did. Over the years, I've watched many of my friends' marriages struggle and collapse. I thought we had a fairy-tale marriage. We grew up together. I couldn't even begin to guess how many times he told me 'he was the happiest man on earth,' and how many times I told him he was 'the love of my life.' People watched our love grow with a measure of awe and envy. When Dad told me what he had done, my whole world came crashing down. I feel like I'm sitting in a mountain of rubble, not sure whether to rebuild or just move on."

"Do you still love him?" asked Bart.

"Of course I do. You can't love a man with all your heart for over 35 years and then suddenly fall out of love, no matter what he's done. Bart, I only hope and pray you and Valerie build the same kind of love your Dad and I have."

Bart smiled. Lauren sensed MJ felt left out.

"And MJ, I know you've had a few issues. But I don't love you any less, nor am I any less proud of you. I hope that one day you will also find the woman of your dreams. You've got so much to offer a woman. Who knows; maybe you'll find a girl just like the one that married your dear old dad."

"Mom, I will. I want her to be just like you."

As the three continued to talk, it became clear that Lauren was planning to stick with Martin through the dark days ahead.

The boys supported her point of view, reminding her that "they were always there for her."

"You know, I remember meeting Alexandria at one of those AFA conferences. She just looked at me funny. You know how a woman notices such a thing. I wondered why at the time. Putting two and two together, I think she figured Dad was going to leave me for her. That's what her pathetic suit is all about. She's out to hurt the two of us, financially and emotionally."

Lauren's observation added perspective to some of Dad's earlier comments.

MJ couldn't help himself. Mom had been his safe-person through his panic attacks. He owed it to her to reveal something. "Mom," said MJ, with Bart glaring at him. "Dad believes you are wondering about his lawyer."

"You're right. With everything that's at stake, your father picks an attorney who looks like she should be on the cover of *Town and Country* magazine. How insensitive is that?"

59.

The real pig-fuck begins.

Moss was relentless. Margo and I agreed he had to be stopped dead in his tracks.

She also knew she needed the cooperation of AFA to bring this increasingly embarrassing affair to a hasty conclusion before it destroyed the AFA culture, the partners' net worth, and the Ruff family.

"Jim, our overall goal has to be the same," said Margo forcefully. We've got to destroy Alexandria's case based on factual misrepresentations. Once Moss realizes he's been duped, I'm guessing he'll want to bail out as fast as possible, so as not to tarnish his never-been-beaten reputation. I'm suggesting that we employ a divide and conquer strategy. AFA has been accused of not having a sexual harassment policy and not acting on employee abuses because of the company's existing 'boys' club' culture."

"That's incorrect."

"I understand, but the courts and Moss don't know that. Martin tells me there has been a written policy for some time, that employees have been given written warnings and been dismissed."

"All true."

"Then you know what has to be done. Those written warnings have got to be shared."

"What about Martin, since the suit is against both of us?"

"That's where I need your help. Martin has given me all the supporting documentation that their relationship was consensual. I understand you have a copy of those documents. What I need to do is show that her loss of income had nothing to do with Martin. You have records which indicate general market softness, her loss of agents, the company's analysis of those losses, her lack of employing new company retention techniques."

"We can help you with that."

"I also need to demonstrate that she is overreaching on her claims of mental duress at the office. In your investigations, while Martin was in Australia, you must have talked to employees who said her claims were exaggerated. She says Martin acted like a jilted boyfriend by throwing pencils and papers at her. Martin tells me that was part of his management style, that there are numerous women at the office like Kate, Kathy, Dee — I'm not sure of their last names — that would support his contention. We need to review prior transcripts or re-interview them.

"And stuff like her Christmas card allegations. I need to prove 'double your income, double your time off' was a longstanding company slogan, that Martin created and managed the broker-dealer initiative, that Martin was solely responsible for evaluating the many partnership proposals you received."

"Gathering what you need should not be a problem."

"Good. Then we should talk about specific details tomorrow. I want to put a case together that depicts Ms. Plummet as a greedy opportunist who will go to any length to cover her shortcomings."

"Sounds like you're planning on getting rough; remember, Alexandria's psyche is probably fragile."

"Fragile! Who gives a rat's ass! She started this. My job is to destroy her and her reputation."

Shamus could see the fire in Margo's eyes. He called Craft. "This lady's a killer with a ton of harassment case experience. I recommend you, Eddie, and Jeremy should appoint her lead attorney for both parties, unless and until there is a conflict of interest."

~

"Burton," said Margo, about a week later, "I think we're prepared to have our pre-filing settlement discussion. Neither Martin nor any of the AFA partners will be attending our first session. It will just be Jim Shamus and myself representing the defendants."

"That seems a bit unusual."

"Well, in our mutual discovery process, we found some factual inaccuracies in your claim that may or may not be intentional. We thought it might make sense for the attorneys to talk first. There are a lot of reputations at stake."

Moss knew he had been professionally blackmailed. "I understand. I'll advise Ms. Plummet to stay home."

~

Moss's slick offices were designed to be professionally intimidating.

The lobby had two big flat screens flashing the latest court news on either side of the receptionist. The remaining walls were filled with client testimonials praising Moss on his settlements, and pictures of Moss with well-known local, state, and national politicians. There were also two computer terminals where visitors could call up Moss PR releases heralding the firm's growth, its record of success, and its philosophy: "Every Plaintiff's Voice Deserves a Fair Hearing."

Silver-haired Burton Moss was a physically imposing figure at 6'3" and 250 pounds, with large hands. "Margo, a pleasure to meet you in person. I've heard a lot about you."

"And you must be Jim."

Jim nodded.

"This is my associate Joe Lo Bosco; he's assisting me on the case."

After a brief exchange of pleasantries, Margo got down to business. "As we see your case, however frivolous it appears, there are six claims. Three against my client, Mr. Ruff, and three against the company." Margo then carefully reviewed each one.

"Correct," smiled Moss, confidently ignoring the "frivolous" comment.

Margo walked to the dry board at the front of the conference room and picked up a marker. "May I? Let's deal with the company claims first. You state that before the alleged incidents, there was no formal AFA sexual harassment policy. Note that I have in front of me an employee handbook dated October 20, 2001, which details said policy. Here also is a copy of the confirmation each employee is asked to sign after reading the handbook. Especially note that acceptance of all its policies includes sexual harassment and conflicts of interest."

She held up a piece of paper. "This is the memorandum of understanding re: company policies signed by Ms. Plummet on October 21, 2001. I also submit for your review letters to the files of eleven male employees dating back to 2001, and four letters of dismissal for inappropriate advances so categorized as sexual harassment.

"I believe this documents the company's longstanding equal opportunity policies. It's also worth noting the company's since-inception employee base has never had a ratio of less than sixty-five percent woman and thirty-five percent men. And the company's three major departments — Business Consulting, National Recruiting, and Marketing — are all managed by women. Women, who I might add, have been promoted from within the ranks."

"May I see those documents?" asked a chagrined Moss.

"Jim," said Margo, "Would you please show them to Burton?"

"Joe," said Moss to Lo Bosco, "Would you mind making a copy of these documents?"

Margo smiled. "Nice try, Burton, but not a chance. If you don't mind, Burton, I'd like to continue. There's more, much more."

Burton squirmed in his seat as he took a deep breath.

"There are numerous other incorrect allegations against the company, but for the sake of time, I'd like to move to the allegations against Mr. Ruff. To begin with, here are the company's current and past organizational charts. You will note Ms. Plummet has never had anything that even vaguely resembles a direct reporting relationship to Mr. Ruff.

"Concerning the accusation that Mr. Ruff forced himself upon Ms. Plummet, I submit a complete schedule of meetings, telephone calls, and other documentation that will show their relationship was entirely consensual. These documents also summarize the content of numerous confidential matters that Ms. Plummet revealed to Mr. Ruff during their friendly encounters. They include the circumstances surrounding the suicide of Ms. Plummet's daughter Shanti; the relationship between Ms. Plummet's best friend, Stephanie, and a married man who changed his mind; and an explanation, in Ms. Plummet's own words, as to why she needed a breast augmentation.

"We also have affidavits from numerous female employees describing Mr. Ruff's management style as intense, but purposely light-hearted. A style which including tossing paper planes and pens and pencils near, but never at, fellow employees.

"Shall I continue? As I said, there is more, much more."

Moss tried one last bluff. "Despite your so-called documentation, the fact is Ms. Plummet's income dropped precipitously because of Mr. Ruff."

"Ms. Plummet lives in a fairyland of her own making. Company analysis after company analysis summarize the major reasons for Ms. Plummet's declining income as her inability to properly coach her advisors through a 28 percent drop in the stock market. Ms. Plummet was not only apprised of her sagging performance in writing, but she also was provided customized remedial action plans, which she ignored."

"Considering some of your new data, perhaps it's best if we reach some reasonable settlement, since going to trial may be a losing proposition for all concerned," said Moss.

"We are prepared to do that today, with one stipulation. Mr. Johnson, who has been dismissed from the company for conflict of interest, receives nothing."

"Agreed."

"We are prepared to provide Ms. Plummet with $100,000, assuming she signs all the appropriate non-recourse documentation."

Moss was prepared to negotiate, since he assumed the settlement offer was a starting point. "Margo, let's be realistic; your offer barely covers expenses. I want to propose…"

Margo leaned over the table and stared straight at Burton. "Burton, this is not a negotiation. That is our first and final offer. If you want to represent a desperate, lying woman in court and destroy the practice you've built, be my guest. We'll bring the unethical nature of the case before the Connecticut

Association, and will make sure the matter reaches the trade and consumer press."

60.

Plummet's version of the truth comes back to haunt.

"So how did we do?"" said a cheerful Alexandria Plummet into the phone.

"How did we do? I was never more embarrassed. They showed document after document refuting every claim you made."

"Impossible."

"Madame, they showed me a diary with documented receipts. You went out with Ruff twenty-two times."

"You don't understand; I was forced."

"How could you be forced to go out with someone twenty-two times, to request gifts and reveal personal information, and to ask for tips and suggestions of a financial and social nature?"

Plummet realized that she had been trapped by her own lies.

"And what about the employee handbook dated 2001 with the AFA sexual harassment policy described in detail? You signed a form, for God's sake."

"But what about the way I was abused in the parking lot? Doesn't that count for something?"

"For all I know, you may have hit on him. Let me tell you something, honey. I don't know what is truth and what is untruth or fabrication. All I know is that Burton Moss doesn't take kindly to being embarrassed in pre-court settlement meetings or court proceedings. They did their homework; they even knew about Johnson's split."

"Johnson's split? What are you talking about?"

"Tell me, didn't you know he was getting 15 percent of my side as a finder's fee and case advisor?"

"I did not."

"After listening to the facts, even I'm convinced — Mr. Protector of Downtrodden Plaintiffs — that Ruff is probably a stand-up guy who made the dumb mistake of being attracted to you. You know, young lady, harassment claims are serious business. You just can't screw with people's lives."

"But I thought the plaintiff always won cases like this."

"Tie always goes to the plaintiff. But this is no tie. We created an out and out misrepresentation. Be thankful. Despite everything, they're willing to settle for $100,000 to close the case."

"What about our two-million-dollar strategy?"

Moss sneered, "If I were you, I'd just take the money and run."

"Well, at least the $100,000 will give me time to rebuild my career somewhere."

"You may have less time than you think. Your share is $50,000. And as far as I'm concerned, I don't owe Johnson a cent. He's your fucking pal!"

~

Margo got the word the next day: settlement accepted; case closed.

"Martin, I just wanted to inform you that we've agreed to settle the Plummet matter for $100,000 plus legal fees, which will be split equally between you and the company. You have thirty days to remit the check to me, and I'll coordinate the matter with Plummet's attorney and AFA."

"All I can say is thank you very much. Now we can get on with our lives."

"Listen, from what I can see, you have a very supportive wife. Stay out of trouble, will you?"

I was so elated that I couldn't wait to tell Lauren. "Just got off the phone with Margo. The case is settled."

"How much?"

"Our portion is $50,000."

"Our portion? Where is the rest coming from?"

"AFA."

"Well, I guess that's a small penalty to pay for your damn stupidity. How much do we have to pay little Miss Pin Up?"

"Her legal fees are about $28,000."

"Christ, no wonder she can afford to wear those clothes."

~

At 5:00 P.M., Eddie Carr, Dawson Craft, and Jeremy Costas were shooting the breeze in Dawson's office when Wasserman entered with his latest *corporate initiative*.

"I took the liberty of bouncing an idea off Jim Shamus. With Martin having resigned, it strikes me we could go after him."

"Why would we want to do that?"

"Well, if I were you, fellas, I would be thinking about all the company time and resources we wasted settling his stupid mistake. And I'm thinking about the bad press among employees and our field producers caused by his sudden departure. Remember, he was quite adamant about not signing those papers, which we drafted collectively and thought was a fair compromise. I've calculated that Martin's ten percent of profit distribution this year should be about a million dollars. We could sue his ass and reclaim those funds for disruption of business, then redistribute them among senior management."

Jeremy was intrigued. "You think we could pull that off?"

"Jim says it's very doable."

"Jesus, don't you think we should give the guy a break?" said Carr. "After all, that bitch and Johnson manufactured the whole thing."

"With all due respect," said Wasserman, "Martin's indiscretion placed the entire company in harm's way.

"My recommendation is to redistribute Ruff's profit distribution among management. Dawson would get an extra $500,000, Jeremy and Eddie would get $200,000, and I was hoping you guys would award me Martin's ten percent."

"I can handle that," said Jeremy. "I'm happy to make a prorated contribution from my annual profit distribution."

"Thanks," said Wasserman. "Makes me feel like a member of the team."

"Let's sleep on it," said Dawson. "Martin's been a friend and a real contributor to AFA. I'm not sure I want to fuck with him any more than we already have."

61.

The pigs try to slaughter one of their own.

"You must be joking," said Margo. "AFA wants to sue Martin for a million dollars! On what basis?"

"Material damage to the business," said Shamus sheepishly.

"I understand business is business, but we just worked together to close the Plummet case. I thought we were done."

"This wasn't my idea; it was Wasserman's."

"I don't understand; isn't he supposed to be the HR guy?"

"Looks to me like he's positioning himself to take over Martin's role," said Shamus.

"Look, I probably shouldn't tell you this, but Wasserman has convinced the guys to give him ten percent of the million as a bonus for his 'good deeds.'"

"But you don't have it yet."

"Margo, let's get real. If Martin doesn't agree, we'll just withhold the payment anyway. Then he's got to spend a ton on more legal fees to sue us. We'll countersue until he runs out of resources."

Margo was furious, but she was also a realist. "Isn't it better if Martin saves the money and aggravation, takes a hit this year, and then gets his future profit distributions?"

Checkmate.

"We're prepared to make it easy. A one-page profit distribution assignment agreement limited to this year's distributions, whatever they may be."

"I'll talk to my client and see what he wants to do."

~

"So, Martin, how is everything on the home front?" asked Margo. "I have some bad news."

"After what we've just been through, what could be so bad?"

"Your partners have decided to sue you for a million dollars."

"A million fucking dollars. For what?"

"Damage to the business."

"Jesus Christ Almighty, this isn't remotely fair. In all my years of being screwed by partners, these guys are the worst."

"I must say, they are a vindictive sort."

"Do they have a case?"

"I'm not sure. But the partners are willing to offer you a settlement rather than go to court."

"I'm listening."

"They'll drop the suit if you assign this year's profit distributions to them."

"That's effectively giving them the million dollars."

"They're also willing to provide you all the appropriate future indemnifications."

"How generous!"

"What do you want me to do?"

I started to mumble, "If I have to, we can absorb a year without the extra cash distributions."

Then I had a potential insight. "Margo, a few questions for you. From your early conversations, would it be fair to say AFA never imagined they would be a party to the suit? And would it be fair to say that my partners assumed I was guilty from the outset?"

"Their actions would suggest that to be the case," said Margo, sounding every bit the cautious attorney.

"Could we also assume they had to interview AFA employees to complete their investigation?"

"That's a reasonable assumption."

"And that there are company documents to that effect? And that we have the right to subpoena those documents and interview those employees, including Johnson?"

"Now I see where you're going, but that could get expensive and embarrassing."

"The way I look at it, if I don't lose this year's profits distributions, I have some spare cash for legal fees. Are you willing to work on that basis?"

"As I mentioned at the outset, our firm doesn't represent contingency cases."

"I'm not talking contingency. It's now October. I'm asking you to defer the collection of most of your legal fees till February, when the company distributes profits. In the interim, I'll also pay $5,000 a month in fees against the final total."

"That would be acceptable. How much do you want to countersue for?" said Margo, knowing precisely what I was thinking.

"I want to sue AFA, corporately, and Dawson Craft, Jeremy Costas, and Eddie Carr, as individuals, for $10 million for defamation of character and emotional distress caused by the possible loss of future wages."

"Your wording is not exactly right, but you're getting pretty good at legal mumbo jumbo," said Margo. "I'll prepare the papers for your review and so notify the defendants of your intent."

"Some more questions. When Alexandria received her settlement, she indemnified us in perpetuity, correct? Did the agreement say anything about indemnifying her?"

"Indemnifying her against what? She was the plaintiff."

"Do you believe that between my documents, statements, company records, and supplemental employee interviews, we could make a case for intentional factual manipulation?"

"Probably. But people usually leave sleeping dogs alone in harassment cases. They don't want to open old wounds."

"At this stage, I'm inclined to throw caution to the wind. I've been screwed by everybody."

"What about Lauren?"

"I can handle that."

"Okay. You're the client. In summary, then," concluded Margo, "we're going to sue AFA collectively and individually for $10 million, and Alexandria for $1 million, for unlawful manipulation of factual evidence. We'll drop our suit against AFA collectively if they indemnify us against present and future claims, if any, and pay one hundred percent of your legal fees and expenses related to the entire matter. That includes actions against Ms. Plummet."

"And, what's our pre-filing strategy with Ms. Plummet?" asked Martin.

"She returns the $100,000, plus we get her mother's house in Nebraska."

"Suppose she's unable to do that economically?" I asked.

"Then we garnish her salary, her worker's compensation, her Social Security, her unemployment, her whatever until we get equivalent value."

I thought to himself, *Thank God she's on my side*!

~

Margo wasn't done; she wanted to know why my partners, Craft, Costas, and Carr, appeared so vindictive. She hired a private investigator (P.I.) to search for clues.

It turned out Colton Wasserman was not Colton Wasserman. He was actually Phil Bernstein, a teacher from Philadelphia's South Side, who had married a Wauneta Consuelo. One afternoon, he came home from class to find his wife in bed with a neighbor. A scuffle ensued; the suitor was armed. The gun went off accidentally and killed Wauneta's lover. Bernstein then took the gun and pistol-whipped Wauneta into oblivion. Her face required sixty-three stitches, followed by multiple plastic surgeries. He was convicted of second-degree manslaughter and served five years.

He disappeared while on probation, somehow stealing the identity of a Colton Wasserman from St. Helena, Montana, who had died about three years before in a nursing home, leaving no surviving relatives.

Margo had an intermediary place an anonymous call to the FBI.

"Jeremy," said the receptionist at AFA, "I have two FBI agents in the lobby. They said they'd like to talk to the company owners. I called you first." Jeremy discreetly sent his longtime assistant Linda to escort them directly to his office. Craft and Carr were coming back from lunch when they noticed the strangers entering Jeremy's office.

Not sure what was going on, they invited themselves into Jeremy's office. He was sitting at his desk, ashen-faced.

One of the men pulled out his badge. "FBI."

"In a nutshell," said Jeremy, "Colton isn't Colton. He's a guy who is wanted for breaking parole after killing his wife's lover and pistol-whipping his wife. They're here to arrest him and extradite him to Pennsylvania."

"Good Christ, we've got to think about how to handle this. The last thing we need right now is another scene," said Craft.

"Jeremy, call Wasserman. Tell him you've got a profit distributions check as a thank you," said Craft. "You fellas — pointing to the FBI agents — stand behind the door. When he gets here, you guys do what you have to do."

"It's called handcuffing and arresting the suspect and reading him his rights," said one of the agents.

Minutes later, a kicking and screaming Bernstein — aka Wasserman —was dragged through the halls to a waiting car.

62.

Costas buries his embarrassment in ballroom dancing.

The Wasserman fiasco left deep scars in Costas's psyche.

He imagined everyone was laughing behind his back since he had identified and hired Wasserman and had been his most vocal internal supporter.

Costas began to eat indiscriminately, sometimes consciously, sometimes subconsciously. His weight ballooned to 280 pounds, transforming his already imposing 6'3" physical presence into a waddling hulk.

His appearance began to affect his relationship with Mona, a workout fanatic who took pride in her shapely body. She hadn't signed up to marry a slovenly middle-aged man. Initially, she was very supportive. "Jeremy, honey, you've got to be a little more aware of your diet, since your job is fairly sedentary." Eventually, though, her motivational prodding became more caustic. "Jeremy, do you see what you look like? People are going to start assuming I'm your daughter."

Mona's incessant chiding continued. Costas gained another twenty pounds. He stood in front of the bedroom mirror, looking at a fat stranger and began to cry. "Look at me, what a mess."

Mona took Costas's self-deprecating comment as an enormous positive. "Baby, I'm so proud of you. You've taken the first step. You can't start to change if you don't recognize the need for change."

"Thank you, Sigmund Freud. Now what? A professionally monitored starvation diet on an uninhabited island?"

"I thought we should try ballroom dancing. My trainer at the Vertical Club was talking about the aerobic and social benefits of ballroom dancing just the other day. She said people who dance regularly have fun while they raise their metabolism and reduce their appetites. And she says ballroom dancing will increase your sex drive."

~

Costas's initial skepticism turned to enthusiasm within a month. He and Mona took some tango, mamba, and waltz lessons with an attractive Latin couple, Louisa and Fernando Batiquitos, who traveled the United States entering ballroom contests. What started as a hobby became a business. Between giving lessons, coaching, and entering competitions, the couple earned almost $500,000 a year.

As Costas's weight declined, Louisa noticed he was becoming increasingly light on his feet. "Jeremeso (her pronunciation of Jeremy)," said Louisa, one evening after practice, "you and Mona are an exceptionally gifted couple. We think you should enter some local contests."

They agreed. Before long, they were practicing three nights a week. Their repertoire and fluidity snowballed, while the weight continued to burn off Jeremy. At the six-month mark, the now 240-pound Costas and his athletic blonde wife, Mona, entered a three-set beginners contest (mambo, tango, and modern jazz) at the Roseland Ballroom on the West Side of Manhattan.

To their delight, they won. The judges gave them a perfect ten for each dance routine. Ballroom dancing was no longer just a means to maintain weight; it became Jeremy's hobby, his passion. The couple practiced and explored new methods whenever they had free moments. Costas's new-found energy also made him more active at the office and a virtual sex machine at home, where two and three times a night, five nights a week, became the norm.

"I've been looking at these American Ballroom Association brochures," said Costas one night over a glass of wine at dinner. "There's an intermediate competition in Las Hadas, Mexico, this spring. It says two hundred sponsored couples will compete for almost half a million dollars in prize money."

"I think that's maybe a little over our heads," said Mona.

"Maybe, maybe not. The entrance fee is $4000, which includes five nights at the resort plus breakfast and unlimited use of the spa. Hell, even if we finished last, it would still be a nice vacation. I've heard the resort is fabulous, though; each casita has a private pool and views of Manzanillo Bay!"

"I'm up for that. But what does 'sponsored' mean?"

"We need a letter of recommendation from a licensed ABA instructor. I'm sure Louisa and Fernando can help there." Once they were approved as entrants, the couple began to practice in earnest. Louisa and Fernando even added a videotape analysis to their sessions. April came, and they were ready.

Upon arrival, they learned there was an orientation session the next day to explain ground rules, practice times, etc. Breakfast was between seven and eight. Each couple was assigned to one of seven lounge areas where they could practice. The contest consisted of four segments, and each couple would be assigned three routines to perform, so contestants had to prepare for every eventuality while maintaining grace under pressure. The four winners in each segment would be those with the most points. The finalists would then compete head-to-head in three additional routines.

Mona and Costas were assigned the mambo, the jitterbug, and the waltz. The increasingly self-confident and graceful couple swept their preliminaries.

"Can you believe all this?" said Costas. "We might win the whole enchilada."

"I'm so proud of us," said Mona, as she reached for his hand. "But, whether we win or lose the competition, we've already won. I've got back that handsome man I married."

~

The first dance of the finals was a waltz. With Costas, Mona glided around the floor as if skating in a puffy pink taffeta gown dotted with silver sequins. The three judges each awarded them ten points. They were tied for first with one other couple.

The second routine was a tango. Mona was dressed in a skin-tight red dress with a slit up to her waist that highlighted her sensual body and long, perfectly proportioned legs. The couple sizzled. Again, they received the maximum scores. They were alone in first place.

The third dance was Costas's absolute favorite: the jitterbug. He was dressed like John Travolta in *Saturday Night Fever*, while

Mona was in a skin-tight miniskirt. As they completed their first over-the-shoulder twirl, Mona slipped out of Costas's hand and landed hard on the floor, breaking the heel of her shoe and severely twisting her ankle. She was unable to walk, much less continue. Costas carried her off the floor. They were both in tears. With no points on the third routine, they finished dead last.

They spent the evening quietly in their room with ice packs on her ankle. "Well, at least we have a few days to relax before we head back," said Mona, trying to cheer Costas.

By morning, Mona's leg had taken a turn for the worse. She had a nasty red streak up to her knee and was running a 103° fever. She was rushed to the emergency room at the Las Hadas Medical Center, generally considered one of the best teaching hospitals in Mexico.

"Very rare," said the doctor. "It is a good thing she arrived when she did. She has a blood clot, and it's moving rapidly toward her heart. I believe she will be fine, but we must make sure the infection is under control and that the clot has dissipated before she can travel, which may be about six days, assuming all goes well."

Costas wanted the best of care for his Mona, so he arranged for a private room and a private nurse to remain by her side during the night.

"I am Consuelo Maria Gomez," said the stunning nurse, who had long black hair and dark brown eyes. "No worries; I will make sure your wife receives special care. My specialty is wealthy women with caring husbands. Senor Jagger stares like you when I watch Bianca. No worries."

Costas wondered how Consuelo knew they had money.

~

The next morning, Costas arrived to find Mona smiling in bed, all made up. "You look great for a patient who almost died last night.

Consuelo held Mona's hand as she said, "Woman must look beautiful for her man, si?"

"Si," responded Costas.

That evening, after Costas left, Consuelo returned carrying a small bag. "Consuelo bring Mona a little present."

"I love presents," said Mona, noticing Consuelo's ample cleavage and erect nipples bursting out of the top of her uniform. Consuelo held up a sheer black nightgown. "Thees make you feel much better than a hospital gown."

Mona looked into Consuelo's sensual eyes. She could feel her heart pounding. Consuelo slowly removed the hospital gown while exploring Mona's equally ample breasts. "Husband a lucky man," purred Consuelo. Mona sat frozen as Consuelo slowly pulled the gown over her head and began to caress Mona's hard, erect nipples in the process. Mona reached to open Consuelo's dress. They explored each other's bodies and then kissed.

"Would the nurse like to help the patient in bed?"

Consuelo nodded. They spent the entire evening making love. Again. And again. And again.

For the next three days, Costas would arrive at 8:00 A.M. and spend the day with his wife. When he left, Consuelo would return for an increasingly uninhibited evening in bed.

On the fourth morning, the doctor proudly announced, "Mrs. Costas, tomorrow it will be safe for you to travel home."

The next morning, when Costas arrived to pick up his wife, Consuelo was present. "Jeremy, I'm not going home," said Mona. "I've decided to stay in Las Hadas and move in with Consuelo." She walked over to Consuelo, held her hand tightly, and kissed her on the lips.

~

Costas' temper returned with a vengeance. First, he beat the shit out of Consuelo, then Mona. The more Mona screamed, the harder he hit. Now a bloody mess, Mona ripped the blow dryer out of the bathroom and pounded Costas, till he also fell to the floor with blood spewing from his lips.

Consuelo than ran out the door. Minutes later, the security guards arrived and summarily threw Mr. and Mrs. Costas off the resort grounds. As the story goes, Mona somehow made it to the airport and got back to the states.

Costas was never heard from again. Eddie Carr weaved a story at AFA that Costas had committed suicide by drowning at the nearby beach. But there was no death certificate and his body was never recovered. Interestingly, his bank accounts were emptied and his Facebook and LinkedIn page disappeared.

Mona — with no assets, no cash, and no visible means of support — declared bankruptcy and went to work slinging hash at a local diner.

Costas's disappearance, the Wasserman fiasco, and my sudden exit all worked to leave the business consultants and their licensed advisors rattled. The exodus began.

63.

Craft's excesses create personal and corporate calamity.

Despite the turmoil and the resulting decline in AFA revenues, the remaining partners, Craft and Carr, acted like it was business as usual. Carr traveled the States looking for miniature antique cars to add to his museum-quality collection, while his wife Evelyn continued to add $250,000 additions to their house like it was popcorn.

Craft, a Las Vegas junkie with a gambling addiction, continued to play craps, blackjack, and baccarat, often losing $50,000 in an evening without breaking a sweat. The MGM Grand and Wynn casinos sucked up to his ego by tossing a broad menu of VIP high roller perks his way. They were like cocaine for his ego.

One of those perks was Amélie Bonard, a charming, intelligent French woman who always seemed to appear when Craft came to visit. Interestingly, she didn't seem to know the difference between snake eyes and boxcars. After a few evenings at the tables, Craft, a 47-year-old confirmed bachelor, was convinced she was the woman of his dreams. They married six months later, with the usually cautious Craft requiring no prenuptial agreements.

Amélie was quite comfortable playing the role of Mrs. High Roller, and she spent Craft's money like water as Craft went from living in a one-bedroom apartment to a $6 million, five-acre estate in Westport with waterfalls and a putting green. To make it homey, Amélie spent another $2 million on furnishings.

Throughout the entire home-buying and decorating process, Craft had only one request — that Amélie add a $750,000 designer cottage on the ground so Amélie's parents — John, a retired policeman, and his wife Martha, a retired schoolteacher — could enjoy their grandchildren. Craft's mom and dad had died in an automobile accident almost a decade earlier after begging him, as an only child, to get married so they could have some grandchildren.

~

Despite his Machiavellian business tactics, Craft's parental guilt made him a dedicated family man. Father-in-law John loved the opera, so Craft had a custom sound system installed in every room of the grandparents' cottage and fifty operas programmed into the system as a housewarming gift. Extended vacations became family affairs with Dawson and Amélie and John and Martha as a foursome.

Within the first year, Amélie became pregnant. Tests showed it was a boy. The plan was for baby Paul to become an immediate member of the Craft vacation entourage as soon as he arrived on the scene. Craft didn't want to miss a moment of his child's growth.

Craft felt his baby's first movement in Amélie's womb. He knew his spontaneous gambling junkets were about to end. "We should plan on early arrival," advised the obstetrician, "since Amélie has gained 37 pounds during the first six months and that baby is kicking up a storm. I would also suggest you restrict her activities a bit."

Craft, who had a history of hearing what he wanted to hear, ignored the doctor's reduced activity prescription. Instead, Craft began planning the junket of a lifetime. He would host a surprise weekend of gambling in Monte Carlo. They would fly by private chartered jet and stay in the presidential suite at the Hotel de Paris, the country's most luxurious hotel, which had every possible amenity including a performing opera house designed by noted French architect Charles Garnier in 1854. Luciano Pavarotti would be performing *La Bohème* while they were there, one of John's all-time favorites. To break up the monotony of a weekend of gambling, Craft had also arranged for his pilot to fly the group over the Grand Gorge in Provence, the French equivalent of America's Grand Canyon, and land at a private airstrip nearby to savor a languid lunch at world-famous chef Allen Ducasse's noted eatery, Bastide de Moustiers.

"Folks, are we ready to go? The car is here," said Craft, noticing the tiny bags his in-laws and Amélie had packed.

"Las Vegas, here we come," smiled Amélie.

As they got to JFK, the limo driver passed terminal after terminal.

"Dawson," whispered Amélie, "does he know where he's going?"

Dawson pointed to a sign: "Private Terminal." The limo came to a halt two hundred yards from a white Boeing Executive Jetliner.

Craft walked over to the staircase. "Ladies and gentlemen, your chariot awaits you. All aboard to Monte Carlo!"

The speechless threesome climbed the stairs to the welcoming smiles of their crew. "Mrs. Craft," said the captain, "We sincerely hope you enjoy your weekend. Best I can tell, your husband has thought of everything."

Over the next seven hours, they were pampered to death with food, drinks, and massages. "That trip was the most incredible experience, I've ever had," said Amélie as the entourage arrived at the Hotel de Paris.

"Don't be so quick to judge," said Craft, knowing there was lots more to come.

They were speechless at spectacular 70-foot hotel entry, and they loved being spoiled by the doting staff as they toured their twelve-room presidential suite.

"I've scheduled massages for about 9:30 P.M.," smiled Craft. That should give everybody a chance to get a little sleep. They're expecting us in the baccarat salon around midnight."

After massages, champagne, dinner, and five hours of private baccarat, the group was pleasantly tired and Amélie was $103,000 richer. "I simply couldn't believe my luck tonight," said Amélie.

Dawson Craft lovingly stared into his wife's light blue eyes. "Me, too."

~

The next day's schedule consisted of flying over the Grand Gorge at 6,000 feet. It was a perfectly sunny day, so the gorge's blue and green veins were beyond spectacular. The plane carefully came to rest on a modest airstrip at the top of the gorge, surrounded by lavender fields, where a waiting limo drove them to the 200-year-old restored stone farmhouse which housed the Bastide. For the next four hours, they sat at a seventeenth-century gilded mahogany table overlooking a hillside covered in yellows and pinks and lavender. Each course of the meal was a masterpiece. The finale was a cheese platter containing eighteen different kinds of cheese.

"You enjoy," said the Chef-Owner Allen Du Casse with a heavy French accent. "I try to make you remember. Maybe you visit my new place in Manhattan. It shall be called simply, Du Casse. But Monsieurs and Mesdames, at the price of New York rents, it will not be possible to do four hours. We do that here. So, you come back."

"Allen, this has been delightful. We will follow your food anywhere," smiled Amélie.

The group returned to the hotel for the performance of *La Bohème,* which left John speechless. At midnight, they returned to play a little more baccarat. The plane wasn't scheduled to head home till morning. They never left the baccarat room. After breakfast, they headed straight to the plane in their formal attire, knowing that they could change, shower, and rest on the way back.

~

About an hour into the flight, Amélie began getting a little nauseous. "Do you want to the plane to turn around and go back to Monte Carlo?" asked a concerned Craft.

"No, I think if I just go and lie down quietly in our salon for a while, I'll be okay." But about halfway across the Atlantic, she started screaming in the stateroom. Dawson ran in. The bed and Amélie were covered in blood mixed with vomit.

"We've got to get this plane down right now!" shouted Craft.

"Sir, I'm sorry, but we are three hours from any place where we could land safely. We're doing all we can. The captain has already called ahead for an ambulance to meet us at the JFK terminal. He has obtained emergency clearance, and he's going almost 700 miles an hour."

There was fear in Amélie's eyes. Martha and John were trying to keep their daughter calm.

"Don't you have anything on board to sedate her?"

"I have two valium injections that I could administer." He did. Amélie fell into a deep twilight. The stewardess carefully administered some oxygen.

The plane landed and Amélie was rushed to New York Hospital. But it was too late; baby Paul Craft was stillborn.

~

About a month later, Amélie filed for divorce. It turned out she had been having an affair for months with an unnamed field producer she met when she was Craft's assistant. She took Craft to court to obtain an obscene settlement. Angered about being a laughingstock, Craft's instinct for self-preservation took hold: he had the stillborn baby's DNA analyzed. The kid was not Craft's.

Craft hired the nastiest lawyer he could find. In the court proceedings, Amélie was awarded zero spousal support. Her attorney appealed the verdict on the grounds that she had been physically abused during their marriage, which caused the stillbirth. Amélie was awarded 50 percent of Craft's assets, forcing him to liquidate almost everything he owed at fire-sale prices.

The messy drama played out in the halls of AFA — the trickle of departures gave way to a mass exodus.

64.

Alexandria searches for life after AFA.

Alexandria struggled to find a job in New York, given the carnage she left behind at AFA.

Her sister, Tori, was having an equally difficult time selling their mother's house in Lincoln. "Alex, Lincoln is certainly not Manhattan. Two more factories just shut down, and with interest rates rising, the best offer we've gotten is $112,000 before real estate commissions and other selling expenses. My guess is we'll have no alternative but to settle for the low bid."

"Sis," said Alexandria, "Remember how you were always saying, 'Why live in New York when your roots are Nebraska?' Well, suppose I told you that I've decided to move back to Nebraska?"

"I'd be skeptical. I thought you loved the action and were making a ton of money."

"It's a long, long story that needs to be shared over bottles and bottles of wine. I'd like to propose a solution on Mom's house. Why don't I come and live there and pay you a 50 percent of fair market value, since we own the place equally?"

"That's okay with me," said Tori, " but be forewarned — Mom and Dad didn't do much to the place in their later years."

"That's okay. After living in apartments for so long, it might be fun sprucing up the old place."

Tori sensed there were financial problems, because in all the years they had lived at home, Alexandria had done absolutely nothing around the house. But since Tori and her family didn't need her share of the house proceeds any time soon and the extra cash flow was found money, she cheerfully agreed.

"Welcome home, sis."

~

The drive to Nebraska gave Alexandria the chance to develop a job search plan.

She concluded that her best job option was her dad's old friend Norman Holbrook, who owned a medium-sized financial services company called Main Street Associates in downtown Lincoln. The thirty-year-old firm had about 125 licensed independent securities representatives. She had done a little research and found he only had one business consultant who communicated new financial product offerings and firm services to the field. Also, the number of representatives and the firm's total revenues had been flat for the past three years. Norman, now 72, didn't appear to have an heir apparent, family or otherwise.

"Norman," said Plummet on her cell phone. "Guess who's little girl is coming to town?"

"Alexandria! I'd recognize that determined little voice anywhere. You've still got the same inflections as your father Fred, may God rest his soul. What brings you back after all these years? Getting bored with the Big Apple?' teased Holbrook.

"Norman, life has been interesting, but I've decided it's time to rediscover my roots."

"Where are you thinking of living?"

"Tori and I have already agreed. I'm going to live in Mom's old place."

"Sounds like you're all set. If there's anything else I can do for Fred and Cecelia's little girl, she need only ask."

"Well, as a matter of fact, there is. Frank Graves said you were growing nicely."

"Ah, the widower Graves, Lincoln's most eligible bachelor. Didn't he take you to the senior prom before that Mary Lou girl snatched him from right under your nose?"

"That was 30 years ago. Right now, I could use a job. I was think my twenty years in the securities industry coaching independent reps might be quite useful on Main Street."

"I'm sure we can find something for you to do. But, Lincoln, Nebraska's pay scales are not like Manhattan."

"I understand that, Norman. I've done well financially, so I'm more interested in finding the right long-term situation."

"Or until Frank pops the question, whichever comes first," laughed Norman.

~

After stopping by Tori's house to say hello and pick up the keys, she headed for the old house, where a surprise awaited her —- two dozen yellow roses and a picture of Frank and Alexandria from the high school prom, signed, "Welcome home, Frank."

Alexandria had another surprise when she arrived at Main Street Associates. The firm was physically more attractive than she had imagined: sleek modern offices located in a shiny glass-skinned building in the heart of a modest but thriving section of downtown Lincoln. And she was surprised by the energy level — flat monitor quote screens, the latest news broadcast on 85" HD monitors, and phones ringing everywhere.

"Is it always like this?" asked Alexandria.

"Friday's our slow day," said the receptionist. "Wait till Monday, when Norman introduces the new variable option series from Templeton on his weekly video conference. The place will be a madhouse."

65.

Some things never change.

Norman was as Alexandria remembered. A Jimmy Stewart look-alike, tall and lean with steel gray hair and a million-dollar smile that telegraphed, *Life is good.*

He had spent his entire life in Lincoln, except for three years in the Air Force during the Korean conflict, where he rose to major and won the Congressional Medal of Honor for providing ground cover to a trapped battalion at less than 1000 feet. Norman had graduated from the University of Nebraska with a degree in finance and married his college sweetheart, Mary Fender. They had five children, all sons, one of whom died in Vietnam. Norman and Mary had sixteen grandchildren.

Along the way, he'd started Main Street Associates, which had made him wealthy. Norman's only regret was that none of his children or grandchildren had any interest in the business. At seventy-two, he had two interests: reduce his twelve-hour days, and groom the next generation of management — or find a strategic buyer.

"Alexandria, you're still pretty as a picture," said Norman as he feigned shock. "Oh my God, am I allowed to say that?" Alexandria had a Martin flashback. " So, what have you been doing all this time in New York?"

Alexandria explained how she had first become a product wholesaler for two securities companies, where she'd called on independent financial advisors as well as broker-dealers. And then about how *she* helped build AFA into a financial powerhouse. She was compelling, articulate, and specific about her strengths.

The two talked for over an hour. Norman introduced her to most of the forty-eight-person staff. One of the young bucks, John Stern at the trading desk, decided to test her wit. "Is it true your Norman's new squeeze?"

"He's a little too young for me," smiled Alexandria. " I like my men a bit more mature."

Norman laughed as they returned to his office. "Alexandria, I don't know if this is fate or what, but you have all these skills and experiences that don't find their way to Lincoln very often. And I loved the way you handled Stern."

"Oh, I wouldn't be concerned about him. He's just an arrogant young man who needs his balls smacked from time to time."

"I bet beneath that highly female facade beats the heart of a woman who could do just that," said Norman lightheartedly. "But a word of caution. My firm has a considerable number of Christian Right married employees, and they attract the same type of licensed field producers. I'm not looking for someone to make a social statement; I'm looking for an experienced financial professional to teach our consultants how to increase their producers' revenue. We've built a familial culture over the last thirty years. If you're going to be a member of my senior staff, I need you to embrace and enhance our culture."

"Shall we talk comp?" asked Alexandria, bored with the chatter about corporate culture and the Christian Right.

"Let's," smiled Norman, amused by and yet concerned about Alexandria's charming directness. "I'd like to make you the director of advisory services, which means you'd oversee everything related to communicating with our reps. I'll give you a base of $70,000 to start, plus an override of one percent on the firm's volume. I'm guessing that would give you a first-year package of about $100,000, plus expenses."

"I'm accustomed to earning quite a bit more," said Alexandria, beginning to haggle.

Norman shut her down. "Alexandria, this is Lincoln, Nebraska. Things are what they are; we don't negotiate."

Alexandria looked at Norman's poker face. He wasn't bluffing. She not only wanted the job; she desperately needed the job. Alexandria reached to shake Norman's hand. "That seems like an extremely fair offer."

"That's what I like: a person who can make a decision rather than lollygag around."

Alexandria decided a little female charm wouldn't hurt at this point — she subtly blinked her eyes. "Norman, if there is one thing I've never been accused of, it's lollygagging."

66.

Frank brings a little sunshine.

"So, how did the interview with Norman go?" said the voice on the other end of the cell phone.

"My goodness," smiled Alexandria. "Frank Graves, how did you know Norman and I met today?"

"Cornhuskers have our ways. How about lunch?"

~

The Metropole Café was a surprisingly authentic French bistro sitting in the heart of the Palace Du Jardin, a formal park filled with gently trickling fountains that were clearly visible through the bistro's large picture windows.

"My, my, Lincoln has grown up," said Alexandria, looking around the restaurant.

"My, my," said Frank looking at Alexandria with a Cheshire grin, "so has Alexandria."

Frank simply meant how attractive she looked. Alexandria misunderstood. She thought he had noticed that she had a breast augmentation surgery since the last time they met at her mom's funeral.

"You men are all alike; its breasts first, brains second."

Frank stared blankly. "Alexandria, what the hell are you babbling about?"

Alexandria realized she had assumed too much. "Oh, I'm sorry, I thought you were referring to my new boob job."

"Maybe you've been in New York a little too long. In Nebraska, men don't typically comment on a woman's breasts the first time they have lunch," smiled Frank. "We usually wait until the second or third date!"

After they were seated, Alexandria said, "Why don't we start all over again. What do you recommend?"

"One of my favorites is the Coquille Saint Jacques."

"That sounds yummy but heavy."

"It's prepared with a surprisingly delicate beurre blanc sauce."

Frank's sophisticated palate impressed her.

"By the way, I meant to thank you," said Frank, "for dumping me on our prom night… all those years ago. When the prom was over, most of us were feeling no pain with all that champagne. You and I and Mary Lou Vuono and her date Jeremy Schrader went to a new night club. Jeremy somehow had gotten VIP passes.

"By the time I parked the car, you and Jeremy had slipped around back and were making out like crazy in the alley. Mary Lou and I were so pissed we just left you having at it."

"I'm so, so sorry."

"It didn't turn out so badly — Mary Lou and I were so mad we drove down to Fisher's Lake with a bottle of cheap wine and made out for hours. That was my first experience with sex on the rebound. Before long, Mary Lou and I were dating. During our college years, we became a serious item. By the time I was in graduate school, we were engaged. Two years later, we got married.

"Mary Lou and I respected our Midwestern values; they were a part of us. We wanted our kids to have the same value systems before they set out into the world. With my Wharton degrees, we could have lived virtually anywhere. But when Texas Instruments came to town, we decided to stay home."

"I know you're a widower, but that's all," said Alexandria.

"Mary Lou graduated from Nebraska Wesleyan while I was in graduate school. By the time I finished getting my degrees, she had established a thriving little commercial design company. After we married, she decided to give it all up and focus on the family." A tear rolled down his cheek. "God, I loved that woman. On her fortieth birthday, we discovered she had an inoperable brain tumor. She was a fighter; never complained. She lived another three years. I raised my two boys, Josh and Edward, by myself. They are fine boys, her gift to the world."

"How long has it been?"

"It's almost ten years, but it feels like yesterday. I know this is going to sound weird, but would you like to take a ride to the cemetery after lunch and say hello? Today's her birthday."

"It would be my honor," said Alexandria politely.

"And what about Alexandria? The last time we talked after your mom's funeral, it was all about work, work, work."

Alexandria looked at Frank. He was unlike any man she had ever met. He was so genuine.

"My story has some of the same highs and lows, mostly the latter. I guess your recollection of Jeremy encapsulates the kind of woman sitting beside you. All my life, I've assumed there was something better. I was happily engaged to one guy, then found somebody else. Married him, had two children quickly. He decided to leave me because he said *he* found something better.

"After a bunch of court fights, he disappeared completely, leaving me broke and penniless. I took whatever jobs I could find. Eventually, through a lot of hard work, I got a decent career started in financial services. Then I met this other guy. He was ten years younger than me. I figured I could have better sex with him than a man my age. Brilliant reasoning, huh?

"Turns out he had a major drug habit. I tried to keep things together, but I got tired of supporting the entire family and his habit. When we divorced, the courts made me pay him a settlement because he had no visible means of support. Along the way, my lifestyle and failed marriages turned my oldest daughter, Shanti, off to men. As you probably know, she hanged herself."

Alexandria paused, rubbed her cheek, and pushed the hair back from her swollen red eyes. "Then I fucked up again. I met this married guy at my last job. I think I loved him. We went out a lot. I tried to force him to leave his wife of thirty-five years. He wouldn't. I cooked up a sexual harassment complaint out of anger. In the end, I embarrassed him; he had to resign. Who knows what I did to his marriage and his relationship with his two sons? They were very nice young men. I'm so ashamed. I wish I could take it all back. Frank, you're a very nice man. You don't want to get involved with a woman like me."

"Why don't you let me be the judge of that?" responded Frank.

67.

Gabby gets involved.

"Gabby, I wish I could take back the other day," Lauren said over lunch in a quiet corner of the cafeteria.

"After you explained what was happening, everything made sense," replied Gabby. "For the last few weeks, you haven't seemed like the Lauren I know. I was starting to wonder if the administration threw too much at you too fast."

"Has anybody said anything to you?"

"No. But then, I'm not sure anyone has the same level of interest in you, personally."

Gabby's relaxed manner made Lauren feel comfortable about sharing her thoughts. "You know, my entire life has been shaped and driven by my *circumstances of life* philosophy. I believe life is divided into three boxes — a business box, a family box, and a relationship box. The trick is to keep them in balance, although from time to time, circumstances cause them to expand and contract. Whenever I have had pressures or crises in a given box, I remind myself not to let it spill over into the other parts of my life. If I encounter a professional problem, I never let it affect my relationship with Martin. I solve the problem in that box."

"Do you really believe life is that neat and orderly?"

She ignored his question. "People resort to shrinks because they've allowed separate and distinct emotional issues to comingle. For the first time in my life, the boxes seem to be opening at the same time, and I'm not sure what to do."

"The more I listen to you, the more concerned I become. Nobody can live their whole life in neat boxes. Life is are too many non-controllables. Besides, if everything is in a neat little box, how can you experience all life has to offer? I believe you're supposed to take life by the horns and enjoy it."

"Gabby, what are you suggesting?"

"Lots of things. But first and foremost, I think you and Martin need to talk to someone professionally before you guys explode in rage and frustration."

"You're suggesting a psychiatrist, a marriage counselor, a psychologist? You may be right, but I don't even know where and how to start."

"Lauren, I've never engaged anyone myself, but I suspect our human resource group might be able to help. Given some of the stuff we see around here, they must deal with patient counseling."

Lauren was reluctant. "The last thing I need are rumors flying around the office that Lauren is in counseling."

"I believe under New York state law, employee confidentiality must be maintained. All you want is a few references; nothing will go into your personnel file. If it makes you feel more comfortable, get an agreement from the HR Director Margaret Graves before you discuss any specifics.

Lauren did just that. She went and talked to Margaret off the record. Margaret suggested three different doctors whom the hospital had worked with before: Reuben Marles, Ph.D.; and Drs. Nancy Cotite and Diana Jones. Lauren spoke to all three. She choose Doctor Jones because she seemed to have considerably more marriage counseling experience.

The doctor insisted that for the counseling to work, both parties had to be present at the sessions. Lauren knew that Martin had historically made deprecating remarks about friends and associates who needed shrinks to help them solve their problems. So, she had to be persuasive and tread lightly at the same time.

"Martin, I want us to talk to someone together. I've heard your explanations, but I think I need an objective third party to listen; some things just don't make sense."

"We don't need a shrink. We've always been able to talk things through."

"I don't need your insensitive, condescending attitude right now."

"I'm sorry. I just want things to be like they were before."

"Martin, I don't honestly know if that's possible."

She told me about Dr. Jones. We met for the first time the following Monday, after business hours. I was nervous and skeptical; I had no idea what to expect.

~

The physical setup at Dr. Jones' office gave me the creeps. Instead of a one-person private office, Lauren and I were ushered into a general waiting room that serviced multiple psychiatrists, each with their own area of specialty.

At one end sat a mother with her fidgety son, who appeared to be about five or six. She was trying to make him focus on his coloring books. The boy had the attention span of an ant, while the mother had the patience of a saint. "Now Jonathan, it's not very nice to color the chair. Please use your coloring book."

To our left sat a couple who looked like they had just survived the Titanic. Their bulging eyes darted around the room, while their hands tapped and shook. They took turns calming each other down.

I looked at Lauren; she looked at me. We scratched our heads silently.

A dour-looking woman in her mid-forties came to the waiting room and called out, "Mr. and Mrs. Ruff." I sheepishly raised my hand. Lauren and I silently followed her down an empty hall to a well-appointed corner office with the obligatory couch and a few large Georgia O'Keeffe prints on the walls, to add a touch of humanity. There wasn't a personal clue anyway: no papers, no mementos, no degrees, and no family pictures.

"Mr. Ruff?" she said, looking straight at me. "Since I've already chatted briefly with Mrs. Ruff about the nature of your situation, let me give you a little of my background. I've been doing marriage counseling for the better part of a decade, so I've pretty much seen it all. Mr. Ruff, why don't you tell us what's transpired to bring you here."

I began to tell the Alexandria Plummet story and the events leading up to the suit.

Lauren interrupted. "Are you lying? How could you go out that many times and never have sex?"

I was surprised by the question. Lauren and I had been over this many times. She even had a copy of my written response to the company.

"Lauren, I'm not sure what you want me to say."

"She wants you to answer the question," glared Dr. Jones, whom I sensed had already taken sides.

"Doctor, we've discussed this same question at home on numerous occasions."

"Lauren either didn't hear you or didn't believe you. Please help her; answer the question."

I turned to Lauren and looked directly into her eyes. "Honey, I told you we never crossed the line."

"But you wanted to?" asked the doctor.

"Yes."

"See, you lied to me again!" Lauren was visibly shaken.

"Honey, I love you. I made a stupid mistake, and I hope you'll forgive me. But I've told you absolutely everything."

"Mr. Ruff, do you know what your wife is asking?"

"Can I ever again be trusted?"

"No, she's asking if you love her. It's amazing how many men are blind to the real issues."

"First of all, Doctor, I take offense to your accusatory tone. Secondly, she knows I love her. I've always loved her and always will."

"Right now, I need to hear that. I'm no longer sure," said Lauren.

"This is not about Mrs. Ruff. Time's almost up, but I'd like to give you a little homework for our next session. I'd like you to tell your wife that you love her in as many ways and as many times as you can during the next week."

"Doctor, I've written love letters and poems to my wife all our lives. I bet my friends I was going to marry her the first time I saw her. I know how and when to tell my wife I love her."

"Apparently not, Mr. Ruff. Might I remind you that your marriage is on the rocks? I'm trying to help save it."

"Did you tell her you were going to leave me for her?" asked Lauren out of the blue.

"No."

"Did you imply it?"

"Not really."

"See, you're lying again! I'm a woman; I know how women think. You couldn't spend all that time together, send her flowers and gifts, and then say there was no commitment."

Lauren had a point. At the same time, the real answer was I did those things with the belief that at some point, I'd get into her pants. "You're right, Lauren. I probably did lead her on."

I could see in Lauren's eyes she wanted to believe me. I could see in Doctor Jones' eyes she didn't want Lauren to believe.

"I think Lauren is right on the point here. Since the time is up, I would suggest you talk that out more fully at home."

Mercifully, the painful session was over. I didn't have the heart to tell Lauren I hated Dr. Jones' guts.

"How did you feel about the session?" she asked.

"Interesting start," was about as tactful of a response as I could muster.

"I feel the same way," said Lauren. "She's great!"

68.

The relationship with Dr. Jones becomes strained.

Unlike session one, there were no prelims the next time.

"Why do you think they hate you so much at AFA? I thought they were your partners," opened Lauren.

"As I told you, honey, it's all about the money. The guys have their life savings invested in the company. We don't. They want to distance themselves from the situation."

"But Evelyn, Amélie, and Mona were my friends. We went shopping. We had lunch together, took trips. Do you know how embarrassed I feel? I can't even look any of them in the face. I'm the one with the husband who cheated. You broke my trust. You lied and cheated. How can you sit there and say that's not an affair? I mean, how would you feel if I did that to you with one of the doctors?"

"Lauren, I believe Martin agrees his actions were unconscionable. Correct, Martin?"

"Yes."

"Is there anything else you'd like to say to your wife?"

"Yes, honey, if I had it to do all over again, this would have never happened. I want to settle the lawsuit and figure out where I stand with my partners. Most importantly, I want to get on with our life. Lauren and I have so many great memories over the last thirty-five years; I promise I will never do anything like that again."

Lauren stared at me for a long time. "All I can do is take it one day at a time. You hurt me so deeply; you have no idea. As for our sons, they'll never look at you the same way again.

Session two was over.

~

Session three revealed Lauren's anger over what she perceived as my vindictive countersuit strategy. "How could you and Miss Pin Up even think like that?"

"Who's Miss Pin Up? Think like what?" asked Dr. Jones, realizing she missed some recent developments.

"First of all, my husband hired this sexy attorney with long black hair and a drop-dead body."

"Is that true, Mr. Ruff?"

"Margo Margoles comes highly recommended as one of New York's leading harassment attorneys. I had no idea what she looked like before our first in-person meeting."

"Recommended by whom?"

"My attorney and friend of over twenty years, that's who!"

"Please, Mr. Ruff, don't get testy with me. I'm trying to help. Surely you realize that, given your wife's fragile condition, selecting an attractive female counsel may not have been the wisest course?"

Lauren sensed Dr. Jones was on her side, which gave her the confidence to continue her verbal assault.

"As I said last night, after working so closely together for five years, how could you hate each other so much? Suing and countersuing and putting liens on people's houses? Dr. Jones, you wouldn't believe what Martin's planning to do."

I was getting frustrated with the process. It seemed clear that whatever I said at home had to be repeated in the presence of Dr. Jones.

"I told you, this is just business. What else do you want me to say?"

"Mr. Ruff, Lauren seems troubled by your Machiavellian sense of ethics. Maybe you can help me here?"

After a few sessions with Dr. Jones, I was starting to get the drill. "Maybe you can help me" meant "What ridiculously stupid thing are you planning to do next?"

"Dr. Jones, we're talking business strategy. It's different from the way people conduct themselves in hospital settings."

"Mr. Ruff, please watch your condescending tone. It doesn't help matters."

"All I meant was that nonprofit hospitals and for-profit businesses are two different working environments. At a hospital, the focus is on helping people get better; in business, the focus is on how to make the most money. People are secondary."

"Mr. Ruff, I'm not sure I would agree with that statement."

"Doctor, at the risk of sounding rude, how many businesses have you run?"

"I'm not sure that's relevant."

"It's quite relevant, because it provides insight into how business people think. My partners are opportunists. They are trying to capitalize on my lapse in judgment with Alexandria to squeeze at least a million bucks out of me. If I were them, I'd do the same thing. Fortunately, I'm a little more sophisticated than they are. The morons left themselves open for a defamation of character suit. I'm going to sue their ass for $10 million."

"On what grounds?"

"Ladies, I don't need grounds. They sued me, I'm within my rights to countersue."

"What are you trying to accomplish?" asked Dr. Jones.

"Simple: pull the suit or I'll bury you. Their attorney will get the message. We'll negotiate, then settle. It's nothing personal."

"Do you think that's normal behavior?" stared Dr. Jones.

"In the context of business, it's standard operating procedure!"

For the first time in three sessions, the doctor was speechless.

~

I had no intention of having another session, but I had to approach the subject with Lauren delicately.

"Lauren, I know you're fond of Dr. Jones, but I've got to be honest with you. I sense she dislikes me, with her accusatory tone and her condescending questioning. She's so anti-men it reeks out of her pores. Without an objective coach, I sense we might reach a state of diminishing returns pretty quickly."

"What do you want me to do?"

"I don't want you to do anything. I love you. I just wanted you to know how I feel."

During the next two weeks, I received hundreds of fantastic cards, notes, and letters from employees and producers alike, thanking me for helping them grow personally and professionally. None was more gratifying than the handwritten note from my former assistant Courtney Street.

> *Dear Martin,*
>
> *As we prepare to go our separate ways, there are so many thoughts going through my mind that I want to convey.*
>
> *Having you as my mentor, I learned so much. You took this punk kid and gave me responsibility, never wavering in your support. You guided me when I needed guidance, weren't shy to point out when I was wrong (sometimes over my shouts and vehement disclaimers), and you challenged me to be the best I could be, always. You taught me the meaning of personal growth.*
>
> *No matter where my career takes me, you will always be the most fantastic boss I will ever have. You are the standard against which all my future bosses will be measured.*
>
> *On the personal side, you were like a father and an older brother. You taught me values; you gave me self-confidence; you made me into a woman that someday will find a man like you to marry and have a beautiful family like you and Lauren. Of course, I know that won't be a small task because guys like you don't grow on trees. You are indeed one in ten million.*
>
> *Love always and forever,*
> *Courtney*

I handed the note to Lauren. A few days later, Lauren told me she canceled the doctor's upcoming sessions via email.

~

Dr. Jones was not quite finished with me. She called Lauren at work.

"I don't normally make a call like this, Mrs. Ruff, but since I received your message about discontinuing our professional relationship, and I thought I at least owed you a verbal debrief."

"That's very kind of you," said Lauren. "This has been a very difficult time for me."

"Mrs. Ruff, my impression is your husband has the classical characteristics of a dominant; by contrast, you are what we call a nurturer. Nurturers have above average intuitions but choose to let others make the final decision, rather than create conflict. Dominants must have the final word. Their primary tactics are fear and misrepresentation."

"Are you telling me I let my husband have his way?"

"Let me answer that with a question. What caused you to cancel?"

"Martin showed me this lovely letter from his office staff."

"Lauren, you're a smart woman. There is something your husband is not telling us. In my professional opinion, unless the cloud hanging over your relationship clears, your marriage will remain strained."

"I think I know Martin pretty well after thirty-six years of marriage."

"Ask yourself something. In all that time, how often have you gotten what *you* wanted when there was a difference of opinion?"

69.

Regaining Lauren's trust becomes more complicated than imagined.

I walked in the door with a single yellow rose and announced, "It's our thirty-sixth anniversary and I've made plans to woo you back."

"That's it? One yellow rose?" she smiled.

"How about a corner suite at the Carlyle Hotel and two tickets in the lounge for a special show?"

"Well, at least you're moving in the right direction," she teased. The Carlyle was Lauren's favorite hotel since our first stay on our wedding night; it was romantic, comfortable, and ultra-sophisticated. I had ordered a dozen long-stemmed yellow roses for the entrance foyer, the living room, and our bedroom. After a brief but intense romantic interlude, we had cocktails drinks in the jewel box lounge, followed by a romantic candlelit dinner in the corner of the dining room.

"Mrs. Ruff," said our old friend Maître d' Jameson Whitcomb, kissing her hand. "How do you do it? Thirty years pass and Jameson has gotten old and gray. But you," he said, blowing a kiss, "Magnifico, you never change."

On Saturday, Lauren purchased a few whimsical gifts for her children and grandchildren at the E.A.T. Gift shop. As we strolled down Madison Avenue, we passed the Max Mara store. I suggested she might like a new dress. She shrugged unenthusiastically. I asked why she wasn't interested.

"That's just me. You should know that by now," she replied.

As the sun began to set, I suggested we return to the hotel to rest and shower before an evening on the town. She stared at me and asked, "Are you serious, or is that your way of saying *let's have another roll in the hay*?"

Dinner was at The Four Seasons, another Lauren favorite. While most people remember the place for its timeless modernity, flawless cuisine, and impeccable service, Lauren had other memories. It was at the bar that we once chatted with comedian Joan Rivers and her cerebral husband Edgar the week before he committed suicide!

I looked at my watch. It was almost 10:15 P.M.; the last show at the hotel began at 10:45 P.M. Lauren insisted on a Four Seasons dessert specialty called Chocolate Decadence — three layers of dark, rich chocolate held together with the tiniest sprinkling of flour-less flour, covered in thick, chocolate frosting.

"Honey, I don't want to rush you, but we've got a show to catch — a surprise."

Our cab stopped in front of the Carlyle.

"This is the surprise?"

"Honey, Steve Tyrell opened at the Café Carlyle tonight." I knew she was mad about his music, so I worked a little magic (a $100 tip) to make sure we had a ringside table. I also wrote Steve a note, explaining that my wife was a huge fan and wanted to wish him a spectacular success on his first engagement at the lounge. I also mentioned we were celebrating our anniversary. I hoped that he might mention her name.

About halfway through his set in the packed room, Tyrell began to talk to the audience. "You know, this old barroom singer never thought he'd get to perform in such elegant surroundings at sixty. My wife Juliana believed in me more than I believed in myself, so I kept plugging. It's too bad she isn't here tonight." (His wife had died of stomach cancer just six months earlier.)

"But, as luck would have it, there's a lovely lady in the front who's celebrating her 35th anniversary this weekend." Jameson had told Tyrell where we were sitting. Tyrell walked over to Lauren, put out his hand, and escorted her back to the stage. Lauren was transformed into a swooning baby boomer. He brought out a barstool and sang his signature song, "Isn't It Romantic," directly to her. An awestruck Lauren sat immobilized. The room roared with delight. But Tyrell wasn't finished. He invited me on stage to dance with Lauren as he sang Carol Bayer Sager's "When I Need You."

Lauren placed her head on my shoulder and closed her eyes. I held her tight. I didn't know it then, but Lauren was thinking about a small, intimate dance floor at the Chicago Hyatt where Gabby Wentworth's strong arms affectionately embraced Lauren for the first time. She could still feel his breath in her ear.

70.

Recalling fundamental values and simpler times.

Alexandria slowly opened the door at 157 Salem Avenue, across the street from Triangle Park. It was as if she had entered a time machine. The morning light seemed to flood the entire first floor of the modest little Nebraska house. Nothing seemed to have changed since she had been a little girl, running around the house and teasing her younger sister, Tori. The blue-green walls, the plastic covered couches and chairs, and the homemade yellow drapes dotted with birds all seemed to reflect Cecilia's celebration of the ordinary.

As she stared at her dad's favorite reading chair, Fred appeared in overalls and bespeckled glasses. "Welcome home, little girl. We'll always be here, but this is your house now." She smiled. His image faded, and she was alone.

The kitchen was more of the same: 1950s Formica counters, painted cabinets with shelves covered in brightly-colored contact paper, a worn ceramic sink, and an old Amana refrigerator with a big stainless-steel pull handle. Momma Cecilia was standing next to her favorite chopping block as the sun flooded the room through the window above the sink.

"We didn't have a lot, child, but that never mattered. This house was full of love. It's still in your heart, you know." Her image also faded as she went to join Fred.

As Alexandria stood silently, she began to realize — perhaps for the first time in years — that she had become a jaded, cynical woman with a limited sense of values. Money had become the center of her universe; it was the beginning and end of each day. She wasn't Fred and Cecilia's little girl. She was a worldly, bleached blonde from the big city, whatever that meant.

Tears started to run down Alexandria's cheeks. At the top of the stairs, she looked down the narrow hallway, which led to three bedrooms. As the older child, hers was the first room to the right. The mural that Fred had painted on the wall, anticipating a son, was precisely as Alexandria remembered —- a big fire truck meant for a boy's room. She walked over to her old blue-painted desk and began to thumb through a few of the dusty notebooks. An envelope fell out of one of the books. It was addressed to Andee. It read simply, "Looking forward to the prom. Will you marry me? Frank."

Alexandria's past again came into focus. She had forgotten her sister had given her the nickname Andee because she knew Dad had hoped for a son. She also recalled the incredible crush Frank had on her as a teenager, and their kiss underneath the bleachers after the homecoming weekend pep rally.

She didn't hear the footsteps coming up the stairs. "So, sis, was I right, or was I right?" said Tori. "Welcome to yesterday! I brought some Starbucks on the way over; let's go downstairs and talk."

Alexandria revealed the missing details and private frustrations of the last twenty years, including her recent sexual harassment fiasco. She also expressed a genuine sense of remorse. "I know I can't recapture the years, but maybe I can be a different person."

"Not a different person," said Tori supportively. "Just the person you were originally meant to be."

Alexandria smiled. "That's a nice way of framing this reclamation project."

Tori became philosophical. "Sometimes, fate works in mysterious ways. Maybe it's time to come home and refresh yourself — physically, emotionally, and spiritually. From what I gather, you're off to a great start in your new job at Main Street Securities. Norman's been looking for the right person for a long, long time."

"How did you know about that?"

"Sis, remember, Lincoln is a small town, and Mike and Norman have been volunteer fireman for almost two decades."

"Do they also run the Lincoln Secret Service?" asked Alexandria, only half-joking.

"I assume that was supposed to be a joke. But you use phrases like that and people will tune you out! Around here, we like to help each other, corny as that may sound. Norman and Mike both want you to succeed. That's all."

Alexandria had an epiphany. The inbred small-town behavior that once drove her to seek her fortune in a larger, more urban setting now seemed appropriate, meaningful, and substantive. The fact that one human being could care about another human being bordered on personal revelation.

~

Norman made sure Alexandria received TLC from the first day at Main Street Securities.

"This is yours," said Norman, proudly pointing to a fully-furnished corner office with large picture windows overlooking the park — and Frank's office in the building across the plaza. Alexandria smiled knowingly.

"And this is Susan," said Norman. "She's your new assistant. Think of her as a mini-Andee."

"I'll bite. What's a mini-Andee?" said Alexandria.

"I think I can handle that one," said Susan to Alexandria. "May I?

"To begin with, I'm pretty intelligent. I graduated cum laude from the University of Nebraska School of Business. I'm entirely computer literate and speak three languages fluently: French, Spanish, and Swedish. I've also spent the last two summers, winters, and spring breaks as an intern at Main Street.

"I've organized a 24/7 paperless advisor communications program and the development of an easy-access website with product information, market trends, operational suggestions, and closing tips that are updated twice a week.

"I've also established the Insiders Club, a real-time interactive quality-control feedback system with key field advisors, which is then re-purposed as content in the communications program I mentioned earlier.

"My goal is to be a senior manager at Main Street eventually, find the right man, have a family, be financially secure, and live happily ever after. In the meantime, I'll do anything you need to be done to make you as successful as possible."

"Talk about focus and determination," smiled Alexandria.

"Well, Alexandria, as you know, we're only here for a short time. I'd like to make the most of it."

"Susan, I think we're going to get along famously. First of all, please call me Andee. Secondly, you've got to turn your aspirational jets down a touch; otherwise, you'll burn out before you're twenty-five. And at the risk of sounding like a depressing older sister, your modest little quadfecta — right-guy, financial independence, happy family, the storybook ending — is about a five million to one shot in today's world."

Susan disagreed, but this was not the time. "Alexandria — I mean Andee — I have your schedule for the day. I tried to get you together with the people I thought you needed to see first."

"Susan showed me what she had prepared. You should be one busy lady today," said Norman.

"*Person*," corrected Alexandria.

"There is one thing we have to get straight right at the outset," said Norman. " I've spent over thirty years building this firm — there is, always has been, and always will be equal opportunity for everyone. Our reps in the field are 50 percent female, which is three times the industry average, and they are happy with the way things run around here. Nobody talks down to anybody, and nobody tries any of that politically correct bullshit! Do we understand each other? You're a member of senior management, so people will be watching."

The rest of the day went as Susan planned. At about 6:00 P.M., Alexandria sat in her office wondering if what she had observed today was real: people seemed motivated, well-informed, and professional. *Could her frame of reference have gotten that distorted? Only time would tell.*

She heard the sound of activity; the sound led to Susan, who was still working at her computer.

"Susan, why don't you go home? I understand pretty much everybody leaves by 4:30, since we open so early."

"I was trying to summarize today's briefings in an orderly fashion. I didn't see you taking notes; I assumed it was my job. You have an early morning meeting tomorrow to brief our staff on the new line of Smith Barney Laddered Bonds. People here want to know the features and benefits, how to pitch them to our advisors, and how advisors should integrate them into their investment practices. I've created some power-point slides and some handout sheets."

"Young lady," smiled Alexandria, "you are good. Very good."

By the time they finished rehearsing, it was almost 7:30 P.M. Alexandria was too tired to cook and too tired to go out. Again, Susan to the rescue. "You might want to consider Panda Express Chinese. There is a kiosk at the Safeway store near your house. The ingredients are fresh, the food tastes good, and it's very reasonable."

71.

An old flame is rekindled.

Alexandria had just finished eating when the phone rang. It was Frank.

"How was your first day, Andee?"

"Oh, not you too!"

"I'd like to make you an offer you can't refuse," said Frank. "I'll make you dinner at my house tomorrow night."

She smiled. "Okay, okay. But I have one question and one condition. Are you going to cook a meal, or are you going to order in?"

He laughed. "I'm a pretty good cook. You'll see. I'm afraid to ask, but what's the condition?"

"That you never again refer to me as Andee. I happened to open a yearbook that was sitting in my old room. Out fell this envelope with a brief handwritten message: 'Andee, looking forward to the prom with you, signed Frank.'"

~

The meeting at Main Street the next day didn't go so well.

Alexandria began to present the merits of laddered bonds, an organized program of selling conservative risk-reward bonds at different maturities and different rates as part of a person's investment portfolio. Their primary goal was to provide a reasonable return with little or no risk to accumulated assets.

She was quickly interrupted by Marcus Slade. Slade, the company's leading coach for almost a decade, preferred to advise his advisors to sell investments that had higher risks, higher potential returns, and higher commissions for the investment advisor — and Slade.

"Alexandria, what do you project the yield to be on a 10-year Smith Barney Laddered Bond?"

"Marcus, that's a difficult one to answer. Normally, a laddered bond is bought as a series in a timed sequence, so you look at the total return of the entire package."

Marcus thought Alexandria was trying to embarrass him in front of his peers, so he took to the offensive. "Frankly, that sounds like a bunch of New York mumbo jumbo. I asked a simple question; can't I get a simple answer?"

Alexandria was between a rock and a hard place. If she just gave him the return on a single bond, it would be misleading. She also wasn't crazy about his snide New York comment. Marcus Slade was your typical wise-ass male trying to set her up. "Marcus, with all due respect, the only mumbo jumbo seems to be in your limited portfolio. A laddered series is what it says. They are designed for the conservative investor, not the cowboy advisor looking for the highest commission. Do you have any field advisors who place their client's interest first?"

The room was so quiet you could hear a pin drop; Marcus and several of his male cronies got up and left. Most of the women in the room stayed and cheered.

~

Alexandria was anxious to see Frank, so she went to his place straight from work and arrived at 6:00 P.M. Frank's home was a tastefully restored two-story Victorian, circa 1910, with a front porch that overlooked a big, wide, quiet street. The first floor consisted of a gallery entrance foyer, a large living room, a formal dining, a kitchen plus family room, a library, guest quarters, and two full baths.

"Let's have a glass of wine and talk while we're preparing some of tonight's ingredients, and then I'll give you the fifty-cent tour while the paella is simmering," suggested Frank.

"Oh, is he here too?"

"Is who here?"

"Fifty Cent. Never mind," said Alexandria, again realizing the continued gap between their two lives. "What do we need to do?"

"I've already shelled the shrimp for the paella, but the swordfish, roasted peppers, and garlic need to be cut into small cubes. I've already started the risotto and shaved the Parmesan."

"I'm impressed! You know what you're doing."

"By the way, I hope you like dessert. How does a Grand Marnier Soufflé sound?"

They clinked wine glasses. "Time for the tour."

As Frank led her through the house, Alexandria discovered Mary Lou's hand was everywhere. "She designed the remodel. The art collections on the walls are mostly me and, since she passed, I've replaced all conventional TVs with high def and installed a home theater system in the great room area. When my daughters and the four grandchildren come over, the house makes for pleasant entertaining."

"This is a pretty big place. Who takes care of it?"

"I have a lady, Jenny, who's been with us for almost twenty years. She comes in twice a week, keeps the place tidy and does the laundry. I pay the bills and enjoy what I've got. The only variation on that theme is when the grandkids sleepover. Jenny comes the next day because the place generally looks like it been overrun."

"The men in my past life have been far less organized and far less reliable, except perhaps for one."

"I'd love to hear more about the 'perhaps for one' fellow."

The aroma of paella filled the living room. "Smells like the main course is almost ready; we can do the second part of the tour later."

Dinner was incredible: the food spectacular, and the company even better, thought Alexandria. "How long has Mary Lou been gone?"

"Eight years. It took me quite a while to get my bearings again. I'm a one-woman man. My friends have tried to match me with their friends. Most of the ladies were very nice, but there were no fireworks, no shooting stars."

"Do you believe in that sort of thing? That there's that one special person out there somewhere?"

"I don't know," said Frank. "When you're over fifty, you're set in your ways. There's the issue of compromise. In a great marriage, ninety-five percent of everything is not important.

That way, each of you knows what is important to the other and will go out of their way to make sure that person gets their five percent. The rest is just an inconsequential collection of wants and desires."

They looked at each other silently for a while. Frank swirled the remaining wine in his glass. "Ready for the rest of the tour?" They headed for the master suite, a complex of three rooms overlooking a lake.

"This is gorgeous. Mary Lou again?"

"Yes and no. We visited the Four Seasons Resort in Chicago once. She liked the décor so much she had it duplicated here. Between my king-size bed, the sitting room, the office, the workout studio, the efficiency kitchen, and the TVs, I could subsist up here until the food ran out."

Alexandria's heart was pounding as she stood in the doorway. Frank walked over to her and kissed her. "You're an extraordinary lady."

She wanted to hold him tight but felt uncomfortable in Mary Lou's room. "I can't, not here."

"I understand; besides, I'm so nervous, I'm shaking. I haven't made love to anyone in four years. I wouldn't want to be a failure in your eyes."

"Relax; we'll only do it when the time is right, for both of us."

~

Alexandria found a bouquet of Peruvian lilies sitting on the middle of her desk when she arrived in the morning.

"Well, it looks like you did okay with at least one guy yesterday," said Norman as he walked into Alexandria's office.

"I had to deal with a male insurrection late yesterday. Marcus Slade and his band of Negativos stormed my office to tell me what an arrogant bitch you are."

"Oh, Marcus. What an asshole."

"Asshole or not, he represents thirty-three percent of this office's production. Figure out how to get along with him. Please remember this is Lincoln, Nebraska. Understand?"

Difficult as it was, Alexandria knew she had to change. This was her last stop. She switched gears and tried to make nice to Marcus by taking him out to lunch. For good measure, she wore a shape-hugging blouse with buttons opened suggestively. As they sat and talked, she could see Marcus attempting to peer at her boobs.

"Like what you see?" she asked suggestively.

"Very much so. Very much so," smiled Marcus, married with three children.

Alexandria knew she had him in her pocket if she ever decided to play that card.

~

With Marcus under control, the rest of Main Street Securities was a piece of cake.

She quickly became the acknowledged queen of product development, who could analyze a client case and offer just the right blend of investment products for an entire portfolio or to fill gaps in existing portfolios. The field reps loved her. Business was up 40 percent over a year ago. Susan was also blossoming into a young superstar, following her boss's example.

Norman was pleased. "You've come a long way from that rocky start. I'm delighted to give you this performance bonus; it's a reflection of what you've done for this firm. At the end of the year, you and I and my advisors are going to sit down and determine how I can make you an equity partner without creating a major, taxable event for you."

Her first thought was that Norman was blowing smoke. "What do you mean by a 'taxable event'?"

"This company is thirty years old. If we establish a fair market value and I award you a percentage of the company, that's treated as ordinary income for tax purposes, even though you didn't receive any cash.

"Let's say we make a case that the company is worth $30 million — which, by the way, is about right. I award you ten percent of the company. You have just received $3 million in income. You will have a tax bill of over $1 million in the current year."

"That's unbelievable."

"That's our tax code. So, if you've got the million dollars you want to give Uncle Sam, I'll expedite the transaction. Otherwise, we've got to figure out something else."

72.

Life is good. Frank is great.

Alexandria's relationship with Frank flourished. She had found a man who made her feel comfortable and at ease with herself, which blunted her jaded view of life.

One evening, they decided to summarize what they had learned about each other in the last forty-five days.

"I loved being a parent," said Frank. "I tried to provide my kids with meaningful value systems, leading by example. Although, with no Mary Lou, it was difficult at times. I guess I'd give myself an A-." His kids had done as he did. The two children both graduated from college, married nice women, had kids of their own, and seemed to be relatively stable financially. One was in Ann Arbor, Michigan, and the other in Cleveland, Ohio.

"I guess I'd give myself a B + at the office," she said.

"Let me guess. That's an average of different grades."

"Now how the hell did you know that? Oh, I know, it's goddamn Nebraska, where everybody knows everybody's business."

Frank was taken aback by the tone of Alexandria's voice. "You need to decide."

"What are you talking about?"

"I'm talking about you deciding which Alexandria you are: the jaded bitch from New York, or Andee the prom date."

"Frank, I'm certainly not the latter, and I'd like to be less of the former. But I don't want to abandon all of what I've become."

Alexandria switched subjects. "I guess I'd give myself an F in the family department. No college degree, a suicidal daughter, two failed marriages. What a mess, and you don't know the half of it."

"Maybe it's time to be completely honest with me." Alexandria had come to trust Frank. She explained what happened with Martin Ruff, why she left AFA, and the $75,000 cloud over her head, compliments of Burton Moss.

"I'm relieved," smiled Frank. "I thought there was another man in your life. The money thing is easy. I'll write Moss a check for the $75,000 and you sign a note to pay me back, interest-free, over whatever number of years you want to specify."

"I can't do that to you."

"You're not doing anything *to* me; I'm doing something *for* you."

~

They both listened to rock 'n roll as a way of relaxing.

"Most people think I'm a little odd, with my headphones and everything," smiled Alexandria. She preferred the early grit of Bruce Springsteen and the E Street Band.

Frank's preferences veered towards the more recent, more mellow Neil Young, sans his Crazy Horse ensemble.

"Have you ever been to the Rock 'n Roll Hall of Fame in Cleveland?" he asked. "It's an amazing experience. Encased in glass are the notebooks of music legends like Young and Springsteen, and Morrison and Lennon. Their handwritten lyrics, their revisions, their creative inspirations, all sitting right in front of you."

"I really love your approach to life," said Alexandria.

"I've never thought about it as an 'approach to life.' I'm happy with my life, my friends, and my community. There's nothing I wouldn't do all over again."

"I guess it comes down to roots," said Alexandria. "You know what yours are. You're here because you choose to be here. I'm here because of the circumstances."

"Trust me. As I've gotten to know you, this town and its values could once again become your town and your values, if you want. Lincoln, Nebraska, may not have the sophistication and polish of Manhattan, but everything that could make you happy is right here, including me."

~

She reached out to touch his hand. Her heart began to race. He put his arms around her waist and pulled her toward him. They kissed. As their passions rose, he began kissing her all over. Her blouse and his shirt fell to the floor. She rubbed her tongue on his ear. He moaned.

"Daddy likes that," she murmured in his ear.

He picked her up, carried her to his bedroom, and dropped her on the bed.

He paused, "I haven't done this in a long, long time; don't expect…."

She placed her finger over his mouth. "Don't you worry about a thing." She stripped him naked, pushed him on the bed, and then finished disrobing herself. She could feel he was ready. She climbed on top of him and pounded until they had an enormous, shuddering climax. She lay still on top as he whispered, "I love you."

Now it was Frank's turn to mount the bucking bronco. Whenever Alexandria thought he was finished, Frank did her again in some other position. After the fourth climax, she quietly rested on his chest, listening to his rapid heartbeat. "I love a man with stamina."

Frank was gentle but uninhibited and unpredictable. It was the kind of love-making she had fantasized about but never fully experienced. She was in love with the perfect partner.

When Frank awoke, it was almost eight in the morning. Alexandria was still sleeping peacefully. He slipped into the other room and called Norman.

"Alexandria is still sleeping. As friends, can you do me a favor and just give her a vacation day, with no questions asked?"

~

After breakfast, Alexandria felt moved to visit Shanti's gravesite. Frank insisted on accompanying her. It was a sunny morning, which made the headstone's embedded silicon particles shimmer.

They stood silently, hand in hand, by Shanti's grave. Frank had a conversation with Shanti, made the sign of the cross, and touched her gravestone. Alexandria started to shake and quiver. Frank grabbed her. "Alexandria, you've got to stop. Let things go. It wasn't your fault."

~

Frank was determined not to lose Alexandria a second time. He planned a special weekend. "We've got an outer berth for the weekend on the Robert E. Lee."

"You mean the steamboat?" She didn't have the heart to tell him she thought that spending the weekend on an old paddleboat was kind of corny. But that turned out not to be the case. They ate and drank until midnight in the old-time Western saloon.

"Have you ever watched a paddle turn in the light of the full moon?" asked Frank. The paddle whished, gently covering them with a light, cool mist. Frank pulled a little red box out of his pocket.

He placed a ring on her finger, "Alexandria, I am deeply in love with you. Will you marry me?"

"Are you sure you know what you are getting into, with a girl like me?"

"You know this means living in Lincoln for the rest of your life."

"I'm very comfortable with that."

73.

Sometimes, even a servant of God wonders why.

The next morning, Frank and Alexandria were sitting on the paddleboat veranda having breakfast when Alexandria's cell phone rang. It was MJ.

"I need to take this call," said Alexandria. Frank remained expressionless.

"What a nice surprise," said Alexandria. "I was thinking about you and some of the things you said to me a while back. Are you all right? Is there anything wrong?"

"No," said MJ, "I just thought you might want to know that I followed your advice and went back into the eye of the storm. I've started a consulting business. To my surprise, I've gotten some referral engagements."

"That's because you're very good at what you do."

"I've even had some out-of-town assignments. Believe it or not, I've been on three planes in the past month."

"I'm so proud of you."

"You don't realize the kind of positive impression you made on me. I'm not the easiest person to converse with," said MJ.

"Thank you for the compliment," smiled Alexandria proudly. "That makes me feel important." Alexandria paused. "I'm sorry about your dad and mom."

"Yeah, he screwed that one up."

"We all screwed that one up! He just wanted your mom to pay attention to him, make him feel important. Men are an insecure lot."

"But she did, she always did."

"Whether you realize it or not, you stepped between them. You took his place. And I filled your mom's. Look, God knows I have no right to point the finger at anyone. I had no business cultivating that relationship, not the way I did. And then to destroy that beautiful relationship for money. I'm so ashamed. What I'm trying to say is that your dad is a decent, caring, sensitive man. Like all of us in this imperfect world, he has his imperfections."

"Have you ever told him that directly?"

"I couldn't possibly. I hope you understand. How is your mom doing?"

"It's getting pretty nasty."

MJ hung up. Alexandria stared at her cell phone, conflicted by the good and the bad news.

"What was that all about?" asked Frank. "At first, I thought it was your daughter Melissa."

"That was Martin Ruff, Jr."

"The son of that guy who harassed you?"

"It wasn't really like that. I lied."

"You what! Why?"

"It's a long, terrible story, and I'll tell you anything you want to know. I've never loved a man as I love you."

"I don't want to know any more. The past is the past. We can't change it. We can only hope to learn from it. All I want to know is, will you marry me?"

~

The guest list was complete and Frank and Alexandria had selected their wedding invitations. The wording was a joint affair.

Frank John Graves and
Alexandria Joan Plummet
Of Lincoln, Nebraska
Cordially Invite You
To Complete a Journey
They Began 30 Years Ago.
The Marriage Ceremony Will Take Place
On the Dock at Lake Fisher
Followed by a Reception
On the Paddleboat Robert E. Lee
From Dusk to Dawn.

~

By the time the couple left the printing shop, darkness had fallen. They were twenty miles from Frank's house. The heavens opened and it began to pour. They could hardly see out the window.

"Robby's Roadhouse is just up ahead. Why don't we have a glass of wine and let this monsoon lighten up?"

Alexandria reached over and gave Frank a soft, moist kiss, whispering in his ear. "This damn rain better lighten up soon. I'm getting so hot, I'm about to fog the windows in the car."

"Frankie, long time no see," said the tall, burly bartender standing behind the empty bar. "Let me guess; this is the blonde bombshell that put the stake in the heart of Lincoln's most eligible bachelor."

Frank smiled, "Alexandria, meet Robbie."

"How about a wedding toast on the house? It doesn't look like anybody else is going to be crazy enough to come out in all this rain."

"I'd like that very much," said Alexandria.

"I've got a bottle of that fancy French vintage stuff, Lafitte Roth, something or other," said Robbie, looking through the bottles under the counter. "I think it was a 1970. I hope it's still good."

"You don't mean Lafitte Rothschild?" asked Alexandria. "That's a collector's item worth hundreds of dollars."

"Now let me ask you a question, Alexandria," smiled Robbie, leaning on the counter with the dusty bottle in front of him. "How many people from Lincoln are going to stop on Route 10 here and ask me for a 1970 Lafitte Rothschild in my lifetime?"

When the rain subsided, the couple staggered towards Frank's car. As Frank put the key in the lock, Alexandria became amorous. "Just hang on, we're less than twenty minutes from my bed. It will be more comfortable than the backseat of my car."

Alexandria snuggled next to Frank as they exited the highway and drove the last five miles down a dark, two-lane asphalt road to his house. She opened the zipper on his pants and began to caress his penis.

Neither Frank nor Alexandria heard the impatient SUV honking its horn from behind. The frustrated driver, unaware of what was going on in Frank's car, sped past the couple on the left, splashing a mountain of water on the driver-side window and the front windshield. By the time Frank regained visibility he had veered onto the other side of the road, where he crashed headlong into a giant 18-wheel truck that was unable to stop fast enough.

Both were DOA at Lincoln Memorial Hospital. Frank was fifty-three. Alexandria was forty-nine.

~

Pretty much anyone that had ever touched Frank and Andee's life showed up at the cemetery. Even Frank's long-time friend, Father Peter O'Mara, was emotionally taken. All he could tell those in attendance was what they already knew. "The couple's demise was *tragic;* even I, a faithful servant of God, wonder why."

74.

The Killer goes for the jugular.

It was Margo's turn to be the aggressor. She called Moss. "Burton, this is merely a pre-filing courtesy call. My client, Martin Ruff, intends to sue your client, Alexandria Plummet, for destroying his business reputation by intentionally lying under oath."

"You're too late, Margo, honey," laughed Moss crudely. "Plummet's dead. Her boyfriend fell asleep or something behind the wheel of a car somewhere in Nebraska, about two weeks ago."

"Well, I guess all well that ends well," said Margo, cynically.

"Not really; Plummet owed me money, so I tracked her down through her sister in Nebraska.

"Let me guess" said Margo, "You were going to sue Ms. Plummet to recapture her settlement, and place a lien on her home."

"Let me save you some time. There are no assets. Her fiancée was originally going to pay me what she owed me., but with him dead too, that's a non-issue. The only asset I can even identify is her mother's house, which she inherited with her sister. It's an old place with a market value of under $100,000, so I don't know if it's even worth the hassle of fighting with the sister to force a sale."

"Where can you get a house for $100,000 today?"

"I guess that's why some people live in Lincoln," chuckled Moss.

~

Shortly after that, Margo filed papers with the courts, simultaneously notifying AFA of her intent.

"Son of a bitch! I can't believe the balls!" said Carr upon hearing Shamus summarize the $10 million suit, with Ruff as Plaintiff.

"Eddie," said Shamus, "with all due respect, you guys threw the first stones. If you remember, I asked you if you wanted to do that. After all, Martin helped get you to where you are today."

"That was all Wasserman and Jeremy's idea."

"Nice try; they're gone."

"Let's cut to the chase," said Craft. "Does he have a chance?"

"I would say if he subpoenas our records and interviews the same people Wasserman interviewed, we may be vulnerable. Who knows what that egomaniac said to our employees privately?"

"But Ruff screwed up our business. People got mad when he resigned."

"But, why did he resign?" responded Shamus. "Because you let Wasserman prepare papers that were ridiculous."

"I thought he worked with you." retorted Carr.

"He did. He told me precisely what to do."

"Now wait a minute," said an upset Craft, "You're supposed to represent *us*."

"When a senior AFA officer tells me that Jeremy, Dawson, and Eddie agreed, what, am I supposed to do? Call and double-check?"

"Is there is a chance he has a case?" asked Craft.

"No, I'm merely telling you he's got a better chance of winning his claim than you do," said Shamus. "You have absolutely nothing. He's got Plummet's misrepresentations, our inept investigation, a reservoir of goodwill among employees and field reps, the fact that Johnson was a crook, and a lawyer we agreed to negotiate with who disbursed unethical kickbacks."

Carr finally spoke. "Fellas, I am sitting here listening, and this is a no-brainer. We fucked up a good guy's life. Then we tried to be pigs. He's just striking back. I'd do the same. Maybe we should talk to him, man to man? Tell him we'll drop our suit if he drops his suit. Then, give him the fucking distributions he's entitled to, when he's entitled to them."

There was dead silence. Shamus looked at Craft, who looked at Carr.

"Pal," said Craft. "Sounds good to me." Craft paused as he looked across the room. "Eddie, you're elected to call Martin and nail down the quid pro quo. You're the last man standing. He hated Wasserman, barely tolerated Jeremy, and he's probably pissed at me for letting things go this far.

"Just get it done quickly," Craft continued. "We've got the tenth-anniversary party coming up. It would be nice to have this all behind us. And while you're talking to him, pal, make a peace offering. Tell him we'd like to invite him and Lauren to the tenth-anniversary party as our way of letting bygones be bygones."

~

Carr sounded like the quintessential jolly old soul when he called me on the telephone. "Hey, pal, good to hear your voice. Your partners believe it's time we talk." The fucker made it sound like nothing had ever happened.

"Fine. Where and when?"

"How about you coming over to the house, and we barbeque a few steaks and talk? Does Tuesday evening around six work? Sans lawyers, sans partners. Just you and me, buddy."

~

I hung up and called Margo. "I just heard from Eddie Carr. He invited me over to his house to talk. I suspect 'the boys' want to do a quid pro quo."

"Why Carr?" said Margo.

"They figure he's the only one who hasn't totally pissed me off. And they're right."

"I suspect he's going to suggest they would be willing to drop their suit if we dropped ours," hypothesized Margo.

"Do we want to do that?"

"That question contains so many other questions," responded Margo. "I'm not sure where to begin. Do we have a plausible case? The answer is absolutely. Should they settle? Probably not. Our countersuit is ten times their number. So, unless we reach a mutual settlement, they would probably be forced to defend themselves in court, if for no other reason than to bring the two amounts more in line.

"I know Shamus well enough to know he has no killer instincts. He never imagined you would sue them. He figured he'd make it easy for the judge by implying the company wanted to be fair by only asking for this year's profit distributions to cover your bad judgment.

"We've also got to ask ourselves: can we head off dueling court actions? I suspect the answer is yes, assuming everybody is willing to give a little. Will you drop your suit if they drop their suit, pay all legal expenses incurred, and indemnify profit distributions from all past, current, and future events?"

"What about my equity position?" asked Martin.

"That's not in play. Tom did a great job. Your position is unencumbered.

"You've also got to think about how all these legal maneuverings might affect your marriage, since they will insist that Lauren countersign all agreements. If I were her, I'd think this was the straw that breaks the camel's back. I'd sign it in exchange for a fair divorce settlement and get the hell out of there."

"Very funny."

"I'm not joking."

I was speechless. Margo's candor took me by surprise. She was speaking as both an attorney and as a woman.

"I have some news myself," said Margo. "Alexandria Plummet is dead. Apparently, she and her fiancé were in an automobile accident during a rainstorm."

"Does this have any impact on our case?"

"Well, we're certainly going to have a more difficult time recovering damages from a dead lady."

"How about suing Bill Johnson and Colton Wasserman for defamation of character?"

"You're kidding, right?"

"Why not? I figure if AFA is paying the legal freight, it's worth letting those bastards stew a little."

"But Wasserman is in some minimum detention facility for a felony, and Johnson, according to Moss, is stone-broke."

~

The steaks were done to perfection. "There is nothing like a good piece of prime meat, eh, buddy?" said Carr. "Listen, life is good. Evelyn and the kids love the new house, all eighteen rooms. The business is going pretty well, and we've all got a few bucks in our pockets as we develop our long-term exit strategy."

"I'm happy for you."

"Happy for *me*? It's happy for *all of us*. You're our partner. You have as much to gain as the rest of us. Listen Martin, Dawson, and I think it's time to bury the hatchet. Maybe we all made a few mistakes in this thing. What do you say we drop the suits, the lawyers, and just have things return to the way they were?"

"Does Jeremy feel the same?" And that was how I found out about Costas's mystery suicide.

"I assume this proposal is over the protests of my friend Colton Wasserman?"

"He's disappeared; he broke probation on a spousal abuse case in another state, under another name."

"Just out of curiosity, did AFA send Alexandria the second installment on the settlement?"

"We're just about to cut the check. Why?"

"Save your money. She's dead. Automobile accident."

"Poetic justice. I told the guys that bitch's suit was bullshit right from the beginning."

"Now that the gang's all gone, here's my proposal. I'll drop the suit. You do likewise. You pay all my legal bills and indemnify me in perpetuity on my profit distributions."

"What's your estimate on legal expenses?"

"About $50,000, roughly the amount you saved on Alexandria's fuck up." I put my hand out. "Deal?"

"Seems fair to me," replied Carr. "Consider it done." He poured us both another glass of wine. "There's just one other thing, pal. Next month is officially the company's tenth anniversary. We're going to have a big bash at Dawson's hacienda. Employees, field reps, guests, etc. The whole nine yards. We'd like it very much if you and Lauren came. It'll be like old times.

"One last thing. Amélie had a miscarriage on a plane. She lost baby Paul."

"They must be devastated."

"Yes and no. Amélie filed for divorce and tried for a big settlement, but it turned out the kid wasn't Craft's."

And that was how I learned about Craft's marital disaster.

75.

Lana's dress reopens old wounds.

The party invitation arrived the next day, before I had a chance to review the events of the last 48 hours with Lauren.

"You're not going to believe what arrived in today's mail," said Lauren angrily, waving an envelope. "We've been invited to attend the company's tenth anniversary like nothing ever happened."

"Why not?" I said. "AFA and I resolved pretty much all outstanding issues: the lawsuits, countersuits, distributions, and the legal fees."

"We've still got Alexandria and her lawyer hanging over our heads," countered Lauren."

"Not anymore more. She's dead, from an auto accident in Nebraska."

"What about that prick Wasserman? He lives and thrives while you have no job."

"Not exactly. The FBI stopped by AFA recently to extradite Wasserman to Pennsylvania. He was convicted of spousal abuse under another name. And the job thing is not an issue. I get my full profit distribution as if I worked full time. The only difference is we get paid in one lump sum annually, rather than as a monthly draw."

"That brings us to the third issue: me. Do you really think things can be as they were?"

"I was hoping."

"You still don't know anything about women. You turned my life upside-down."

"I know this isn't a perfect answer, but let's go to the party. See how you feel. Take it one step at a time."

~

The tenth-anniversary party was as billed: six hundred employees and friends, enough food stations to feed an army, a seven-piece jazz band, speeches, merrymaking, and company memorabilia everywhere, including pictures of Lauren and me with field producers and conference speakers.

Lauren mingled with old friends while I was besieged by many of the young employees I had hired and given advice to over the years.

One employee I had mentored was Lana Stewart, a bright Boston College MBA whom I had persuaded to join the entrepreneurial world of AFA, rather than the staid organizational world of investment banking giant Smith Barney. In the three years I had known Lana, she rose through the ranks in the marketing department to become, at age twenty-five, the company's youngest marketing manager, with sixteen people reporting to her. It was common knowledge that I was her mentor. She saw me as the father she never had, and I saw her as the daughter I never had.

She gave me a big hug. "It's so good to see you. I've missed you." I couldn't help but notice that she looked terrific. We talked for about ten minutes. She was contemplating a move to San Francisco. "Suppose the West Coast is not for me. Do you think I'd be precluded from the New York job market?"

"At your age, it doesn't work like that," I replied. "You have impeccable educational credentials. You've been exposed to things in the last three years at AFA that people in New York's financial services training programs never experience. And the fact that you want to experience another professional and personal culture outside of the Eastern seaboard should only enhance your maturity and marketability."

Lana was skeptical that I was giving her a shallow pep talk. "Listen, don't take it from me. Talk to my son Bart. He's a financial services powerhouse. He's closer to your age and has lived what you're talking about." I took one of her business cards and wrote Bart's phone number on it.

~

While I was chatting with Lana, Lauren had found Evelyn Carr and began to chit chat like old times. "We've missed you.

Eddie tells me everything is settled, and now things can get back to normal again."

Lauren rolled her eyes as if to say, we'll see. She wanted to change the subject. "I don't see Amélie and the baby."

"You don't know?" asked Evelyn. "She had a miscarriage; lost the baby, and then filed for divorce."

Lauren was embarrassed that I had neglected to mention the Craft family affair, but that was short-lived. When she saw me give Lana a good luck hug and hand her my card with a handwritten phone number, she was pissed! I could see it in her eyes as she approached. "So, who's this pretty young thing?" said Lauren, feigning pleasantness.

"Mrs. Ruff, don't you recognize me? I'm Lana Stewart. You guys were nice enough to invite me to your house when I first arrived from Boston."

"My, my, you're all grown up," said Lauren, glaring at me.

"Well, that's thanks to your husband. He's helped me grow in the job. I hope I'm lucky enough someday to find a man like him."

~

On the way home, I tried to make small talk. Lauren broke her silence.

"Why did you give Lana your phone number? Do you take me for a complete fool? I heard you tell her to call if she wants to talk. Is that how it started with Alexandria?"

"You're so far off base, it's unbelievable."

"Oh, really."

"I gave her Bart's number, not mine. She's thinking of moving to San Francisco for lifestyle reasons, but she's also concerned that if it doesn't work out, she wouldn't be able to return to the New York job market. I told her that with her credentials, it shouldn't be a problem, but she should talk to a younger person, like Bart, who's been through the situation. If you have any doubt, ask her yourself."

Lauren began to cry. "I'm confused; I don't know what to believe anymore."

"Honey, you've got to stop going backward. You can't be thinking that every time I talk to a woman you don't know, I'm trying to get in her pants."

"And what about Amélie?

"Oh, honey. I'm sorry. With everything that's been going on, I forgot to tell you. Forgive me."

"Are you trying to sit there with a straight face and tell me you didn't purposely try to embarrass me with Evelyn?"

76.

Decisions have been made.

Lauren made her decision.

She wanted her children, Bart and MJ, to be the first to know, so they met at Bart's office.

"So, Mom," said a cheery Bart, "Dad tells us things are slowly getting resolved."

"It looks like all the legal mumbo jumbo will be a thing of the past. And Dad and his attorney somehow managed to get everything paid for by the company, including the legal fees."

"That's great. We should all go out and celebrate."

"What about Alexandria?" asked MJ.

"Why?" asked Lauren.

"Wait till you hear this, Mom," said Bart. "That broad's been working with MJ to step into the eye of the storm."

"Look," said MJ defensively, "She's been through this panic disorder thing too, and none of you have. She's also helped me with my issues with Dad, and wants to help me get back into the game of life."

Lauren was upset about MJ's fondness for Alexandria. "First of all, MJ, Alexandria's dead."

"Dead! I just spoke to her last week; she sounded so happy." The tears trickled down MJ's cheeks.

"All I know is that she and her fiancé were fatalities in an automobile accident."

"Well, I guess that's one less thing to be concerned about," chuckled Bart insensitively.

"Yes, it is," said Lauren. "That leaves only one remaining item — Me!"

Lauren put her hands through her hair and rubbed her face. "I don't know if it's right or wrong, but I've decided to divorce Dad. The wounds are too deep."

The boys were speechless.

"Is this a final decision, or can we at least talk it out?" begged Bart.

"I've made up my mind."

"But there are thirty-six years of memories, of sharing, of time invested," said MJ. "Please, don't throw it all away."

"I'm not throwing anything away. Memories last a lifetime, and I still have my children. I love you very much. A part of me will always love your dad, but the world he and I built together has changed. I don't want to live in that space anymore. About the only thing I'm sure of is that I'll make it a fair and amicable divorce. I owe that to all of you. Including Dad."

"Does he know?" asked Bart.

"No. I'm going to tell him at dinner tonight."

~

Lauren's dark brown eyes never looked more beautiful. The flickering candlelight lent incredible dimension. I said, "You look beautiful tonight." And I meant it.

"Thank you," she responded warmly. I reached for her hand. She pulled back. "Please don't make this any more difficult than it has to be. I've done a lot of soul-searching these past weeks. I'll always love you, but I can't live with you anymore."

"You can't be serious. After all the years? One mistake. I understand I'm not the perfect man of your dreams, but it's not like I've spent decades running around behind your back."

"I'm no longer sure of that. I'll always have doubts."

"Is that your way of saying you want a divorce?"

"Yes."

And there's nothing I can say or do or promise?"

"No."

"That's your final decision?"

"Yes."

~

Our divorce was fast and friendly, as these matters go. And a bit unorthodox. We agreed that Margo Margoles would represent both of us.

Lauren kept the house and furnishings in Southport, while I kept the apartment and furnishings in the City, since both were appraised in the $4 million range. We split our remaining cash and investments evenly and made sure all commingled assets and liabilities like cars and credit cards were properly cleaned up.

She also generously assigned one hundred percent of AFA equity and profit distributions to me, and I disavowed all rights to accumulations in her hospital investment programs and bonuses.

Two months later, our divorce was finalized.

~

As I prepared to leave my Southport home, I looked around one last time. The walls were covered with memories. I stood emotionally frozen in time, reluctant to leave those beautiful bits and scraps of everyday life.

I began the next phase of my life by driving into Manhattan, surrounded by bumper-to-bumper traffic, which made the trip even more depressing. Bob Dylan kept me company on the radio with clues of what had been and, in some ways, would always be.

In the still of the night, in the world's ancient light
Where wisdom grows up in strife…
We live and we die, we know not why
But I'll be with you when the deal goes down...
I laugh, and I cry and I'm haunted by
Things I never meant nor wished to say
Soul to soul, our shadows roll
And I'll be with you when the deal goes down.
©Bob Dylan

77.

Love may be lovelier the second time around.

A glum Lauren sat by herself at a table in the hospital cafeteria. Gabby walked in.

"May I share this table?" he smiled.

"Suit yourself," she said.

"Wow, what a vibe."

"This is not a good time."

"Do you want to talk about it?" he asked.

"No, not here." She wasn't prepared to discuss her divorce, particularly in the hospital cafeteria.

"How about over dinner?"

"Gabby, I'm still married."

"What has that got to do with anything? Lauren, this is the twenty-first century. Professional colleagues do share meals, even after work."

"I'm sorry. I didn't mean to be so rude."

"Relax. I have a plan that will protect your reputation," whispered Gabby. "About 5:30, after most of the employees have gone home, you discreetly slip out of the hospital through the secret passage behind the laundry room," deadpanned Gabby. "I'll have an unmarked black town car with tinted windows waiting by the clothing chute to whisk us to the one restaurant in the entire city where New York Hospital employees are banned."

She finally smiled. "Fine."

"By the way," said Gabby. "The restaurant's called Tutto Bene. It's on the corner of 54th Street and Ninth Avenue. I've been going there for years. It's nothing fancy, just an eatery run by a charming couple from Northern Italy."

~

After ordering a bottle of Montepulciano, Gabby started the conversation with a simple, "So." Desperate to share, Lauren just started talking.

"The psychiatrist sessions were dreadful. I did nothing but attack Martin. I think his betrayal not only shook my trust, but it also shattered my self-confidence," said Lauren.

"Recently, we were invited to the company's tenth-anniversary party. I spotted Martin talking to this twenty-something hottie in a skintight dress. I heard him say 'so call when you get a chance.' It turns out he was merely advising his protégé to talk to our son if she had questions about the benefits and pitfalls of relocating."

"That certainly doesn't sound like the end of the world."

"The following week, I did it again. We met at a restaurant for dinner. After we were seated, an attractive waitress took our drink order. She said, 'Hi, again. Small world.' She went to get the drinks. I sarcastically said, 'So where did we meet that one?' He explained they had met in the parking garage when he was looking for the private elevator to the restaurant. The fact that she turned out to be a waitress in the place was a total coincidence.

"He asked me, 'Are you going to chastise me every time I talk to another woman?' If I was him, that's a reasonable question. I said I didn't know. He said, 'I can't live with that answer.' We agreed to disagree. Permanently."

"So."

"So, "continued Lauren, "we are getting a divorce. The final papers have already been filed. We're down to little details. It's amicable and fair. He gets New York; I get Connecticut. We split everything else fifty-fifty. Except I keep my deferred compensation, and he keeps his company stock."

"Lauren, are you sure you want to throw thirty-six years down the drain?"

"Yes."

Gabby wasn't sure about the timing, but he didn't want the moment to slip away. "Lauren, I think you've felt our chemistry. You're intelligent, beautiful, charming; you're this doctor's dream."

"Gabby, I think you're wonderful, but I'm too old for you."

"Lauren, don't be ridiculous. I'm 42, and you're only 53."

"I've already lived a large part of my life," said Lauren. "I have kids, a grandchild. We live in two different worlds. I shop at Bergdorf's and have cocktails at the Four Seasons. You go scuba diving, camping, and mountain climbing in exotic places all over the globe. Besides, I'm just getting divorced. It's too early. What would the kids think?"

"Lauren, are you attracted to me?"

"Yes," she said with a sigh of inevitable resignation and sheepish guilt.

"Why don't we take it a step at a time? Let me make dinner for you Friday night at my apartment." Gabby wouldn't take no for an answer. "Come on; everybody's gotta eat. What are you going to do after a long week at the hospital? Go home to that big empty house in Southport and reward yourself with a take-out dinner?"

"I've got to hand it to you,' she said with another big sigh, "you've worn me down. I accept your invitation."

"Wonderful."

"Do you have a garage in your building where I can park my car? I doubt I'm going to be in the mood to ride on Metro-North to Southport."

"Lauren, I've got tons of room at the apartment. Stay over. Just bring a change of clothes. I'll drive you back to Connecticut on Saturday."

Before heading for work, Lauren packed her overnight bag. She found a sheer negligee she hadn't worn in ages and put it in her bag.

~

Lauren arrived at Gabby's building at 7:00 P.M., not knowing what to expect. She pictured everything from a sophisticated working loft to a funky building, but she never imagined a white-glove condominium in Manhattan sitting on the East River, down the block from the United Nations, with an elegant Ritz Carlton-style lobby, twenty-foot ceilings, polished redwood paneling, brass accents, burgundy granite counters, and millions of dollars in original art.

"Madame, you're here to visit whom?" said the concierge behind an imposing desk.

"I'm here to see Dr. Wentworth."

"Jonathan," said the concierge, "Please escort Ms. Ruff to the Wentworth Penthouse."

The elevator opened to a gracious entrance lobby on the 44th floor.

"Lauren, I'm so glad you could make it." He kissed her on the cheek. "You smell delicious. Let's put your bag down. How about a glass of wine and a tour? Then you can help me put the final touches on dinner."

"After putting in a full day at the hospital," she joked, "You want me to slave overtime in the kitchen?"

The 4,500-square foot apartment — three bedrooms, three baths, living room, dining room, kitchen plus den, media room, and maid's quarters — had tasteful, understated modern Italian design and soft defused lighting.

"The views are breathtaking," said Lauren., looking out ten-foot floor-to-ceiling windows with a panorama that stretched from the East River to the Empire State Building. "I feel like I'm sitting in a precious jewel box on top of Manhattan's glittering lights, and yet the apartment feels like a real home. Who decorated the place?"

"Me. Honest. Every room, every piece of furniture, every last detail. Probably time to finish dinner preparations."

They walked down the hall past the den. Lauren stopped to stare at a wall full of pictures. "Is that who I think it is?" she asked, staring at a picture of Fidel Castro standing next to an unfamiliar gray-haired man.

"That's my Papa, Hernàn. Before the revolution, he was a doctor and a prominent sugar-cane farmer in Cuba. He was also one of the country's few aristocrats who believed in what Castro wanted to do. All his friends fled to the United States. But he gave up his holdings and decided to stay in Cuba, where he dedicated his life to providing quality health care to our citizens. He and Fidel were quite good friends. In case you haven't figured it out, I could never have afforded this apartment on my own. When Papa died, the state discreetly bought this apartment for me as a thank you for Papa's years of service."

"Did you ever meet Castro?"

"On many occasions. He's nothing like the depiction in the American press. To some extent, we are still living in 1961, while the rest of the world has recognized Cuba as a tiny country of eleven million people, just trying to make a better life for all its citizens."

"And who's this beautiful woman by the airplane?"

"That was my wife, Moravita. She was so committed to Fidel's vision of quality health care for all that she used to fly her plane into the island's more remote regions to deliver drugs and medicines. That picture is particularly ironic; she crashed later that day doing what she loved to do."

Gabby touched the picture. "But life moves on, doesn't it?"

~

The kitchen was a gourmet's delight filled with every accessory one could imagine, all wrapped in white marble and stainless steel.

Gabby walked to the center island, proudly pointing to a series of copper pots and pans. "Tonight's first course is Wentworth Bisque. It contains freshly shelled Maine lobster — by me, of course — simmered in puréed Chilean heirloom tomatoes with a light cream sauce and a hint of mascarpone cheese. You have three kinds of sherry and a plate of coriander and saffron. Be my guest — flavor to suit.

"Our second course," said Gabby, pointing to the oven, "is Alaskan Halibut Wentworth. It's my variation on Beef Wellington. The fresh halibut is topped with a light beluga caviar sauce and wrapped in phyllo dough and baked in brown rice paper. It will be accompanied by white asparagus Hollandaise and French pearl potatoes. The asparagus are steamed, and the potatoes are baking; both await your final touches.

"Dessert consists of dark chocolate soufflés with a fresh raspberry sauce and a little Turkish espresso."

"I'm impressed," said Lauren, leaning provocatively. "Do you do this for all the girls you lure up here?"

"Absolutely. Gets them every time," joked Gabby.

"So, what did you do with the rest of them? Coffee and a quickie?"

"Enough," said Gabby. He walked around the counter, took Lauren in his arms, and kissed her until their passions reached the boiling point. Gabby picked up Lauren and carried her to his master suite, gently placing her between the soft satin sheets as he slowly removed her clothes. She lay ready and waiting as his muscular, tanned, nude body stood seductively in front.

"Isn't the food going to get cold?" teased Lauren.

"We'll reheat it for breakfast."

78.

Lauren lets herself go.

Lauren woke up to the aromatic scent of lobster bisque and freshly baked halibut. She slipped on her negligée and covered herself in one of Gabby's thick Turkish bathrobes.

The famished couple devoured every last drop of the first two courses.

"Are you ready for some dessert?" asked Gabby, referring to the soufflés cooling on the counter.

Lauren stood up and shed her robe. The sun glistened through her sheer negligée. "The real question is, are *you* ready for some dessert?"

They made love again — this time on the couch in the den, just below Fidel and Papa.

~

"I think it's time to share and share alike," said Gabby, sitting in Lauren's office.

"Did I miss something? I thought that's what we've been doing."

"I know you're a big Four Seasons aficionado, and you know I love scuba diving. So, I did a little research. The Four Seasons just opened a place on the island of Nevis. It's secluded, exclusive, just four hours from JFK Airport, and there is no phone service."

"Now *that's* exclusive."

"We've got a four-day holiday weekend coming up, so I figured we could kill two birds with one stone. I'll show you the wonders of the sea, and you can show me why you give the Four Seasons such rave reviews."

"But I've never scuba dived. I'd be scared to death."

"I'll be with you every step of the way. I'd never let harm come to you. Ever. Trust me."

She smiled. "I do."

"Frankly, if anybody should be cautious, it should be me. I've been to a Four Seasons or two. The word around town is you wield a wicked credit card."

"Hey, look at it this way," she said. "Worse case, I spend too much, and you have to sell the apartment to pay the bill!"

~

"I'm frightened to death," said Lauren, staring into the crystal-clear water with an oxygen tank strapped to her back.

"Just hold my hand as we jump off the platform. If I lose you when we hit the water, stay in place; I'll find you and we'll submerge together. You are not going to believe the world below."

Fifty feet down, Gabby pointed to the spectacular colored fish meandering in and out of the gorgeous coral reefs. *I've never seen anything so beautiful*, thought Lauren. *It's so quiet and peaceful down here, away from the cares and worries of the world above.*

Gabby had brought a camera. He signaled to Lauren to let go so that he could take a few solo pictures of her with a school of fish. Then he turned the camera around and took shots of them together amid blankets of vibrant reds, blues, and yellows.

Gabby also talked Lauren into windsurfing and an unescorted sailboat ride to an uninhabited alcove, where they lunched among a friendly group of dolphins.

Lauren made sure they ate the most expensive dinners on the island, had a couples' massage every other day, and ate a romantic lunch by themselves on an isolated bluff overlooking the island, prepared and delivered by the Four Seasons. She also bought Gabby, MJ, Bart, Valerie, and Bianca resort caps and shirts.

The bill came to almost $12,000 for the four days. "The rumors about your proclivity with a credit card were all true," laughed Gabby as he scanned the bill.

"You're not looking at the big picture," smiled Lauren. "How many times did we have sex?"

"Believe it or not, I wasn't counting. Let's say six. What's your point?"

"It was eleven. That's approximately $1,096 per session. I defy you to produce a Manhattan Madame who could deliver a comparable combination of uninhibited, on-demand sex, five-star meals, and abundant drinks."

~

"Mom," said Bart, "we were starting to get worried. We hadn't heard from you in four days. Where have you been?"

"Oh, I just took a spontaneous little vacation. There are four messages on my voice mail from you. What was so urgent?"

"Next weekend is Thanksgiving. MJ and I thought it might be appropriate if we had the family dinner at our place this year."

"Sounds wonderful. I have a friend I'd like you to meet."

"No problem. I'm sure we'd all love to meet *her*," said Bart.

~

Lauren thought it would be better if she and Gabby arrived last. "Everybody, I like you to meet a good friend of mine from the hospital, Dr. Gabriel Wentworth."

"Just call me Gabby," he said with a smile. MJ noticed his mom reach for Gabby's hand.

"So, Gabby, what's your specialty?"

"I'm an orthopedic surgeon."

"Does Lauren give you preferential treatment in the OR?" Bart smiled. "That is one busy, busy place."

"I think she tries to please all of us. You know doctors can be a little full of themselves."

"How did you two meet?" asked Bart, realizing that Gabby was considerably younger than his mom.

"You know how these things start. Right at the hospital."

"Well, we're so glad you could join us at the last minute," said Bart's wife, Valerie. "I spent the entire weekend trying to find my mother-in-law. Her cell phone went right to voice mail.

"Nevis is probably one of the last places in the world without cell service. That's one of the reasons I selected it."

The kids now realized Gabby was more than a friend. Lauren felt awkward. "Mom was great; she even went scuba diving and windsurfing."

"Mom!" said a wide-eyed MJ. "How did she do?"

"You would have been proud of her, after she got over her initial nervousness. I've got some terrific pictures in the car. Would you like to see them?"

"Absolutely."

"Here she is underwater with her tank, playing with a school of fish."

MJ remained stone silent.

~

Gabby spotted a Sony PlayStation 4 in the corner of the media room.

"You know PlayStation?" asked MJ.

"Know PlayStation? Every kid that ever went to college knows about PlayStation. At Amherst, I was the class champion. Guys used to challenge me in *Madden Football* all the time. In my junior and senior year, I think I made over $2,500, which kept me in beer and broads."

It turned out that Gabby hadn't lost his touch with *Madden Football.* He beat Bart 47 to 7 while MJ laughed his ass off. Gabby's enthusiasm about PlayStation reminded Bart about the age difference between his Mom and the doctor, he didn't want her to get hurt again.

~

Gabby and Lauren got married on the beach on a sunny Saturday in July in Southampton, New York.

About fifty friends and family had been invited to attend the ceremony and stay the weekend at a historic bed and breakfast, the 1708 House in the heart of town. Graciously, even I was invited.

Dr. John Savarese, president of New York Hospital, was Gabby's best man; our daughter-in-law, Valerie, was Lauren's maid of honor, and granddaughter Bianca, now two, was the flower girl who led Lauren to the water's edge by dropping yellow rose petals.

As waves crashed and Lauren slowly walked towards the group in a flowing yellow taffeta dress, Gabby read "How Do I Love Thee." Lauren never looked more radiant.

How do I love thee? Let me count the ways.
I love thee to the depth and breadth and height

My soul can reach, when feeling out of sight
For the ends of Being and ideal Grace....
Smiles, tears, of all my life!— and, if God chooses,
I shall but love thee better after death.

After the ceremony, the group returned to the 1708 House for an elegant, yet simple, meal. Local restaurateur Eddie Plant, a fixture for more than thirty years at his Southampton Gardens, served mountains of his signature lobster rolls (fresh Maine lobster salad on French baguettes), his secret recipe Caesar salad, and his homemade country pâté spiked with white truffles.

We laughed and ate and drank till dark, since we had closed the B&B for the weekend; then we retired to the inn's gracious public rooms, where we devoured an endless array of homemade pastries and drank cappuccinos, espressos, and after dinner drinks till the wee hours of the morning.

79.

Money is no longer a concern.

"I've got some great news," said Craft over the phone, just days after the wedding. "Pat Defoe at Appalachia Life has come back around with a generous offer to buy the company — $250 million!"

"Any contingencies?"

"None other than the usual due diligence, and the fact that I have to stick around for two years to help them with an orderly management transition. They want to meet each of the equity partners separately as part of the due diligence. I also need you and your attorney to look at the contracts. We're all going to have to sign the final documents."

"What's the curveball?"

"You've got to stop thinking like a goddamn cynical New Yorker. Other than paying us over two years with interest at eight percent, the deal looks clean. They need to expand their distribution system, and we have the biggest and best around."

"Are they stable enough that we can handle the debt service and paydown equity?"

"Martin, stop. This is a $10 billion company. There isn't going to be notes or periodic distributions; it's a straight cash deal. For tax reasons, they would like to close before the end of the year; they need the deductions. I'm also sending you a draft copy of the definitive letter of agreement. As a public company, this is a substantive economic event. They have to notify their shareholders."

"I'll get on the documents as soon as I get them."

"I thought you'd sound a little bit more excited. Do you realize you're going to be getting checks totaling nearly $30 million? Christ, you and Lauren will never have to even think about money again."

"I forgot to mention; we've had a recent development. Lauren divorced me."

"Join the club," laughed Craft. "Damn, that means she gets a $15 million windfall."

"No, not really. Our deal was that Lauren keeps her pension and deferred assets, and I keep the AFA stock."

"Pal, what a fucking brilliant move! You're in Fat City. That's a prenuptial agreement with zero emotional hassle.

~

Suddenly it hit me: I would never have to worry about being dependent upon anybody in my old age. I had all the cash flow I would ever need, and our children and grandchildren, current and future, had a dowry.

The money did raise two issues: Should I create an income-producing trust for MJ right now, so that he would have one less hassle in his panic-disorder-prone life? Had our divorce agreement accidentally screwed Lauren financially, and should I do something about it?

~

Since Gabby was not exactly scraping the bottom of the barrel, and from what I could see, Bart and Valerie were doing just fine, I decided to make MJ the priority. I paid a visit to MJ to deliver the good news.

"Dad, what a surprise," said MJ at the door of his apartment.

"MJ, I've got some terrific news," I blurted enthusiastically. "I just learned that my partners had received a fabulous offer from Appalachia Life to buy AFA."

"I'm happy for you, Dad."

"Do realize what that means? Dad is set for life; and, you kids never have to worry about money."

"Great! That's just what Bart needs: more money," said MJ with a hint of sarcasm.

"Forget about Bart. I'm talking about you."

"Me?" said MJ defensively. "Don't you think I can take care of myself?"

I paused, not sure if candor was the best course. I decided to gamble; I let the love flow and hoped for the best. "Honestly, MJ, I'm not sure. But you need to realize that I love you with my whole heart and always will. Maybe I've never been the perfect father or even the father you wanted me to be. But you're my flesh and blood, my firstborn, and nothing will ever change that.

"I've proud of the way you've handled life's curveballs. I know you're doing everything within your power to stay in the game, and sometimes it's not easy. That's why I'm going to put $3 million into an income-producing trust in your name. My attorney, Tom Morrison, who is now your trust executor, tells me you should receive about $150,000 a year without invading the trust's principal. And after I'm gone, the $3 million is yours to do with as you please."

MJ began to sob. "Dad, you don't *have* to do that for me."

"MJ, I *want* to do that for you."

We stood silently for what seemed like an eternity. I opened my arms. MJ wrapped himself tightly in my embrace for the first time in thirty years. I could feel his body quivering. My mind returned to a more innocent time. Little three-year-old MJ was sitting in bed as we sang his favorite song:

The itsy-bitsy spider went up the waterspout

Down came the rain and washed the spider out!

Out came the sun and dried up all the rain

And the itsy-bitsy spider
Went up the spout again!

I began to sing the song quietly into MJ's ear. He held me tighter. His body stopped quivering, and he smiled shyly.

"You remembered."

"How could I ever forget? I love you like crazy."

"Dad, that's all I've ever wanted to hear. I've felt for so long that you loved Bart more than me."

At that moment, I felt I had wasted half a lifetime as a father and a human being. "MJ, this entire experience with Alexandria and your Mom have taught me so much about my flaws and the impact they have had on those I love the most. All I can tell you is that I've tried to be a decent person, although I'm not perfect."

It was MJ's turn to spread some positive reinforcement. "Dad, even though you're a bit wacko, you're a great dad," smiled MJ. "And, I want you to know I'm proud to be your son."

It was my turn to cry as we hugged one more time.

80.

Visiting Gabby's Cuba for the first time.

The newlyweds' first six months together flew by in the blink of an eye. They spent most of their evenings at home, discovering more about each other, since this was a later-in-life gift.

Gabby felt God had granted him the gift of a new Moravita — the perfect wife. And Lauren felt she had found a sensitive, professionally compatible man who made her feel alive every minute they spent together, something she craved after her personally humiliating ordeal.

One of the things that surprised both of them was Lauren's growing curiosity about Gabby's Cuban heritage, and his interest in the country's medical reputation throughout Latin America.

"When Papa turned over his wealth to the state under Castro, I'm told his friends laughed at him as they exported their own wealth to possession-driven lifestyles in South Florida."

"Was it worth the sacrifice?"

"Papa was always a doctor who cared more about his patients than his fees. He used to say '*dios prove para ellos que conteparter su buena fortuna* [God provides for those who share good fortune].' When he died, Castro provided a State funeral as a way of recognizing his sacrifices to respect the dignity of all Cubans, regardless of educational or financial status."

"Did he know Castro?"

"They were old friends. Papa was a resident at Havana School of Medicine when Fidel first came to power. He was one of the few people Fidel could trust during the hectic early days of the revolution. In time, Papa became an unofficial advisor to Fidel on medical matters. President Castro dreamed that no citizen should ever want for medical care; it was Papa's vision that the University of Havana Medical Center be recognized as one of the leading teaching institutions in all of Latin America. Papa wanted me to study aboard, then bring back my knowledge of international ways to Cuba."

"Which you did, right?"

"I did my residency in Havana but then left after Moravita died and Papa passed away. I was a thirty-three-year-old doctor with shaken cultural roots."

"What about your mother?"

"She passed away when I was eight. She contracted a rare form of pneumonia that Papa couldn't cure. He was devastated. I only remember bits and pieces about her. I decided to go to America to hone my professional skills and become financially independent. My original plan was to return, but I never did. And probably never will."

"Why?"

"America's wealth has a way of mesmerizing you. The country also has such a distorted, ignorant view of Cuba and Castro; I rationalized it would be a hassle to go back and forth."

"Let's never say never, fair enough?"

"Fair enough."

Gabby pulled a book from the shelf. "Our conversation reminded me of something. This is my diary from my residency in Havana. Would you like to see the ravings of a young idealist?"

"I would love to."

He handed her the tattered, blue hardcover book. As he did, a small letter fell to the floor. She picked it up.

She began to read the letter, which was one-part broken English, one-part Spanish.

> *Dear great doctor Gabriel,*
> *Muchos gracias for saving MAFA.*
> *I was so afraid she was going to die, like Papa,*
> *Leaving me all alone.*
> *I hope someday to be a*
> *especial' medico like you, so*

I can help save somebody
else's MAFA.
I pray that your gift comes to me.

Love always,
Benito Fernando Carnita

"What a charming note," said Lauren.

"Ahhh, little Benito. His mother suffered from an unidentified virus that had attacked her nervous system. I rode a donkey into a mountain village that was known to mix some rare herbs into a powerful natural formula that had the same effect as a manufactured antibiotic, which simply was not available in Cuba at the time."

"How in the world did you even know about the formula?"

"In those days, anecdotal stories traveled by word of mouth. I figured she was dying, so it was worth a shot. It worked."

81.

Meeting THE Fidel Castro.

"Lauren, there's been a development at AFA that you, Gabby, and I should discuss," I said.

"*Mi casa es su casa*," responded Lauren.

"Let me guess; you're practicing your Italian for your next vacation!" I said, not knowing the difference between Spanish and Italian.

The following evening, I was sitting in the living room of Lauren and Gabby Wentworth, explaining the $25 million-plus surprise and what I had already done for MJ.

"Martin, Lauren and I are delighted at your good fortune. And we applaud establishing a trust for MJ. But what does it all that have to do with us?" said Gabby.

"I just feel that in good conscience, some of that money belongs to Lauren."

"We appreciate the gesture, but as I understand it, you two made a deal. And a deal is a deal. Lauren, if you feel differently, please speak up."

"No, I agree, the money belongs to Martin. But, I do have a thought," said Lauren. "Martin, how much did you want to give me?"

"Is this a negotiation?" I joked. "I was thinking about five million."

"My God, that's incredibly generous." She turned to Gabby. "Remember what you and I were discussing the other night? You said you had a strong emotional attachment to Cuba and the University of Havana Medical School. Why don't we make the $5 million a gift to the medical school to increase the teaching facilities, update the physical infrastructure, and create a foundation that provides worthy students — like little Benito — the opportunity to become *especial 'medicos*?"

"What a spectacular idea!"

"Hey fellas, I have no issue with your intent, but given America's Cuban embargo policy, I can't just write a check or transfer funds to a Cuban bank."

"Fortunately, this is an issue I've dealt with before," said Gabby. "I have dual citizenship."

"I had no idea," I responded.

"You make a gift to me, which I deposit in a Haitian bank where I maintain certain intermediary accounts. Papa established them many years ago because Fidel did help him transfer some funds to those members of our family who decided to leave."

"Fidel Castro?" I gulped.

I wired the funds to Gabby and Lauren's account at UBS the next day.

~

About a week later, I received a call from Gabby. "Martin, I have been talking to the State Department about your generosity and our situation. We have been granted an exception to visit Cuba and deliver the check personally. Although it still has to be wired through Haiti, as I explained."

"That's wonderful. You and Lauren must be delighted.

"You don't understand. I said *we* had been granted an exception to travel — you, me, and Lauren. Lauren and I want you to come with us. What do you say?"

I was honored.

Soon, we were on an Air Viasa flight to Caracas, Venezuela, where we boarded a connecting flight to Cuba. It was a bit inconvenient — a twelve-hour journey to an island just ninety minutes from Miami.

~

We were greeted at the Havana airport by a driver in a 1951 Chevrolet, which looked and ran perfectly. Since the American embargo some forty-four years ago, Cubans have become master auto restorers.

The city was not what I imagined. Everything was old, but not dilapidated. Neighborhoods were colorful, the streets seemed orderly, and people seemed happy; there was lots of street dancing. There were no honking horns and no abject poverty.

Fidel Castro's office, the Bureau for Maintenance of the Revolution, was in the Headquarters of the Communist Party of Cuba, an unassuming eight-story, gray concrete structure that sat directly behind the José Marti Monument in the Plaza de la Revolución.

Upon arrival, we were informed President Castro was just concluding a meeting and would be with us shortly. Displayed prominently on the wall outside his office was a picture of Castro at the Palace of Nations in Geneva, receiving the Health for All Medal from the World Health Organization. Below that picture was his speech:

> "Your Excellencies, officials of the WHO, distinguished delegates.
> How much is a human life worth?
> Why are the children who die and could have been saved are almost 100% poor?
> Why are 200 million children under five years of age undernourished?
> Why do 110 million not attend primary school, and 275 million fail to attend secondary school?
> Why do 2 million girls become prostitutes each year?
> Why do developed countries, with 14.6% of the world's population consume 82% of the medicines? The rest of the world's five billion people — consume only 18%.
> Why do countries spend $800 billion a year on military projects designed solely to kill while the world cannot find the $25 billion annually to provide access to the cost of universal access to basic health care services?...
> ...The WHO is fighting heroically against these realities, and it also has the duty of being optimistic.
>
> As a Cuban and a revolutionary, I offer optimism for the future. Despite the cruel

> blockade we have suffered for more than 50 years, Cuba has successfully fulfilled the WHO Health for All 20-year program goals. We have reduced current infant mortality to during the first year of birth to 7.2 per thousand, which is lower than the European Union; there is one doctor for every 176 inhabitants— the highest level in the world— and our citizens have life expectancy of more than 75 years of age. … The world can also fight and win."

I had no sooner finished reading the speech than a bearded man in uniform, older and much frailer and more gracious than I imagined, approached our group. It was Fidel.

"Ahhh, Gabriel, my Gabriel. It has been a long, long time. Welcome home, amigo." Castro hugged Gabby.

"President Castro, I'd like you to meet my wife, Lauren Wentworth."

"Ah, Senora Wentworth, I knew your *marido* (husband) when he was simply Gabriel Wentas," smiled Castro. He turned toward Gabby and nodded, "Hernan would have approved."

President Castro looked at me with an equally warm smile. "This must be Mr. Martin Ruff, *lo adinerado americano con cheque grande* [the wealthy American with the big check]. A pleasure to make your acquaintance."

I addressed the President. "Hopefully, Gabriel's donation will help Cuba remain a healthcare model for the rest of the world."

"No, no, no," said Castro raising his hand and eyebrows.

I was alarmed. Had I somehow insulted President Castro?

"We know the gift is yours. Gabriel is merely, how you say, *intermediario*," smiled Castro. "We propose the people of Cuba know your generosity. With your permission, these funds will be used to expand our teaching university. The extension will be named the Ruff College for Advanced Medical Studies."

I was overwhelmed with emotion as Lauren, Gabriel, and President Castro all gave me hugs.

Fidel Castro died on November 25, 2016, about six months after we met.

82.

Life is a journey to an unknown destination.

One day, I was sitting on my favorite park bench in Central Park near the 59th Street pond when my cell phone rang. The number was unfamiliar. My first instinct was to let it go to voicemail. But something told me no.

"Martin, how are you? This is Margo Margoles; do you remember me? I was walking by Barnes and Noble on 53rd Street. I saw your book featured in the window."

"Yeah, I decided our little journey might make an interesting read."

"I bought a copy. I figured I'd give you a call and see if I could get an autograph."

"Absolutely. By the way, how's your practice doing since our little case?"

"Thanks to your book, word has gotten around about our success strategy. My phone hasn't stopped ringing. Everybody wants to be represented by 'The Killer.'"

"I bet your husband's pretty proud."

"I'm not married. Never have been."

"But the pictures in your office?"

"Just stock photos. I have an image to protect. I mean, what wife is going to let her husband hire an attractive, unmarried attorney in a harassment suit?"

"But you answered Lauren's questions."

She chuckled. "Remember, I'm an attorney. If you listened closely to what I said, rather than what you thought I said, I was very clear. I spoke about my interest in hiking, mountain climbing, and camping. I never mentioned a family."

"If that's the case, I'd like to make a suggestion. Have you seen the new multi-billion-dollar restoration of the Palm Court at the Plaza?"

"No."

"How about we meet there for a book signing and a cappuccino?"

There was a pause on the other end of the line.

~

My first cappuccino with Margo was like the Spanish Inquisition.

"What made me stray off course?" She didn't buy my mid-life crisis explanation.

"That's a cop-out. People don't just throw away thirty-five years."

"Didn't I realize my untidy workplace indiscretion would inevitably be discovered?" I mumbled, "It wasn't really like that."

She smirked, "Are you that dumb? From day one, she had you pegged as an insurance settlement. What women genuinely falls for a guy, and then keeps all his voice mails?"

"And, what about your 36 years with Lauren? And that lame 'I really didn't mean to hurt you' nonsense?"

It was my turn. "For the past hour, we've been sipping cappuccinos while you beat the crap out of me. Why are you here?"

Margo's response was vintage Margo. "Let's just imagine we were in a relationship, and I stress 'imagine;' I'm trying to figure out if I could ever really trust you."

"And the answer is...?"

"I don't know."

My cell phone ended an awkward silence; I had forgotten to put my phone on vibrate. My ringtone, Bruce Springsteen's "Waiting for a Sunny Day," turned heads as I fumbled through my pockets. Margo's big dark brown eyes bulged angrily.

"Lauren, can I call you back? This is not a good time."

"MJ's dead," she blurted. "He committed suicide."

I sat there stunned, then slowly lowered my head. Margo, who had no idea what had just transpired, signaled to hang up. "Stop with the damn cell phones." I waved her off. She left in a huff.

"What happened?"

"I don't know for sure. We had just finished a nice dinner. Gabby suggested we all go to the Four Seasons for a nightcap, since we all had a no-call weekend at the hospital.

"MJ told us he'd 'have to take a pass.' He mumbled something about having an international conference call with some Chinese software developers. Gabby knew it was a smokescreen to avoid socializing. Gabby told MJ he was never going to lead a normal life unless he confronted his demons directly. MJ started to scream, 'You just don't understand, and you never will!'

"I tried to calm things down. I told MJ, 'Mommy understands.' Gabby suggested he use our den for his conference call, then stay over in the guest room.

"I said, 'In the morning, Mommy make will breakfast. You know, egg white omelets with lots of vegetables, and a little cheese on top, just the way you like it.'

"MJ just smiled and nodded. I figured the worst was over, so we went out for a few hours. When we returned, MJ was lying in bed, lifeless."

83.

Dumb, Dumber, Dumbest.

It's been three months since that call. I have been seeing my new best friend, psychiatrist Randy Jamerson. But I'm no closer to the answers, or any answers really, since we started this process twelve sessions ago.

Dr. Jamerson says men are unusually unfaithful for one of three reasons: the tawdry thrill of an affair, boredom with the relationship partner, or the feeling that emotional needs are somehow being ignored.

I can't speak for all the men in the corporate world, but I know there is another reason. Once you are in a position of power, indiscretions are like cocaine addiction. Once you're hooked, you do stupid things.

~

My first thoughts every day still revolve around Lauren. I must have told 1,000 people over the last thirty-six years about our love-at-first site meeting back in college, and how we spent a lifetime building a partnership and parenting two kids. My former twice-divorced sister-in-law called us "the fairy-tale marriage that only existed in books and movies."

I used to delight in bringing home little surprise gifts and writing love poems. Her enthusiastic responses made me feel like the most important guy in the world. The greatest tragedy is that I willfully and consciously traded this lifetime of highs, and for what?

Of course, it no longer matters what the answer is, because it's too late. One part of me — the good part — wishes Lauren and Gabby the very best. He got the catch of the century.

~

Then there are the unanswered questions about Alexandria. Did she have genuine feelings for me, or were those ponderous titillations just a sideshow for her own mid-life crisis? Was her flight to Fred the real thing? Did it matter, now that she's dead?

My titanic ego, the one that got me into this mess in the first place, could live with any of those explanations. But suppose I was nothing more than the victim of a sophisticated sting to extract a big payday from today's low-hanging corporate fruit — a substantial insurance payoff. Could my ego live with that?

Given that the defendant just *happened to record* a series of personal phone conversations, and got in bed (professionally) with Burton Moss — the undisputed, undefeated champion of sexual harassment lawsuits — I will always wonder what the hell went on behind the scenes.

~

Finally, there is MJ. He was our first. Lauren and I showered him with love. He was intelligent, witty, athletic, and respectful. You couldn't ask for more in a son.

I yearned for the kind of relationship with him that I never had with my own father, a blue-collar workaholic who died at age 60. Somehow, I lost my way, and in turn, MJ lost his. I will always feel guilt. Where did I fail? How did I miss his subtle pleas for help? Did *I* drive him to Lauren as his lone safe person? Did I abrogate my responsibility as a father? In the end, was I just a clone of my father?

~

As I reread my final words, I don't like myself very much. I've lost everything important, yet I'm still not sure if I've been totally transparent with myself.

As a reader who has shared my unplanned journey to this peculiar place, what do you think?

Request for Review

Dear Reader,

We want to thank you for taking the time to read our book.

We realize *Indiscretion* is somewhat unconventional, and we know you have many choices. We have tried to do everything we could to create a book that entertains and informs, a book you will not soon forget.

We recognize everybody lives busy lives these days, but we would appreciate you posting a short review with the retailer from which you purchased *Indiscretion.* It will help other readers to discover my library of 13 books.

If you'd like to join my monthly mailing list, there's an interesting free book offer on my website www.mgcrisci.com, or learn more about me, put ***mg crisci*** into your google search bar.

Thanks again. See you somewhere along the way.

M. G. Crisci

THE WORLD OF
M.G. Crisci
Stories that entertain. People you'll remember.
Literature that matters.
Twitter.com/worldofmgcrisci
YouTube.com/worldofmgcrisci
Facebook.com/worldofmgcrisci
Buy now at
amazon.com >
7 DAYS IN RUSSIA
M.G.CRISCI
TRAVEL PHOTOJOURNAL
CALL SIGN WHITE LILY
M.G.CRISCI
WOMAN'S ACCOMPLISHMENT
DONNY AND VLADDY
M.G.CRISCI
POLITICAL SATIRE
ERGONIA
LAND OF THE GIANT ANTS
VLADIMIR ALENIKOV
KIDS ADVENTURE
INDISCRETION
M.G.CRISCI
PSYCHOLOGICAL THRILLER
MARY JACKSON PEALE
M.G.CRISCI
SUCCESS AND EXCESS
ONLY IN NEW YORK
M.G.CRISCI
BIG APPLE SHORT STORIES
PAPA CADO
M.G.CRISCI
INSPIRATION AND WIT
PAPA CADO'S BOOK OF WISDOM
HUMOR AND WISDOM
PROJECT ZEBRA
M.G.CRISCI
WW2 HISTORY
THE SALAD OIL KING
AN AMERICAN TALE OF GREED GONE MAD.
M.G.CRISCI
WHITE COLLAR CRIME
SAVE THE LAST DANCE
M.G.CRISCI
PERIOD ROMANCE
SHE SAID. HE SAID.
M.G.CRISCI
PSYCHOLOGICAL THRILLER
STILL STANDING
VICKI FITZGERALD
M.G.CRISCI
PERSONAL MEMOIR
THIS LITTLE PIGGY
M.G.CRISCI
INSIDE WALL STREET
Learn more at www.mgcrisci.com

www.ingramcontent.com/pod-product-compliance
Lightning Source LLC
Chambersburg PA
CBHW030812310726
48980CB00006B/470/J

* 9 7 8 1 4 5 6 6 3 0 5 5 3 *